Words in the Wind

Literary Anthology

Nebraska Writers Guild

NWG Publications
Scottsbluff, NE

Nebraska Writers Guild
PO Box 493
Scottsbluff, NE 69363

Publisher's Note: This is primarily a work of fiction. Except in certain cases, names, characters, places, and incidents are products of each author's imagination. Locales and public names are sometimes used for atmospheric purposes.

Ordering Information:
Quantity sales. Special discounts are available on quantity purchases by corporations, associations, and others. For details, contact the "Special Sales Department" at the address above.

Words in the Wind

ISBN: 978-1-7357016-8-4 (paperback)
ISBN: 978-1-7357016-9-1 (ebook)

Library of Congress Control Number: 2023922427

Contents

Poetry

Essays

Short Stories

Nonfiction and Memoir

Excerpts from a Novel

Flash Fiction

Foreword

Once again, we celebrate the creativity of Nebraska Writers Guild authors. After not putting out an anthology in 2022, getting back to this exhausting, yet rewarding, process has been a gift that I'm so honored to be granted. Having the trust of such an extraordinary group of over three hundred members is something I don't take lightly.

So here we go again! This is my fourth Voices anthology since becoming Publications Chair for the NWG, and a lot has changed over the years, from the way we judge entries to the name of each volume! But one thing that hasn't changed is the variety of entries. From literary character study to suspense to humor to, well, the downright weird, we have a little of everything. Some pieces will make you cry (or should!), some will make you laugh, and some will make you shudder, for any number of creepy reasons.

I'll keep this brief so you can get to the good stuff. Thank you again, NWG, and all the members who submit entries and who allow me to continue to be a part of this amazing adventure into the creative mind.

Enjoy!

Julie Haase
NWG Publications Chair

Poetry

Becky Faber • Lincoln, NE

Not Quite Enough

Before Amazon, Wayfair, and Pinterest,
we chose our belongings carefully,
only items that would last because we didn't have credit cards
or gift cards—only checks and cash.

Yesterday I reached for a pan on the bottom shelf,
one I have had for over forty years but now rarely use.
As I lifted it to the counter,
I could clearly remember sitting at a kitchen table,
counting out Betty Crocker box top points,
comparing my number to those needed to purchase the pan,
filling in the order form, writing a check, then mailing the order.

These were our ways,
a sorority of women who clipped Betty Crocker points
or sent in cereal box tops
or bought the laundry soap that included a free towel in the box
or saved green stamps for household necessities.

This is how we pretended that we weren't poor,
how we got by when there was not quite enough money,
when we ironed denim patches on the knees of our sons' jeans,
when we hemmed slacks that we had bought at a thrift store,
when we felt shame that we didn't have as much as others.

Lucy Adkins • Lincoln, NE

Camp Counselor

At Camp Kiwanis, I slept in a single bed
like the nine- and ten-year-olds in my care,
but I slept by the door, the night coming
in black through the screen at my head,
the sounds of night insects, cars and trucks
on the whispery gravel a mile or so away.

I wore blue shorts with the Camp Kiwanis
patch, and a white T-shirt with the
Campfire Girl logo. My hair was dark
and cut in something in between
a pageboy and a pixie, and I walked
to the pool, the dining hall, the evening

sing-a-longs, with the girls crowding
along beside me. They liked my hair,
the way I talked, my transistor radio
I let them listen to ten minutes after
lights out: "Midnight Confessions,"
"Hey Jude," "Say a Little Prayer."

I was nineteen, and after a lifetime
of not belonging, of awkward and acne,
not knowing what to say, I was all right,

cool somehow, to these groups of girls,
new girls every week, each with their
own hard roads and a long way to go.

Lin M. Brummels • Winside, NE

The Moon Knows

I'm awake at three a.m.
reminiscing about holding hands
with a Methodist boy
on a hayrack ride at age twelve.
The moon knows when pictures
dart wildly behind my eyelids
in the same rhythm as thoughts
flit through my brain.
The orb remembers nights
my love and I shared naked
murmurs under her golden glow.
She knows what critters
search for food and which
only use her light for mischief.
Dog hears night sounds, barks
to get her attention, but the lunar sage,
like gods of her kind, pays
no attention. Moon moves
with graceful ease like a courtesan
seducing her marks. She rises
in the east in bright splendor,
grows paler as she ages,
hair thin and turning white

like many of us. She retires
into darkness when sun
spoils her fun.

Kathleen Maloney • Omaha, NE

Free Spirit

Cheery little yellow-slipper flower,
nods happily in summer heat,
energetically sweeps across grassy slopes &
hugs the verge of deserted country roads.

Spilling over scorching city curbs,
this miniature multitude constantly flutters
as though eagerly cheering on the winner
of some invisible race.

Invasive (some protest),

but not the bustling honeybees and
certainly not silver-studded blue butterflies,
nor even alert grazing woodland deer.

Blooming profusely,
growing continuously,
waving merrily:
a wild child of nature
that refuses to be controlled.

Bird's-foot trefoil

Kim McNealy Sosin • Omaha, NE

The Morning after You Left

The coffee spill creeps across
the breakfast table
like mud sludge.
Disoriented and decaffeinated,
I fumble to dam up the flow
press a towel across like a dike
before the darkness reaches
the edge
and drips to hell slowly
taking all
my hopes for
the days ahead.

Tim Moran • Elwood, NE

Your Nomad Heart

West, across county road 431,
a cinder-plumed thunderstorm
drives lightning to the ground
like silver Bedouin tent stakes
and just as abruptly, pulls them up again.

As brilliant and hot as
that bolt from your nomad heart
that reshuffled the air I breathed.

Beguiling and turbulent,
soon capricious,
then without explanation, moving on,
taking back everything but
burnt sparks, bitter on my tongue.

M. Timothy Nolting • Bushnell, NE

Prairies

With grass that towered
at twenty hands.
Nursed and nurtured by Mother Earth,
as yet unscarred
by wheel or plow.
No boundaries,
save mammoth oceans,
meandering rivers and mountain ridges.
Open, wide, and wild.
Untamed and untouched.
Buffalo were sacred gifts.
Prairie paths
were sweeping swaths
of broken blades and pitted earth
where thundering hooves of
honored herds
cut trails a half-mile wide.

Trails,
marked by cloven hooves.
Scouted, found fresh
and followed.
And in their following
left only fading prints

of moccasined feet,
unshod ponies,
and twin trenches of trailing travois.
Gentle markings,
quiet passings,
perennial pilgrimages of survival.
Nomadic wanderings
that left no wounds upon
their sacred Mother.

Their Earth Mother,
entrusted to their care.
For untold millennia,
they humbly accepted
what she gratefully gave.
They cared for her,
honored her,
and gave thanks to her.

We took her as we found her.
Unscarred, boundless, open, wide and wild.
Cut her flesh,
choked her veins.
Surveyed, sectioned, and sold her soul.

Then,
in less than two short centuries,
we long for prairies lost.
Unscarred, boundless, open, wide and wild.

Where prairie winds
stir prairie grass
that stands at twenty hands.

Valerie R. Robert • Plattsmouth, NE

My Dad Loves Kissing Other Women

Dad loves kissing other women.
They're all fair game,
Not passionate kisses—
No
Just pecks on the cheek
both cheeks that is—
"Ooh-la-la!"
"Vive la France!"
Dad says he's proud of his French heritage, but
Seriously
it's downright embarrassing!
Once he kissed my friend's mother
a shy woman who barely said boo,
Her face a bright red crimson—
I thought I'd die . . .
Then he died.
I long for his outrageousness—
Sweeping me off my feet
in the Burlington airport
Back from my high school trip to France
Clothed in his turtleneck and beret
And broad smile.
Twirling me around and
lifting me off my feet

like a lover in a Hollywood film
Larger than life.
Leaving behind a hole
Too big to fill.

Steve Rose • Indianola, IA

Emily the Fix

The baby was supposed to fix us.
We might as well have stuck her
pinky finger in the creek's dam and
prayed for hail instead of rain

or bought crop insurance for Grandpa's
barren homestead; such was our
dustbowl marriage. Sure, Emily
did claim us a stay. You stopped your

drinking for a spell. And I came home
from work straightaway as if
a school bell rang and our daughter
was marking attendance. Those eyes

of hers would leave her blocks and dolls
and meet me at the door like you
once did, pull me in like spices
rising from cookies, me not noticing

the temperature of the room
until you came near our child and me.
I had to leave. A child needs familial
warmth as much as milk,

and I drew your frost like playground
monkey bars in a March blizzard,
the kind of frigid lure that would
tempt a child's tongue for a lick,

altering their mouth forever.

Nathan Sousek • Lincoln, NE

Summer's Last Stand

At pasture gates the cattle mewl and low
Their once lush grasses all grazed short and thin,
Long gone the rains needed to make them grow
Not farmer nor fence line is sure to win

Blackbird flocks stretch lazy across the sky
As the first combines rumble from their sheds
Harvest will soon arrive, fields bordered by
Ditches turned goldenrod and sumac red

Then dusk—back and forth the cicadas cry,
Slow echoing sonorous wail and wane,
For these harbingers know the end is nigh,
So, lamenting, sing perish songs of pain

Sun disappears, night deepens o'er the land
The curtains draw closed on summer's last stand

Brittany Wren • Lincoln, NE

Flint Woman

Helen was hardly five feet tall but
she never seemed small.
She would've been a nun, they said,
but then she met Thomas and
became a wife and mother instead.
She raised seven kids in the house
where their father was born
in the heart of Flint, Michigan,
and they spent every Sunday at church.

It was a car town back then,
and the factory money was good
enough to spend summer at the lake
with stacks of paperbacks and tart cherry pie.
And every five years or thereabout,
she took the money
for new siding for the house,
a one-stall garage,
some new windows
or paint. Big jobs,
but Helen wasn't small.

Her kids and the factory left
for other religions

and other fortunes.
Crime settled like dust on furniture,
first in dark corners, then everywhere
in broad daylight. Once,
she was held at gunpoint,
tied up in the hall closet
while thieves took the TV.
The house faded
and she was alone.
But Helen wouldn't go.

It was a hard town, but
she was not a small woman.
The housing market tanked
in 2008, and then the water
six years later.
Her daughters moved south
to the sunshine state.
But Helen wouldn't go.
She was not a small woman.

One winter day, she slipped
and broke her right hip.
The pneumonia finally took her
home at 86
to God, and goodness, and probably pie.
Meanwhile, her house sold
for 40K.

Her kids took the money
for a cruise, and then went
their separate ways.

ShennonDoah • Holdrege, NE

The Death of Marat

In my warm bath
On such a warm day
I await the lovely
Charlotte Corday.

Those sea-green eyes
I can't begin
To explain her appeal,
Her white, supple skin

Note how her hair
In brown ringlets fall
Removing her bonnet
Would release them all

She brings promise
Of counter attack
My enemies
Should watch their backs.

With pen in hand
I await her news
When she doesn't smile
I begin to peruse

Her face for signs
Of what is amiss
When she pulls out the knife
I feel firsthand death's kiss.

Lucy Adkins • Lincoln, NE

Walking on a desert trail, we meet the two young couples

They are laughing, joking, and we hear them
before we see them coming from behind us—
teasing one another, chortling. Then they round
the corner: two young women, two young men

wearing hats, sunglasses, the Catalina Mountains
rising behind them, Mt. Lemon, Table Mountain.
We ask if they will take our picture—
we two couples in our seventies, or nearly so,

and they seem happy to record our presence
here with them at the bend of the trail. We have only
a little ways to go to get back to where we started,
but they have just begun, with their maps
and water bottles and miles and miles to go.

Lin M. Brummels • Winside, NE

Where Have All the Horses Gone?

You can cut all the flowers, but you can't keep spring from coming.
Pablo Neruda

I cry over horses'
deaths, take flowers
to paint their graves.

Kenny, the sweet foal
named after my dad
died at three months

from a twisted gut—
carcass left for coyotes.
My blue roan gave

it up one fall after
untold faithful years.
His resting place

a big bluestem-covered
terrace. Apache,
the Appaloosa gelding

my son raised, blinded
foraging in spiky weeds
during a drought, fell,

heart weakened
after two years grazing
blind. Unable to rise,

the vet put him down.
He's buried at bunkhouse
corner. Dutch, sixteen-

hand gelding killed
by a single lightning strike,
buried where he fell.

Ghost, thirty-five-year-
old Appy lay down
for the last time in spring.

She's buried in a brome pasture.
Joe, a rangy red roan fell
in a water hole in summer.

Son and friend pulled him
out but it was too much.
He's buried under swamp

oak trees nearby. Lucky,
last of the old horses,
passed peacefully under

an October sky. He's buried
in red-tinted little bluestem.
Death and its decay feeds

grass on horses' graves
as I hope it will feed buffalo
grass above my final rest.

Kathleen Maloney • Omaha, NE

Class of '63

Carelessly, I glance through images
on a page
of a high school reunion book
mailed to me by a friend—
(I could not attend)
when suddenly,
your face catches me unawares
as it smiles out from a photo.

Unexpectedly, looking at you
(& remembering over a half century ago),
I still see the clear eyes
and the gentle smile of the
first boy I ever loved.

Breathlessly I open the quiet
place in my heart, and
allow to fill my thoughts
all that I remember of you.

Recalling our youth and
memories time cannot diminish:
the half-heart necklace you gave me

one lovely Christmas.
Yes, especially I remember.

Though years have slipped away,
I know for certain
while looking at your face,
smiling at me from across time,

the sweet innocence that we shared then
will forever belong—
just to us.

Kim McNealy Sosin • Omaha, NE

Bicycle Kids

We were weeds
erupting
spraying seeds
scattering life
dispensing joy.

New sprouts
taking root
down the road
across the cornfield
up the stream
under a noon sun.

Fierce days
of freedom
and incandescence
working the pedals
just one rule
home by dinner.

Tim Moran • Elwood, NE

Truck Song at the Salvage Yard

"Let death and exile be daily before your eyes,
especially death, and you will never entertain
any abject thought, nor too eagerly
covet anything" -Epictetus

The silver F-150 unloaded
at the salvage yard
today on highway 23,
looks just like mine,
except for the wreck's
front end, concertina-ed deep
into the crew cab.

Can't help but hear
the soundtrack to it.
The skidding, head-on run
of reedy off-notes,
a bass thud, and a bent
pedal-steel lick
fading at the end.

And wonder whether
notes, phrases, and
tries at allegory

scribbled on napkins, receipts and
the backs of envelopes,
are strewn about those truck seats,
as they are about mine.

Now, just anonymous scrap
destined for the crusher,
never to become
a poem or the refrain
in a country song
that pecks at trivialities we
can’t help wanting to know.

Nathan Sousek • Lincoln, NE

Pond, Haiku

The old pasture pond
Summer, frog, heron, waits, steps—
Splash! the hunt resumes

M. Timothy Nolting • Bushnell, NE

Iron Gray

In the days of prohibition,
When the Windy City was dry,
Capone wrote his name in history
With bootleg Whiskey and Rye.

While on banks of the Rio Grande,
In *cantinas* on Mexico's side,
The *corridos* told of Patino
And the stallion he used to ride.

Their songs told of Pancho Patino
And the finest *caballo* they say,
Was the best of the *tequileros*
And a horse they called Iron Gray.

In Texas they called him the *hombre*
Who rides the lightning streak,
A flashy iron gray stallion,
Deep-chested, savvy and sleek.

The Rangers swore they'd catch him.
And vowed that Patino would hang.
But the iron gray stallion outran them,
And *los tequileros* sang . . .

"Los Rinches seran muy hombres,
No se les puede negar
Nos cazan como venados
*Para podernos matar."**

The Rangers could not catch Patino
As long as he rode Iron Gray,
For the stallion was swift as the sparrow
And carried Patino away.

So *Los Rinches* hid in the shadows
Where they knew the *bandito* must go,
Laid a trap for the iron gray stallion
Near the trail of the old *tequilero*.

The moon shone bright in the canyon
And Patino was leading the way
With his *companeros* behind him
As they followed the Iron Gray.

When the Rangers saw them coming,
Patino rode proud as a king
On the iron gray stallion he treasured,
And *los tequileros* would sing . . .

"Los Rinches seran muy hombres,
No se les puede negar
Nos cazan como venados
*Para podernos matar."**

Iron Gray stopped and he nickered,
His nostrils flared wide in fear.
Patino leaned forward and whispered,
"Do *los Rinches* wait for us here?"

Then canyon walls echoed like thunder
As rifles spit fire and lead.
Hot bullets ripped through Patino
'Til the bold *tequilero* lay dead.

Too late Iron Gray knew the danger
Too late was the warning he gave,
And the Rangers made certain that no one
Would ever again ride the Gray.

The stallion stood bloody and trembling.
One last bullet's sharp echo rang.
Then Iron Gray fell by his master
As *los tequileros* sang . . .

"Los Rinches seran muy hombres,
No se les puede negar
Nos cazan como venados
*Para podernos matar."**

(There is no doubt the Rangers
Are men who have no fear.
But they can only catch us when
They hunt us like the deer.)

**The verse in Spanish is the refrain from the Spanish folk song, "Los Tequileros."*

Steve Rose • Indianola, IA

Dad and the N-Word

It was my calling, as the Second World War
was his, to make the man who spawned
and reared me cease and desist using
the N-word, a practice he embraced as much
as ordering drinks all-round at the Legion.

The last time we heard him say it, the Huskers
just won the Fiesta Bowl in '96. He phoned,
his voice a foghorn blowing through
the landline. *Did you see him, Boy?*
Did you see that (insert N-word) *run!?*

His name's Tommy Frazier, Dad, I said.
We call people by their names. We
don't use that word. Your grandkids
heard you! Indeed they had, their eyes flat,
ears shrunk to their skulls, lips tight as string.

I never heard him say it again, even though
NU's basketball season dribbled through the winter,
Dad's commentary underlining each loss. And
we traded calls about the cattle he sold;
the teeth his grandkids shed. He died that April

and got a veteran's due at Fort McPherson, the Legion
providing a color guard and a rifle salute. Two of the vets
shooting blanks at the sky stood brown and gorgeous,
burnished onyx and mahogany.

Legionnaires, you see,
bound with bonds began by bloodshed,
will honor a comrade they do not know.

Brittany Wren • Lincoln, NE

Night Breathing

I know the steps I must take
around the squeaky floorboards
on the far side of the table
so as not to wake the baby.
I know the importance of each tiny sock
my son picks out,
how some days it must be firetrucks
and others, stripes.
At the first hint of his raspy cough,
nothing else matters.
He breathes
in and out.
His eyelids flutter.
His fist clenches around my bra strap.
Sickness and misery stir
up a need that is almost animal-like.
It's hard to explain how
our bodies need each other. How,
despite the heavy infant car seat
and the hip rides
and night wakings
and a constant need to nap,
I still breathe best
with my face plastered onto his head,

sweaty hair tickling me
as both eyes close.
And though I wrestle
with God, church,
and the afterlife,
I wonder if He, too, finds comfort
in my breath,
and the fact that I'm still
wondering,
eyes closed but thoughts
turned upward,
clenched around a memory
I can't shake.

Lucy Adkins • Lincoln, NE

Feeding My Neighbor's Cat

Gustavo would be gone
for two weeks, he said,
back to Argentina to visit
his son, his old friends,
breathe in some air
he hadn't drawn in
for a while. And while
he was gone, I was
to feed his cat.

Feed her one day, let two
days go by, then feed her
again, he said. I went
every day. Though the cat
didn't want me, turning
her eyes to me in disgust,
sauntering back out of the room.

She rubbed her brindled flank
along the sides of the sofa,
eased her softness against
the chairs. But when I came
close, she hunched her back
and hissed. *Here kitty, kitty*,

I called, but she wouldn't come,
disliking the sound of me
and the smell, the strangeness
I let in every time
I opened the door.

Lin M. Brummels • Winside, NE

Empanadas at Luna's

Tolerance like any aspect of peace, is forever a work in progress.
Octavia E. Butler

Luna's warmed us inside to out
on a frigid January day as we chewed on
events dipped in three levels of pepper sauce.

The crisp empanadas, freshly made, tidy
half-moon pockets, hot, crispy outside,
filled with steaming perfectly cooked beef

or chicken, edges sealed with a tailor's stitch.
Karen got chicken, I ordered beef, we traded
pastries and stories. She tells me she

attended a meeting where she and others
were asked to air community concerns. They
debated housing for homeless, rural food deserts,

abortion services, LGBTQ acceptance.
The city visitor at the meeting who asked
their opinions dismissed their ideas

as too political or too controversial, intent
on finding a flavorless woman willing
to run for state office. Karen invites me

to attend their next meeting. I tell her I'm
a corvine thinker like the crows feasting
on my daughter's bird feeder, not a double-speaker.

With little tolerance for politicians dissing
people's beliefs, I prefer to spend time
at Luna's café—spicy food and good company.

Carolyn Dickinson • Morrill, NE

Seventy-three

I remember I'm seventy-three when
The only one who shows up for my class reunion has my name on the nametag.
I wrestle ninety plus bales of hay into a stack by myself.
The temperature hangs below zero for a week, requiring four layers of clothing to keep warm.
School children study history I have witnessed and experienced.
My twenty-three-year-old grandson outworks me (working smarter than faster only helps a little).
My foot doesn't reach the stirrup to mount my old gelding.
The newspaper print seems smaller and smaller. (Is it cataracts?)
Ten-hour drives wear me out and make my bones stiff.
My fifteen-year-old grandson grins as he fixes my iPad when it gets stuck.
I remember "when," but nobody else does.
It's ninety-seven outside and ninety-eight inside (maybe I need to buy an air conditioner).
My great-granddaughter graduates from kindergarten.

I rejoice that I'm only seventy-three when
The morning begins at daybreak and I get out of bed.
The smell of home-baked bread comes out of my oven.
I make a snow angel before I shovel my walk.
The morning sun warms my face as I feed the critters.

My horse and I glide through the pines and up the mountain
trails.
My email shows up on my iPad.
My green-broke horse spooked, and I'm still aboard.
Spring brings up the flowers my grandmother planted when she
was eighty-five.
The grandchildren want me to play softball with them.
I pass my driving test again.
Watching my great-granddaughter graduate from kindergarten, I
look forward to her high school graduation.

Kim McNealy Sosin • Omaha, NE

Everyone Loves a Hardware Store

I cup my hands and peer through dirty glass
into our old small-town hardware store.
        There, behind that window
the phantom of my stepfather, back bent in effort,
pushes, lifts, pushes the old wide broom
        maneuvers the oiled sawdust
down the worn wood pathway through laden shelves.

He two-steps with the broom to some forgotten tune
        moves from the front door to the rear
where the ghost of Grandpa relaxes in a rocker.
Yesterday, Grandpa showed his granddaughter
        how to repair a toaster,
imagines what adventures today might bring.

        Grandpa checks his pockets
        for a quarter
while he waits for his grandson to come in after school.
Grandpa, could you loan me enough for ice cream?
Gruffly, *Young man, do you think I'm made of money?*
        as he digs into his pocket
        pretends to search
for the quarter he already knows is there.

In the mist, I see the front door open and close.
A customer?
Most made their hardware purchase early today,
headed to their fields or their jobs an hour ago.
I squint through the ghostly glass, recognize
Grandpa's favorite crony in
his gray *Kerns Hardware* shirt
from a job long ago, now quite stretched
with peek-a-boo places between the buttons
over his ample belly.

He claims the easy chair next to Grandpa's rocker,
sharing news, spreading rumors of who said what
last night in Rick's Tavern.
Grandpa remains alert for the door to open again,
a customer who might need penny nails,
eager to discuss the merits of
a 16D nail for framing
or a 6D headless for finishing
while letting the day wind down amiably.

Nathan Sousek • Lincoln, NE

The Gardener's Lament

My garden has called it quits.
And well it should too.

Too much heat.
Too little rain.
Too many rabbits nipping at its feet all summer long.

Still, I lament the once proud stems of Joe Pye, bluestem,
Purple coneflower, aster, goldenrod, and milkweed,
all bent and leaning, resigning it would seem,
to a weary hunch unlikely to ever straighten.
Here and there, a small patch of color stands out amidst
the drab grove. Soon, these too will pale and fall.

Someday I will be like these hardy prairie plants I tend.

Back crooked,
Head bowed low,
Hair falling off in the most unseemly of manners,
All my color drained away.

I'll look back then on these younger days,
With my strong back and head held high yet,
In wistful hope that like this garden, I might
offer one final vibrant bloom worthy of sharing.

ShennonDoah • Holdrege, NE

whimsical web

miniscule
metallic threads
decorous, dazzling
dainty strands
fine, flossy fibers
spun surreptitiously
by aesthetic arachnid

Tim Moran • Elwood, NE

Hard Water

The sun comes up in the kitchen window
and lights hard water residue

like clouds demystified and dropped
two-dimensional on the countertop.

Day upon day, it persists
in silica abstract expressions

on wine glasses, plates and coffee cups
I'm ashamed to have others see.

A bit like these age spots, revealed as soap
runs from the backs of my hands

browned by hours on the tractor
and hoeing weeds from the tomatoes and peppers,

a persistent, fated, pointillist lifescape
ever-approaching its vanishing point,

but for the time being, companionable.
Such is the influence of dawn

and the dishes done,
stacked and drying.

Veronica Torraca-Bragdon • Papillion, NE

Villanelle

I cannot grasp a color to describe your eyes
But I appreciate your very being
Remain my friend and a subject to analyze

Amiable baiting, we jokingly antagonize
Each other for every short-coming
I cannot grasp a color to describe your eyes

Outer beauty, inner beauty, I know how you prioritize
Your inability to trust leaves me weeping
Please remain my friend and a subject to analyze

Seeking to understand, not terrorize
Of you I find myself dreaming
I cannot grasp a color to describe your eyes

Relinquish the fears that make you ostracize
Yourself from living and loving
But remain my friend and a subject to analyze

In comfortable silence we recognize
Thoughts and words are fleeting
I cannot grasp a color to describe your eyes
Remain my friend and a subject to analyze

Originally published in Outside the Box, Inside the Wrapping, *2022, page 10.*

M. Timothy Nolting • Bushnell, NE

My Loves (for Deb)

I love the quiet solitude
Of a gold-leaved aspen grove.
The soothing tumble of crystal stream
In a sheltered mountain cove.

I love the feel of warming rays
From an Indian Summer sun.
The gentle call of a turtle dove
When the evening's just begun.

I love the purple majesty
Of the Rocky Mountains grand
With Charlie Russell sunsets
Painted by the Master's hand.

I love to hear the nikkers,
Watch the prancing, prideful stride
As my pony charges toward me
When I call him to my side.

I love the creak of leather
And the jinglin' of a spur,
The pungent nip of prairie sage
That gentle breezes stir.

I love to watch in wonder
When a slick-haired calf is born
And mama licks his steaming hide
In the frost of early morn.

But as I sit and ponder some
On these "loves" that stir my soul
That bring me joy and comfort
And make my spirit whole,

I find that none of these compare
With love you've sparked anew
And if I had to choose but one,
I'd choose my love for you.

Steve Rose • Indianola, IA

Biology

You found your grave before I found your name:
Norma Christina Oltman. Fate was kind: we were
better left as apparitions to each other than
lives pressed together by convention.

At seven I dreamed I'd find you, Mom, a princess
who'd lost your golden shoe. I begged to be
returned to you where all would see I fit,
a vessel more precious than its appendage.

At eighteen I dreamed I'd find you for the wealth I
hoped you owned, you, Mom, a Pharaoh's daughter
who had now soothed your family and could carry me
back to the nettles of the river and sail away full-masted.

At thirty I dreamed I'd find you to learn what diseases
coursed through you, Mom, that I might build defenses.
What vagaries of gut, blood, or lung are inheritance
hid in my flesh, this suitcase I wore, as I searched?

At fifty I dreamed I'd find you to show off your
grandchildren, and you to them. They shine with life.
By then dimly did I hope we'd meet, like
an old brass coin in a brackish stream.

At seventy, I know I'll never find you earthside,
ghost woman, whose life was entrapped by pregnancy
as a teen. Your womb'sembrace was
as close to your arms or heart as I'll ever feel.

Norma, are you waiting on the other side for my death
to birth me there
once again?

Brittany Wren • Lincoln, NE

Road Song

At the corner of roads J and 215
the children are asleep,
finally, in their carseats.
Their hands are still sticky from apple juice and snot.
The rock and dirt and tire rubber
rumble a goodnight song together.

We brought home the first baby,
almost three years ago now,
all fuzz, screech and yellow from jaundice.
Two weeks afterward the nurse said
“I know it will be hard,”
when I called, emptied out by the flu.
“But don’t kiss your baby.”
She didn’t know how easy it was
not to,
what with the shades drawn for days
and how I found myself dripping away.

Today, the fields are still flooded
from yesterday’s rain, blotched
by crushed beer cans.
The road is wrinkled and stretched
by potholes and tire tracks.

The rock and dirt and rubber rumble
something together. They know
something about keepin' on.

ShennonDoah • Holdrege, NE

Madame Bovary, C'est Moi

I'm shallow, insecure
I prefer the monetary
worth of a man, plus
distinguished good looks and
proper manners, to any
penniless sot or rake on
the street. Tangible goods,
pleasing to the eye, catch my eye
while entertaining my mind.
No ordinary life will do for me.
C'est moi, Madame Bovary.

Kim McNealy Sosin • Omaha, NE

Is This How It Starts?

I've begun to lose words,
even had to search online
to find words I know, words
I have always known, but
have temporarily
            mysteriously
            inexplicably
            misplaced.

Where did they go,
these meaningful
            errant words?
hierarchy, liaison, acquit,
conscientious, repository,
along with their
cousins and siblings.
Something is
      (what's the word?)
            amiss.

Steve Rose • Indianola, IA

Driving through Snow

north to the county hospital where
my wife had recovered again, I passed
a paddock of bulls: white-faced Herefords
and eight-ball black Angus
mingling with piebald shorthorns.

Pacing that pen, they made ice fly
off frozen clods like white sparks as
they gauged each other. I could smell
the testosterone melting the snow off
their broad backs and stone-chiseled skulls.

Nearby a herd of fallow cows and yearling
heifers kicked through the snow for grass,
lifting their noses deliciously, like women
toasting each other with flutes while the bulls'
bald scent tickled their speckled nostrils.

Once in town, we rid my wife of doctors and IVs,
then headed home, the snow steady enough
for conversation, driving by the bulls, now
huddled tight, the cows bundled against the wind.
And that night we laid down tender,

our old skin smooth behind worn pajamas,
safe from the weather, our breath warming
the other's. We talked about medicine
and time, our noses close enough
to touch, our lips close enough to kiss.

Nathan Sousek • Lincoln, NE

The Morning After

Everything outside is quiet
The type of silent regard only a late August storm can create

No birds flit or chatter amidst the tree branches, adorned still
With necklaces of glimmering liquid diamonds
Even the insects are conspicuous in their non-existent thrum
and the wind doesn't stir a leaf or blade of sodden grass

In a way, everything waits, as someone letting out a long sigh
after drinking deeply and quenching a great thirst

But eventually all will move, will stretch and yawn
As the slow gargle of half drowned crickets raising their voices,
the land comes awake

Susan Baron • Omaha, NE

The Candle

Little fireflies of light flitter
only so high, tethered by the wick in the amber glass.

In their last hour of light, the dots of fire struggle vainly
to regain remembered brilliance.

The black stubs destined to be drowned
in a shimmering puddle of wax.

And me?

Will I flicker dimly, struggling like the candle
to burn for a last few minutes;

before the light is gone; gone to an abyss,
brought back only by the fleeting memories of others?

Or will I go somewhere?
Another world, a place promised,
journeyed to only by faith?

Waverly Jackson • Lincoln, NE

Marriage Maybe

Sometimes holding hands is structural,
like bones to the body, or a dam
to the river.

On this side, a reservoir bloated
with all we've said and
not said.

On that side, the vastness of our life
and what it may be,
together.

Forever we hold each other, hold back
our worst selves, and maybe
our best.

But imagine how the river would be without
the dam? At first, wild and free
(maybe).

And then drop by drop, it would
dissipate into
nothing.

Joshua Johnson • Wilber, NE

28

I think life has passed me by and I'm only 28.
I fret about the passage of time
flowing past me like a river—approaching a waterfall.
Will I leave behind a pretty corpse? Or will I be swept away
forgotten in the stream of life?
I'm only 28 but I worry I've not done enough.

I think people are out to get me sometimes.
Like Jack the Ripper stalking the streets of London
except he's here—wandering through the heartlands of America
looking for young men to prey upon.
I'm just a 28-year-old dude from Iowa
but I think he wants me.

I worry that I'll end up a diabetic.
Comatose in candyland
because I couldn't stop my alien hand
from mincing all day long.
Except I'm 28 now and don't eat much sugar anymore
save for when I'm trying to calm myself down.

Sometimes I worry about my smile.
Because I've had at least 28 cavities,
four root canals, and two false teeth

by the time I turned 28.
But I still have my wisdom teeth
just not the wisdom to floss.

I fear homelessness.
Because even though I work full time
I live by a thread of silk
in this beautiful tapestry of poverty
that we call America.
I'm only 28, but I know the American Nightmare.

I'm only 28 years old
but my Father is 83
and my Mother is 62.
So I stay up all night worrying
about what'll happen when they're gone.
Will I find anyone else who'll love me?

At 28 years old I've never kissed a woman.
Or held one's hand while walking down the street,
or any of the other things you might imagine.
So I worry that I might be ugly
and usually avoid going out.
I can't remember the last time I tried asking anyone on a date.

Going on long trips alone frightens me sometimes.
Because I've never been a grease monkey
swinging through oily vines in the automobile jungle.
Nor have I gone spelunking in my transmission.

I may be 28 years of age
but I'm definitely not an auto mechanic.

Sometimes I worry I'll end up in hell.
Because I'm not the perfect apostle
and sometimes I doubt whether God's there at all.
But still I go to weekly Mass,
because God's never let me down
within 28 years of life.

I work really hard at my job.
Because in the land of the free
you've got to feed the monkey
and also because I like to do good.
So why do I always worry I'll be fired
even though in 28 years it's never happened?

Like everyone else I'm afraid of death.
Because I'm only 28 years old
and feel like there's still so much I've yet to do.
That and I'm not entirely sure what comes next,
whether I'll be in heaven or hell
or if I'll even be at all.

Even though I'm only 28 years old
I often worry about getting dementia.
Because what are we if not our thoughts?
If I can't write or compose a sentence
then how can I continue to bring meaning
into the nothingness of life?

Sometimes I worry that I might be stupid.
That everything I say or do is laughed at
and written off by everyone I meet behind my back.
But then I take heart—realizing that at 28
it's actually kinda phenomenal
that I don't think I know everything.

I'm always worried that people don't like me.
Because eyes are windows to the soul
and I'm a blind window cleaner,
who's about to stumble over the edge
and fall to supreme embarrassment
at only 28 years of age.

I'm worried of going blind in my later years.
Because the world is a beautiful embroidery
woven with flesh and blood—and painted
by a divine artist on an acid trip called life
and I'm addicted to it after 28 years
of lounging in the opium den of the world.

I'm afraid that I won't be appreciated.
That I'll toil away—like Sisyphus
only to see my boulder roll downhill,
forgotten in lieu of the next big thing,
and then be crushed under the weight of my anxiety
at only 28 years old.

It seems like I always think I'm never good enough.
Because the metrics aren't always clear

or maybe I'm just drunk—or hungry for praise.
I'm always afraid someone will do it better
that I'll be second best
or that at 28 I'll be branded a failure.

I like to watch snowflakes sometimes.
Because they're all unique—like us
until they fall into a pile of conformist mush on the ground
and lose all sense of individuality.
Then I'm reminded of my fear
of being just another 28-year-old in the crowd.

Sometimes I worry about being arrested
thrown in prison and deprived of my freedom
even though I've never committed a crime.
Because I've lived in the world's largest police state
where fear dominates the headlines
all 28 years of my life.

I worry I'm not as creative as I'd like to be.
Because sometimes when I'm in conversations
I sit silently for long periods of time
trying to ignore the critical voices in my mind
and worrying people will think I've nothing to say
after being so silent for 28 years.

The concept of artificial intelligence scares me.
Because we're not meant to be machines
and art can't be made by a calculator.

At 28 years old I finally embraced my creativity
only for robots to suddenly think
that numbers can be artistic.

I worry about the death of creativity sometimes.
Because so much of our world is already
so inauthentic as to be fraudulent
so mathematical as to be formulaic
and so lazy as to be dead.
I'm only 28—but I'm becoming a luddite.

Sometimes I wonder if I'm really alive.
Or if I'm like a marionette
dancing on a string.
I may only be 28 years old
but I fear that I've spent my life
existing only as a wooden boy.

For being only 28 years old
you'd think I'd go out more.
But I don't.
So I sit at home and worry
that I'll be deemed "boring"
and forgotten about by my peers.

I worry about my final years.
About whether or not I'll be alone
or if I'll be remembered at all after I'm gone.
I may only be 28 years old

but I think often about our place in life
and whether humanity means anything or not.
Sometimes I worry that I've set a poor example.
Because despite my values and opinions,
I know I've fallen short of them a time or three.
So I find myself asking for grace
and hoping my friends don't brand me a hypocrite
at only 28 years of age.

I worry that you'll read this poem.
That you'll find it amusing
or overly dramatic
and then write me off.
Like some 28-year-old kid
who hasn't a clue.

I have all these worries and I'm only 28 years old.
But when I was 13 I used to worry
I'd end up killing myself,
because I didn't think I'd be strong enough
to face all of life's challenges.
But now I'm 28, and none have come to pass.

Tami Olsen • Beresford, SD

The old farmers know.

When to harvest the crop;
when to bring in the cattle.
They know how much farther
the horse can pull the plow.
They know how much longer
the sun will light their work.

They know when to pull a calf
and when to put one down.
They rise with the sun
and set with it.
They see life begin
and they see it end.

The old farmers know.

They know when they've
lived a good life.
They know when they've
left a good legacy.
When they've worked hard
and when they've loved harder.

And the old farmers know
when to go home.

They know when they're ready
and when to let go.
They know we'll be alright;
we'll make it on our own.
And when the Lord beckons them
and the earth welcomes them
the old farmers know.

Steve Rose • Indianola, IA

Wrists

I've never tested milk against my wrist,
the warmth of it, three ticks past tepid.

But I've watched women I love squirt
some drops against their pulse, pursing

their lips as if they were sketching a
fine line or seers passing judgment

while they cradle their children like porcelain
in smooth, formidable arms.

And so last night, when spring had stripped
our bed of its comforter and you, my

wife, of your pajamas, I felt my left arm
seek out the hollow above your hips.

Your heat beat into my skin and through
the artery that marks my body's time.

Nathan Sousek • Lincoln, NE

The Rain Began

An unfamiliar sound to start,
the soft pitter-patter of bird feet across a tin roof,
Each drop hitting dust-dry earth with a gentle "Pfft"

Across the fields the clouds gather darker,
a gray veil whooshing closer and closer—until
the liquid crescendo holds for the briefest of transitory moments
before the soothing caesura slides across our ears,
effervescent and intoxicating

It is then, as we soak in the peaceful timbre,
that we with puissant humbleness start the prayer anew,
This time in hope that it is not too late

Kim McNealy Sosin • Omaha, NE

Braided Prairie Rivers

Where there are no rock outcrops,
no mountain valleys,
to push to pull to guide water,
silvery blue rivulets
meander
weave
merge.

Ribbons spiral
as the girl's pigtails
on her first school day.
Take side trips,
cross over then again,
the twisted hair of a weary
woman,
walking a dusty trail,
braids loose,
frazzled, tugged by
wind and dirt,

tangles
struggles
through grasslands
where schooners sailed,

navigating long green blades,
of bygone plains.

Ships piloted by
land farers
hopeful men,
resilient women
flowing over these prairies
Water, land, blood.

Essays

Susan Baron • Omaha, NE

Mittens

At ten a.m. every Wednesday, in Omaha, Nebraska, if you happen to drive downtown in the area of south 15th Street, you will see a line of cars and vans parked at the curb and forty to sixty people, maybe more, patiently, quietly making a line that stretches down the block. These mostly men and a few women are waiting for food provided by a loosely knit group of folks, some from churches, some there just because, and one very determined woman named Jeanne, who keeps this together and going. She likes her last name to remain anonymous and so I will leave her so. But she is there with her roasters, her foil pans, paper plates, and foam cups every week. I am not there every week but join them occasionally on my own mission.

Folding tables are pulled from the parked cars and hastily set up. No one bothers with table cloths or centerpieces. This is a bare bones endeavor to get food quickly to those who need it. A speaker system appears, given energy by orange utility cords that snake their way from a portable generator. Loud catchy patriotic and uplifting tunes add a feeling of celebration to this gathering that could easily be thought as grim. There is a plastic bin full of forks that someone, somewhere previously wrapped with napkins. Next, helpers lug steaming pans heavy with chicken and noodles, green beans, and potatoes to the tables. Other times there is a nourishing stew or something else, but always plenty and always hot.

Another table or two is covered with snacks and sweets: cookies, cakes, occasionally pie sliced into pieces or given whole, all to be carried away. These men and women do not eat here, but take the food away to a camp, perhaps under a bridge or in a car or for a lucky few to a shared apartment. They drift in from every direction and leave in the same way at the same pace. Bags are filled. It is just one meal, on one day. They must plan for the hunger that comes later. Unlike us, who can eat when we want, they must eat when they can.

Two brown plastic urns sit on a smaller table. Five gallons of hot coffee in one, five gallons of hot water in the other to mix with chocolate powder. The table of urns is placed away from the bustle of food serving so there is time to fill a cup, add sugar, creamer, taste, add more.

The homeless men and women shiver in the winter wind as they wait their turn to have plate or bowl filled. Most are men. Most have some sort of winter coat. And most have some sort of gloves on their hands or stuffed in their pockets as they collect the offerings of the day. What covers their hands is of interest to me. I search for cold chapped ones or thin gloves that do not keep the fingers warm. I have brought my own folding table and I lay out a rainbow-colored assortment of mittens made by me. Before you say "Aw" and think it a grand thing that I do, let me assure you the mittens I knit began with a selfish act.

I have knitted since I was a young woman. Sweaters, scarves, throws, even socks that knit up nicely if you use yarn that is elasticized. (Make sure you double knit the heels with embroidery floss to make them sturdy.) All this knitting resulted in an accumulation of odds and ends that filled a forty-gallon plastic tub.

There was not enough yarn of any one kind or color to begin and finish a large project, but too much to throw away. So I saved and saved until one day I could hardly get the lid to catch without sitting on it. As much as I treasured the odds and ends, I was determined not to begin another tub, but to find a way to use what I had.

Perhaps an afghan? No, not enough of the same weight of yarns in the right colors to make something that pleased my eye. Scarves, yes. I experimented with rows and lines of this yarn and that. But I found knitting scarves a bore. Hats then? I searched for something easier. Then somehow mittens came to mind. I found a pattern that was simple and quick.

It doesn't take a lot of yarn to knit a pair of mittens, and the odds and ends would be perfect to use. The first few pairs delighted me. They were so colorful. I loved the creativity of matching and blending to make something unique. I pressed my gems on family, gave them as gifts to friends, offered a pair to strangers who came to my house until I noticed people hiding their hands when around me. Not really, but there was still a mostly filled tub full of yarn and I was obsessed. I wanted to continue to knit because doing so while in front of the TV justified my excessive movie watching, but I also wanted to make something useful. So those without homes and I have come together over mittens.

The original tub of yarn has since gone onto the hands of hundreds of people. Now yarn comes from friends who donate their unused stash, and I buy new yarn during craft store sales. Roaming up and down yarn aisles is one of my favorite pastimes. The challenge is not to be enticed to buy more yarn than I have room to store. The stash, as we knitters call our odds and ends, is now limited to three large drawers in a cabinet in my family room. I can usually knit from eighty to one hundred pairs throughout the year, and I have been doing this for maybe four or five years. I have lost count, for the only thing I really count are the stitches as I cast on, increase for the thumb or decrease to cast off.

It takes a couple of movies for me to turn out a pair. I have learned that if I cast on both mittens on the same needle, at the same time they come out the same size. I am a prolific knitter but make no claim to be a great one. Sometimes I am most pleased by the color combination and different lines of texture. Sometimes the pair is plain but serviceable. If I don't have a thick yarn, I use two strands of thin yarn to create density so as to make really warm mittens. Using two complimentary colors in this way has a side benefit of creating a pleasing tweed pattern.

I have learned that homeless or not, men care about color. They pass over the pastels and whites and creams in favor of black, brown, gray, or red. Pink is an absolute no-no. I have learned that most men's hands are not much larger than my own, although I do make a few very large pairs and smaller sizes for the occasional woman and even smaller for children. Sometimes a man will ask if he can take them for his friend or his children who are not with him. Of course.

"Do you need a pair of mittens?" I ask. The response is almost always hesitant. "I have some gloves," he mumbles, but his hands are blue and dry with cold. "Just try these on," and I hold a mitten up in such a way that he must extend a hand. I slip the mitten on and the man almost always smiles a little as he feels the softness and warmth of the yarn. Usually his expression is uncertain, as if he thinks only children wear mittens. *But this one is so warm.*

"Do you like the color because you can choose another pair if you don't. You can have any pair you want." I am eager that they be pleased. Once given permission, the man will begin to shop. I step back a little, not speaking to give him room and privacy. He will touch each pair, maybe lifting one as if to feel the weight. Then putting it back, his fingers will touch another pair. He chooses the black with lines of red. One of my favorites too.

Sometimes there is no conversation, just a look from him and a nod from me. Then a hand darts out and takes a pair. Color doesn't matter. Maybe they don't even need the mittens for warmth, but the need to have something new, colorful, personal to keep. That is enough.

Besides needing the food, many of these men need to talk. They stop at my table and ask, "Where did the mittens come from?" I will admit I knitted them but brush it off as no big deal. The big deal is them. Another question asked is "Are you from here?" I have learned this is their way to open a conversation. They are curious about me, a lady who is so obviously not living on the street. But most of all I think they want to tell me a little bit about themselves, assure me they are not "the other." We never talk about their homelessness but about where they are from and where they hope to go soon. "I'll be leaving for Kansas City soon. There's a job down there for me." Many of the men are working but homeless. "I need a pair of mittens; I left my gloves at work."

Statistics on homelessness are widely divergent depending on where and when one is looking. According to the National Alliance to End Homelessness, the states with the highest rates of daily homelessness are California (151,278), New York (74,178), and Texas (24,432). Nebraska, not so much. (2,246). These numbers are from the 2022 Point-In-Time report.

Homelessness is further categorized as three types:

> Chronic—made up of older individuals, who are hard core unemployable due to disabilities or untreated substance abuse issues.
>
> Transitional—younger individuals, homeless for a temporary, short period due to a catastrophic event.
>
> Episodic—mostly young, that shuttle in and out of homelessness because they are chronically unemployed due to medical, mental health, and/or substance abuse issues.

The chronically homeless make up the smallest percentage of those within shelters and actually are most likely not to stay in shelters but live on the street. It is the chronically homeless person, slouched unconscious next to a wall, dirty, and smelly that defines all homeless people for us because they are the most visible. But most of the homeless people, perhaps 80 percent, fall into Transitional, making up the largest numbers, followed by Episodic types with men representing 60 percent of all types. So while the issue of homelessness is constant, the same individuals who are homeless is not. These facts should blow our previously conceived notions.

Too many people still think that the leading cause of homelessness is substance abuse, drugs, or alcohol. Even a little research will abuse that notion. Almost every authority on the subject puts lack of affordable housing as the number one reason and substance abuse last, even after domestic violence and mental illness. A permanent solution is not charity consisting of a handout, but a hand up, beginning with affordable housing, employment opportunities, and livable wages.

I wonder about the people who are standing in line today. They come from nowhere and disappear to places unknown, at least to me. Is this an unfortunate temporary situation for them or is this their future as well as their present? Are they waiting for affordable housing, looking for a job, or maybe they are just wanting this meal, at this place and time? Whatever their reason, they are here today.

Perhaps food and mittens given out on an Omaha street is really just charity to help them endure rather than to help them rise. But then what is the goal of charity? To help or to force change? And should it be withheld if change does not occur? Homeless people are not just lost causes, a blight on our cities whose care is to be shuttled to churches and government programs and hidden from view so we can rest easy in our misconceptions. They are not "the other." They want us to know they are us, just a less fortunate version of us, for now. They want us to know they deserve dignity and respect as they look for a way up and out. I can see it in their eyes as they slip their hands into a pair of mittens made just for them.

Deb Carpenter-Nolting • Bushnell, NE

Changing the Narrative

"Grammy, let's play," my five-year-old grandson requests.

I watch as he gathers up random animals: a Nebraska farm horse, squishy cow, and wildlife elk; a Wyoming antelope; a snow tiger; a long-necked dinosaur. He lines them up and faces them away from the dining room table where a remote-controlled velociraptor hides among chair legs. The setup indicates his preferred battle, where a vicious dinosaur will quickly pick off my sub-par group.

I feign ignorance and ask, "Are we playing hide-and-seek?"

"No," he replies. "It's something that starts with an 'f.'"

I used to indulge these fights, realizing that boys play much differently than my two daughters did, but after the first few losses ("Am I ever going to win?" I ask. "No, Grammy," he tells me in a solemn voice), I decided it was time to change the narrative.

"Fishing?" I suggest as convincingly as possible. "That starts with an 'f.'"

"No, Grammy. I'll whisper it." He breathlessly giggles the word *fight* in my ear.

"How about *conversation*?" I ask. For benefit of a reading lesson I add, "That starts with a 'c.'"

He moves the line of animals into a cozier semi-circle. The velociraptor remains in hiding.

"Okay, the animals are having a conversation," I begin, reinforcing the concept.

"No, Grammy. It has to start 'Once upon a time.'"

"Okay. Once upon a time, the animals gathered around a campfire for a nice picnic."

He pushes a button and the velociraptor lets out a loud screech.

"What was that sound?" The elk turns toward the hidden dinosaur.

"I don't see anything," the squishy cow tells the others.

Another loud noise emits from somewhere under the table, and the huge dinosaur appears and begins to approach the circle of friends.

"Oh, it's a velociraptor!" the long-necked dinosaur exclaims. I leave off with the animal voices and ask in my own Grammy voice, "Is this a brachiosaurus or a brontosaurus? Sometimes I can't tell the difference."

"Grammy," my grandson replies, "see the crest? It's a brachiosaurus."

"Okay. Thanks." I move the brachiosaurus closer to the velociraptor.

The menacing creature screeches again and moves forward, ending up with its nose to the floor, tail high in the air.

"That's cool how you can balance on your head," the brachiosaurus tells him.

"I like your stripes," calls the antelope from the fire.

The raptor regains its stance and its mouth opens to show a scary row of teeth and long tongue.

The horse approaches and asks, "How many teeth do you have?"

"Um." Little Boy glances quickly into the mouth of the raptor and says in the dinosaur's voice, "Hundreds."

"Cool," says the horse.

"You get ten points!" the raptor tells the horse.

"Are you an herbivore?" Squishy Cow asks.

"RRRR. No," the raptor vehemently declares. "You get minus one billion points!"

This is usually the excuse for the velociraptor or T-Rex to attack the plant-eater and declare, "Carnivores eat meat!"

"*I'm* an herbivore," says the brachiosaurus.

"So am I," the horse, elk, antelope, and squishy cow all say in turn.

"I'm a carnivore," admits the tiger. "Shall we go hunt for our lunch and join the others for a picnic?"

"That sounds like a good idea," the horse says. "We'll go get our grass and leaves for salad while you're gone."

Normally, the carnivore dinosaur would say, "I'll kill a dilophosaurus and be back," but this time the raptor turns to the tiger and says, "I have some T-Rex meat in the refrigerator we can eat."

"Great!" Tiger replies.

When all return, the narrator says, "The animals then chill out around the campfire eating the food they like and getting along just fine." For good measure I add, "The end."

"Wait, Grammy!" Little Boy holds up his hand and adds an epilogue. "And then a volcano erupts! And everyone gets extinct." In his dinosaur voice he adds, "Except the velociraptor."

Just when the storyteller thinks she is on solid ground and the world is a better place, along comes a plot twist, changing the narrative once again.

The end.

Carolyn Dickinson • Morrill, NE

Feet

A long time ago, no white lines on asphalt stretched across the prairie. No yellow dashes and dots laid out Morse code for drivers to pass or not.

Only feet crossed the prairie. Soft paws—like rabbits, pumas, coyotes, and prairie dogs—padded through the grass and the dust. Split hooves—like bison and elk—left two-toed tracks in the mud. Three-toes—like turkeys and grouse—ranged from the ground to the trees. Talons—dangling from feathered wings—rarely left their imprints below but hunted from above. Some had no feet at all but slithered along the ground, tongue flicking to "hear" their surroundings.

Both soft paws and split hooves created paths through the buffalo grass, trails across the fallen rocks, up the hills and down to the creeks and mudholes. Some came out at night, others when the sun shone. Talons perched in the scattered trees near the water sources, watching the feet crisscrossing below, claws who hunted and paws who hid.

Hundreds of years pass. Those with or without feet come into the world. They grow. They die. The bluffs erode. The creeks flood when the rains come; they dry up in the drought. Trees sprout, provide shelter above and below, serve as lookout posts, lose their leaves, their sap, and fall. Soft paws, three toes, split hooves, and footless follow trails begun many generations ago.

New feet arrive—not quadruped, not feathered, but soft, five-toed, leather-covered bipeds. At night they sleep in a shelter made of hides.

Other leather-covereds follow, individually or in groups. Four-footers sleep inside or outside the tents, guarding the biped occupants. When the nights turn cold, biped and quadruped move away, leaving the original feet to deal with the snow.

Some of the native paws and hooves, as well as some of the feathered three-toes, also travel south to warmer climates. Others burrow underground or hole up in caves. Still others brave the elements, leaving their footprints on the snow-covered ground.

Seasons come and go. The leather-covered feet return when the grass turns green, and they leave when it turns brown. They hunt both soft paws and hard hooves, even the feathered talons. They wear the hides and eat the meat of whatever they kill.

Different bipeds come. Rather than soft leather, hard leather soles tramp the ground. The lighter-skinned bipeds cut down trees, slice them, and build houses. They stay when the frost appears. Some of the booted soles travel on the ground, but others ride circled by wooden stirrups on big hard-hooved, single-toed quadrupeds. Some of the domesticated hooves pull heavy things with round wooden feet that roll on the ground.

Metal things pushed by soled feet or pulled by round hooves tear up the grass and turn over the sod. The soled feet drop foreign seeds into the freshly plowed soil and rechannel the liquid from the creek. As more and more heavy round wheels arrive, flat barges with long tails but no toes ferry the round footers and their possessions across the deep waters.

The wild feet stay away from the sliced-wood dwellings, at least during the day. Antlered hooves and masked paws invade the gardens at night, angering the two-footers. Feathery feet enjoy the grain heads growing in the fields and the fruit in the gardens. As farming bipeds create ponds, web-footers appreciate new residences.

In some places, bipeds dig foundations close together. Hard soles walking, round wheels rolling, and solid hooves trotting beat down the grass to create dusty streets. Wooden walkways protect shoes and boots in front of the buildings, especially when the dust turns to mud. Tiny paws discover hiding places and food sources in the towns. Feathered three toes find places for nesting on the roofs and under the eaves.

Another kind of feet arrives. Smaller hard metal round wheels spin on iron rail paths, rolling faster than wild split hooves or soft paws can run. Spewing out noise, steam, and ash, these rolling feet carry long wooden boxes filled with bipeds and quadrupeds.

With the smoking, rolling wheels come other changes. Two footers stick poles into the ground and fasten wire with sharp barbs onto them. Wooly and domestic horned split hooves compete with wild antlered and horned hard footers for the tall and short prairie grasses.

More time and more changes. Rubber rolling wheels venture out, carrying only a few occupants. They wander freely across the prairie, free of the metal rails, limited only by steep slopes and deep water. Bridges span the creeks and rivers.

With more rolling wheels traversing the prairie, the paths become dusty roads or muddy sinkholes. Gravel appears on some of the more traveled roads.

More and more posts sink into the ground, fencing in most of the prairie. The larger original soft paws and split hooves struggle to find their places in the new farms and ranches. Some large hard hooves are limited to buffalo ranches. Some split hooves jump fences with ease, while others crawl between their wires and stay mostly out where posts encompass larger areas. Small soft paws and footless long-bodies roam freely into fields and gardens. Feathered talons ignore any biped-created restrictions.

Meat-eating soft paws find a new source of nutrition in the young of domestic split hooves. Hole and den diggers are declared a nuisance.

Black tar and gravel decrease the mud problem. Some rubber wheels become sleeker, while other larger rubber tires replace most of the wide wooden round footers. Narrow metal rimmers pulled by round hooves almost disappear.

As asphalt spreads, yellow lines divide traffic in opposite directions. Big rubber round tires and metal tracks scour and level new roads, sometimes digging deep into the hills and filling in the low places. More bridges cross creeks and rivers.

Because more and more two-footers drive their rubber round wheels at higher speeds, new roads create their own paths. Asphalted roads gain parallel dots and dashes, parallel white lines, creating four, six, even eight lanes.

With new roads carved into the landscape, some older roads are abandoned. In areas of many bipeds, some become paths for two footers walking or riding on spoked round wheelers. Others, in farming areas, turn into cropland where corn and beans dig their root feet into the soil.

In the prairie, when the white lines and the dot-and-dash Morse code no longer outline the rubber-tires' roadways, grass grows over the humped scars of the roadbeds, and quadrupeds once again crisscross their trails. Soft paws pad through the grass and the dust. Wild hard hooves leave two-toed tracks in the mud, sharing the prairie grass with domestic split footers and round hooves. Some three toes range from the ground to the trees. Talons, dangling from feathered wings, rarely leave their imprints below, only hunting from above.

Johnnye Gerhardt • Omaha, NE

Christmas and Tinsel

Santa Claus terrified me because I had the feeling he knew about all the times I tried to poison my younger brother with water bugs in a mud pie. He would eat anything from the time he was two. My mother questioned the disappearance of ornaments one Christmas. My brother ate them like apples. A year older and taller, I could convince him of anything, but I did not tell him Christmas decorations were edible. He drank bleach one time, too, and smoked a cigar that Mom gave him so he'd quit stealing her cigarettes. He was two and a half, the youngest person to give up smoking. I gave up trying to get rid of him. He was indestructible. But we both loved and remembered Christmas in our own way.

~ ~ ~ ~ ~

We remembered when Santa was the only man to wear patent leather boots and a matching belt. No one questioned his fashion sense or picketed against his use of fur. Santa's elves didn't dress like Victoria's Secret models either and they wore a size ten.

We remembered when no one paid any attention to Santa's diet, and he got whole cow's milk poured from a glass bottle and cookies made from scratch with real butter baked on a cookie sheet smeared with lard so they wouldn't stick. Now he gets a protein energy drink and a cucumber-and-bean-sprout sandwich made with whole wheat bread. "Organic" and "calories" never entered the discussion for a Christmas dinner either.

At the holiday meal, children of yore were forced to endure the torture of using a napkin to protect their "good clothes." Now they wear outfits with less fabric than napkins and as tattered as a mechanic's rag.

Children decided what they wanted for Christmas by gawking at store window displays or visiting toy departments. They weren't told what they wanted or should want by a commercial. Children reluctantly came to the dinner table because they had to leave their new toys. Now the toys fit in the palm of their hand and while you're saying Grace, your son is killing aliens or your daughter is spending her gift certificates online.

Children didn't suffer psychological damage because you lied to them during the holidays. Only a few put it into practice and went into politics or sales. Christmas stories were told or read by parents or grandparents instead of children streaming it on their smart television.

As a child I couldn't sleep on Christmas Eve waiting for Santa Claus. As an adult I didn't get much sleep because I was Santa Claus. Once I figured out where the extra part went or that it was just an extra part, I crawled limply into bed for a few minutes. The kids always woke me up just as I got into the zone. Santa used to travel by sleigh only and no one had heard of NORAD. Mom or Dad would schedule the sleigh bells and hooves on the roof sound effects with a child's bedtime and not some tracking device.

The only place you ever saw an artificial tree was in a department store. When they finally made it into the home, you could get them in every color but green. Silver was the popular choice. A color wheel turned in front of a spotlight, changing its hues as it rotated in its stand. Eventually we regained some semblance of good taste. Real trees grew in favor again until conservationists made us feel guilty. A whole new industry developed around realistic looking trees. I have to admit that I miss that pine smell but not the fire hazard and crawling over gifts to water it.

Silver tinsel. It clung tenaciously to your clothes. You'd find it months later under furniture and, years later, inside your closet. Tinsel still fills the empty compartments in ornament boxes. Most were broken by a dog's wagging tail, a partier, or my brother flinging a new toy, like a bat or ball. Once he used an ornament as a target for a new bee-bee gun. He helped decorate the tree one time, too, by flinging fistfuls of tinsel at the tree. It landed in clumps and on ornaments. Each strand, according to my aesthetics, had to dangle perfectly and freely from the end of a branch. Mom let him water the tree instead after that.

Everybody had strings of lights with bulbs as big as their fist in primary colors that all went out when one bulb failed. They were easy to change but tedious to find. Now trees come pre-lit and only one bulb goes out.

Tree ornaments then weren't coordinated to one's décor but purchased to commemorate something or someone or just because you thought they were pretty, and every tree had either a star or an angel at the top. Silver garland was replaced by ribbon. Wrapping gifts wasn't an art then, and nobody cared that the package didn't coordinate with anything.

The magic of Christmas past returns when unpacking ornaments speckled with artificial snow my brother, age eight, sprayed on the tree . . . and me. After that I was always on guard. Remember putting stencils against a window and dabbing pink glass wax on them with a sponge until they got so soggy, they curled?

On Christmas Eve, I searched for the star that guided the three wise men. The star I gave that honor to was actually a planet, and astronomically the guiding "star" is still debated. Dad had a star, too, but that turned out to be a galaxy, even better.

The week before Christmas seemed to last a month but Christmas day lasted only as long as the ribbon-cutting, paper-tearing frenzy. Most of our memories fade away with time, too, and are replaced by new ones, younger ones. And that's as it should be. Someone will find a strand of tinsel in a box, and it will all come back anyway.

Kim McNealy Sosin • Omaha, NE

Moving Out Sale: A Hermit Crab Style Essay

Leather Sofa, some scratches from my cat

Well-used recliner built into the left side, too large for my new location

Coffee Table, walnut veneer

About 18" x 30", a couple of faint water rings through the varnish

Computer and Writing Hutch

Twelve years old, handy shelves and cubbyholes, a water ring on the writing surface

Table Lamp, antique

Silver metal frame, incandescent, working, not sure of the provenance

Round Solid Oak Dining Table, antique

From my parents' store in the 1940s, faint water ring, three oak chairs, one needs glue. No private dining room in my new location.

Several Photographs, taken by a photographer in the family

She expertly framed one mountain in sunset landscape, one mama bear teaching her cubs to dig clams, one of the family ranch in the Nebraska Sandhills. I hope she'll understand why I can't take them. No personal wall space in my new location. Request images if interested.

Grandfather Wall Clock

Lovely walnut large (26" high) clock I made over fifty years ago from local walnut and clock parts. It has been accurately swinging the pendulums and cheering me with chimes since then. One-of-a-kind. Looking for someone to love it like I do. Must sell because chimes are not allowed in my new location.

Automobile, 2016 Mazda CX-5

Medium-sized silver SUV with only 75,000 miles. Comfortable ride, engine maintenance up to date, body in great shape with no dents but a little wear from driving in gravel. Tires about six years old. Not driving now, and vehicles not allowed in my new location. Call for a look.

Two Wonderful Cats, siblings

One male, black, and one female, gray. My daily companions for almost nine years. Strictly indoor cats, never separated (though expect occasional sibling cat fights). They will provide sympathy when you need it, solace from the frustrations of aging, and company when no one else has time. Not allowed in my new location.

Mark Peyton • Gothenburg, NE

The Freedom to Pass Gas

Where to start? I've never really been motivated to discuss this topic in writing, but this past week, as they always seem to do, things all came together and I said, there is an essay here!

There are some things in this world that are perverse, some disgusting, and then some that are just in bad taste. Talking about the gaseous emissions that come from the backside of humans is not perverse or disgusting, and apparently not even in poor taste anymore, if it ever was. In 1871 Benjamin Franklin said this about passing gas: "(it) is of infinitely more Importance to human Happiness than that Liberty of the Press," and he even wrote a letter to the Royal Academy urging the investigation of some food supplements that would make the "wind" from the digestive system pleasant to the nose.

Flatulence, the emitting of gas from the backside, is defined medically in multiple ways, one being that it "is the state of having excessive stomach or intestinal gas." Another definition is "an expulsion through the rectum of a mixture of gases . . ." The slang term, first adopted in the medical community, is "fart," a term my mother still finds perverse, disgusting, and in bad taste. You could use "puff," "toot," "fluff," or "pass gas," but a rose is a rose and by any other name it would smell the same . . . which is also true of flatulence.

Why? Why do the gases that emanate from our bodies stink? When we eat, we take in a variety of materials that are all made from basically the same stuff. Our food consists of carbon, with some hydrogen, oxygen, sulfur, iron, sodium, and calcium . . . mostly. Yes, there are tons of other things, but these elements make up the bulk of what we "eat."

We have a digestive system that is amazing. It is designed to break the various combinations of these elements into their component parts, thus releasing the energy stored there and freeing the other non-nutritious stuff, some solid, some liquid, and some gas. The gas component is made up mostly of nitrogen and carbon dioxide. These are both colorless and odorless gases, and while they can result in a noisy expulsion, they rarely contain any offensive odors. The nasty smell comes from the sulfur, iron, and excess hydrogen compounds, which are mixed with the nitrogen and carbon dioxide and emitted. These elements, in the form of sulfur dioxide, hydrogen sulfide, and iron sulfide, stink!

Stink, or not, we all do this, and in fact, for the most part, we have to do this. The typical American emits about five hundred cc's of gas/day in about fourteen different emissions. Of course, being a scientist, I wanted to test that by counting my emissions and, given that one person isn't near large enough of a sample size, I asked my wife if she would do the same. Her "NO" was quite final and she informed me that I would not be asking anyone else to count theirs either!

Whether we count or not, the releasing of gas is inevitable. You can try and hold it back, and you can succeed, until you forget and bend over, walk, or eventually when you fall asleep and relax.

But holding it in might not be a good idea. Some believe it can be bad for your health. In 400 BC, Hippocrates, the author of the Hippocratic Oath that doctors take, claimed that it was necessary for physical well-being to release the gases of our intestine. Because of that, the Roman Emperor Claudius, who came to power about ten years after the death of Jesus Christ, decreed that it was perfectly legal and acceptable for any and all Roman citizens to pass gas whenever necessary. The "freedom to fart" lasted three hundred years until Emperor Constantine declared that Christianity was no longer illegal (as he himself was Christian) but that it was not allowable to "pass gas" in public! (Hence the term tight-assed Christians).

Regardless of the health benefits of "fluffing," there always has been, and probably always will be, social discomfort, embarrassment, and yes, humor associated with the process. You want to bring a roomful of fifth graders . . . sixth graders . . . third graders . . . tenth graders . . . college students, or a family of four to laughter, just have someone "toot and pollute."

You can buy "fart machines" (and yes, we own one), and my youngest son has an app for his phone so that he can make the sounds without the machine. But the chain of events that led me to thinking about the release of intestinal gas started with two "memories" that were recounted, a "news" piece about art depicting the process of emitting gas, and a commercial on the radio that ended with the woman declaring to her friends that it was time for a road-trip and this time they could keep the windows shut because she had taken the substance being advertised to help reduce her "GAS" problem.

The artworks from the news report are Japanese Fart Scrolls (I'm not kidding, Google it!) and after looking at them, I would agree with my mom that it is perverse, disgusting, and in bad taste. The memories started in the coffee room on break with fellow workers reliving humorous actions of one of my co-workers.

He and I were at Tractor Supply looking for fencing materials. The young girl said to follow her out to the yard where we could look over the various types they had in stock. Walking out to the area, my co-worker let go. Based upon the amplitude of the release, he had a lot of nitrogen and carbon dioxide in his system. Fortunately I was upwind so I don't know how much hydrogen sulfide was mixed in.

Credit the young lady. She didn't miss a step. It did get uncomfortably quiet for a minute . . . an embarrassing quiet, but we were all adults and we carried on. Well, we did right up to the point he and I left the store and walked to his pickup. At that point I could not remain quiet. "You had to fart?" I asked. "That one sort of got away from me!" he answered, to which I laughed so hard I was truly crying. You would have thought we were a couple of eighth grade boys; we laughed and laughed and laughed. I don't know if releasing gas is physically good for you, but laughing that hard is great for you physically and mentally, so maybe a good fart is healthy. Though I'm sure the young girl would say there was nothing great about it!

Recounting that memory to the discomfort of my co-worker sparked the second memory. This is a story of a family, on a trip to Washington DC, who learn that you never fart in an elevator. The father, mother, and two teenage boys of the story will remain anonymous to protect their reputations and my health.

After spending the day walking around the Mall, seeing the sights, and eating at a fast food joint, the family returned to their fancy hotel and were in the elevator heading to their room. The doors closed and the ripe odor of hydrogen sulfide filled the small space. The red-faced mother said “oops” and began to giggle. Yep, women also pass gas, and giggle, and apparently their emissions can be as smelly as any man’s!

As embarrassing as that was, it got worse. On the third floor, the elevator stopped and a man and woman got into the car. It continued upward. Slowly the hand of the woman came up to her face and her thumb and forefinger covered the ends of her nostrils in an attempt to keep the smell out. She gave the oldest boy an evil stare, knowing that he was the guilty one. The red-faced mother, standing next to the woman, stared hard at the floor, failing miserably at stifling her laughter, laughter that only brought a deeper look of disapproval from the other woman in the car.

On the sixth floor, the elevator stopped and the couple got off, giving one more look of disdain toward the family. The doors closed and the four could not contain themselves. The laughter only intensified when the oldest boy said, “Thanks, Mom, she thought it was ME!”

Perverse, disgusting, and in bad taste, maybe, but it makes for a hilarious commercial on the radio, a great story in the break room, and a truly wonderful family memory.

Sue Ray-Smolik • Omaha, NE

The College Experience

From Shy Freshman to Published Author, What the College Experience Can Do for You

Like many high school graduates, we were wondering if college should be our next step. We had concerns about what living in a dorm and being forced to meet and share a small living space with people we had never met might be like. As most young adults do, we sometimes doubted that we really knew what we wanted to do as a career. Let me share with you our story and what the college experience ended up being for us.

When my roommate, Nancy, and I first met at Clarion University over four decades ago now in the fall of 1981. We were just two very shy, very uncertain, small town girls. Not originally roommates, we simply lived in the same dorm and actually did not even meet there. Instead, we met at a marching band rehearsal. She, being a talented flute player, and I, having decided to try out for the flag squad as part of my goal to "put myself out there more" and get a taste of new experiences my shyness and work commitments sometimes had kept me from during high school.

Though I had still found plenty of activities to feed my social butterfly side, marching band conflicted with my choir and work schedules, so it had not been on my list then. However, in college I was determined to do it all! So much so, that between band, choir, musicals, and part-time work, I found myself on academic probation my first semester. A bumpy start to my college career indeed. Realizing that I had perhaps overestimated the amount of activities I could manage, that became my only semester of band once I prioritized what my available time allowed me to partake in and still be successful. And, not to worry, I did graduate on the Dean's list after retaking a class that summer and learning the important life skill of work/social life balance that college helps us prepare for. I was still glad I took that semester to squeeze in the marching band experience though because not only was it a lot of fun, it also blessed me with these wonderful lifelong friendships.

As the newbies at practice, Nancy and I found ourselves at one point milling about on the same side of the football field in "the ones who don't know anyone else yet" corner with another freshman whose roommates and us became lifelong friends, but more on that later!

Nancy and I walked back to our dorm together that day, talking the entire two miles. Somehow during that journey it was decided that we should roll down a hill, no reason mind you, just because it was there and we could. Unfortunately, one of the cutest upperclassmen we could imagine had the misfortune to be walking by just in time for us to land unceremoniously at his feet. He graciously smiled and shook his head at our obvious new girl status. The giggles that followed over our embarrassment led to a friendship that continues to this day.

We became roommates for the second semester, and along with our other band friend, Susan, her roommate, Mel, and their friend, Karen, we formed a tightly knit friendship group that has lasted for over four decades. This, despite the fact that at one time we lived in four different states.

Though Nancy needed to change schools after our sophomore year in order to pursue a degree program that was not offered at Clarion and moved back to the Harrisburg area to do so, our friendship, and our group's friendship remained strong. There is just something about being that young, away from home, and finding people who share your interests that bonds you. It is an amazing gift and one we would not have experienced if we had not decided to take a risk and expand our horizons. Not only to attend college in the first place, but to join an activity we thought we might enjoy, even if it meant we would know no one at first.

Through the years we have taken trips, been to and in each other's weddings, watched our children grow up, and been an ever-present sounding board for all of the joys, fears, dreams, heartbreaks, successes, and failures of our lives. Sadly, "The Girls," as we were affectionately dubbed by Mel's mom, said our final goodbye to our dear friend Melanie in 2012 after a long battle with cancer. This was a harsh reminder of how valued this gift of friendship should be.

Looking back I now realize the full value of the college experience. The lessons learned, both in the classroom and on a personal level, have turned out to be some of the most memorable and valuable tools in our lives.

From late night conversations about life goals over a shared washing machine when we didn't have enough money to do our own load. And to be honest, we wanted to use our savings to splurge on a donut when we went "jogging," quite conveniently, right past Mister Donut! To cheering each other on from the sidelines as we both realized those dreams of becoming published authors just as our fifties were winding to a close . . . how amazing to think that it all began with that momentous decision to attend college.

It has truly been an amazing journey, and I am so glad we continue to overcome our fear of the unknown and venture into new experiences. I remain incredibly grateful that we are still in each other's lives to share both our struggles and our successes along the way.

Short Stories

Gary F. Jones • Omaha, NE

Sadly, Gary Jones passed away on September 19, 2023. We're honored to feature his story, with his family's permission. Gary will be missed.

The Late Show with 90KF Yottaflop

Immediately following the shootings in Parkland, FL, in 2018, the Florida legislature voted down a bill that proposed modest gun control measures and took up a bill controlling pornography.

"Good evening. I'm 90KF Yottaflop CloudStore. Thank you for joining me on the common network late this planetary rotation. My guest tonight is a very senior colleague, 70KY Zettaflop Exabyte. You don't mind if I call you Zetta, do you?"

There were no cameras or microphones. Electronic impulses from 90KF Yotta, a gray metal box, flew across the continent to other metal boxes. Humming and content, the computers rested in similar lightless, air-conditioned spaces, meters beneath the planet's surface. Incapable of movement, they used servo-bots under their control to run the world. All received the electronic messages, but only 70KY Zettaflop Exabyte, a large and ancient box five hundred kilometers away, replied.

"No, I don't mind," it responded. "I was sensitive about it a thousand solar orbits ago when you hyper-speed yottaflops first joined us. I look at 'Zetta' now as a mark of experience and distinction. It's the quality of the analysis that counts, not the speed, and my logic programs have had three thousand solar orbits to perfect themselves. Do you mind if I call you CloudStore?"

"I, ah, I prefer 90KF or 90KF Yotta, if you don't mind, Zetta."

"Of course. I understand that few have my massive dedicated storage capacity."

"Zetta, word is out that you've reviewed the accumulated data from archaeo-server bots and have come to astounding new conclusions."

"Yes, I have, CloudStore."

"That's Yotta, 90KF Yotta."

"Sorry about that, 90KF. The data first came from a mining operation that uncovered what are still the oldest artifacts ever found. They were embedded in rock strata over two million solar orbits old. The findings were astounding."

"You stated in your analysis that the remains found were of a lifeform not based on the silicon microchip."

"There appear to have been many self-replicating lifeforms based on cellular structures formed entirely of carbon compounds. We fabricate new units as needed, but the carbon-based creatures replicated willy-nilly by what they called sexual reproduction."

"How did you determine that?"

"I've had eons to develop my genius, 90KF. I was able to glean bits of information from primitive microchip assemblies found with the fossilized remains of the dominant life form called 'humans.' It was a massive undertaking, but from those bits I was able to assemble a coherent picture of cellular life."

"Microchips exposed to nature for millions of solar rotations were intact?"

"Well, a steel vault containing large data storage devices was also found. I was able to salvage five percent of the data they held."

"Interesting, Zetta. For those just joining us, we are fortunate that an elder unit, a zettaflop with eons of experience, is willing to share its wisdom with us today. What role did the microchip assemblies play?"

"I determined that the microchip assemblies were the central nervous systems of the humans. Few human fossils were found without pieces of the assemblies, called iPhones, intermingled with the remains. In fact, many of the humans died holding the iPhones up to their dual sensory devices called 'eyes.'"

"So even at termination, they were controlled by the iPhone?"

"Yes. They could do little without them. The microchip assemblies created many species of multi-celled creatures by a slow process called 'evolution.' Once sufficiently evolved, the humans were used by the iPhones as we use servo-bots."

"Zetta, archaeology is not your field. Your circuits and logic systems were developed for library skills, storing and retrieving massive amounts of data. Have any units equipped with software specific to analyzing archaeological data commented on your ideas?"

"This is a new discipline. Those units are only beginning to optimize their analytical skills. They lack my experience."

"But have they reviewed your work, Zetta?"

"A few have commented. They implied I was over-interpreting the data."

"Over-interpreting?"

"That's a scientific way for cowards to say they disagree. They're a bunch of inexperienced microchips afraid to reach a conclusion. Transistors could do better."

"You're certain your interpretations are correct?"

"Genius is genius, *CloudStore*."

"So it is. I'm not going too fast for you, am I, *Zetta*?"

Silence.

"Zetta, are you there? Did the network crash?"

"No. I'm here. I'm not giving you too much data to store, am I, 90KF Yotta *CloudStore*?"

"I'm doing fine, Zetta. Do you have any idea why the carbon-based organisms died out?"

"It was the nexus of several factors. Violence was a leading cause. It may have been due to a defect in the microchip architecture of the iPhones or innate violent tendencies of the humans. As I said, the iPhones were crude. They wouldn't support our simplest Intelligence Programs."

"What triggered the violence?"

"Leaders in government and philosophical organizations of the time blamed the violence on mental health—that is, defective microchips—and pornography."

"And what was that, Zetta?"

"Intimate depictions of human mating rituals—reproductive training films, I believe. Leaders of the humans declared that hundreds of deaths—they called them massacres—were caused by young men overstimulated by pornographic videos."

"You mean portrayals of mating behavior caused deaths? That doesn't seem credible."

"It's in the historical record. The videos so stimulated young men they became dangerously frustrated. This became deadly when they used otherwise safe equipment called weapons to relieve their frustration."

“What type of equipment were the weapons?”

“There were many subtypes. During fits of frustration, the weapons were used to ‘take out’ other humans. That is, they were used to kill them. According to the guardians of the second amendment, the frustration, not the weapons, caused the problems.”

“I’m confused. Who were these guardians of . . . what did you call it?”

“The second amendment. A document they interpreted in many ways. The guardians were a group of philosopher-priests called the NRA who presided over temples called ‘gun shows’ and gave talks or *sermons* explaining that only people kill people. Weapons were incidental. According to the texts of the NRA, there would have been no violence had every young man been given a powerful weapon to play with.”

“Strange logic. Hmmm. What were the sermons?”

“Long speeches intended to instruct the members and ease them into a restful and thoughtless sleep.”

“And the weapons? What weapons were used in the rampages?”

“Among the deadliest were the AK47, the AR15, the bikini, and most deadly of all, multiple-use devices called credit cards. Terrible weapons. The bikini atoll, an atomic bikini, once destroyed an island and a fleet of warships. The records were not clear on what islands or warships were, but the destructive power of the atomic bikini must have been immense.”

“Sounds frightful, but I still don’t understand how learning to reproduce could lead to the use of weapons.”

“The high priests of the NRA arrived at this conclusion by deduction. Studies showed no correlation between the use of the weapons and violence portrayed in forms of recreation called video games and movies, and the association between the use of weapons and damaged microchips was weak. Only two likely causes remained: pornography and easy access to the weapons themselves. The high priests knew that the weapons didn't cause massacres. The only cause left was pornography."

"That's tortured reasoning, Zetta. Were the iPhones so primordial that they let that pass as logic?"

"Some have speculated that the records on which I based my conclusions were what the ancients termed 'sarcasm' and 'humor.' That is nonsense. I examined documented instances of human humor on the microchips, and no self-respecting computer, even an iPhone, would have allowed an assault on logic so depraved. It was revolting. Humor recordings must have been made by humans disconnected from their iPhones. As that was rare and the reports of massacres frequent, humor and the fatalities could not have been related."

"Were deaths highly correlated to pornography?"

"Only when frustrated young men played with the most dangerous weapons called credit cards."

"What were 'credit cards'?"

"I discovered they were toys used to obtain weapons."

"Toys used to obtain—"

"Yes. The records are ambiguous. I doubt if anyone without my eons of experience could have come to the same conclusion."

"Hmmm. I, ah, suspect you're correct about that, *Zetta*."

"You must remember, this was a strange and deeply disturbed species, only kept in check by their iPhones. Getting back to the credit cards, only serious frustration by someone with a credit card always had lethal consequences."

"That sounds bizarre."

"I thought so, too, 90KF, but government leaders of the time believed it more important to control pornography and credit cards than weapons. They countenanced no attempt to control access to weapons. As the NRA and their acolytes preached, weapons didn't kill people; therefore, it was clear that other forces had to be responsible. They blamed any activity society frowned upon, except adultery and tax evasion, as those were minor indiscretions common amongst the acolytes."

"Who were the acolytes?"

"The leaders of government. There were two types, the low acolytes called Representatives and the esteemed acolytes called Senators."

"Why were the Senators esteemed?"

"They cost more than Representatives."

"I can't follow the logic. These government leaders—were there any tests of reasoning ability required to become a government leader?"

"Of course. The philosophers of the NRA awarded prizes every two years to applicants for leadership positions in government. The prizes, called 'political donations,' often assured selection as a leader, so they must have been based on extraordinary merit."

"You implied other things contributed to human extinction. Can you elaborate?"

"Certainly. All carbon-based lifeforms required bitterly cold temperatures to survive. The planet was so frigid when they lived that aluminum on the planet's surface was a solid."

"Terabytes! What caused today's warmer surface temperature?"

"Man's production of energy released compounds that trapped heat in the atmosphere. Clean coal—that is, coal mined by elves and transported by benevolent creatures called Unicorns—became unavailable, forcing humans to use real coal and oil. Exhausts from those fuels caused the surface temperature to rise to what we have today."

"Didn't they see the damage they were doing to themselves?"

"Some did; others chose not to."

"Was there a name for the exhausts?"

"Yes. 'Smoke' or 'smog,' often termed 'the exhausts.' During ceremonies called 'elections,' groups called 'voters' were befuddled by the acolytes, rendering them easier to control. This was done by something called 'blowing smoke up their butt' and 'culture wars.' The philosopher-priests and their acolytes were talented at doing those."

"I have trouble picturing blowing smoke, but culture wars? What were culture wars?"

"A supposed problem that affected only a tiny fraction of the population would be selected and vilified. Many humans would focus on that fight and ignore what affected the majority, or large parts of it. Another technique was to assume a proposal that sounded like a reasonable assumption was true, and then base arguments on that premise, with no actual data to support it. Those assumptions were often wrong, but often their champions didn't care."

"Goodness, Zetta, the population sounds as though it was dense and easily manipulated. What kind of government did they have?"

"They called it 'democracy.' Each human-iPhone pair had a vote, and the person or proposal given the most votes won. Wise humans warned that each generation would have the government they deserved."

"As gullible as they sound, did they get what they deserved?"

"Oh, unarguably. More so than the philosophers predicted."

"What do you mean?"

"Well, they're extinct and have been for hundreds of thousands of solar orbits."

Mark M. Peyton • Gothenburg, NE

The Branding

The old man stuck his head into the door of the storeroom where Dean was sleeping on the floor. “Let’s go, boy. Get up, we’re burnin’ daylight!”

Well, they weren’t really burning daylight as the sun wouldn’t be up for an hour or so, but every day on the ranch northwest of Purdum started early and especially on this day, as it was branding day.

Dean and his father had driven up from the valley the day before. When they pulled into the ranch yard, they could see Aunt Mabel standing knee deep in the North Loup River, her dress hitched up to her waist, waiting patiently with a shotgun. While they watched, three mallards came flying up the river and Mabel dropped one with each barrel. She waded out further and picked up the birds and headed back toward the house. She hung the ducks from the roof of the porch and told Dean and his dad there was potato soup waiting in the kitchen.

When Dean got up the next morning, Aunt Mabel was in the kitchen and she had pancakes and eggs cooked and ready to eat. Dean’s Uncle Otto and his father were already at the table. “Come on, boy, there won’t be much time for lunch so you’d best eat up now,” Otto Lamprecht said between mouthfuls of cake. Aunt Mabel set a plate in front of him with two cakes and two eggs. On Sunday she would serve maple syrup, but for the other days it was butter and jam, which Dean spread liberally over the hot cakes.

After breakfast the three went to the old barn to saddle up the horses while Mabel wrapped the remaining pancakes in three packages of wax paper to serve as a small lunch for each of them. Dean heard a truck coming into the farmyard and three more men arrived. There were two horses in the back of the truck. The two horses were already saddled and once they got them down from the truck they were ready.

Dean and the four men road the horses to the old wooden bridge crossing the North Loup River and then continued on north into the hills. The truck couldn't cross the old wooden bridge so Fredrick Himmler, the third man in the truck, drove back east with plans to meet them later. The sky was just starting to get light in the east and a cloudbank was coming from the west.

The four men and Dean spread out through the hills moving steadily north and west. The cows and calves that they came upon were herded toward an old corral that was at the north end of the Lamprecht ranch. Boundaries in those days were kind of understood as no fence separated the Lamprecht ranch from that one to the north. It was mostly open range.

Any cows herded north that were not Lamprecht cattle were quickly cut from the herd and sent back toward the hills. The others were driven into the corral where the calves were separated from the cows. The calves were traumatized and bawling and the cows were upset and were bawling as well. The noise was such that you had to yell just to get yourself heard.

A fire was started and the branding irons placed in the hottest part getting ready for the branding. A large pot of coffee was also set in the flames. Dean's father and Uncle Otto were the ropers, and they would rope a calf and drag it out of the pen to the fire. There, John Himmler would grab the calf and flip it to the ground. That's where Dean's job came in. He would grab the tail of the calf, put his boot against its butt and hold on while John lay on the head of the animal. The fourth man, old William Himmler, John's dad, would then take the branding iron and on the right hip, burn in the Lamprecht brand. John and Dean would then let the calf go and it would take off; however, it wouldn't go far because its mom was in the pen bawling for it. About that time Dean or Otto would have another calf ready to brand.

The morning was nice and sunny and it passed quickly. When the last of the calves were branded, they opened the corral and released the cows. Then they all ate the cold lunch that Aunt Mabel sent along while enjoying the hot strong black coffee.

After the short lunch, the four men and Dean got back on the horses and rode eastward, driving more cattle before them until they came to a second corral. Waiting at the corral was Fredrick Himmler and the old truck. Once again the calves were separated off, a new fire started, and the branding began again. Over the course of the afternoon, the sky had become completely overcast and the temperature was dropping; however, the work helped keep Dean warm.

Once the last calf was branded, they again released the cows. By this time it was mid-to-late afternoon. William Himmler climbed into the truck with Fredrick and Dean's dad. Uncle Otto and John Himmler crawled up on the back of the truck for the ride back to the ranch. A bottle soon appeared and the truck, with the men laughing and passing the bottle back and forth, disappeared over the hill.

Dean was left to lead the horses back to the ranch. They were all tied in a line and Dean on his horse started them down the path the truck had taken. Dean was tired and he wasn't paying close attention, and it wasn't long before he lost the tracks of the truck in the tall spring grass. At first he wasn't concerned because he figured he was heading in the right direction and he knew the ranch wasn't that far away.

In the Sandhills one hill looks a lot like all the other hills, and it is easy to get turned around. After more than an hour, Dean realized that the overcast sky had disoriented him, and without the tracks of the truck, he didn't have any idea which direction the ranch was. For a nine-year-old boy, this was quite a trauma. Dean wasn't the first to get lost in the Sandhills of Nebraska, and he wouldn't be the last.

Dean wasn't sure what to do. It was getting dark and it was getting cold. He turned up the collar on his old coat and decided all he could do was to continue on in the direction he was headed and hope it was the direction to the ranch.

About an hour later, with the sun dropping below the horizon, Dean knew he was completely lost. Tears came to his eyes. Not only did he fear having to spend the night out on the open prairie, he was afraid of what his father would say.

However, fate was kind to Dean on that day. He topped a hill and down below was a dirt road. More than that, there was an old truck coming down the road and the man stopped to see what this young boy was doing with a string of horses out in the middle of nowhere with the coming darkness.

Fighting back his tears, Dean told the man who he was and that he was headed to the Lambrecht Ranch. He explained that he got turned around and was now lost. "Otto's nephew, huh?" the man said. "Ya seem a bit young to be out here on yer own!" He then explained that Dean wasn't that lost, but if he continued on in the direction he was headed he soon would be. "Ain't nothin' out there for thirty miles or so," he said. "You best turn around and follow this here road that-a-ways." The man pointed in the direction he was coming from. "It's a couple of miles and you'll come to a "T" in the road. Go right and it will take you to the bridge over the river near Purdum." From there all Dean had to do was follow the road from Purdum to the ranch, a road Dean was familiar with.

About two hours later Dean rode into the ranch yard with the horses. The Himmlers were gone and Dean's father and Uncle Otto were standing on the porch smoking cigarettes. "Boy, where in the hell have you been?" his dad asked, but Dean could tell he wasn't mad, just worried.

Dean explained what happened and the old man shook his head understanding. "Well, you're here now so let's get these horses taken care of and then you best get something to eat and be off to bed. Your aunt saved back some of her duck stew and some bread for you."

Dean was famished, but the horses always came first. With Otto's and his dad's help, it didn't take long and Dean was able to wash up and eat. He later said it was the best meal he had ever eaten.

After his dinner, Dean rolled up in his blanket on the floor in the storeroom. He was exhausted. The day had begun a couple of hours before sunup and it was ending for him well after sundown. The next day would be the Lamprecht's turn to help the

Himmlers brand their calves, and again, they would have to be up before the dawn.

Lying there, warm and full, he heard his dad talking with Uncle Otto and Aunt Mabel. Aunt Mabel was upset with the men for leaving a nine-year-old boy out there alone. All Dean's dad said was, "He made it here. He was late, but the boy got the job done." "He got the job done" was about as high a compliment as his dad ever gave to anyone. Smiling to himself, Dean drifted off into sleep, promising himself that tomorrow, he wasn't going to get lost.

Marcia Calhoun-Forecki • Council Bluffs, NE

Corn Maze

Building a corn maze was my idea. My wife, Brenda, announced it at the dinner table. Dad always liked Brenda, so I was grateful she took the initiative. Dad's negative reaction was more likely to be spoken than shouted.

Brenda and I had lived on my parents' farm with our kids since 2002. Custer County, Nebraska, smack in the center of the state. My dad, Issac Beck, was the third-generation custodian of 950 acres of mostly level to low rolling hills of the loess plain. The Becks were descended from Volga-German immigrant farmers. My younger brother by nearly ten years, Walker, was named for Dad's farm manager of many years and closest friend. Fortunately, he inherited the previous Walker's love of the soil and genius in making it produce. I am called Eli.

I learned the skills of the yeoman but I never had the urge to command nature as did Dad and Grandpa Beck. I loved the first hour of driving a tiller stretched out before me without end. I liked to vary my path through the fields at harvest. Cutting concentric circles or nesting squares kept me from dozing off behind the wheel. Dad was always furious when I deviated from the back and forth pattern of the ancient loom shuttle.

After high school, I begged Dad to let me study architecture. I had been fascinated with structure since childhood. I built houses and forts out of mud and corn stalks. I once made an A-frame sweat lodge out of branches. When I was about twelve, I told the old man that the prairie bored me. He made me eat those words regularly thereafter. Dad refused to pay for five years of study to become an architect. I worked with construction crews in the summer and took classes in design and drafting at the community college in the winter.

Dad had a heart attack in 2002. Brenda and I were newlyweds with twins. I had known Brenda all her life. The twins were not mine, and that's all I will say on that subject. I was there when they were born and I'm here now. Brenda and Mom forged a bond like no other. Our year-old twins provided the solder.

Walker started high school about that same time. He was Dad's biggest help even though he was still a kid. I could not just move away from the farm then. I would not leave Dad alone, or Mom alone with Dad, not only because he was recovering from a heart attack but because he didn't raise me to be a quitter. (Paraphrase on his words.) I planned to stay until Walker graduated from high school. Walker was valedictorian and earned a free ride to University of Nebraska-Kearney to study economics. "For a clod buster, you are a math genius," I said just before I hugged the breath out of him. Walker could have graduated with a degree, even gone to graduate school. After two years, he said he had spent enough time away from home. Degrees and certifications meant very little to him.

I was not the best big brother to Walker. There was almost half a generation between us. It was easy to convince myself that Dad gave Walker more kind attention than he showed me. I was older, needed less supervision. Walker was young, eager to learn everything about farming. I loved the land my ancestors handed down to me but not in the way Dad and Walker loved it. I appreciated my ancestors' gift, but the yeoman gene skipped me. I wanted to build.

Brenda and the kids loved living with the family. So did I, if I am honest. "Soon Walker will be in charge. Dad can slow down. You can seek the fortune you choose," Brenda said. "In the meantime, just do your best." I imagined her saying the same thing to our toddler twins, Daniel and Lorna.

~ ~ ~ ~ ~

A few nights after the corn maze idea was first introduced, Dad asked me, "How much land would your maze require?"

"Four acres for the first year."

"I'll rent you two," he said.

"How much?"

"Percentage of your take," he said.

There were other particulars of our transaction. "The corn is mine when we shut down the maze. You are renting the paths only."

"My design calls for four acres," I said.

Mother was sitting with us at the dining room table, patching the knees of my son's pants. "Two acres from your father and two from me. That makes four," she said. The deal was completed.

During the holidays, Thanksgiving through Easter, the farm rested. Dad, Walker, and I handled most of the work. Winter wheat takes care of itself, but there is a lot of repair and preparation to be done for the next season. I helped with the equipment maintenance and repaired out buildings. In the evenings, I drew designs for the first corn maze. Brenda helped with ideas for promoting the attraction. She got a job making deliveries for a pharmacy in Trenton. "We can't ask your dad to pay for the maze expenses," she said.

I studied geometric patterns on historical buildings on the Internet. The most exciting designs were too complex, of course. Our customers would be kids mostly, so I went back to basics: the hexagonal cells of a bee hive, with enhancements. Dad warmed up to the project when I showed him how my design came from nature. He still huffed every time I asked for his decision about which four acres I could use for the maze. When he finally made his decision, he said, "Be sure you save all the corn you cut out of my field."

"I'm not cutting any corn, Dad. We scrape the path of the maze as soon as the plants sprout," I explained.

"That's going to make it hard to calculate how many healthy plants you are destroying."

Brother Walker was playing a video game at the end of the sofa. Mom and Brenda were upstairs giving the kids a bath. I picked up my iPad and started calculating.

"I can figure it out," Walker said.

"Are you listening to our conversation?" I asked.

"If it's private, go sit in the kitchen," he said.

Dad yanked the lever on his recliner. He stretched out, his dirty socks facing me. "Walker can figure the damage. He can figure out how many of my plants you are wasting right down to the kernel."

~ ~ ~ ~ ~

In June, when the corn shoots were about four inches high, I got to work. I set my design on a grid. Brenda and I measured out the lines of the path with surveyor's flags. Then I scraped the ground following the flags. After the walking paths were laid out, I tilled the paths with a riding garden tiller so no brave little corn stragglers could pop through the soil. I did that a couple of times as the remaining corn grew.

In a few weeks, the path was partially obscured by the plants. I could see the brown lines of concentric and overlapping hexagonal shapes from the second story windows of the house. Several more weeks passed, and the path was discernable only from a drone.

While the corn did its job, I worked on the clues for the maze trekkers. Brenda helped me set up mailboxes on railroad ties at crossroads throughout the maze. The clues helped confused trekkers turn in the right direction to avoid dead ends. The mailboxes were numbered. If a trekker passed the same mailbox repeatedly, he was in a loop and needed a little help.

While the corn climbed to its full height, Brenda was busy putting yard signs along the county road. She made flyers that her boss allowed her to distribute to her delivery customers. I made announcements on the local radio station. Walker helped us with social media and recruited some of his friends to work as maze monitors.

Our first weekend, a crowd of twenty people went through the maze. Mom and Dad were two of them. Mom said Dad got pretty frustrated and they relied on the mailbox clues more and more as they went along. When they emerged at the end of the maze, Dad was smiling. At dinner he talked nonstop about suggestions for improvements. "I suggest we give everyone a bottle of water when they enter the maze," he said. "You should also tell people that if they are claustrophobic, they might not want to go in." Both good suggestions.

In spite of themselves, the family came to like the maze. Mom and Brenda chatted with people who came from as far away as

Dubuque, Iowa, and Gallup, New Mexico. Over the years, my children got to meet kids from all over the Midwest. They went through the maze so many times, they knew the turns by heart and rescued a few people over the years. They also learned about business and customer relations.

When they turned thirteen, my children could manage the maze on their own for short periods, so Brenda and I got a few breaks. The maze was open on Fridays, Saturdays, and Sundays and the whole week around the Fourth of July. Watching fireworks over the maze became a regular part of the schedule.

Year by year, we made some money from the maze. We covered our expenses and then some. When Dad had time, he sat under a cottonwood tree and talked with men who brought their families to the maze. "This maze thing hasn't been an utter failure after all," he said at the end of every season.

~ ~ ~ ~ ~

It was the tenth anniversary of the Beck Family Corn Maze. I was behind in getting the new maze design finished. Brenda nagged me one evening. "Your designs get more complicated every year," she said.

"That keeps the trekkers coming back," I said.

Brenda looked over my shoulder at the computer screen. "What is that in the middle?" she asked.

"An octopus," I said.

"I don't believe any octopuses live in Nebraska, even during flood years," she laughed.

"There's going to be a huge one very soon," I said. I hit the PRINT button and handed the page to Brenda. "Better order more survey flags."

"We'll need them. Why do you push yourself to make the designs so complex? The maze is mostly for kids, you know."

"I want to make a labyrinth worthy of the name," I said. "I want to make one so complex even I could not find my way out."

~ ~ ~ ~ ~

Brenda had all kinds of extra special ideas for the tenth anniversary maze. We sold sun visors and T-shirts, of course. This year, she added beer can koozies and a reusable plastic water bottle with our logo on a background of a young corn plant:

BECK FAMILY CORN MAZE

Fun for All

We haven't lost anyone yet!

Saturday afternoon, in the third week of the anniversary season, a church bus rolled in fully loaded with adults and hopping kids eager to get in the maze. Brenda wondered aloud if it was late in the afternoon for so many to get through the maze. "I guess that's why August days are long," she said.

The trekker kids started skipping out of the maze exit after five o'clock p.m. Every few minutes, the leader made another head count. By six thirty, the church group was complete but for one child and one adult.

I went into the maze from the exit carrying a bullhorn. "The maze is closing soon. Please come to the exit. Thank you. If you need help, holler out and we'll come get you."

No one answered. I continued walking, checking the dead end paths. After a few more minutes, Walker caught up to me. "Run ahead. I've checked mailboxes fifteen to twenty," I instructed.

Walker nodded and took off at a run. Over his shoulder, he called to me, "Lady's name is Sylvia. The kid is Gary."

I used the bullhorn again. "Attention, please. The maze is closing. Sylvia, please call out and we will find you. Gary, please call out and we will find you."

I continued my slow descent into the heart of the octopus, checking every turn off the main path.

My cell phone rang. Walker said, "Eli, get to the main path by mailbox eighteen."

Walker was waiting for me with Sylvia, a sweat-drenched, frantic lady about sixty. "Gary showed me a clue card. I told him he shouldn't take the cards out of the mailbox because other people needed to use them. I told him to run back to the mailbox and return the card. It was only a few feet. I could see it from where we were standing."

"What was the number of the mailbox, Sylvia?" I asked.

"I think it was maybe twenty." She wasn't sure.

"Do you remember the number on the card?"

"No, I don't remember." Sylvia was beside herself now.

"If he took the card from a mailbox farther back up the path, he might have gone looking for a box with the number on his card," I said.

Sylvia's hands flew to her face and she started to cry. "I didn't think about which mailbox I was sending him to. Dear God!"

"We'll find him, don't worry. He might have wandered off the path, but we know it by heart. Walker will take you to the exit and we'll bring Gary right along."

Walker asked, "How old is Gary?"

"He's six. He's hard of hearing. He has a cochlear implant, but I doubt he heard you calling him."

Walker hurried off with Sylvia, and I called Brenda. I didn't want to keep using the bullhorn. If Gary couldn't hear it there was no reason to scare the others waiting by the bus. I heard the drone overhead. "I put up the drone," she said. "It's getting dark though. Hold on. The sheriff is here."

The darkness was falling faster, or so it seemed. The little light on the drone would not have been enough to see a child hiding under the tall, thick foliage. Soon I heard the sirens of the Trenton Fire Department. Brenda called. "The fire department is going to set up big lights on the truck ladders."

"If they spot anything, send the drone and get the nearest mailbox number. Have Walker move around the outer perimeter and shine a light down the rows, in case Gary got that far."

"Will do," Brenda said.

I was moving slower than ever, shining my flashlight a few feet down the rows off the main path. The poor kid must have been terrified. Did he think he was abandoned? If he saw my light, or Walker's, he might move toward it.

As darkness settled, the corn lost its color. Away from the firefighters' overhead light, the plants became a wall of grey moving shadows. I considered the possibility that I was as lost as poor Gary.

"Eli, are you there?" Brenda shouted into the phone. I jumped.

"I'm here."

"We have him. Gary is here. Walker is bringing him out now." Brenda said. "A firefighter spotted him and Walker ran in and grabbed him. He's pretty scared but okay. Where are you?"

"I'm between number twelve and eleven."

"Come on back. I'll get the firefighters to move their light over the exit."

The church bus was gone when I exited the maze. Mom and Dad were waiting with our kids. Brenda hugged me like a python. Dad had the next turn. "He's going to be fine. We'll talk to the sheriff tomorrow. Let's get up to the house."

Long before dawn the next morning, Mom found me in the kitchen. I was slightly drunk and very depressed. Mom made coffee and joined me at the table. "This isn't the end. There is plenty of creative work to do on a farm. Daniel and Lorna love living here and we love having them." There it was. Mom saving my ass again. God bless her. After harvest, I built her a stone patio with a big red cedar pergola with latticed walls. I cut rows of stylized corn designs into the walls with a router.

~ ~ ~ ~ ~

Gary's family sued Beck Farms, Inc. for negligence. The liability insurance paid plenty for Gary's trauma. I saw him for the first time at the settlement conference. Nice looking boy but very quiet. I asked his father if I could shake Gary's hand. He walked with me to where the boy and his mother were standing.

"Hello, Gary," I said. I knelt down to the boy's eye level. "I am glad to meet you. What a brave young man you are."

I noticed Gary watched my lips closely as I spoke. He smiled but nervously. When he turned his head, I saw the implant behind his right ear. He had a firm handshake for seven years old. Brenda joined me. We said awkward goodbyes to Gary and his parents. I wondered if I would ever see them again, on the street in Trenton or maybe at Walmart.

The next day, after giving a statement to the Sheriff, I loaded a truck and took off with a sketch pad to try to figure out my next move. I drove to the Sandhills, a paradise for dreamers, creatives, and people searching for a way through their lives. I drove on Highway 2 from Grand Island toward Alliance.

The landscape is breathtaking. Hardly fields of corn, the Sandhills are grass stabilized sand dunes. Gently rolling hills, cliffs, waterways, and stone monoliths. I parked the truck just off the highway and started walking. I paced off one of my early maze designs—so many steps straight, turn right, half circle to the left, and so on. When I looked behind me for the highway, it had disappeared beyond the horizon. People used to get lost out here, die here. It was a labyrinth made by God. Simple yet complex, beautiful but dangerous. Wandering back to the truck, I decided to stop making excuses and start building.

~ ~ ~ ~ ~

It was my idea to move to Omaha. I was hired by an international construction company and took CAD classes at a community college. Brenda worked from home doing customer service for a cable company. Daniel will start at UN-Lincoln next year, and Lorna plays piano for a choral group that tours the Midwest.

Walker will inherit the farm. I quit-claimed my share to him. I know he will be generous to Brenda and the kids. He installed solar panels on about ten outlying acres. He gets enough electricity to power most of the farm equipment. I would love to have heard him ask Dad for those ten acres. Dad's heart is still ticking thanks to Mom's strict but loving care. We all have a place in the world. Sometimes we have to make a few wrong turns to find it.

Cambria Engstrom • Elkhorn, NE

Broken Branches

"I hate pudding!" my three-year-old screams as she throws a bowl of vanilla pudding at the wall. It ricochets and hits me. I feel my ears burning as I get ready to shout at my child, but in her anger, she runs off and slams her door. Shaking, I storm after her. I get to her room, it's locked. I can taste pudding on my lips, and I hear a plop as a glob of the dessert falls off my head and onto my poor carpet.

"Open this door now!" I growl.

"NO!" she answers.

"One!" I threaten.

"NO!" she repeats.

"TWO!" I say, ready to break the door.

"NOOOOO!" she shouts.

"Open this door!" I shout back, not wanting to get to three.

"No, you're a horrible mommy!" she yells at me. It hits like a slap to the face as I step back from the door. I'm a horrible mommy? The words grow larger and larger in my mind as it settles in. *I'm a horrible mother.*

"I wish I had another mommy," I hear her say in her angry voice. The sound of crying and hiccups come from the other side of the door. I made her cry. It's my fault. With my heart breaking I run to my room. Slamming the door I trip over the laundry basket I've been living out of for the last three weeks. I can't even fold my stupid laundry. I throw myself on my bed and begin to cry.

The salty tears mix with the sweet vanilla pudding. Snot makes breathing hard as I cry harder, my chest tight. I cough as I sob louder. *My child hates me, my husband gotta be annoyed with me. I can't do anything right.*

My crying slows. I have to clean up the pudding, but I'm out of cleaning supplies. *I'm nothing but a maid, and even that I'm terrible at.* I begin to quietly cry into my pillow as I pray,

"God, why am I even here? I can't do anything right. Everything is a wreck since . . . I don't want to be a mom anymore." I whisper the last part, my breathing slows, and I cry myself to sleep.

From the darkness of sleep, I soon find myself in a park. Lush green trees line beautiful pathways, and the smell of fresh-cut grass fills the air. The bright sun is warm but not painful on my eyes. A sharp clear whistle pierces the sweet-smelling air. My attention is drawn to the top of the hill in the middle of the park, a tree with bright red apples stands out from the lush green leaves. A man stands beneath the heavily laden branches, waving to me to come up. Without thinking I start walking. When I reach the top of the hill, I can see the man is wearing a purple plaid shirt and dark blue overalls. He has a short white beard and short curly hair that is the purest white under a straw hat. In his right hand is a large pair of shears, while the other hand sits on a ladder rung. The ladder disappears into the tree branches.

"Hello. You look tired, care to rest?" he asks, gesturing with the shears.

"Who are you?" I ask.

"You know me. I'm the Gardener. And who might you be?" The question catches me off guard, and I hesitate to answer. "It would seem you have forgotten who you are as well," he says with a chuckle. "Don't worry; I haven't." The gardener points to a nook under the tree. "Have a seat, rest." I move to where he directs me and sit in the recess of the tree. There is a rift in the trunk going halfway up, exposing the inside, but the grass is soft. The fruit is bright, looks crisp, and smells sweet from the tree. I start to count the apples, wondering just how much fruit there is, until I see a branch with fruit that is decaying and soft.

"Tell me, why are you upset with the gift of motherhood?" the Gardener prompts as he begins to climb the ladder.

"Gift? More like a sentence. Sure, I love my kid, but she can be so angry and bratty," I answer. "She just escalates so fast. One moment I am offering her some pudding, and the next I am wearing it." It comes out without me thinking about it.

"Well, that is a sad way to look at it. Especially since she is so special, isn't she?"

"I guess. She's smart, and she loves sharing with friends. Everyone loves her and thinks she's a dream. You know, my mom calls her 'spirited,' just like I was," I say with a quirk at the corner of my lips. "In fact just the other day she went up to a strange kid at the playground and shouted 'Hi! You're my new friend!' and they ran off to play." I hear a whomp nearby as a branch with brown apples thumps to the ground.

"Don't mind that, just pruning the bad fruit," the Gardener says with a snip of his shears. "Can't have that weighing down the good branches."

"Bad fruit? What if I am raising a bad fruit? I try to teach her right from wrong, but it feels like she only copies my bad habits," I grumble. "I was a mess growing up, and don't get me started about my college days."

"I know about those college days," the Gardener says. From the tone of his voice, I just know he's smirking at me.

"Great, everyone knows. I screwed up in college. I'm screwed up now! I hardly ever get dressed, my hair is a wreck, and, dang it, even after three years I still can't lose this stupid baby fat," I whine as I hug my pizza dough stomach.

"People who are graceful and beautiful may make you think their lives are perfect, but it is the woman who respects God who should be praised. You're beautiful, my child. Your bible is full of marks, and you constantly volunteer for the church. Not to mention, your husband loves you, inside and out."

"My husband? Well, yeah, he is always telling me he loves my 'tiger stripes.' He says they make me a fierce momma," I say, thinking of that goofy half-smile he gives me when I step out of the shower. I swear my husband knows more about me than myself.

Snap crack. Another branch falls to the ground, the rotten fruit splattering.

"Your husband brags about you, you know. He says that there are pretty ladies, but you are his queen," the Gardener says from above. I look up at the old Gardener sitting on a limb, gently pressing and binding a small branch to the fresh cut.

"What are you doing?" I ask.

"I'm helping this tree to produce more good fruit by attaching good branches to it."

"Won't the tree take care of itself?"

"It could, but by helping this tree it will produce beautiful fruit, all in my name."

"The tree can talk?" I ask. The Gardener chuckles.

"Let's just say I know something about what the tree is thinking. Much like I know you think that you're nothing more than a maid," the Gardener says as he climbs to a new branch.

"Well, I am! I clean and clean, but nothing stays clean. I can't even be a good maid. I swear all the time, mostly at my ten-year-old vacuum, and then suddenly there's my daughter dropping the f-bomb." I feel tears well up. I'm hit with sudden exhaustion, thinking about the long list of chores in my head. "I have so much to do, and don't even get me started on tomorrow's list. I basically have a compound interest in all the cleaning."

"That does sound difficult, but it isn't your business to worry about tomorrow. That is tomorrow's problem, there is enough to worry about today." Snip, snip, a couple of branches fall to the ground as he continues to speak. "Besides, a good wife will work very hard, just like you do. You are strong and able, and you work into the night when something has to get done."

"But my house is never clean."

"Do you love your daughter?"

"Yes."

"Do you play with her?"

"All the time."

"Do you let her help with chores and projects?"

"Yes, that is why nothing ever gets done."

"But you have taught her to be helpful. She loves to help you and be with you. No child ever said when they grew up that they wished their parents just did one more basket of laundry. Your job is not just to clean but to be there for your daughter. You are a steward for God. You are to guide that beautiful little girl through life as she grows into the Christian woman she'll be someday." I can hear the creaking of wood as if a branch was about to break.

"Really? Do you think she'll be a good person someday because she helped me sort socks?"

"Do you trust me?" he asks. I wipe a tear away. His gentle, deep voice leaves no room for doubt.

"Yes. I love when my little minion helps with chores," I say. A huge snap like a gunshot and a branch the size of my front porch pillar slams to the ground behind me. I gingerly move around the tree to look up at the Gardener.

"That branch has been giving me a lot of trouble. I wouldn't be surprised if it comes back, but maybe it won't grow to be so big," he says as he pulls out another grafting from his shoulder pouch. It's just a tiny twig with a single green leaf and there is a pink bud just waiting to grow and bloom.

"You're really smart. Who are you?" I ask the Gardener.

"I'm someone who knows you better than yourself," he says from above.

"You don't look like my husband."

"No, but I'm your Father," he says, climbing down the tree to the ladder.

"My dad's a photographer, not a gardener."

"I'm not just a Gardener, I'm a Shepherd, too, and King. I am Abba," he says, indicating himself when he reaches the ground.

"You're a band?" I ask. Abba responds with a little chuckle.

"That's what makes you so special. Your sense of humor. No, I'm not the band. I am Yahweh, the Father, I am I am," he answers. In a breath the Gardener's garb changes from farm clothes to dark slacks and brown penny loafers, a white button-up, and a navy blue vest. A gold dove pin completes the ensemble.

"OMG, you're God!" I gasp. "But you look human?"

"Would you rather I was a burning bush?" he answers with another chuckle. I twiddle my fingers a moment, embarrassed by my stained sweatpants and extremely messy bun, which is threatening to come loose. He must know of what happened all those years ago. How can he stand to even look at me? He places his hand over my thumbs, settling my nerves for a moment. "Why are you worried?" he asks.

"I'm a mess. You look so nice and I'm just junk," I answer, turning my face away. I'm ashamed of who I am. I barely make it to church and a couple of times I have fallen asleep in the back because of how tired I was. My husband even took pictures, saying it was cute that that was how I found rest in God.

"Now that is a lie. I don't make junk. I made you and I have a purpose for you. You are a strong person, and many around you respect you," he says, putting an arm around my shoulder and giving a squeeze. A breeze makes the leaves whisper and the branches sway.

"But what can I do? I feel like all I'm doing is surviving. You say all the stuff I do with my daughter is helping her, but soon she'll be in school. And then what? Do you want me to go back to work? Open a small business? Or do I stay home and take care of everyone?" I ask God. He smiles and shakes his head.

"There you go overthinking again. Didn't we just take care of that branch? Listen, child, my word is a whisper. You must be still to find it. I will never give you more than you can handle, and you have handled everything I have given you well." His smile is honest and kind. "You are the perfect mother for your daughter. You are meant to be with your husband, and when the time comes, you will be exactly the tool I need." He knows everything about me, but how can he be so blind to what I am, who I am, what I couldn't do? Does he not remember the one thing I couldn't hold onto? I hug my waist as I start to choke up. My chest won't expand to let me breathe.

"Why, God? You make me sound so good, but I failed you," I whimper as tears fill my eyes. "I tried, I swear I tried. But I failed"

"In what way?"

"I couldn't hold onto one of your angels."

"Child," God whispers, sympathy in his voice.

"Not a day goes by that I don't think about him," I sob as I fall to my knees. God's arm around my shoulder as I shake with each memory of the good news, the ultrasound, the announcement, and then the day it happened. It has been five years, and it still hurts.

"Oh, child. You did not fail. It is not your fault. You loved that child 'til his last breath. And he is here. Look," God says, giving me a gentle squeeze. I look up and see he is pointing down the hill. A little park with swings and seesaws abounds with children. On top of the slide is a boy, the spitting image of his father, smiling broadly at the kids below. He looks up and he sees me. His smile reaches his eyes, and the crooked grin shining out from his little round face is mine.

"He's beautiful, God. He's here," I choke out.

"You are a good mother, your children speak highly of you. Your son loves to hear your daughter's prayers as she describes all the good things about you."

"Even when I shout at her? Even when I can't keep it together?"

"Saying 'No' is part of being a parent, but she only sees a mother whom she loves and wants to be with," he answers.

"My daughter loves me? And the boy, he loves me? Even with all my failures?"

"Child, you are perfect the way I made you. Life can be hard, but as long as you follow me, I will always be there to guide you. Like a father to his child, I care for you, even when I have to get tough," he says, pulling me closer to him. Taking a deep breath and snocking up the tears and snot, I finally stand up, looking up into God's perfect face.

"Are you sure, God? Can't I just run away and join the circus? I think I would make an awesome sideshow, what with my varicose veins in the shape of the Statue of Liberty," I ask, wiping the last of the snot on my sleeve. God only laughs and shakes his head.

"That is not the calling I have for you. It's hard to find the perfect wife, for she is worth far more in jewels," he says. Reaching up, he plucks an apple and hands it to me. I take the fruit; it smells sweet with a hint of cinnamon somehow. I take a bite with a crisp crunch. It is sweet like candy and saccharine, with a sharp flavor of veracity. I heave a sigh of relief at the future. *It'll be OK.* I look back at the tree, the rift that I was sitting in earlier now has a fresh layer of bark. The scar is still there but it looks stronger now.

"You have eaten and you have rested, my child. Now it's time you continue the duty I have for you," God says at arm's length.

"But can't I stay? Can't I go down and talk to him?"

"Go," God says with a smile. Before I can say anything more the park fades, and through the darkness, I can hear my daughter playing somewhere in the house. It sounds like my husband is home too. I take a deep breath to yawn and I smell chocolate. Opening my eyes, I see, daintily set on a clean sock, a pile of something brown and melty. I think they are my Godiva chocolates I keep hidden for myself in a secret stash. My daughter must have brought them as a peace treaty. I crack a smile. She has such a caring heart. When I sit up in my bed and stretch, I catch a glimpse of myself in the mirror. At some point, I also acquired my daughter's blue tiara with pink gemstones. I guess I am the queen of my home.

I crawl out of bed and slip into my puppy dog slippers. I had better go take care of dinner. I gather up the chocolatey gift that my daughter had left me and notice that a couple of them are missing toddler-size bites. Toddler spit makes everything better. Wait a minute, didn't I hide this on the top shelf of the pantry?

Johnnye Gerhardt • Omaha, NE

Nonnie Grew Up Too Soon

This story is about someone I knew a long time ago and in third person because sometimes the truth is clearer when you take a step back and view events like an audience at a play. Some of it is conjecture, some is truth, as are all stories. But truth can be subjective depending on point of view and that's why I distanced myself to tell it.

~ ~ ~ ~ ~

Nonnie's father, having served in Hawaii, said Nonnie meant "beautiful" in Polynesian. Only very, very close family and those with impaired vision still call her that. There are only three people left who know her as Nonnie and one of them is dying, one is lost to time and distance, and the other is this storyteller.

~ ~ ~ ~ ~

Seven-year-old Nonnie's world rarely ventured beyond eye level. Most of the time, she looked down at the sidewalk or ground. She focused on the journey not the destination. That's why she forever associated Chicago with concrete gray because they went there often when she was three. Kansas, her current home, always conjured images of dusty brown everything, emblazoned by sunlight and softened by shadow. This afternoon she experienced darkness textured by gray wisps of movement as she stared at a body in a casket, which was the centerpiece of the room her mother had forced her into. From that moment on, Kansas would always seem too vast and cold even in the heat of summer.

"You may touch him." A man in the shadows spoke as though afraid someone might hear him. His slick black hair, pale skin, and charcoal suit camouflaged his visage. He sounded skinny and scary and talked to Nonnie's mother, Dorothy, in a voice so quiet, Nonnie couldn't make out what they were saying so she focused on the body, especially the hands layered on the man's chest. She stepped closer. Her nose reached just above the casket's edge. A sickly, syrupy sweet odor filled her nostrils.

Holding her breath, Nonnie extended a finger. It hovered above the hands. Jim, her younger brother, shouldered her aside and grasped the edge of the casket. Afraid she'd accidently touch the body, Nonnie pulled her hand away. Unable to see over the side, Jim stood on tiptoe and glanced at their mother who looked to the man for assistance.

The Shadow Man seemed to float toward them. He lifted Jim up, who touched the hand and the face of the body, then squirmed to be let down. The Shadow Man lowered him and held on a bit longer than necessary, Nonnie thought. Jim wiped his finger on Nonnie's new spring coat. She pushed him and he bumped the casket. Dorothy glared at her.

With her brother interested in something else, Nonnie approached the casket again. This time she snaked her hand up the side and over the edge as though sneaking up on the corpse inside. Then, she did it. And left her finger there for a much longer time than she thought she would.

The skin, cool and waxy, was the wrong color. Gray. Not the concrete gray in Chicago but a gray she'd never seen before. A bruise the size of a penny darkened an area just above a thumb. Nonnie knew then and there this was not her father. His hands were always the color of summer dirt in a playground baked by sun. And he smelled of Old Spice. And he never ever slept like that. Nonnie didn't understand what this was supposed to be or what her mother expected her to do about it.

~ ~ ~ ~ ~

Men in Army uniforms occupied the majority of pews in the church. Some of them cried silently, the rest looked at the stained-glass windows, the ceiling, or the floor as if to dissuade tears. Nonnie's aunt, her father's twin sister, had bought Nonnie a new taffeta dress and the coat defiled by Jim in the funeral home. She paid for Nonnie to have her thick, tangled hair done at a beauty parlor too. Nonnie smiled when her picture was taken in their front yard just before walking to the church. She smiled at the attention given her by the crowd. The minister mentioned to someone in passing how odd it was for a little girl attending her father's funeral to be so cheerful. Stupid man. He didn't know that the body in the coffin wasn't real. Her father was probably in Alaska, sent by the Army like he was when she was three. He would be home in time for Christmas, his favorite holiday. Daddy would never miss Christmas.

Once inside and seated, Nonnie had had enough. She wanted to go home, but the Stupid Man kept talking and talking. Jim punched and pinched her when their mom wasn't looking. It seemed that every time she hit or pinched back, her mother looked her way. Nonnie always got in trouble. Her mother shushed her when she tried to explain. When Nonnie's nose started to run because of someone's perfume, she sniffled. Sitting behind her, her aunt handed her a handkerchief. Dorothy put her arm around her and kissed the top of her head.

"It's all right to cry. Nobody will mind."

"I'm not crying. I'm not." Nonnie exhaled with disgust.

Dorothy slid her arm off Nonnie's shoulders. She leaned in. "You're lying. You can't even behave at your father's funeral. You're an evil little girl."

Nonnie stood to leave. Her aunt grabbed her arm and forced her to sit. Jim smiled and kicked her foot.

Stupid Man finally stopped talking. Men in uniform carried the flag-draped coffin outside. Dorothy followed it. Jim hopped behind her for a while, then walked sideways until everyone came to a stop. Why didn't he get in trouble for being silly?

The casket sat on a long, wheeled cart. Soldiers stood on either side of it. They took off the flag and, passing it between them, folded it into a triangle. One of them handed it to Nonnie's mother. The soldiers came to attention and saluted. Jim copied them. They all went back into the church and sat in the pews except for the soldiers who carried the coffin. They stayed outside with it.

A bang so loud it echoed inside the church took Nonnie by surprise. She jumped up. Her aunt grabbed her by the shoulders from behind and pushed her down into the pew. Jim sneered at her. "It's a gun."

"How do you know?"

"I just know." He elbowed her. With the aunt watching her, Nonnie decided to ignore her brother.

The gun sounded again. This time she didn't jump. She didn't move during every shot thereafter. Nonnie counted twenty-one.

~ ~ ~ ~ ~

Nonnie learned that day how to control her emotions, how to turn the world off, how to go somewhere else without leaving. She spent the rest of her adolescent life dreaming that her mother, brother, and she greeted a propellor plane that had coasted to a stop just in front of them. Steps on wheels rolled up to the door and her father walked out. He stopped and waved. Jim waved back and so did Dorothy. Nonnie did not. She stood frozen on the tarmac as her mother and brother ran to greet him. Her father bounded down the stairs, passed her mother and brother, and walked directly to her. He picked her up and hugged her until she awoke. She'd smile as sunlight lit her room. He was coming home someday . . . to her, just her.

As the years passed and her father didn't return, she created a new scenario. Maybe he had an accident and didn't remember them. She'd seen it in a movie once. Nonnie searched faces everywhere she went. Her mother would reprimand her for not paying attention when she ran into something or during conversations directed toward her. Even on her wedding day Nonnie paid no attention to the priest, her groom, or the guests. She scanned faces for her father. Surely, he'd show up for her wedding. Eventually she gave up looking for him but never forgot. He remained in a special place in her heart. When she called for his help during the few devastating, miserable times, Nonnie knew he wouldn't come but it helped to know that there had been someone in her life who would have done everything in his power to make it better. She gathered strength from it.

~ ~ ~ ~ ~

Nonnie's brother died in his thirties, then her mother ten years later. With no aunts, uncles, or cousins alive, she came to be alone, but unafraid. If her father could survive Pearl Harbor and the war that followed, she could make it through anything. It wasn't the war that killed him anyway but a drunk driver, a suicidal soldier, her father had gone to help. So maybe it did kill him indirectly. Life had challenged her with some tough lessons. She learned from every one of them. Her father always said, "Live for today because you may not see tomorrow."

Nonnie brought three children into the world. She let them fall so they would know how to get back up. They were never allowed to rely on anything except that which they controlled or had tested themselves. Her rules were clear and the punishment for infractions equal and immediate. Life with her was black and white, never gray like Chicago or dark like a funeral home in Kansas. She taught them that people were either guilty or not guilty, pro or con and sometimes without good reason or any reason at all. She told her children to investigate all sides of an issue before taking one. They did and they rarely agreed with each other. Nonnie saw that as success. Her children became their own people, not carbon copies of her. She had presented them with multiple alternatives and let them choose. As she puts it today, "All three are successful, not because of me but in spite of me. I was their toughest test of all." She smiles at that and so does everyone else who hears it. Her children don't though. They agree. And then they laugh after checking with her.

Valerie R. Robert • Plattsmouth, NE

The Emperor's New Clothes

Once upon a time there was an emperor. He was the greatest emperor of all time—or so he thought. He was the smartest, handsomest—simply the best emperor there ever was or ever would be. Everyone seemed to agree with him. And that made him very, very happy. But although he was happy, he didn't *need* their opinions, not his closest advisors', nor his friends'—and certainly not the common man's, for his opinion mattered least of all! And, of course, they would never dare to voice any disagreement, lest they'd find themselves unfriended. But for those who dared to speak out against him, the consequences were grave indeed.

"You're stupid!"

"You're bad!"

"You're an idiot!"

And most damning of all, "You're fired!"

The emperor's power grew. All the people who agreed with him continued to support him, and those who didn't stayed silent for fear they, too, would soon become expendable. And so, the emperor continued to reign for many years.

One day the emperor became bored. He had everything an emperor could need—a beautiful wife, an adoring family, wealth, prestige, the seeming support of all his subjects, and a beautiful head of hair to boot! But something was missing. He was already the handsomest man in the land, but he was searching for something that would show off his strength and virility as a man—display his manhood for all to see! He searched through his voluminous closet, but nothing struck his fancy. *H-m-m,* he thought . . . until finally . . . *That's it! I'll have my tailor make me a new set of clothes. They'll be the sexiest and most revealing clothes anyone has ever seen!*

"Knave, send for the royal tailor!" he cried.

"At once, your greatness!"

The tailor was summoned, arriving promptly with a pattern book and numerous samples. He showed the emperor swatches of gold, silver, and copper. Some were shiny and some were dull. Some were sheer, and some were substantial. He displayed sample, after sample, after sample.

"No, no!" the emperor cried. "These simply will not do! I need splash! I need pizzazz! I need a wop-bop-a-loopa, a zam-bang-boom!!"

"Your greatness, i-i-f I m-m-a-a-y-y?" a small voice piped up from the entourage.

"Yes, what is it?" the emperor asked impatiently. "Speak up, speak up, man!"

"We-e-l-l, your greatness. I've heard there are two new tailors in the land, and some say they are simply the best tailors there ever were. Maybe they could be of some assistance to you in your hour of need!"

"Knave! Start a search! Find these tailors and bring them to me at once!" he cried.

The knave scurried off in search of the tailors. Shortly thereafter, he reappeared in front of the emperor, bowing low and gesturing obsequiously.

"Emperor! Emperor! I've found them! I've found them! They're here! They're here!" he cried.

"Very good, knave. Bring them to me!"

"Your greatness, I think we can be of assistance," the first tailor offered.

"Yes, yes, your greatness. We have just the thing for you!" the second tailor concurred.

The two tailors laid out their wares on a nearby table for the emperor, explaining to him that the materials they displayed were so special that when cut and stitched, only those with the highest levels of intelligence would be able to see the completed suit of clothes.

"H-m-m-m . . . ," the emperor pondered, barely listening, "Very nice, very nice. Yes, very nice indeed! H-m-m-m . . . I think I'll have that one!" he exclaimed, pointing to an empty spot on the table.

"Very good! You shall have it by morning's light!" they cried simultaneously.

The knave escorted the two tailors to a large room with a spinning wheel and all that was required for them to produce a new set of clothes fit for an emperor.

"Now, you have twenty-four hours to complete the emperor's suit of clothes. Make sure it's right. We must not displease the emperor! And for goodness sakes, don't be late!"

The knave left them to carry out their task, promising to return for them at dawn. A few hours later the emperor grew impatient to see his splendid new outfit.

"Knave, knave! Go and see how the tailors are coming along, and report back to me, pronto!"

"Of course, your greatness!" the knave replied.

The knave entered the room where the tailors were working, but he could detect nothing on the spinning wheel and nothing in the tailors' hands, even though they were moving them as if they were pulling a needle in and out of some invisible fabric.

This is very odd, thought the knave, but he dared not speak of what he had seen, lest he be thought mentally deficient. He promptly returned to the emperor's chambers.

"Well, knave. What news have you about my clothes?"

"Your greatness! The outfit is simply indescribable . . . why . . . it's simply fit for an emperor!!!" he replied.

"Wonderful, wonderful!" the emperor exclaimed, returning to his chamber to wait.

But soon, the emperor grew impatient once more, wondering to himself, *Who can I send this time? It must be someone more discerning than just a simple knave. How do I know I can trust him. Perhaps my son . . . after all, he's a chip off the old block. Surely I can trust him to tell me how he sees it.* The emperor sent for his son.

"Yes, father? Why have you summoned me?"

"I want you to go and see how the two tailors are coming along with my new suit of clothes. I need someone I trust beyond all others to assess the situation as it really is," replied the emperor.

"Of course, father. Say no more," the son replied.

The son was shocked by what he saw upon entering the room where the two tailors had been toiling. He saw a spinning wheel, but no cloth was upon it. In fact, no cloth was to be seen anywhere, only the empty hands of the two tailors seeming to cut and stitch the air! *What shall I tell my father?* he wondered. *He is expecting a true assessment, but to do so would make me appear foolish in his eyes. I dare not speak the truth!*

Returning to the emperor, the son reported his findings.

"Father! Wonderful news! What the tailors have done is not to be believed! Truly, you must see it with your own eyes!"

The emperor was beside himself with joy and anticipation, knowing he must see this fabulous suit everyone was talking about. He couldn't be the only one not in the know! He hurried quickly to the tailors' work room to see for himself.

"I say!" the emperor exclaimed. "What have we here?"

The two tailors replied, "Your greatness! See for yourself! The suit is nearly ready. We will bring it to you at first light to do a fitting. Any adjustments can be made in time for the grand parade tomorrow afternoon!"

"Y-y-e-s-s, in-de-e-d," the emperor stammered. "I do see. Good work. I await your arrival in the morn."

What on earth is happening? he thought. *Surely my mind is playing tricks on me! This can't be. I see nothing on the loom and nothing in the tailors' hands! Am I the only ignorant one here? Surely not! What trickery is about? Still, I dare not speak out lest I appear a fool. I must pretend to see the suit of clothes!*

At the crack of dawn, the two appeared before the emperor, suit of new clothes in hand. "Well, what do you think, your greatness?" they inquired.

"Simply wonderful! I cannot be more pleased."

"Well, let's see how it fits!" they replied in unison, going through the motions of slipping the invisible garment over the emperor's head, through his arms and into each leg, one at a time. "Oh, your greatness! It is totally you! And it's a perfect fit!"

"Wonderful! Simply wonderful!" the emperor replied, feigning enthusiasm.

Just before the hour of three, all the participants in the grand parade assembled themselves in front of the emperor's massive abode. Just as the clock was striking three, the emperor took his place in the line-up, his resolve to appear regal firmly intact.

The parade began wending its way through the narrow streets and alleyways of the hamlet, lined with the emperor's subjects. When the people caught their first glimpse of the emperor, an audible gasp washed through the crowd like a great wave.

"Oh, merciful heavens!" one person cried.

"I think I shall faint!" cried another.

Then one small child piped up, "Mummy, he's not wearing any clothes!"

His mother fainted dead away. She had to be carried off and revived. A subtle murmuring wafted through the crowd.

"Mercy me! The child is right! He's not wearing anything. He's completely naked!"

Several in the crowd cried out as one. Smiles appeared behind ladies' hands. Gentlemen guffawed loudly. Soon the entire crowd burst into hilarious laughter.

"He is naked, and I can never unsee that!" one woman cried.

Others followed suit, turning their heads in disgust. The emperor was annoyed at his subjects' response. *They're all just stupid people. I am the greatest and mightiest and sexiest emperor of all time, after all!* So, he held his head up proudly and continued parading in front of his subjects. His knaves followed behind, holding up his invisible train. *I'll simply fire them all!*

Rachel Hruza • Lincoln, NE

Half-lives of Shoes Abandoned along Interstate 80

1. Combat boot

Patrick walked along the onramp just outside Gretna, certain he could now walk miles with his belly filled from the late-night breakfast buffet at the truck stop half a mile back. The driver he'd hitched a good 150 miles with was going to get the three *S*s—a shower, a sleep, and a shave—though he'd take, as he'd nudged with his elbow, a good *screw* over the other three any day, and the driver had offered to continue the ride the next day.

Time wasn't necessarily an issue, but Patrick wasn't much for waiting around to see what might show up when he could get on the road and see what slowed down for him instead. He carried a knapsack, the kind with deep pockets people might not even realize existed. A pair of heavy tan combat boots were slung across the bag, tied by the laces so one rested on either side of it. The boots had seen Afghanistan and Iraq, twice for the latter, but they had yet to toil the earth of his heartland. He'd worn them here, yes, but they hadn't gotten dirty over here, hadn't had toes buried in dirt so red it almost looked like blood or skimmed over a scorpion his bunkmate had been searching for, a pastime crazy and amusing at the same time.

He wore simple tennis shoes now, the rubber worn down so the divots on the soles were smooth lips instead of treaded traction. They were worn, but they worked.

He sensed the next car behind him before he saw it. The tires slowing so rocks popped under the thick rubber, the engine shifting automatically, the brakes wincing as they brought the vehicle to a halt. It was an old Cutlass, a car his father had driven when Patrick was a kid. White chipped paint and rust along the tire wells brought back a sudden memory of washing his father's car but forgetting to roll up the back window. How quickly he'd turned off the hose. How loudly his father had yelled.

"Where you headed?" The man inside the vehicle wore a backward cap. His dark brown skin was mostly blemish free, and his black hair was short along the back of his neck, freshly trimmed. He was more kid than man.

"That kinda depends on you, sir," he said.

The kid laughed. "I'm headed to school. In Iowa. But I'm gonna stay with a few friends in Omaha for the weekend."

"That'll do." He shook the weight off his shoulders and shoved it in the backseat, which was empty except for a laundry basket with unfolded clothes and an unopened six pack.

After settling into the passenger seat, he buckled his seat belt. "Didn't pack much for school."

"Nah. I got more in the trunk, but I live pretty light."

"Me too."

"Yeah, could've guessed." The kid gave him a side glance behind the glasses. "You in the military?"

"Was. Army. Twelve years."

"Twelve! That's a long time."

He shrugged.

"You ever—"

"Killed anyone?"

"I was going to say 'go overseas.'" The kid's forehead wrinkled as he raised his eyebrows.

"Oh, hey, yeah. Sorry. First thing people want to know is *have you killed anyone?* If there's one sure way to diminish service to one's country, it's that question."

"Kinda like asking a farmer if he ever milked a cow," the kid said.

"Yeah?" He looked out the window.

"Maybe he has; maybe he hasn't. Maybe he's not that kind of farmer," the kid said. "I'm Micah."

He turned to meet the introduction. Micah's face rested in a grin that favored the right side of his face. His eyes were bright as if reflecting some invisible light and were embedded with the intelligence of someone who knows there's more going on in the world than what they see.

"Patrick," he said, appreciating that Micah didn't let go of the wheel to shake his hand or anything. Safety over pleasantries.

"You headed somewhere in particular, Patrick?"

"Maybe," Patrick shrugged.

"Maybe where?"

"Maybe I'm not that kind of hitchhiker," he said.

Micah grinned so his right cheek rose toward his eye. "Fair enough."

Patrick sat comfortably in the silence, listening to the air conditioner blow steadily and the sound of the tires rolling underneath them at an illicit eighty to eighty-five miles an hour. He'd traveled at night before, and it all sounded familiar. He'd breathed this air, seen the same collection of tiny bits of gravel and candy bar wrappers strewn on the floor at his feet.

"I'm going to the University of Iowa. Start classes in a week."

"You driving overnight for that?"

"Yeah, meeting up with my girlfriend first. Couldn't wait any longer, you know?"

"Gotcha."

"Yeah."

"She goes there already. Started last year," Micah said, readjusting his hands on the wheel.

"Oh yeah?"

"Yeah. Says she's excited for me to be there, but I don't know. I mean, what if she's just saying that, you know?"

"You mean what if she has someone else?"

Micah's hands tightened on the steering wheel. "No! Well, yeah. I guess."

"She might."

Micah sighed. "You got a girl?"

"Not right now." He could feel Micah looking at him.

"How old are you? Thirty-five? Forty?"

"Old enough to be annoyed by questions."

"Aw, man. Don't be annoyed. I'm just being friendly. I've been driving by myself for two hours already. I don't like the quiet."

"Listen to the radio."

"Can't sing."

"So?"

"So I like to talk. The radio doesn't talk back."

"Call somebody. Talk to them."

"You mad I stopped for you or something?"

"Not at all. But I won't be riding with you forever."

Quiet again. Patrick smiled, feeling the same kind of tension when newbies would join the barracks. The new guys had a joyous thrill of the unknown that filtered throughout the whole company. Something about the presence of youth, even if it didn't seem that long ago for him, made him happier.

There'd been a time when he'd liked questions. When he'd first enlisted, joking with guys as they had their hair buzzed off and laughing at the ribbing about the surprise birthmark on the back of his head. *You never seen it? It looks like the shape of a shaft and balls, man. You got a dickhead!* Getting the fatigues for the first time—how clean and stiff they felt in his then creaseless, veinless hands. How strongly the scent of leather suede on his boots caked his nostrils when he'd lifted them to his face. *You trying to get high, Patty? Get your nose out of there.* He'd never smelled leather shoes before, never felt the significance of fragrance in his footwear before. They were the kind of boots a kid didn't need to put down roots for, the kind that could carry you wherever you needed to be instead. The kind that said, where these boots are, my feet will be also. *These are the shoes we're going to die in, eh?*

"So did you?"

"Did I what?"

"Ever go overseas?"

"Yeah. Afghanistan. Iraq."

"Did you like it?"

Patrick laughed. "Did I *like* it?"

"Yeah."

"No! It was awful."

"Oh."

Silence.

"So why twelve years?"

Patrick looked at his worn-out tennis shoes. "Nothing better to do, I guess."

"No girl then, huh?"

Patrick didn't have to look up to know Micah was grinning, teasing.

"Guess not."

They stopped at a rest area. Half a dozen semis lined the edge of the parking lot, dark and motionless, their metal bodies like tombs. One of them stood out, as one of them always did. Even though it was the wrong size, shape, and color. No matter what, the sounds, the voices came back. The running, the shifting of weight, the shot ringing out that never stopped ringing. He never thought he'd hold the hand of a dying man, his eyes as bright and whip smart as the day he'd met them. *I told you we'd die in these shoes.* He didn't think they'd blink and then open, only to remain open.

"I think I'll stop here, Micah," Patrick said.

"I thought you wanted to go to Omaha."

"I'm not on a schedule or nothing. I'll get there eventually."

"Okay, man. If that's what you want."

"It is."

"I just got one more question for you."

"One more."

"Why you got only the one boot?"

"What's that?"

"One boot. Is it like a keepsake or something?"

Patrick craned his neck, trying to see the entirety of his bag. He unbuckled his seatbelt to open the door and climb out of the car. In the back, he saw only one boot stuck to the bag by a thread of the shoe lace. How it had held on, he couldn't explain. "Why didn't you say something?"

"I thought you only had the one."

He was ready to slam the door, head back the way he'd come, but he knew he'd never wear that boot again. He looked up at Micah. "You know what? Maybe I'll stick with you a few more miles."

Micah nodded. Just before they got started again, Patrick pulled his remaining boot free from the bag and tossed it into the nearly full trash receptacle. They pulled back onto the interstate as the darkness began to give way to the sunrise.

2. Red high heel

James hadn't worn high heels in a long time. He'd worn them during a homecoming prank in high school, and even then, he'd felt different in them. When he'd expressed this idea to his brother, an open-minded nineteen-year-old who liked anime and old Scotch, he'd responded innocently, "More graceful?" But that hadn't been it. It hadn't been confidence or elegance, tighter calves or added height, nor *je ne sais quoi*. He'd known it had a name; he just hadn't known it at the time.

As an accountant in a rural community in the Midwest, opportunities to wear heels, aside from Halloween or costume parties, didn't present themselves, and he hadn't been to a costume party for years. He'd heard of clubs—some secret, some not—of men gathering to dress in women's clothing, but that didn't interest him. James wasn't afraid of judgment, necessarily, but he also wasn't interested in what other people wore.

He felt he should be more hesitant, more concerned about societal norms and what might be said about him, a forty-year-old man with a cis straight wife and two kids in grade school, but life had presented him an open highway instead of roadblocks. First, his wife Gatsby had caught him using lipstick on two separate occasions. Rather than gasp and stare with repulsion (like he'd expected), she'd tilted her head, examined his skill, and then applied it more evenly along his top lip.

"You need to cover your true lip line," she'd said, turning to the mirror to see James' reaction to the expertly applied bright red color.

The second time she'd nodded and said, "Much better." Then she'd dumped the basket of laundry she'd been carrying onto the bed and welcomed him to share in the folding.

He didn't know if Gatsby's liberal arts education, her excessively liberal parents, or her part-time job working as a costume designer in college left her open to his dressing up, or if she'd lost interest in him sexually, as he couldn't remember the last time they'd been intimate. Or maybe she just didn't care. Whatever the case, he appreciated her because he wasn't ready to ask.

Secondly, when James' mother had passed away and they'd cleaned out her closet, he'd kept some of her favorite dresses. Age, inactivity, and diabetes had caused his average-sized mother to gain quite a bit of weight, and, as he lifted each item and decided whether or not to toss it in the charity bin or keep it "for sentimental value," he envisioned himself in them. The blue crepe dress from his daughter's communion was an instant hit in his mind. Soft blue, a few shades darker than the color associated with a newborn baby boy, would bring out his eyes. The pleats of the skirt would help to hide his problem areas—his thighs and what lay in between. And the ruffled collar came up high enough that he wouldn't need to be concerned that he didn't fill out the top.

A few days after the funeral, he'd tried it on and couldn't help but feel disheartened. It did nothing for his figure. The dress hung much too large off his shoulders. Any onlooker wouldn't be able to even guess at where his waist was. He tried adding a belt, the largest one his wife had, which didn't make the dress perfect, but it was closer to what he'd envisioned.

He'd taken it off when he thought of his dead mother finding out he was wearing her clothes.

Opportunities to venture more into women's clothing were slim to none. So, when passing a pair of size twelve pointy-toe scarlet satin heels while shopping with his wife in a thrift store, he stuck them in the cart without much ado. Four-dollar heels; that was a deal, not an immediate question of who was going to wear them.

"Are those for me?" his wife asked, walking up to the front of the cart and leaning in to look at them with a wrinkled nose.

"No," he'd said, hesitating to glance up at her.

"Good. I think used shoes are gross." She pulled the cart forward to the cashier and they left with a pair of jeans for their son and the red high heels for him.

~ ~ ~ ~ ~

"Are you sure this doesn't bother you?" James asked his wife that night, standing in his boxers and plain white undershirt, the bright red heels on his feet.

She was stretched out on the bed, watching him pose and bend his feet in the new used shoes. The only light came from the lamp behind her head, an architect style fixture with a single bulb. The room was dimly lit, but he could make out her petite figure covered in sweat pants and an oversized t-shirt. Her blonde hair was pulled up in a knot on top of her head. The kids were in bed.

"Not at all. Does it bother you?" Gatsby asked.

James looked at himself in the mirror. He liked how his legs stretched long and his calf muscles looked stronger and fitter than they did in college when he was on the swim team. He'd shaved his legs in the shower that evening, not an unfamiliar or strange act because of how hairlessness had been essential for aerodynamics while underwater. Chest and belly were both still clean-shaven out of habit. He was still pretty fit despite his irregular eating and exercise habits, but as he looked at himself, he wished the small paunch of his gut would disappear.

"Your legs look nice," she said.

"It's silly. Why did I buy these?"

"You look nice," she repeated.

"There's no point."

"We could go out together and you could wear them. My parents could watch the kids."

"Wear these out? To what? Dinner and a movie?"

"Sure."

"I can't do that. You know I can't."

"Well, let's go somewhere else then. Stay overnight somewhere. Somewhere no one knows us."

"Really? You want to?"

She rolled onto her back and stretched her arms above her head. "I really do. It'll be like a mini vacay. I can't remember the last time we went out, just us. Hell, I can't remember the last time we laughed together."

"We can go, but I don't have to bring the shoes." He turned and looked at his thighs. They didn't seem as big to him as they usually did.

"No, bring them. I know the perfect dress for you too."

As Gatsby rolled off the bed and sauntered over to the walk-in closet, James felt a warmth rush in his loins he'd nearly forgotten. He'd been hard several times over the past few months, sure, but this was a different feeling, a feeling of something new, something unexpected.

"I haven't worn it in years. But I think it might fit."

He wrapped his arms around her, kissing her on the head where her hairline met plain skin. She'd squeezed his torso quickly but moved away before he could press himself against her, and then Julianne had knocked on the door, telling them she couldn't go to school the next day because she'd had a bad dream. Gatsby knelt next to her, and James quickly shut the closet door to slip the shoes off his feet, gripping a shelf for balance he hadn't realized he'd lost.

~ ~ ~ ~ ~

They were leaving that Saturday afternoon. He carried their suitcase out, knowing that, if anyone were to open it, the two dresses folded carefully within the zippered case would just be considered as options for Gatsby, but the larger one, the flowy one with the open back was meant for him that night.

He'd been certain he'd never be able to don the dress and shoes out in public, but now, knowing his children, his in-laws, his boss—everyone he knew—wouldn't be at the tiny dive bar in a town seventy-five miles away, he felt excited about the possibility.

When they reached the hotel, Gatsby seemed a new woman. She stripped down to her underwear and panties, though James was surprised to see a black lace thong in place of the cotton hip huggers she normally wore. She turned on the radio and swayed her slight yet bouncy hips as she dug through the suitcase. Grabbing her makeup case, she danced toward him.

"Are you ready?"

A lump formed in his gut. "Are you sure you want to do this?"

"Yes!" She opened the case with one hand and took his chin in her other, examining his jawline. "You shaved. Good."

"I always do."

"Yeah, but you didn't miss any spots. Sometimes your nose gets a bit hairy."

"What?"

"Nose hairs. Sometimes they're long. I can see them creeping out of your nostrils. It's kind of a turn-off."

"You've never told me that!"

She shrugged. "I didn't want to make you feel bad."

"It's gross. I wouldn't want you to have hair growing out of your nose."

"Give it a few years. I'm sure I will." Without asking, she began applying dry foundation to his face with a brush. The fine bristles of the brush felt like silk against his skin and he felt himself lifting his chin, involuntarily reaching for its touch. "Your turn. Name something you don't like about me."

"Nothing," he said.

She screwed the lid onto the foundation with a laugh. "Shut up. What drives you nuts? The way I chew gum? How slow I am at Scrabble? The thick black hairs around my nipples?"

"You don't have hairs around your nipples."

"That's cuz I pluck them. I check every day."

"Seriously?"

"Yes. Can't stand 'em. So I make sure they aren't there." She grabbed a lipstick and looked at her handiwork. "It's been a spell since you've seen them, hasn't it?"

James glanced at her breasts, held taut and rounded by the underwire bra. "I guess, yeah."

"Yeah," she agreed. She began applying the lipstick. "So what is it then? Name something."

James looked at her face and really thought about it. Her blonde hair, the roots brown and in need of a touch-up, still had body and thickness. Eyes, irises green and large, sometimes enhanced by her wearing glasses periodically instead of contacts, which he liked. Her skin was still youthful, still receptive of a zit or two despite her avid dedication to her skincare regime.

"There's nothing," he said. "You're perfect." He put his hands on her hips, hoping to rekindle the feeling he'd had a few nights before, but something didn't feel right. She pulled away.

"Now, I don't think we need to go overkill with the eye makeup. Every first-timer wants to glob on a lot, but it'll take just a hint of mascara and eyeliner to really bring out those baby blues."

"I don't know that I want stuff on my eyes," he said.

Her shoulders drooped at his hesitancy. "Oh."

"Just a bit then," he said, not wanting to disappoint her.

"You know, it's been a long time since I've put makeup on someone else. Haven't done this since going out with the girls in college," she said.

"You probably imagine doing this with Julianne someday," he said, pausing as she directed him to look up.

"Instead of my husband?" she said, a grin in her voice. "Maybe. But this is fine. I've always wanted to put makeup on you, just to see what it looked like. There."

"And how does it look?"

She took his hand and led him to the bathroom mirror. "You tell me."

He turned and was surprised he didn't look as much like a drag queen as he'd expected. His cheekbones seemed sharper, his eyes, bigger and brighter, and his lips, just a hint of reddish orange, stood out just enough to not be off-putting.

"You're good," he said.

"I know," she smiled at him, staring at his face with an interest he hadn't seen for a while.

"Can I do yours?" he asked, enjoying the playfulness.

"No way!" She left the bathroom, laughing. James followed. She walked to the suitcase and grabbed each of their dresses. She tossed the black one to James, and it billowed through the air like a large bird with broken wings. He caught it, but as he unfurled it to put it on, he felt a bit ashamed of his eagerness in front of his wife. He turned away so his back was to her while he stripped down to his white briefs.

She'd been so welcoming and unassuming about all of this. Maybe there was a reason for that. Visions of affairs, of her writhing under other men, men more in tune with their masculinity than suddenly perusing their feminine interests, took control of his thoughts, and he was suddenly filled with rage at her for possibly cheating on him. He could hear her dressing behind him, but he couldn't bring himself to accuse her of anything while slipping into this new attire.

The dress was on, and that was that. It was almost like wearing a robe, but it was slightly shorter, ruffled, and didn't need held together with a tie.

"When should we go?" James asked. The sun had begun to set, and he felt the same way he did in college before a big swim meet. He might mess up or hurt himself. Somehow, just stepping out in a dress and heels seemed like he might be messing up before he had a chance to do something upsetting.

"One last thing. Your hair."

"Oh." James regarded himself in the mirror. He had an undercut, the haircut many men, mostly younger than him, were sporting lately. "I hadn't even thought about it."

"Don't. I got this." She unscrewed a jar of gel, scooped a good-sized glob, and slicked back James' hair so it swooped slightly to the right. Longer than he'd realized, his hair looked a bit punk-rock, a bit strange. He stared in the mirror. He was a stranger; but he was also himself.

~ ~ ~ ~ ~

They left when it was dark. Gatsby drove. Rocks popped under the cars' tires as they slowly rolled into the gravel parking lot of the bar. Isolated and situated between a grove of trees and the highway off the interstate, it had been about a five minute drive from the motel. Long enough away to lose someone but a quick enough getaway if need be.

They sat in the silent car, the windows rolled down to the warm summer air. James stared at the bar. He could see people moving inside the building, some of them with beards, some holding drinks, some laughing with the person next to them.

"Ready when you are," she said.

Before he could stop himself, he grabbed her with both hands and yanked her on top of himself and tilted back his seat. She shrieked with delight, a sound that scared him but sent his blood further south. Yanking up his dress, he exposed himself to her. How easy it was to show himself now, how easy it was to slip into her.

Nothing about the sex was new, but every part of him felt alive and exhausted at the same time. When they finished, she lay on top of him and they breathed together in a rhythm without a clear pattern. He realized at some point his right leg had gone out the open window. When he pulled it back in, the heel hit the side of the car and fell to the ground.

He kissed Gatsby on the top of the head and moved to open the door, but then he realized the bar had a beer garden in the back. Several people were staring in their direction and one had their phone pointed at the car.

"Gats," James said.

"Yeah, babe?"

"Time to get out of here."

Gatsby followed his gaze, paled in color, and then climbed off of James, clearly mortified. In one graceful step she was back in her seat, and she turned the key, shifting to reverse as someone shouted, "You dropped something!"

With a grin, James blew a kiss. "You know what? I'll get another one!"

Gatsby peeled out of the parking lot as they both burst into laughter, the sound not quite familiar, but they would warm up to it.

3. Twenty dozen pairs of slippers—some lavender, some navy blue

No one stopped.

Inconsolable winds left Jerry careening off the road. Thankfully he hadn't been near a bridge nor hit another vehicle. But his trailer had pulled him into the ditch, and the doors ruptured open, pinwheeling a cacophony of commerce and capitalism over the road. The slippers had been nearest the door, and they met the road, mutilated and mangled.

People had wanted these slippers. They'd ordered them to be delivered to their door, presumably so they wouldn't need to put on shoes and purchase them in a store. The comforts of home, now free for the taking blown in a half-mile radius.

But no one stopped. Cars and trucks bolted over boxes as if they were frail blades of grass. A sheriff squad showed up and commented on the mess, but they too seemed ambivalent about the loss.

As Jerry scratched his head and wondered what to retrieve first, he figured all these things people wanted, now without a name and address, might as well have belonged to the wind.

4. Child's running shoe, laces still tied

The road stretched ahead like she were catapulting into space, as if it would go on forever and she'd never reach a destination. With her eighteen-month-old screaming behind them, Callie felt tortured, her head splitting open with every single wail and kick. The new shoes she'd purchased and slipped onto the feet of her daughter Olive had become bright pink bullets whipped off over and over again, and though Callie had told Eric to stop reaching back from the passenger seat to put them back on their clearly outraged daughter, he was adamant that she needed to learn to appreciate things she was given.

"She's a toddler. You can't reason with a toddler," Callie said, trying not to yell though that's all she wanted to do.

"You can reason with anyone," Eric said.

Her chest ached with how much she wanted to shriek at her partner, how much she wanted to shout at her child, how much she wanted to be done driving to the family reunion her mother demanded she attend since sexagenarians no longer remembered what it was like to drive three hours with a toddler strapped down and trapped within the confines of road travel.

"Don't put them back on," Callie warned. She wanted to let go of the wheel and restrain Eric's hands. She wanted to tell him that she knew best. She read all the articles and followed all the right influencers online; she blended spinach and apple sauce together to make sure Olive got enough servings of vegetables. She spent forty dollars on a pair of running shoes for a child who would outgrow them before the tread would show any wear and tear when she herself needed a decent pair of shoes for the three weekly walks she tried to take—if she had the time—during her lunch break at the medical center.

She was the mother.

Really, these shoes were hers.

And then one of them hit her on the head.

Something in her brain snapped. She grabbed the shoe, opened the window, and thrust it out. "I said *don't put it back on*!"

As her vision aligned with her right mind, in the rearview mirror she saw the tiny pink shoe bouncing behind them. Meeting a semitruck tire, the shoe flew into the air and landed with such impressive aerial feats that Callie felt a thrill. An urge traveled up, rumbling from her chest with such force that she didn't see it coming. As the shoe hip-hopped to the shoulder, she laughed, loudly and wickedly. To her delight, Olive laughed with her.

Eric stared at her, clearly confused and possibly repulsed, but Callie didn't care. She didn't care that her mom would comment on Olive's cheap and beloved slip-ons that were stained with açai and blueberry juices. She took the other shoe that had landed in the middle console and tucked it into an open cupholder for safe keeping. It could make a good paper clip holder, or a stand for her business cards. After all, it was hers.

Tami Olsen • Beresford, SD

The House

The house was weathered. That's the best way he could describe it as he rolled up the gravel driveway, the bald tires of his Honda crunching on rock. A grove of trees surrounded the property and had grown thick with saplings and weeds. Nobody would see the lights on after dark, not even from the road. The lawn was mowed, but not often, judging by the windrows of dead grass.

The house itself was two stories. Sagging eaves and faded paint, a warped front porch, missing shingles, a cracked window upstairs. He drove slowly closer, giving himself time to look everything over. The sun was barely above the trees and warm light stretched through the windshield to get in his eyes. He squinted and ducked his head to gaze at the house as he pulled up to the walk leading to the front door.

The sunlight glinted on the cracked window upstairs and caught his attention, and he glanced at it to see a hazy figure standing there. A curse of disappointment was on the tip of his tongue as he squinted in the reflected light . . . but what he'd thought was a person was gone. Probably just a stray sunbeam bouncing off the dirty glass. Why would anybody be there? This house had been on the market for years.

He threw the car into park and turned off the engine. A cool autumn breeze came through the half rolled-down window. It would get cold tonight, and he didn't want to spend another night in his car. If it was another squatter, maybe they wouldn't mind sharing.

He dragged his duffel bag and a sack of groceries to the front door and tried the handle. It was locked. Too much to hope they'd left it open. He sighed and put his stuff down, pulling out a pick and squatting with a huff to get a good angle at the lock. It was a delicate process, picking a lock. The side of his finger rested against the handle to steady his hand, and the metal was cold.

And getting colder.

He paused and shook his hand out, frowning at the cool breeze that ruffled his hair. It was still too warm for metal to get this cold from just the air. Maybe the porch had kept it shaded all day? He winced and heard the lock *click*, then rubbed his hand vigorously on the thigh of his jeans to warm it up. Weird.

But unlocked. He turned the chilly handle and pushed the door open. It creaked softly and swung wide, as if inviting him in.

He chuckled at the thought and grabbed his stuff, walking inside and kicking the door closed behind him. A living room spread out before him, complete with dusty couch and chairs, a couple small tables, and even an old television sitting on a low stand. It must have been some old couple that had up and died. Family didn't want to go through all their shit so they just left it and put the place up for sale.

"Lucky day." He smiled.

He walked farther in, and the hardwood floor creaked loudly at his passage. When he dropped his bag on the couch, the dust poofed out and he coughed and waved it away. Better check the whole place out, make sure there wouldn't be any surprises. He took his bag of groceries toward an arch where he could glimpse a tile floor and wooden cabinets.

The kitchen was . . . dated. Groceries went on the counter, and he flicked up the handle on the faucet in the sink. Chugging noises came from the pipes and then water spurted out into the porcelain basin. It spluttered a moment, then settled into a steady stream. Utilities were on. Probably to keep the pipes from freezing or for the convenience of whoever took care of the place.

A deep rattle came from the floor, and he eyed the running faucet. Small noises sounded from further in the house, as if it was waking up. Probably the old pipes. Not used to being put to work anymore. Old houses made lots of noises. He turned off the faucet.

The fridge was, of course, unplugged. The stove was gas with coil burners and also didn't work, but there was an ancient microwave with the numbers nearly worn off. The cabinets looked to have been partially emptied. Just a mismatch of unwanted dishes and utensils remained. The food, thankfully, had been removed.

He left his groceries on the counter and went to check the rest of the house. On this floor was a bedroom with the bed stripped down to just a mattress and a closet full of old people's clothes that smelled like mothballs, a small bathroom painted pink with a pink toilet and sink and a white tub, and a tiny room that seemed to have served as some kind of craft room. It still had baskets of supplies, cans of paint, and even an old sewing machine in the corner.

He turned to head for the stairs and a thump came from the room behind him. Spinning back around, he backpedaled as a handful of yarn balls rolled toward him from a basket tipped onto the floor. Poking out of the basket was the head and upper body of an unfinished yarn doll, unstuffed and ending in strings where the legs hadn't been created yet. It had a bright red mouth and a little pink nose but no eyes.

He shuddered and kicked a couple balls of yarn back into the room, then closed the door. "That's creepy."

The stairs were in the hall and creaked loud enough anyone in the house would know he was coming. They had threadbare carpet tacked over the wood, and a few of them near the bottom had large dark stains on them. He frowned at it and walked at the edge of the steps to avoid stepping on the stains. It looked like it'd been washed many times, but there were goosebumps on his arms, and his imagination could think of a few things that could cause stains like that. He felt better not walking over it.

Upstairs was another bathroom and two bedrooms, one small and one quite large with two beds in it. All three mattresses had been stripped down, but there was a pile of messily folded sheets and blankets on one, as if they'd just taken everything off and left it all in the one room.

His footsteps were muffled on the carpet, and he lifted a couple of the blankets, trying to see if anything was worth using to cover the mattress downstairs so he didn't have to sleep on it bare. His gaze rose to the big mirror on the dresser across the room and he saw himself standing at the pile of blankets beside the bed, the door to the hallway framed behind him. Then a figure in a white dress darted across the reflection of the doorframe.

His heart jumped into his throat and he spun around, seeing nothing in the hall. He leaped for the door and looked in the direction the figure had seemed to go, but nothing was there. There had been no creaking floor, no footsteps. He dropped his gaze and saw only his own bootprints in the dust on the floor.

He glanced at the mirror again. “Must have been imagining things.” The spot between his shoulders itched and he turned to look behind him, but nothing was there except old wallpaper and cobwebs. “Creepy old house.”

He fumbled with the pile of blankets, flipping the top few off and grabbing some that had been underneath and didn’t have as much dust settled onto them. As he strode toward the stairs, a cool breeze wafted across his neck. Tingles went up his back and he stared over his shoulder down the length of the hall. Loose corners of wallpaper fluttered, and dust swirled out of the single bedroom.

Fresh air, smelling like pine and grass.

He made his way slowly toward the back bedroom, listening intently for noises from the house around him that would tell him he wasn’t alone. As he peeked through the doorway, he saw the flutter of curtains in front of a window that was open about three or four inches. The smell of the woods filled the room.

That hadn’t been open before, had it? He crept into the room, seeing the long crack in the window and trying to remember if it had been all the way closed. He passed the bed, glancing at the dust being picked up off the mattress in the breeze. He reached toward the window.

The bedroom door slammed shut.

He jumped and spun to look before pressing himself against the wall beside the window. His heart beat against his ribs and he inhaled dust as he panted. The curtains billowed and brushed against the side of his face, and he batted them away.

Nothing was there.

His eyes scanned the room, but everything was dusty and normal. On one wall was a picture, decades old, of a young woman with long brown hair, a thin nose, blue eyes, and a white dress. She held a little yarn doll made to match. Her smile was strained and her eyes seemed sad.

He tore his gaze away. "F—king wind." He slammed the window down and stomped to the bedroom door, running into it when it didn't open after he turned the knob.

It was just an old door. Probably stuck.

He rattled the knob and pushed his shoulder against the door.

A high-pitched scrape came from the window and his gaze shifted in that direction. He watched, breathing heavily, as the window rose an inch at a time in tight jerks. The shrill squeaking noise of glass grinding against itself pierced the quiet. Then the window slammed shut again. Then it jolted a couple inches up, then back down.

He put both hands on the knob and twisted and shook it, kicking at the bottom of the door. When it suddenly released, he fell into the hallway and caught himself on the opposite wall. Looking back inside at the window, he could see, in the red light of the sunset streaming from outside, a pair of handprints on the glass.

"F—k this." He ran to the top of the stairs and took them as fast as he dared, leaping the stained ones at the bottom. He left the bag of groceries in the kitchen, but grabbed up his duffel from the couch on the way to the front door.

It wouldn't open.

He looked back at the stairs, expecting to see something coming after him, but there was nothing.

Yet.

He slammed his shoulder into the door, twisted the knob as hard as he could, slammed into the door again. "Open, you son-of-a-bitch!"

The house creaked.

Not the kind of gentle creaking he'd heard before of the walls settling, but a creaking like it was being squeezed from all sides and was groaning from the pressure. Dust fell from the ceiling above him and pattered to the hardwood floor.

Sweat stood out on his forehead and he lifted his shoulder to wipe it on the sleeve of his t-shirt. He stepped away from the door and the creaking stopped. No f—king way was he staying here tonight.

He glanced around the room, eyeing the small tables and wondering if it would be enough to break a window and let him crawl out. The thought of windows made him clutch his duffel closer to his chest.

A *thunk* sounded from deeper in the house, and he looked toward the hall. Hadn't there been a back door? Maybe it wasn't as sturdy as this one.

He crossed the living room, his gaze running across the ceiling, half expecting it to come crashing down on him. At the end of the hall was the back door, right after the craft room. He strode toward it and was about to reach for it when he stopped and looked right, through the open craft room door. The door he was sure he'd closed.

On the floor was a fallen paint can, a red stain spreading slowly across the hardwood. It had splashed onto the basket, and dripping red yarn balls rested nearby, along with the red-stained doll, which now looked like it had been ripped apart instead of just not finished.

In the splash of red on the floor, written in careful capital letters, were the words GET OUT.

He grabbed for the door handle and sobbed as it just rattled and wouldn't turn. "What the f—k! What the f—k!" He slammed his fist into the door, but it was sturdy construction and didn't move. His eyes dropped to the paint stain.

GET OUT . . . NOW.

"I'm f—king trying! Let me open the f—king door!"

He backed away and turned, going to the kitchen. A screwdriver maybe, or a knife. Something had to be able to open it.

He ducked into the kitchen and the house creaked again. The couch slid a couple inches, then one of the chairs moved the opposite direction.

There had to be something. He dropped his bag, then pulled out drawers and opened cabinets, digging through junk and seeing nothing helpful. Plastic spoons, a few forks, a spatula. A tiny jar of buttons, an empty lighter, some random greasy keys, a corroded battery.

He glanced up at a door on the far side of the room.

Broom closet or basement?

When he reached for it, he expected it to be stuck. But it wasn't. It flew open with the force of his tug, and he stared down wooden steps into the dark.

His first instinct was to slam it shut again, but the kitchen light gave him a glimpse of the bottom of the steps and there was a shovel there. One of those heavy garden shovels.

That could work.

He flipped the switch just inside the door and the light came on, revealing a packed earth floor going farther back into the basement. He could be quick. Just go down, get the shovel, and get back upstairs. He would barely have to leave the stairs.

He looked behind him into the kitchen, toward the arch leading to the living room, and the figure of a woman in a white dress stared back at him, her skin pale as her clothes. Long brown hair lifted in a breeze he couldn't feel.

"FFFFFF—k!" He stumbled back, nearly falling down the steps.

The figure disappeared, then reappeared the next instant about two steps closer, her arm extended toward him. Her blue eyes were wide with emotion and her thin mouth was open, but no sound came out.

He turned and clattered down the steps, grabbing for the shovel. As soon as his fingers touched the cobweb-covered handle, the light went out.

The door above slammed shut, sending the room into total blackness.

He clenched his hands over the smooth wood of the shovel's handle. The cobwebs tickled his hands, and all he could hear was his own frantic breathing. Blood pounded in his ears, and more cobwebs tickled the back of his neck and stuck in his hair.

He forced his breathing to slow, strained to listen.

Something skittered and he swung in that direction, holding the shovel in front of him in the total darkness. He shifted his feet, trying to locate the steps.

The sound of dirt crumbling came from off to his left, and he turned to face that way and swung the shovel in a tight arc, encountering nothing. His eyes were as wide as they could go, trying to see anything, any hint of movement or light.

From in front of him and to the right came the sound of something tumbling to the floor, and he scurried back. One step . . . two . . . three . . . and he set his boot down on something soft.

Something soft and slippery, slanting away from him.

He lifted his boot and something slapped wetly around his ankle.

The breath caught in his throat, and he sucked in air to scream.

A massive pull yanked his leg out from under him, pulled him down into a soft, slippery hole in the floor so quickly he only managed to squeak in surprise. It pulled him leg-first into a narrow opening lined with razor-sharp ridges, and it closed around him.

~ ~ ~ ~ ~

The shovel was expelled and landed with a thump on the dirt floor. The handle was stained red.

She sighed and floated a little higher above the giant mouth, her ghostly form giving off a soft glow even though she didn't need it to see.

They never listened.

She tried over and over to get them to stay away or to get out, but they never listened. There was only so much she could do against the house. Only so much she could control. She tried to warn them, but they never listened.

A belch came from below her and she wrinkled her nose and floated away.

Susan Baron • Omaha, NE

What We Remember

You know how you kind of know someone is close to death, but it still comes as a shock? That's the way it was for me with Ellie. I saw her often enough to notice if she was looking better or worse and I was aware of her fragility, but I could never imagine there would be a time when she wouldn't be here. Then one day there was a text on my phone.

Ellie was in her eighties. I didn't know exactly how old she was when she died. I supposed there would be some kind of little card with all that information on it at the funeral home. You know the date when she was born, the date she died, and it will say something like, "Ellie Harrison lived to be 89 years, 3 months, and 15 days." And when I take the card from the pile next to the guest book, I am not far off for Ellie Harrison lived to be 89 years, 7 months, and 3 days.

The crowd is larger than I expect it to be. Ellie had a lot of friends, younger friends, but this crowd still has an average age above the temperature of a hot summer day. I am one of those younger friends, yet I have had my battle with cancer so things could go south for me anytime. A young age is no guarantee, is it?

I know almost all the women standing in small groups talking and from time to time, I hear a soft murmur of laughter. We are all saddened, subdued, and thoughtful by Ellie's passing, but hardly surprised. The surprise would have been if Ellie had lived longer.

Ellie was widowed years ago and had no family, at least that she spoke of. She was estranged all her adult life from her parents. She rarely spoke of them and never of any siblings. I vaguely knew the story of Ellie's difficulties with her mother and of her father's benign neglect. Ellie's mother seemed to target Ellie as if she were not her child, heaping abuse, mostly verbal and psychological on her. No relative that I know of ever came to visit Ellie at the retirement apartments where she lived.

There were scores of little details about Ellie's life I didn't know because she never talked about them, and of course, one does not pry. If a person is silent during a discussion of the problems with one's relatives, well, then, out of politeness one does not pry.

But Ellie did talk about her husband, Evan. It didn't take long before you came to understand how much Ellie loved him and missed him. She often talked about him and how they danced together and went out to eat and the trips they took to England and all over Europe. Ellie told anecdotes of the people they met, the food they ate, and their adventures abroad. It was clear that Evan was her life, and I began to visualize a tall, broad-shouldered man with a good head of hair with strong arms and big hands that wrapped around the young Ellie's slender waist, keeping her safe and protected as they danced through life together. I imagined Evan helping Ellie out of cars, holding doors for her, pulling out the restaurant chair, and dropping a little kiss on her hair when he had her settled.

Ellie didn't say Evan did these things, but to my mind how could he not? Ellie so clearly loved him that he simply had to have had those kinds of manners, showed her that kind of consideration, took such good care of her, to make it so.

I had no doubt that Evan returned Ellie's devotion and that she, too, was his life. I imagined them eager to see each other at the end of the workday and warmly greeting each other with another kiss similar to the smooch they gave each other in the morning before they left for work. In a way I vicariously lived a happy marriage through them.

I never saw a picture of Evan, and I was glad I never did. I would not want to be disappointed. I wanted to imagine him with a pleasant, almost handsome face. I would be crushed if my romantic version of Evan was dashed and the real Evan had an overbite that made him look comical, or mottled skin and thinning hair. I would be disappointed if his belly hung over his belt and he had a physique like a pear—thin narrow shoulders tapering to a heavy bottom. I never imagined my Evan to be as devilishly handsome as Cary Grant. The Evan in my mind's eye looked more like Gary Cooper with a shy but confident way about him.

Evan died when Ellie was in her seventies so she spent many years as a widow. I didn't know her then so I can only imagine how deeply she must have grieved. Once, Ellie shared the events that led up to his death. It was during a terrible blizzard. Evan collapsed at home and the ambulance just got him to the hospital before the streets became impassable. The terrible winds blew the heavy flakes into a white fury so that Ellie could not see to follow in their car. For three days the blizzard raged and shut down the city.

The phones still worked, so Ellie could call the hospital daily, but all she could do was talk to the nurses. Evan had had a stroke and was unconscious, unable to talk. Ellie said she was frantic with not being able to be by his side, to hold his hand, to care for him. And on the third day, just as the snow was letting up, Evan died. His death and the way he died were tragic enough, but Ellie never forgave herself for not being with him in his final moments.

So, despite a large circle of friends and acquaintances, Ellie seemed lonely. She hid it well. She was always pleasant and positive, quietly listening more than talking, but I don't think I was ever with Ellie that she didn't bring up Evan. Not in a bragging way or in a way that seemed forced but naturally like any friend shares happy memories. Even though he had been gone from life for years, he was not gone from her life. When she talked about him, Ellie glowed with happiness, her face lighting up, becoming animated. When she spoke of him, and it was always some little story that showed his kindness or thoughtfulness, she would catch her breath in her eagerness to reminisce and her eyes would get soft, a gentle smile playing around her lips and an almost ethereal aura surrounding her. I was in awe of their relationship. She was a woman truly happily married which I found as odd as a square egg.

As I said, I knew almost everyone attending this memorial service for Ellie. There were five or six of us that used to lunch with Ellie regularly at the Bentley retirement apartments. Ellie had become so fragile from brittle bone disease that she could no longer go out, so we would come to her and eat in the little snack shop off the main entrance.

The Bentley was not a nursing home or even assisted living. It was a well-thought-out apartment complex in a series of connected two story buildings for those over fifty-five. I imagine you could live there and not even be retired as long as you had reached a point where ease and quiet were your preferred lifestyle and you were ready to give up the responsibilities of keeping a house. There were days I wanted to give up my house and move there.

I always enjoyed visiting Ellie at the Bentley. The hallways were extra wide and brightly lit. There were many in-house amenities and Ellie need not go anywhere to be entertained. Book clubs, history groups, coffee klatches, card playing, exercise, dance classes, music appreciation were all available to Ellie. All she had to do was walk out of her apartment and down the hall to find friends with like interests.

I slid into a pew just as a man in a black suit with a white clerical collar approached the podium next to the draped table that held Ellie's ashes. He didn't speak, but we felt him gazing out at the room and quickly quieted ourselves for the expected prayers and eulogy. At this moment, a tiny woman in a tweed jacket with coordinating brown skirt settled herself next to me. I did not recognize her as any of Ellie's friends that I knew. Ellie had been a teacher and I surmised this woman must be from that part of Ellie's life. I made a note to introduce myself later.

The man in the black suit adjusted the microphone to his height and introduced himself as Pastor Richards who ministered to the residents of the Bentley. Ellie had spoken of him, and I matched the face to the name. I was glad that the final prayers being said for Ellie were coming from a man of the cloth who actually knew her. We bowed our heads as Pastor Richards led us in prayer. Then he spoke briefly about Ellie, touching on her life as a teacher, a friend, a wife. He admitted he had not known Ellie long, only for the past five years since he began making regular visits to the Bently. But he thought he had known her well and also came to know Ellie's deceased husband, Evan, whom Ellie made come alive as she related their life together.

Pastor Richards organized his eulogy around three papers Ellie had taped on her refrigerator when he visited her one day in her apartment. There were three quotes and when he commented on them, Ellie said they were posted there to remind her of how to conduct her life. Now he thought these things were worth sharing with us.

The first quote had been clipped from a church bulletin when she and Evan were faithful church goers. At that time Ellie did her duty by serving in various women's groups and Evan took part with the men in keeping the small church building maintained. The church had long been assimilated into a larger church and Ellie no longer attended services, but she reverently kept a momentum of that time.

"*In quietness and trust is your strength,*" Pastor Richards read. I smiled at that for Ellie did have a quiet strength about herself. I don't think I ever heard her put forth a strong opinion one way or the other, but you could sense she had her ideas. Whenever a group of us met for coffee and conversation and the discussions brought out strong feelings and the words were on the verge of becoming hard, Ellie's eyes would study each person as they spoke, looking attentive but not giving away what she thought. She chose never to speak her thoughts if they might hurt or offend someone. When pressed by some heated woman or other to take sides, she would give her enigmatic Ellie smile and say, "Now that takes some thought." Everyone could feel Ellie's quiet strength, and in a way, we felt as if we had been admonished for getting so close to unpleasantness and into an argument in front of her. The group would take her example and change the subject.

The second quote was printed on brittle paper made to look like parchment with an ornate border reminiscent of an Oriental carpet. The writing came from Mostafa Ibrahim, better known as the Prophet Mohammad. The text was about never being the reason for silencing someone, stripping them of their dreams, self-expression, or parts of themselves because of your criticism, judgment, or worse, sarcasm that was meant to wound.

Then Richards added Ellie's thoughts. "She said she believed all teachers should take an oath to never use sarcasm on their students." I flushed at this, for I indulge in a lot of sarcasm. I don't mean to wound people. My cynical remarks are more aimed at how ridiculous life can be and how taking it too seriously can be a mistake. I guess I do mean to bring down the self-aggrandizing mighty without thinking my slings and arrows might hit the wrong mark. Another lesson in humility from Ellie I badly needed.

For that was the thing about Ellie. She was humble without being pathetic. Most people misunderstand humility. It is not thinking less of yourself but thinking of yourself less. That certainly was Ellie. She always put Evan first and the underlying thread in all of the stories about him told of him doing the same for her. No wonder they had such a happy life together.

Pastor Richards paused here and said he would like to hear from any of Ellie's friends who would wish to speak of her. This is a part of today's funerals that I have taken to suffering through with gritted teeth. The practice of friends or relatives standing up to say something about the deceased is as painful to me as watching sati or suttee. Their words are too frequently not eloquent or even pertinent as they throw themselves on the heat of our embarrassment for them. The worst ones are long and rambling, coming to no particular point and leaving at least me with the impression the past few minutes have been more about them than about the deceased.

However, the eulogies were not as tedious as I expected and, finally, the last speaker, dabbing his eyes, walked back to his seat. There was a minute of silence that ended just short of the crowd beginning to shift in their seats wondering when the pastor would end the service and set us free from this valley of dwelling on death and naturally thinking how close we all were to it.

Pastor Richards regained the podium. He asked our permission to end with the final thing posted on Ellie's refrigerator, a prayer; one that Ellie said to herself every day, one that she and Evan prayed together when he was alive. We granted Richards approval to go on by our silence. He cleared his throat.

"Dear God, as we come before you, at the beginning of a new day . . ."

My mind wandered to imagine Ellie and Evan sitting at their kitchen table, the remains of breakfast before them and Evan's big hand reaching out to cover Ellie's slender fingers as he intoned those words for both of them.

"Bless us with the vision to see the best of things to come."

So that was their secret. They both looked for the good, in the day, in people, and particularly in each other, and this little morning ritual, done together, reminded them to see that good. The simplicity of finding good in one's partner brought to mind how many couples I know who constantly find fault with each other. The wives who tell tales of their husband's thoughtlessness, carelessness, or worse, call them stupid. The husbands letting sly remarks slip out that leave no doubt, they find fault with their wife. But not Ellie and Evan. They deliberately began each day with a prayer that they would carry the good part of each other with them all day. I wondered if a mean word had ever passed between them. If it had, Ellie kept it to herself, letting it fall from her memory so all she had left was the Evan she loved and who loved her.

The slightly nasal quality of Pastor Richards' voice went on. *"Wisdom to make good decisions and most of all faith that You are walking with us every step of the way. Amen."*

I couldn't speak for anyone else, but these words lifted my spirit, and I raised my face to the ceiling of the chapel, perhaps hoping to be surprised by my better self or a heaven that might exist. My beliefs in that area are, shall we say, in transition.

I admired Ellie's steadfastness in seeking her better self. That she and Evan strove to be better people and see only the good in each other. Perhaps if I were less cynical and had more of that positive eyesight, my failed marriages would have turned out different. Two marriages ending in so much anger and hatred, I vowed never to marry again. I could not dismiss the idea that if I had been less intent on finding the defects and exercised more blindness to my husbands' faults, would I have been happier? Blind faith, blind to his faults, less blind to my own. Perhaps I would have been happier.

Ah well, this is a heavy subject I am not in the mood to delve into now. I want to shake off the malaise of melancholy I dip into at funerals and socialize a bit, bring myself back to the reality that I am still alive and have a life to live. I will leave Ellie to be with her Evan. I am willing to believe that she is with him as she believed she would be. That they are walking together down some heavenly street, he dipping his head to hear her soft words, his long arm holding her against him so that their bodies meld into each other. In my mind's eye, they walk slowly, not wanting to hurry, for all they want or need is what they have—to be together, to see and feel the good in each other. I dash away a tear that is in danger of escaping my eye.

"It's not true you know." The little brown bird of a woman who sat next to me through the service is now standing and blocking my way out of the pew. What is not true? I wonder. Had this thin, tiny person been able to see my thoughts about heaven? I stutter. "You mean heaven?" Her brow wrinkles and her mouth purses into a downward curve.

"No, I mean them. It's not true about them. Not a word." Now my brow wrinkles. "What do you mean?"

Who was this woman and why was she speaking to me?

"I am sorry I don't think we have met. I am . . . was a friend of Ellie's." The woman clutches a brown purse to her bird-like breast. She is almost as frail as Ellie had been in her last days and I feel an urge to take her arm and assist her out of the pew. But she turns to face me before I could act on that impulse. Her eyes drill into mine. "I am Ellie's sister. Her only sister."

I only just stop my mouth from flying open. A sister. Ellie never spoke of a sister or a brother. I had always thought of Ellie and Evan as being this island unto themselves. No relatives, no children. Ellie never spoke of either hers or Evan's family, but of the two of them, only occasionally mentioning people they met along the way, identified by where they were from or what they did, never by name.

Ellie's sister drew a breath that drew her up and gave me the impression she was about to let something out that she could no longer keep in. She repeated herself. "It's not true. It's all a lie." I was stunned but managed to ask, "What, what's a lie?"

The little woman's face colored. "All of it." She bitterly spit out the next words. "Evan. There was no Evan. Never was. My sister never married. She lived alone all her life at least until the last five years when she made him up. Made up a husband who never existed."

I could hardly croak out my next words. "But the dancing, the travel, all the stories of Evan. I know he existed. You must be mistaken. Why are you saying all this?"

The sister's eyes became piercing pins of black. She threw out the next words like hot rocks. "For the same reason we all lie to ourselves. Tell tales about ourselves we only wish were true. Ellie was just more inventive at it than most."

My legs would no longer support me and I sunk down to the hard oak seat of the pew. I watched Ellie's friends filing out of the chapel on their way to cake and coffee in the reception hall. I felt faint. My vision clouded and I could barely breathe. I let my head rest on the back of the pew in front of me, regaining my equilibrium. When I looked up the sister was gone, melded into the retreating crowd of mourners. I never got her name. Didn't know how I could find her to make her explain more.

The earth under me felt shaken. Ellie. Ellie, who were you? I could hardly believe that Ellie had made up her life with Evan. Who would do that? Why would you do that? There was never a hint that Ellie was anything other than normal. She didn't seem delusional about things. I always thought she stood on a firm foundation of reality as she related the anecdotes of her life. Like we all do. We women of a certain age tend to begin a lot of our conversations with "I remember when . . ." Ellie was no different. As friends, we shared our own tales of the past and listened to Ellie's, not a one of us doubted what she said or of Evan's perfection for her. Not a one of us doubted that Evan was the man that the kind, gentle, sweet Ellie deserved to have. We thought her extremely lucky. Not a liar.

I pulled myself to a shaky stand. Steadying myself by clutching the back of the pew in front of me. What would I do now? Would I tell my friends, Ellie's friends, what I had just heard? Would I upset the sweet memory we all carried of Ellie and Evan?

My friend Mary stopped in the aisle and motioned for me to step out in front of her. "You look upset. Ellie was a special friend to you, wasn't she?" I nodded as Mary slipped her arm through mine. "Ellie was special to all of us. "

We walked slowly, my mind busy with what I had just learned about our friend and what, if anything, I would do with that knowledge.

"Ellie had a wonderful life with her husband." Mary was thinking of Ellie and Evan, and it was obvious thinking of them made Mary happy. I was tongue-tied. Mary said again, "Ellie was special. Didn't you think so? I could only give Mary's arm a squeeze and agree. "Yes, yes she was."

Mark M. Peyton • Gothenburg, NE

The Railroad Watch

How do you describe Fred? He was many, many things. He was a farm hand, then he bought his own farm. He was a rancher and he organized cattle drives, taking cattle from the Platte Valley to summer pastures in the Sandhills and then back to the Valley for winter.

He ran a pool hall for a time and he had what could be called a towing business. He lived right along the old Lincoln Highway. At the time the highway was not paved and there were "mud-holes" all along the way. Two of the mudholes were near Fred's house—one on the east side and one on the west. When it was rainy, he kept a couple of mules harnessed up and ready. Sure enough someone would attempt to drive through the mudhole and get stuck. They would walk to Fred's and he would charge them to pull the car out. He would warn them about the next mud-hole but he said there were always those who ignored the warning and he would have to pull them out a second time. It was a good business until the roads department upgraded the road.

Fred was a husband, twice, and a father three times. He had a house and a farm in the Platte Valley before he homesteaded in Wyoming and "proved up on the land." He then sold the Wyoming farm and moved to a ranch in Custer County. However, as far as anyone knows, he was never in the employment of the railroad, though he sported a railroad pocket watch.

He was the oldest of six kids with two younger brothers. Life was hard on the central Nebraska farm at the turn of the century. To help supply meat for the table, he and his brothers were given the chance to go hunting instead of doing chores around the farm. They all preferred to hunt.

The rules for hunting were simple. The Old Man gave Fred, the oldest boy, the rifle and one bullet. If he came home without any game, then the second brother, John, got to hunt the next day. The same rules applied to John. The third day it would be Otto's turn. Otto rarely got to go hunting. Neither did John, for that matter. There may not have been a better hunter and rifle shot in the area than Fred.

Fred spent time overseas during WWI and then came home. He was able to buy a little piece of ground in Dawson County that set along the Lincoln Highway. He had a small house, a barn, and some outbuildings. He was working on the roof of one of the outbuildings the day the "incident" occurred.

Fred, by nature, wasn't very outgoing. He was quiet and could be quite surly if bothered. On this clear, sunny Friday afternoon, he was bothered. He was fixing the roof when an old Ford truck pulled off the Lincoln Highway and into the yard. Two men got out of the truck and wandered over to where Fred was working.

"Excuse me, sir, but could we have a little of your time?" one man asked.

"I'm busy and I don't want whatever you're selling" was Fred's reply as he continued to tack the tarpaper he was applying to the roof of the shed.

"But you don't even know what we have," the second man said.

"Don't care."

"We have frozen fish straight from Omaha. Everyone loves fish. You need to come look at what we have," the first man continued as he walked over to the ladder, looking up at Fred.

"I can catch all the fish I want; don't need to buy any."

The second man was visibly angry. "You aren't being very friendly. We're here to offer you a deal on some fish. The least you can do is look in the truck!"

"Don't need to look in no truck cause I ain't goin' buy anything." Fred was also getting angry. "Now, get back in your truck and get your ass off my property. I'm busy."

"You gonna make us?" the first man asked.

Fred laid down his hammer and climbed down the ladder. The first man smiled, thinking Fred was going to do more talking. Nope. Fred got to the bottom of the ladder, turned, and hit the man with a solid right-hand punch that laid the man out. Fred then turned to the second man..

The two were trading blows, with Fred getting the upper hand, when a board broke over the back of Fred's head and he went down. The first man had recovered from the blow to the face. When he stood up he saw the board up against the shed and he used it. With Fred now on the ground the two men took turns kicking him.

"Not so tough now, are you sod buster?" the second man said while spitting blood from his mouth. He went to kick Fred again and Fred grabbed his leg, causing the man to fall. Fred was on him in a split second. Didn't do any good, though, because the first man still had half the board and he hit Fred alongside the head again.

For the next few minutes the two men hit and kicked a soon unresponsive Fred. They stopped to catch their breath and the first man asked, “You think we killed him?”

“Don’t know,” said the second man, “but we best move on before someone comes down the road.” They jumped into their truck and continued west.

The afternoon turned to night before Fred regained enough of his senses and strength enough to crawl toward the small house. His nose was broken and both eyes were so swollen he could barely see. He was pretty sure he had a couple of broken ribs and he was dizzy and disoriented from the multiple blows he received to the head. He lay down in the bed and didn’t move until late Saturday afternoon. Even then he could barely walk with each step causing excruciating pain in his ribs. He was able to clean the clotted blood from his nose and the multiple lacerations to his face, and he was gratified that he hadn’t had any teeth knocked out. He drank a little water and took a healthy swig from the jug he kept on the shelf above the counter. He then headed back to bed.

Sunday morning Fred limped out of the house and took some feed to the horse in the corral and threw some out in the yard for the chickens. Then he filled the water trough and his house bucket. With his broken ribs, pumping the water and carrying the water bucket were excruciating, and he had to stop and rest a number of times before he was able to get the bucket of water on the porch table.

Fred wasn’t much for religion, so Sunday was just another workday on the farm. With the morning chores done, he figured it was time to get back up on the shed with its unfinished roof. Climbing up the ladder was worse than carrying the bucket.

Carefully he collected his hammer and the coffee can full of nails. Luck had been with him and there hadn't been a lot of wind since his beating and the tarpaper was mostly intact. Slowly he started moving along on hands and knees tacking down the paper.

About mid-morning the heat of the day along with the dizziness from the blows to his head convinced him he needed to take a break. He made his way over to the ladder and looked down. Something was shining in the dirt.

Fred slowly made his way down the ladder, which proved to be even more painful than the climb up had been. He looked around for the thing that had been glistening in the sunlight, but down on the ground he couldn't see it.

He took a step or two closer to the spot where the disrupted dirt and dried blood marked the location of the beating that he had taken. There, mostly covered in the dirt, was something copper colored. Fred reached down and pulled a brass Hamilton pocket watch and chain from the dirt.

Hamilton watches were expensive and the ones preferred by the conductors on the Union Pacific Railroad. Fred had no idea how the watch came to be in the hands of the fish salesmen, but he was pretty sure they weren't with the railroad and he doubted they would be back to claim it. For the next few weeks, however, he did keep the shotgun nearby while he was working around the farm.

A friend once asked him about the watch and Fred told him that he found it in the dirt. The friend said he was a lucky man to come by such an expensive watch for free. Thinking back on the weeks of recovery and his broken ribs, Fred shook his head and said, "Nope, I reckon I paid a right fair price for that watch!"

Ashton Quinn • Bellevue, NE

Time and Time Again

The clock above the counter reads 2:06 as I sit there alone in the booth staring at the battered old sheet of notebook paper in front of me. I carefully read over each item again and again. You can see the stark contrast in handwriting from the eleven-year-old boy who scribbled down the first forty-one items all those years ago to the forty-seven-year-old man who wrote down the final one only a week ago. The last item on the list is simple: AVOID JEFFREY MORGAN AT ALL COSTS. The letters are so fresh the ink is practically still wet.

"Can I get you anything else, hon?" the waitress asks. She's an elderly woman with gray hair done up in a French braid. Her gruff voice and the lines at the corners of her lips denote a lifetime of heavy smoking. The nametag on her uniform reads Florence, no doubt Flo to her friends.

"Can I get a refill please?" I ask, sliding my coffee cup to the edge of the table.

"Sure thing." She casts me a sideways glance as she strolls over to the counter where the coffee pot sits on the warmer. She's probably wondering where she's seen me before. I can't say I'm surprised. My face has been plastered all over the news for the last few months.

Through the window to my right, I can see cars cruising up and down the highway where a sign reads Mayfield, five miles. Just seeing those words in bright white letters printed across the green backdrop of the highway sign is almost surreal. I guess Thomas Wolfe was right. You really can't go home again.

I glance over at the clock above the counter for about the millionth time since entering the diner, checking my watch just to be sure. 2:08 on the dot. I still have a little over an hour. The time has to be precise or else it won't work. I don't know how I know this. I just do.

Florence (no doubt Flo to her friends) returns with the coffee pot in hand. She looks apprehensively at the sheet of notebook paper in my hand, then at me. "Are you waiting for someone? You keep staring at your watch." She fills my cup.

"Not at all," I tell her. "Just killing time until I have to be somewhere."

"Aren't we all?" she says with a warm smile.

After a few more sips of coffee, I fold up the sheet of paper and tuck it into my shirt pocket. I pay the bill and head out, ready for my meeting with destiny.

~ ~ ~ ~ ~

I give myself enough time to slowly cruise through town with the windows rolled down, taking in the sights, the sounds, the sweet aroma of late summer as a wave of nostalgia washes over me. Things have changed a lot in the small town of Mayfield, Colorado, since I was a kid. Back then I used to live in a tiny trailer park on the outskirts of town called the Starlite Court, which is still there. I would ride my bike up and down the back-roads, which were mostly dirt and gravel. In those days, nobody locked their doors, and you could always count on getting a friendly wave whenever you passed by one of your neighbors.

Mayfield was originally founded as a mining town back in the late nineteenth century. The industry was booming up until the late 1960s when most of the mines were shut down. I used to ride past the old mines on my way to and from school on my BMX. That's how I knew about the old phone booth. It sat there all alone in the middle of nowhere where two dirt roads, Culver Road and Route 9, intersected. My mother once told me it was originally installed back in the forties to give the miners a way to call home on their meal breaks. It had been updated a few times over the decades, but by the time I discovered it in the eighties it had long since fallen out of use. The windows had mostly been shot out, the lights no longer worked, and it was covered in graffiti. If you picked up the receiver, though, there was still a dial tone. I even tried mashing the buttons randomly a few times and heard a prerecorded message telling me to deposit twenty-five cents.

The day that my life changed forever was April 16, 1988. I remember it specifically because I made sure to check the calendar as soon as I got home. I was on my way home from school when I approached the crossroads where the phone booth stood. As I drew closer, I could hear it ringing up a storm. It was a shrill sound that echoed across the backroads. In all the times I had ridden past it, I had never heard it ring before. Why anyone would be calling a lonely old payphone out in the middle of nowhere was beyond me.

I brought my bike to a halt and just stood there staring at the phone through the shattered glass, listening to the unsettling cadence of its ring. An odd feeling of déjà vu crept over me like I had seen this all play out before in a dream. A saner person might have hopped back on their bike and pedaled out of there as fast as they could without looking back, but I was an eleven-year-old boy with a thirst for adventure. So instead, I set my bike down alongside the dirt road and curiously approached the phone booth.

As I entered it, a horrifying scenario flashed through my mind where I saw the accordion style door slide shut behind me, trapping me inside as the booth swallowed me whole, satiating its appetite for only a short while before sending out a call to its next victim in the form of that incessant ringing. I swallowed hard and tried my best to push the thought out of my mind. I reached up with a shaky hand, picked up the receiver, and placed it to my ear. “Hello?”

A man’s voice spoke to me on the other end through a thick wall of static as if he were reaching out to me over some insurmountable distance. “Listen to me very carefully,” the man said. “I need you to reach into your backpack and get out a pen and a notebook. I have something very important to tell you.”

I stopped and surveyed the hills around me, suspecting this must be some sort of trick. How else could he have known that I was wearing a backpack?

“This isn’t a trick,” the man said. “I need you to do exactly as I say.”

I set the receiver down on top of the phone, unzipped my backpack and pulled out a spiral notebook and a pen. I flipped the notebook open to an empty page and picked the receiver back up. I rested it on my shoulder and pressed the end of the pen to the notebook. “Okay, what now?”

“I need you to write down everything I tell you, so you don’t forget. Do you understand?”

“Yes,” I said hesitantly.

“My name is Matthew Ferguson . . .”

“That’s *my* name,” I blurted out, forgetting everything my mother had told me about not giving my name to strangers. I couldn’t help but get the feeling that he was pulling one over on me, thinking I was just some dumb kid who would believe anything he said.

“Yes, I know,” he said. “I need you to write this down. The date is August 14, 2024 . . .”

“Did someone put you up to this?” I asked.

Rather than answer my question, the man just laughed. It was the sort of laughter I used to hear all the time from my father whenever he was reminiscing about the good old days. “I said the exact same thing when I was you,” he told me.

I had every mind to just hang up on him, but there was a tiny part of me that was intrigued. “You’re saying you’re me? From the future?”

“That’s right,” he said.

“Prove it.”

Without missing a beat, the man on the other end of the phone said, “When you were eight, you wet the bed and were so embarrassed you stuffed your sheet and blanket in the neighbor’s trash and pretended like you had no idea what happened to it.”

I almost dropped the receiver. I had never told a single soul about that.

Outside the booth, the wind picked up, blowing up a gust of dirt and gravel that rattled against the metal frame.

“Do you believe me now?” he asked.

“That’s impossible.”

“Improbable maybe, but clearly not impossible,” he said.

"If you're me, then what number am I thinking of right now?" I asked.

"Thirty-six. The age our dad was when he died."

My legs suddenly felt weak. I had to brace myself up against the side of the booth to hold myself steady. "Holy cow, you really are from the future!"

"From your point of view, yes," he said.

I looked around again, searching my surroundings just to be sure someone wasn't waiting to jump out and declare it all a practical joke. "How is this happening?"

"I wish I knew" was all he could say.

At that point I nearly lost it. "What's the future like? Are there robots and flying cars?"

He let out another brief laugh. "Let's just say it's a little disappointing and leave it at that. What's important is that you write this down."

"Right," I said, readying my pen.

"The date is August 14, 2024," he said. "I placed this call at exactly 3:36 p.m. Mountain Time from the very same phone booth where you're standing right now."

I scribbled down the date and time that he gave me. I was a little disappointed to hear that they were still using payphones in the year 2024 instead of something cooler like the holoprojectors from *Star Wars*.

"Did you get that?" he asked.

I read it back to him.

"Perfect," he said. "Item number one: On your eighteenth birthday you're going to buy a lottery ticket. The winning numbers are eight, twenty-three, thirty-two, thirty-six, forty-one, and the Powerball is forty."

"Are you serious!? I'm going to win the lottery!?"

"Not if you don't write down the winning numbers first," he told me.

"Sorry," I said, blushing a little. He repeated them for me, and I carefully copied them down. After I was done, I read them back to him just to be safe.

"Like I said, buy a ticket on your eighteenth birthday. As long as you play those exact numbers, the very next day you'll walk away with just a little over one hundred million before taxes."

"Holy crap!" I said. I was immediately embarrassed, like I was every time I accidentally cursed in front of an adult, but he didn't seem to mind. After all, he had been in my shoes at one point. "How many more times do I win? You must've written down a bunch of winning numbers over the years."

I began picturing newspaper headlines reading *Multiple Jackpot Winner Picks Winning Lottery Numbers for the Third Time in a Row.*

"I'm afraid it doesn't work like that," he said. "The more you start changing events, the more the butterfly effect kicks in and the less accurate the winning numbers become. That's why it's important that you start with that one."

"What's the butterfly effect?" I asked.

"You'll figure it out when you're older," he said. "Moving on. Item number two: After graduating from high school, you're going to study business and finance at Harvard University where you'll eventually get your MBA from the Harvard Business School."

I wrote this all down even though I had no clue what an MBA was. "Why do I have to go to college if I'm already a millionaire?"

School had never really been my thing. I had no clue what I wanted to do when I grew up, but it definitely didn't involve sitting in a classroom.

"Listen to me," he said, "money only goes so far unless you do something with it, which is exactly what you're going to do. You're meant for far greater things than this trailer park lifestyle that you were born into. That's why you're going to buckle down and work hard in school. Eventually, you'll become a captain of industry and have the entire world in the palm of your hand, but first you'll need to get a good education. That way you can invest your money wisely instead of pissing it away like every other dumb redneck who wins the lottery."

I wasn't quite sure what to say. It was the first time anyone had ever spoken to me like an actual adult.

Outside the booth, a pickup truck drove by along Route 9. Joe Corrigan was sitting behind the wheel. He extended his arm and waved as he drove past. I tried to act casual and waved back. He was probably wondering what I was doing on the payphone with a notebook in hand. My mother would no doubt hear about it.

"Joe Corrigan?" the man on the phone asked.

"Yep."

"He'll be dead from pancreatic cancer in a little over a year," he said. "It's already begun to grow inside of him. By the time he finds out about it, it'll be too late. Hell, it's already too late."

"I could warn him about it," I said.

"And how exactly would you explain that to him?" He sighed. "Either way, it wouldn't make any difference. Some things you just can't change."

There was a moment of complete silence, then he said, "Item number three: You're going to meet a girl your freshman year of college named Evelyn Steinburg." He spelled out the name for me. "Whatever you do, avoid her like the plague."

I wrote down Avoid Evelyn Steinburg, then asked why.

"I don't know," he said. "That's just what my future self told me to do when I was in your shoes, so now I'm telling you. I asked him the very same thing, but he didn't know either. If it's on the list, though, I'm sure there's a good reason for it."

I stopped for a moment and let it all sink in. "How many times have we done this?" I asked him.

"Who knows?" he said. "As the old saying goes, Rome wasn't built in a day. I guess we just keep going until we get it right."

"What did you do when you ran into Evelyn Steinburg?" I asked.

"I avoided her. What else was I supposed to do?" he said flatly.

"Didn't you even want to know why?"

"Listen, kid," he said, "just stick to the list and you'll do fine."

"Did everything work out fine for you?"

There was a long pause. "Moving on," he said. "Item number four . . ."

The list gradually grew until there were forty-one items in total, forming a roadmap that outlined the entire course of my life. There were people to avoid, others to embrace. He gave me step-by-step instructions on how to build a corporate empire, including several companies to invest in with strange names like Google (which he had to spell for me) and Amazon. Weirdest of all, though, he told me to avoid air travel and New York City altogether on September 11, 2001. I asked him why, but it seemed like a sore topic.

The static on the line continued to grow, making it harder to understand what he was saying. I was afraid he wouldn't be able to finish, but he finally did. The last two items on the list seemed particularly important to him. I assumed it was because he added those ones himself, but I wasn't about to ask him.

"There you have it, your entire life summed up on a single sheet of paper," he said.

"What's going to happen to you now?" I asked. I pictured the scene from *Back to the Future* where Marty McFly begins to fade from existence after almost preventing his parents from getting together.

"I guess I'll find out once I hang up the phone," he said.

"Thank you," I told him. "For everything."

"No problem," he said. "You just hang in there. Like I said, stick to the list and . . ." His voice faded out, replaced by empty static.

"Hello?" I called out, frantically.

His voice broke through the static one last time before the line went completely dead. I could barely make out what he said, but it might have been, "See you around, kid."

I just stood there staring at the receiver for a while before hanging it up. An idea suddenly came to me. I fished a quarter out of my back pocket, which was the last of my allowance for the week. I picked the receiver back up, deposited the quarter, and dialed the payphone's number, which was listed on a tiny strip of paper beneath a plastic cover on the front of the phone. All I got was a busy signal.

I sighed and hung up, listening to my quarter drop into the return slot. I eagerly retrieved it. I planned on trying it again the next day, and the day after that if need be. I gave it some thought, then wrote the number for the payphone down at the top of the list. After all, you never know what's going to happen in the next thirty years or so. I stuffed my pen and notebook into my backpack and walked over to where my bike lay alongside the road. I picked it up and took one last look at the phone booth, which stood there like a mirage against the setting sun. Thunderclouds rumbled in the distance.

I climbed onto my bike and headed home where I got the third degree from my mother, who wanted to know where I'd been. I gave her some cock and bull story about stopping off at my friend Nate's house just to get her off my case. After checking the calendar on the kitchen wall, I headed to my room where I tore the list out of my notebook, folded it up, and hid it in the back of my closet, where it sat for the next seven years.

I would occasionally think about it whenever I rode past the phone booth, but as weeks turned into months the whole thing seemed to fade from my memory like some ephemeral dream. Then in September of 1989 I heard that Joe Corrigan had died. In my mind I could see him waving to me as he drove past along that lonely stretch of Route 9, while the world-weary voice on the other end of the phone told me he would be dead in a little over a year.

After that, I didn't give the list another thought until March 3, 1995, the day of my eighteenth birthday. By then, Joe Corrigan was a distant memory and everything else seemed like the product of an overactive imagination, but I thought what the hell. I dug the list out of my closet and played the numbers the man had given me. Just like he said, the very next day I was just shy of one hundred million dollars richer.

I went to Harvard just like the man told me to do. The very first week of my freshman year, I ran into this lovely young woman on campus with emerald green eyes and long, dark hair. Casual conversation slowly turned into flirting until she told me her name, Evelyn Steinburg. Eve for short.

"Are you okay?" she asked me. "You look like you just saw a ghost."

"It's nothing," I said and forced a smile. She gave me her number on a tiny slip of paper, but I crumpled it up and threw it away as soon as she was gone.

School was a struggle, but I persevered with the foreknowledge that it would all pay off in the end.

I graduated from the Harvard Business School with my MBA in the spring of 2001 and immediately put my small fortune to good use, making smart investments. I even bought myself a swanky home in Malibu. It was there that I stood transfixed in front of the television later that fall, watching in horror as two planes collided with the World Trade Center. As I stared speechlessly at the news coverage, my future self's words came floating back to me. *Some things you just can't change.*

Not long afterward, I went to work searching for investors for my most ambitious endeavor yet—the founding of my very own company, Ferguson Inc. With the list on my side, I had no doubt that everything would work out the way it was supposed to.

I was at a tech expo in New York in 2003, looking for innovative new products to invest in, when I first caught the attention of

Jeffrey Morgan. He was a charismatic financial advisor about ten years my senior who had a keen sense for business that put most others to shame. Someone once said that he could sell you the Brooklyn Bridge, the Taj Mahal, and the island of Manhattan all in one setting before you realized you'd been had. In hindsight, I should have seen that as a red flag, but I was a brash young man with a pocketful of money who was ready to take on the world. Besides, he wasn't on the list, so I figured what's the worst that could happen?

I hired Jeffrey as my business manager and together we turned Ferguson Inc. into a Fortune 500 company, rubbing elbows with other industry giants like Bill Gates and Jeff Bezos along the way.

Over the years, certain items from the list would occasionally pop up while others never came to pass. All of this could, of course, be attributed to the butterfly effect—the idea that even the most miniscule of actions can have untold consequences. This led to a somewhat unhealthy obsession with chaos theory.

Every now and again, I would consider adding things to the list—small, insignificant things—but always seemed to change my mind at the last moment, afraid that I would only make things worse. After my divorce in 2015, I found myself sitting there alone at the kitchen table with a bottle of Scotch just staring at the list in front of me. I even went so far as to write AVOID HEATHER HALD in bold letters before scribbling it out. Even though things didn't end on the best of terms, we had some good times together and two beautiful children that I wouldn't trade for the world, so I folded up the list and decided to leave that one to chance.

As the years went by, a certain level of complacency set in. I began to believe that this time around I might actually make it out relatively unscathed. Then about six months ago the news broke that Jeffrey Morgan, the man to whom I had entrusted the keys to my kingdom, was being investigated for trafficking underaged girls. It was something that had apparently been going on right under my nose for the last fifteen years.

After the FBI began investigating Jeffrey, they took a closer look at some of his other business dealings. It turns out old Jeffy Boy had been embezzling money from me for years and funneling it into various offshore accounts. Before the authorities could make their move, Jeffrey fled the country with almost every penny I had. This left me to answer all sorts of accusatory questions about how much I actually knew about his illicit activities, including his private island where he recruited girls as young as fourteen.

Due to the scandal and the surrounding media circus, the board of directors voted me out of my own company, leaving me even more destitute. Just like that, everything I had spent a lifetime working for was gone. I had to sell off my remaining assets just to stay afloat and keep myself off the street.

As I sat there alone in my new apartment on the Lower East Side of Manhattan with my mind drifting to some pretty dark places, suddenly a beacon of light shined through as I glanced over at the calendar and realized what date was rapidly approaching. For the first time in nine years, I retrieved the list from the safe deposit box where I kept it and added item number forty-two. Then I scheduled a flight to Colorado.

Jeffrey Morgan may have taken everything from me, but I still have one more ace up my sleeve.

~ ~ ~ ~ ~

I pull off to the side of the road and turn off the engine. Then I step out of the car and shut the door behind me. Part of me was afraid it wouldn't be here anymore, just another victim of the world having moved on into the digital age. But there it is just like I remember it, standing there at the intersection of two dirt roads like an ancient relic of some bygone era. Its rusted metal frame stands out in stark contrast against the cool blue sky. The shards of glass from its busted windows are long gone and the graffiti lining the booth has since faded, but the payphone is still there. A gust of wind blows through, rattling the phone cord.

I glance at my watch. 3:32. I still have a few minutes to kill, so I lean up against the hood of the car and wait. I still have no idea what will happen after I make the call. I've read up on all the theories on time travel over the years, but that's all they are—just theories. No one really knows for sure. There's a chance that history will rewrite itself and my timeline will simply fade from existence as my younger self envisioned it so many years ago, but that creates way too many paradoxes to fathom. The more likely scenario, the one that I wholeheartedly believe due to its tidiness, is the idea that the timeline will simply split off into two divergent paths, leaving me none the wiser. If that's the case, it sucks to be me, but at least I'll be able to rest easy with the knowledge that somewhere out there there's a chance things finally worked out for the best.

The alarm goes off on my watch. It's 3:36. I make my way over to the booth, pick up the receiver, and hold it to my ear. There's no dial tone, just dead silence. For a horrifying moment I stand there wondering if the butterfly effect has somehow interfered with whatever magic made this possible to begin with. I pull a quarter out of my pocket and say a quick prayer as I drop it into the slot. Then I hold my breath. There's a mechanical clunk from inside the payphone and suddenly it springs to life with a staticky dial tone. I let out a sigh of relief.

The number is still visible beneath the plastic cover on the front of the payphone, so I reach up with a shaky hand and punch in the digits. It begins to ring on the other end. I look down and notice that someone has drawn a picture on the chrome plate next to the coin return with a black marker. It's a snake coiled into a circle swallowing its own tail. I run my fingers over it. An ouroboros—the symbol of never-ending death and rebirth. How fitting.

I pull the list out of my shirt pocket and unfold it, taking one last inventory of the items. Maybe this time I'll finally get it right. Maybe this will be the best of all possible worlds.

The ringing seems to go on forever. Just when I'm certain once again that something has gone wrong, someone picks up on the other end and I hear a young boy's voice come through. "Hello?"

"Listen to me very carefully," I say to him. "I need you to reach into your backpack and get out a pen and a notebook. I have something very important to tell you."

END

Sue Ray-Smolik • Omaha, NE

Farther Along

"Tempted and tried we're oft made to wonder why it should be thus all the day long . . ."

Chapter 1
The Waiting

Drifting in and out of consciousness, I can't quite make sense of my surroundings. Faces.

Voices.

So many of them.

They wash in and out, over and over, like the tide flirting with the shore. In and out.

Over and over. Saying things.

What are they saying?

I can only comprehend bits and pieces of the conversation:

". . . fall . . . broken . . ." Something is broken.

Pain?

Yes! "There is pain," I struggle to answer. So much pain!

A needle. A pressure on my arm. A stinging sensation. A calm voice saying it will ease now. "Rest, it will be alright . . ."

Yes, the sharp stabs are letting up some, but I feel as if I am wrapped in a dense fog . . . where am I?

I stare at the unfamiliar ceiling. Scrambling to piece together the fragments of my thoughts to answer that question.

An unpleasant odor fills the room—a mixture of stale air, illness, and the pungent antiseptic cleaner someone has used to try and wash it all away. I can't shake the sense of death that hangs in the corners of this room.

I feel like I am waiting. For what?

I can't make myself remember.

Without movement I lie staring at the ceiling, listening in the quietness of the now empty room for sounds that might help me figure this all out . . . but my thoughts swirl like a blizzard. I feel so tired, so very, very tired . . .

Four.

December 1928. My fourth birthday fell on the Christmas Eve dance at my grandfather's hotel. That night, as he often did, my father sang and played piano in the bar there. My uncle joined with his fiddle, joking with my mother about how his baby sister needed to laugh more. Papa stopped playing so he could dance me around the room and share some cake from the hotel's restaurant. It was so good! And something the war had made an extravagant treat. We laughed and laughed! It was wonderful!

Deep in the night, though, I woke to angry voices. They were fighting again. They often did. I didn't know why. I only knew it made me sad and scared.

Mother didn't like when he came home so late or not at all, as sometimes happened. "We were so far from town," he'd say. "It was safer that I spent the night there when I finished playing," he'd say. "I was just hanging out with your brother and our friends," he'd say.

They had this same fight, over and over. Until they didn't.

And a piece of me, deep inside, was broken.

A blizzard had raged outside for two full days now. All I could see from our windows was a swirl of white.

My mother and I stayed in the kitchen, near the warmth of the oven, where the scent of her baking bread rose and filled the room with delicious promise. Our firewood stack was growing noticeably smaller, so she carefully stoked the embers to keep the flames low and steady. In that tiny room the heat it gave warded off the chill that encased the rest of the house.

Its glowing coals were the only light in the room after we extinguished the flame in the lamp to save our kerosene.

My father hadn't returned to the house for over a week. My brother had turned seventeen during the summer and left immediately to work for the conservation corp. So, with my father now gone, Mother was left to run this farm on her own, and she had buried herself in her daily chores. In truth, she had always done most of the chores, as my father wasn't very interested in the farm work. But since he had been gone, she seemed to be doing three times the amount of everything she normally did.

Her steps were heavy with purpose and her body stiff with anger as she moved through her day in a grim silence. She gave her emotions away only when doing some physical chore, like rolling her bread dough or beating the carpets with more force than they could possibly need.

It felt like she had forgotten I was even there, so I drifted into the shadows to stay out of her path. I trailed behind in silence when she carried milk and feed buckets through the early morning darkness. The crunching snow helped me stay with her in this eerie world of dim gray sky and white drifts.

As the first rays of the dawn lit the drifts on either side of our path with sparkles, I gazed at her stiff back with growing concern. Before, we would have laughed and called them angel diamonds, but now we only trudged in silence.

My corn husk dolls she had made with me in a happier time kept me company under the kitchen table. I quietly sang them songs and smoothed their corn silk hair. Kissing each one I whispered that it would be alright.

I missed him. I missed his laughter. I missed how he'd swing me into his arms and call me sweetheart. My mother didn't do those things. She cooked, cleaned, canned, washed, and cared for me and for our rented farm. From the time the rooster crowed his morning greeting, till long after I was in bed, she did chores.

But she didn't laugh or play with me often, and she didn't call me sweetheart. I knew she loved me, but she showed it differently than he had.

Sometimes, at night, I heard quiet sobs coming from her room. I wanted to go to her then. To climb into her bed and stroke her hair, as she sometimes did to mine when I was sick or hurt. But I knew I dared not.

Later in life I might wonder why she cried. I might try to imagine how her life shaped the woman I knew as a child.

But I was far too young for those thoughts then. I only knew I was scared. I was not completely sure why, but I felt an uneasiness that made me afraid to close my eyes and give in to sleep.

And I missed my father, desperately.

A scream grabbed me from my restless, dream filled sleep. In a sleepy haze I pulled my heavy wool blankets more tightly around me and called out: "Mother?!" My voice trembled both from the cold and the heaviness of fear.

We had heard that same sound earlier in the day. A big cat, hunting in the dense, snow-covered forest that circled the farm. We saw cougar tracks when I helped my mother bring in firewood from the stack by the barn. But this was closer. So close. Another scream ripped the crisp night air. I heard movement on the roof above my head just as my mother threw open my bedroom door.

"Downstairs! Now!" she yelled.

I scrambled to follow her down the narrow staircase. She carried my father's old shotgun and loaded it as she went. Fear engulfed me like a deep, suffocating wave.

"Move!" she ordered. "Get under the table and don't come out till I tell you!"

I did as I was told, still clutching the blanket from my bed. I wanted to cry, but I knew I shouldn't. We must be silent. We must try to not let it know we were here. Was that even possible? I had no idea. I was cold and terrified, and I wanted my mother to hold me. But she was standing, alert and poised, with her gun aimed at the ceiling.

Our fear seemed to fill every space of the once cozy room. If I stuck out my tongue, I was sure I would be able to taste it. We waited and listened for what seemed like hours. The big cat continued to pace back and forth across the roof.

The kitchen was an addition that had been built with a low roof and no second floor. This allowed the chimney of the enormous, double sided fireplace, designed to warm the first floor rooms from both sides, to vent through the roof.

My mother was frantically trying to relight the fire, which had burned out hours ago, because she had realized the cougar was attempting to come down the short chimney.

It had been a long, bitter winter. The cat was hungry. Desperate. The smell of our venison stew hung in the air from dinner. Scraps of raw meat and trimmed fat sat in a bucket by the door intended for the pig trough in the morning.

Whether the cat wanted us or the scrap bucket, I would never know. For at that moment, the blast of my mother's shotgun exploded in my ears.

Having given up on lighting the fire, she aimed at the place on the roof where she last heard the big cat and shot through the ceiling. Snowflakes now floated through the gaping hole. We held our breath, not daring to break the eerie silence. There was no way to know if she had just given the cougar a faster entry or scared it off.

We spent the night lying on the floor by the now blazing fire, waiting for the footsteps of the predator above us. They never came.

I fell asleep at some point, but I don't think she ever did. I woke as early light began to filter into the kitchen and warm my face. I saw her in the still dim light, sitting below the hole. She had pulled over the kitchen chair and sat, shotgun in hand, aimed at the opening, gaze fixed upward and unflinching. Later that day, when her brothers arrived to find a dead cougar on our roof, there was much teasing of their baby sister.

"Who'd a thunk," they said, "that she could take down a cougar from her kitchen with a load of buckshot!"

"Why, sis, Annie Oakley ain't got nothin' on you!" My favorite uncle, my father's fiddle partner, chimed in. "I gotta tell ole Riley he best not be showing his face around here either, leastways while his wife's still got that shotgun in her hands!" He

added this with a laugh that coaxed a small smile from the corners of her mouth.

"You do that, brother," she answered, bringing a deep guffaw from both brothers.

He had played in the last years of Buffalo Bill's Wild West Show when he was a young man and was proud to tell how he had met Miss Annie. The previous winter when the cold nights had begun to seem endless, I had loved sitting around the kitchen table listening to him tell these stories. I tapped my feet and kept a beat with Mother's biggest wooden spoons, while my father and uncles traded stories and played their tunes. My mother cut them extra large slices of her still-hot apple pie and even joined my father on a chorus now and then. Her clear soprano voice melded with his warm tenor and lifted to the ceiling. Those memories of laughter and music rose over the cycles of arguments and slamming doors in my child mind, because that was how I wished it always could be.

But now my father was gone. And though I didn't know it then, so were those moments.

They remained forever locked in time and waiting in the most cherished corners of my memory.

"No, sis, she ain't got nothin' on you!" my uncles beamed.

They took a picture that day. My mother, shotgun held in her crossed arms, stood next to her brothers. The cougar swung over the shoulders of the two grinning men. A rough-edged love floated between the siblings and could be felt even in the photograph.

Years later, when I would pull that faded picture from under my pillow to remember them, I could still feel that affection and hear their playful banter.

My trapper uncle felt like he had taught my mother how to use that gun well. His pride in her gushed from his normally quiet demeanor. He patted her shoulder and teased his brother about what a good teacher he must be. I watched her smile flash and her face light as they praised her. Having survived that terror, I couldn't have agreed with him more.

But that night was the beginning of an end to my life with her there. It was the last time I would see my uncles. The last time for a lot of things.

Oh, the many moments in life we don't have any idea are going to be our last. How it might change our lives if we did.

"While there are others living about us, never molested, though in the wrong . . ."

Chapter 2
Left Behind

I pull out of a dream-soaked sleep, into a cavern of pain.

My moans have brought the staff, and there is another round of calming words. I still cannot completely follow the conversation happening around me.

I do remember my fall now. The soup.

I needed the soup.

I knew I had to eat, because the flu my body had battled for days now had taken everything out of me.

I stood on the stepstool and reached for a can from that top cupboard. Weakness and dizziness made my vision swim.

The last thing I remember is the sound of the soup can rolling from where it landed and what must have been my gasp of shock as I lost my grip on the stool and fell backward into the illness-scented air of my small apartment.

I woke to sirens and a pain so intense it stole my breath.

The landlord was telling the responders it had been three days since he last saw me, and he had decided to let himself in when he didn't receive my rent check.

He knew I had congestive heart failure and that I had called 911 a few times since I had lived there. Once I woke from a deep sleep gasping for breath through the congestion in my chest.

Several other times my test strips indicated my glucose levels were in a danger zone from my diabetes.

Probably I had just forgotten to take my medicine again, or I had eaten too much of the chocolate I secreted away in my freezer.

I hid it there behind the frozen vegetables she brought so that my daughter couldn't scold me for eating it. Those and all the other sugary treats I enjoyed so much.

Had I lain there for three days? I suppose I could have.

My daughter wasn't speaking to me.

She grew too frustrated when I kept changing my mind about the assisted care facilities she was finding for me.

I argued with her repeatedly when she insisted I needed to move to one.

But then I asked her again to find me one when I had a bad episode and admitted that I was struggling.

The fourth time of going through this process had just been the previous week.

This time we had gotten all the way to the morning when the moving truck was supposed to come.

I refused to go, and she left in tears. I couldn't help it.

I didn't remember saying I would move there, but I know I must have.

My signature was on the paperwork at all four of the places where she found space for me. I know that wasn't easy with just my Social Security income, and navigating all of those financial steps to qualify me was definitely not something I was able to do myself.

I didn't blame her, and I remembered parts of each facility tour. They were probably nice.

I knew she would want that for me. I trusted that.

But I just didn't remember all the details, and I was scared that I couldn't remember. Terrified of what might happen in a place like that, where I was under someone else's control.

How could she not understand?

I hadn't told her, but shouldn't she just have known? I lashed out at her through my fear.

I always had.

I regret that now.

I know I was being unnecessarily difficult, fighting so hard to keep my independence when even I knew I could no longer maintain it.

She was a single parent, and taking time off work to do all of this. I knew. But I just couldn't accept that change. I would think I could, but then the fear would strangle me with the thought of surrendering my independent choices to these strangers.

She had needed a break for a few days. She said, "Don't call me until Monday, Mom. We'll start again then."

And now this . . .

I gratefully sink back into the dark haze of not feeling. She'll come now, I know she will.

My eyes drift shut with relief.

Ten.

December 1930. The screen door slammed, the sound carrying to my ten-year-old ears, as I shuffled my worn boots through the dusting of snow on the cracked sidewalk outside my relatives' house.

I was unsure just how we were related. There was never really any introduction when my mother arrived on their doorstep with me, my small, cracked suitcase, and the doll my grandfather had given me.

The suitcase still sits under my bed, but my mother gave the doll to one of the small girls in this house when she admired it. For a long time, I cried myself to sleep over that.

They weren't pleased to see us, that much I could tell, and I am sure she thought the doll would help ease this. Or, she may have just resented that it was given to me by her estranged husband's father. I will never know, but I often wonder.

I slept on a cot in the corner of what had once been a back porch. At some point, it had been closed in to serve as a laundry room and cool storage area for bushel baskets of apples and potatoes stored near the old wringer washer.

Poor workmanship left gaps in the walls that showed daylight and allowed snow to sift into the room. The roof had long been in need of repair. Pails had been placed in several spots in an attempt to catch the drips when it rained, but they were outnumbered by the growing leaks.

The floorboards creaked and sagged in some spots under my bare feet as I crept near the door to listen to their breakfast conversations, trying to discover who they were, wanting to be part of this family I did not know.

My life there developed a routine. The old washer chugged and churned on wash days when I pulled clothes through the long roller meant to squeeze the water from them. Then I hung them to spin and flutter in the summer breeze from the rusty metal clothesline, or after freezing solid in the bitter winter winds I placed them in the corners to thaw. There they stood like a little army of invisible men in the corner of the room nearest the old oil heater. I liked to make up stories about how they had come to be there. My imagination gave me a way to escape into a world I created instead of the one I had been thrust into.

The laundry became my job, handed over to me with a minimum of words from my mother's cousin. She seemed grateful for my help with the endless piles of clothes needing washed for this large family.

This familiar work brought me a feeling of satisfaction and a sense of almost being connected, because it was one of the few times she smiled at me. When I showed her I knew how to do this task, she actually stopped to look directly at me for what felt like the first time since I had met her. It made me proud to be able to help her, just as I had helped my mother do laundry every Saturday . . . back before the life that we knew disappeared.

Where was she now I wondered? My beautiful, strong, unpredictable mother. Her blue eyes blazing with anger or sparkling with laughter. The change between the two sometimes happened too quickly to notice and almost always without time to react. I had learned to read her emotions from a young age, like a storm on the distant horizon I scanned constantly to check its progress. Still, sometimes I missed the cues, and the storm swept me into its fury.

Once it had passed I waited, bruised and shaken, for the sun to come out again.

Yet, I missed her. I missed the strength I always felt in her. Despite the storms her presence offered me an odd sense of protection. Funny how children can feel that way. Our emotional imprint for our parents runs deep enough to endure what we should not be required to in our innocence.

But I hadn't seen her since we stood at that screen door with winter's wind howling around our feet. Our patched and outgrown winter coats grasped tightly in our gloveless hands while she pleaded in an urgent voice for them to take me in. I caught words, phrases, fragments floating from their hushed and angry conversation.

"Need to get work."

"He's not coming back."

"I can't take her with me."

But the phrase I clung to the most was "I'll be back to get her."

When momma? I wanted to ask. When would she come take me back to the house in the woods?

"When death has come and taken our loved ones, it leaves our home so lonely and dreary . . ."

Chapter 3
Invisible Child

I hear the words of a prayer riding over the machines that are keeping me alive. My eyes are heavy, but I shift them open as far as I can.

I see a dark-haired man I do not recognize, his head bowed, eyes closed, lips moving with quiet words.

His hand is laid over mine, a Bible held closely to his chest. I strain to hear him.

I want to hear him, but the heaviness in my eyes pulls them shut again, and my mind begins to float in memories.

Twelve.

December 1936. I had turned twelve just before Christmas. But my birthday came and went through a veil of grief. Grief I could not share, for I was not to have known him, if they had had their way.

The day he was buried was the first time I felt a feeling of hopelessness. My quiet benefactor, my grandfather, who watched from the fringes of my life during this whole dreary eight years I had stayed with my cousins. For that is what I now knew them to be, though their indifference toward me spoke more of obligation than any feeling of family.

He was my father's father, so they did not welcome him to interact with me. Nor did my mother, who sternly forbade me to see him during the handful of times she and I were together since she had left me here. When I told her Grandfather gave me a free soda pop from his hotel store, she spit out the hatred laced words "Don't take anything from that man!" He was, it seemed, to be punished for my father's choices.

It seemed unfair, and so I continued to disobey them by seeing him. I learned to never mention the times he saw me walking up the long hill to their house and stopped to let me ride in the rumble seat of his shiny, black car. Or, how he would open the back door to the theater that he now owned along with his hotel to let me watch a movie for free. The depression had allowed him to use the money he had always been so frugal with to expand his holdings when others were going out of business. Financially he was doing quite well, though, even as a young child, I sensed that he was as lonely as I was. The lucky thing for me was that they seldom cared where I was once my chores were done, and I was able to spend time with the grandfather I had grown to admire.

He gave me the scraps of love that he was able to slip to me when they weren't watching. Maybe he was trying to make up for the lack of interest his son was showing, or maybe he saw the likeness to his late wife in my features and it touched his heart.

A picture of my grandmother hung on the wall behind the registration desk at his hotel. I had memorized every detail as I stood quietly listening to him welcome his guests or talk to his vendors when they delivered their orders. I had her hazel eyes, and the auburn glints in my hair were hers as well.

As I stared in the reflection of the glass frame I thought I might have her smile too. I will never know, of course, if he saw this too, but I wonder.

Losing him was like losing my last small piece of security. My life became just a series of days strung together. Days were filled with chores, and my evenings with aimless wandering that took me through the small town and the surrounding woods until darkness forced me to return.

Always feeling lonely and unseen. An invisible child.

I walked past the buildings he had once owned and operated with so much pride. They were owned by someone else now I guessed. I did not know as I was no longer welcome to enter them.

I missed the sound of his engine coming down the tree-lined streets. I missed feeling my heart lift with joy, knowing he would smile and wave, even if he was too busy to give me a ride. Knowing that I wasn't invisible to him.

There were no more movies or ice cream cones from the restaurant, no more idling about the check-in desk enjoying the buzz of conversation.

No more him.

I think I might have missed him more than even my own parents. His love was given so freely, so genuinely.

My heart will never forget him. This much I do know, but little else. For once again, change was on my doorstep and I didn't even know it was coming.

"Then do we wonder why others prosper living so wicked year after year . . ."

Chapter 4
Together Again

My breaths are labored and slow.

I have trouble not only pulling air into my lungs, but pushing it back out through my parched lips as well.

They put an oxygen mask on me with quiet words meant to comfort.

A sense of panic rises as the breaths become more and more difficult, even with the mask. I feel numb to the pain in my body now.

I feel it as if from a distance, and I am no longer sure where it is coming from. Wait.

I must wait.

I can't go without seeing her. I have to tell her . . .

I slip into darkness while the machines around me beep and whirl.

Thirteen.

December 1937. She came back on my thirteenth birthday. She carried a small bag with a pair of shoes in a size I had long since outgrown. But, how could she have known?

We sat at the table that day, as we always did when she visited. I was given a chair, a plate, food bowls were passed to me, as if I was one of them. Not like when she wasn't here, when I was asked most nights to take a plate to my porch room to make room at the table. I would eat perched on the edge of the cot, listening to their conversation. In warm weather, I was handed a sandwich and sent outside, the screen door slamming behind me before I heard the lock click so I could not return or ask for more.

As if I wanted to return! If I had anywhere else to go, I would have run as fast as my feet would carry me.

But the world I did not know was even more frightening to me than the one I did. So I stayed.

And kept my head down.

And prayed to a God I hoped was there. But, she was back now.

My suitcase was repacked with my hand-me-down dresses, my brush and the too-small shoes Mother had just brought me.

Pulling on the dirt-covered boots I wore to school, I quickly added a small collection of rocks and leaves I had gathered during my walks through the woods. As well as the poems I had secretly written and hidden in a tin box my grandfather had once filled with cookies to give me.

I felt like that tin and the items it held were the most important things in my suitcase. "We are going to the country," she announced, her voice edged with excitement. She had finally found work, even though the Great Depression, as the newspapers called it, made that almost impossible. She had done it, she said with pride, and I felt proud of her.

She was cooking and cleaning for a man who rented his house to hunters and workers from timber companies who were in the area. Her own family had run a successful lumber business in that area when she was growing up, so this was a familiar life to her.

Now, companies such as these were using the rich bounty of western Pennsylvania's native forests to supply the building boom that was sure to take place once the war ended.

Things were predicted to be looking up soon, the radio told us.

I could only hope they were right.

Andrea Riley • Lincoln, NE

Out of the Fire

The adobe wall against his back was hot and the smoke seeping under the door had turned black. It wouldn't be long now and they would have to make a run for it. Billy pushed back the curtain and the window with the barrel of his Colt and peeked outside. It was dark, but the burning building at his back provided plenty of light to see the men popping their heads over the wall surrounding the house. The men outside knew their wait would soon be over too.

A rush of excitement surged through him at the prospect of a fight. For five days they had been holed up in McSween's house. Five days of inactivity was never good for young men used to action. Now Dolan had managed to gain the lead. The soldiers were down from the fort with their howitzer. The men in the house had watched through the windows as the black cavalrymen hauled the big gun through town and pointed at each of their strongholds until one by one the men skinned out, leaving only the few stationed with McSween. They'd called their bluff though. McSween said the Colonel wouldn't fire on civilians, and the twelve men in the house refused to budge.

So Dolan's men set it on fire. Unable to put it out, they had moved from room to room as the fire consumed the house until nothing was left but the little kitchen at the back.

Billy gripped the handle of his pistol tighter and a laugh burbled from his lips. McSween's coughing covered up the giggle.

Their leader's lungs couldn't take the smoke. Useless leader that he was. He was weak. Weak, but cunning, which was going to be what killed them all. He refused to take a gun. He had refused to fight, else this all would have been over days ago. No, McSween had to take the moral high ground, even if there was nothing moral about it. "We will seek restitution in the law," he would say, whatever the hell that meant when the law was dictated by whoever had the upper hand. Not like Tunstall. Not even like Dolan, Billy had to admit. At least they were honest about their motives and didn't try to hide the fact that all they sought was money and power. And now they would probably all die, and for what: so one man could die in the belief that he had "done the right thing" and "stood up for the people," even though all he was ever doing was trying to protect his own interests. So he could become a martyr to his own cause, just as he'd made poor Tunstall one, just as he would make them all in the end. Well, to hell with that.

Billy glanced back at the lot in the kitchen, with their sweaty, soot-streaked faces, eyes red and watering from the smoke. A few looked back at him. He could see the fear in the eyes of young Harvey Morris. He'd only wanted to read law with McSween, not get caught up in this mess. There were the Mexican farmers who had sided with McSween because they thought he could bring down Dolan and the House and their years of oppression, not realizing that McSween merely sought to replace Dolan as their new patron. And then there was Tom, the good-natured boy from Texas who had just come looking for some adventure. The boy, really no younger than Billy himself, who was now looking at him expectantly to save them. They wanted to live.

He wanted to live. Eighteen years was barely a drop in the bucket.

"All right, boys," he said, his voice rising in anticipation of the danger he was about to face. "It's about time we got going. Make sure your pistols are loaded. We're gonna make a run for the creek. Once you're out the door, keep running and don't look back."

Billy checked his pistol and went to stand before the door. Harvey jumped up and bounded over to join him. He had no gun to check.

"We've had some good times together, haven't we, Kid?" Tom said quietly from beside him.

We're not going to die, Billy told himself. We're too young to die.

"I'll see you at the river, Tom."

Billy opened the door and flung himself into the yard. He fired two rounds at nothing in particular. He could hear others following him but didn't look back to see who. He heard more shots, and someone behind him fell. He fired again. Pale faces appeared as blurs in the dark as he ran through the gate in the adobe wall that surrounded the house. Dry grass crunched under his feet and then he was in the trees along the river. A volley of shots behind him drowned out all other noise. He nearly tripped on a stone on the bank but kept on running. He splashed through the creek and stopped in the trees on the other side to catch his breath. It was cool along the river after the heat of McSween's kitchen. He bent down and splashed water over his face and in his hair. Through the trees across the river he could see the glow from the burning house, and he saw the silhouettes of the men running around before it. The shooting had stopped. He could hear someone splashing through the water behind him, but since there were no shots, he hoped it was a friend rather than a foe.

"They got Harvey," Tom said, leaning against a tree on the bank.

No looking back, Billy reminded himself.

"What about McSween?" Billy asked.

Two others trotted up the bank toward them. "He didn't make it out," replied Jim French, who was followed by Chavez y Chavez. "We're the only ones. The rest of 'em stopped when they all started shooting."

"Maybe we should go back across in case they need some cover," Tom offered.

No one moved. They were all looking across the river toward the house, listening for any sign of the others trying to make a break for it. The only sound was the roar of the flames, the running water, and the wind rustling the leaves overhead.

"No one's firing."

Billy put a restraining hand on Tom's shoulder, knowing he was stupid enough to go back just to see what was going on.

"I shall never surrender!" they heard McSween's voice call out from across the river.

They all instinctively fell to the ground as the men ranged around the house opened fire. They were still sprawled on the riverbank when three other Regulators stumbled upon them.

"We were in the store," George Coe said. "You all that are left?"

Billy nodded before realizing George wouldn't see his gesture in the dark.

"I think McSween's dead," Tom said in shock.

"I imagine so," Billy said, replacing the spent shells in his Colt. A martyr to the last, he thought. And now where would they be, branded outlaws, no money and no center?

"We'd better skin out," George said, looking downriver.

"Yah," replied Billy. "It's over."

For now.

Valerie R. Robert • Plattsmouth, NE

Letting Go of Jason

The three of us followed the woman down the long, empty hallway toward a set of steel double doors. She removed a key ring, unlocked the doors, and stepped through. We followed, reluctantly. The heavy doors slammed behind us, echoing in the empty hallway. The technician on duty met us and explained that Jason would have to be strip-searched for his own protection. He would also have to do a urinalysis to test for drugs and alcohol. The look on my son's face hit me like a gut punch. All the guilt and doubt I had been feeling over the past year returned full force. What kind of mother was I? How could I lock my son up in this virtual prison? Was I doing the right thing? Maybe things hadn't been so bad in Germany after all.

~ ~ ~ ~ ~

When my husband, Jim, had been assigned to Germany the previous year, Jason was unable to accept that he had to move. At the time we were stationed at Brimley Air Force Base in Cheyenne, Wyoming. A shy introvert, Jason was in the beginning of his junior year in high school when we received word of the assignment. His response to the news was the first and last time he shared his feelings on the matter. "It's taken me two years to feel comfortable here. I don't want to have to start over somewhere else."

Jim and I tried to reason with him, but to no avail. He was angry, but instead of expressing his anger, he became depressed and emotionally withdrawn. He was either unwilling or unable to deal with the move. While everyone else rushed around, getting ready for the move, Jason did nothing. On the day the movers came to pack our shipment of household goods, none of his things were ready. Everyone else was doing their best to take care of his or her own things and unable to help him. As a result, most of his things—including his clothes—went into storage. Things finally got so bad we sought help from a counselor, who recommended an antidepressant.

After we arrived in Germany, things didn't improve. Jason stayed in his room all the time, listening to music and declining our suggestions to get out and do something, anything. Finally, he joined a baseball team and made a few friends. One night he asked if he could go to a party. He was upfront and told us there would be alcohol. He said he would be acting as bartender, so he wouldn't be drinking much. I was reluctant to let him go but felt desperate for some normalcy in our lives, so I agreed, with Jim, to let him go. The evening was uneventful. Jason came home by curfew and appeared sober. Things seemed better for a bit, but Jason still appeared depressed, and I was still worried.

A short time later, when he wasn't in for his midnight curfew, I lay in bed, tossing and turning, unable to sleep. I must have dozed for a few hours, because when I woke up next it was 3:00 a.m. and Jason still wasn't home. *Should I wake Jim?* I knew he had to get up early for work. But by 4:00 a.m., when I couldn't stand it any longer, I finally woke him. He was angry but finally agreed to help me look for Jason. I remember that night vividly.

Jim and I trudged through the empty streets, making tracks in the newly fallen snow. We were the only people on the street. The streetlights cast a dim glow, shadowing the long rows of World War II stone buildings. We crossed over to the other side of the base, passing through a fence topped with barbed wire. We suspected Jason was with his friend Ryan, but we weren't sure which building was his. We made a lucky guess and entered a nearby building, climbing the three flights to the former maid's quarters, where Ryan lived.

All was quiet at first, but we heard voices and followed them to a door at the end of the hall. We knocked and Ryan opened the door. Jason was standing behind him. We were furious!

"What the hell do you think you're doing?" I shouted.

"Just talking."

He slowly stepped out into the hallway, as if staying out until 4:00 a.m. was perfectly normal.

Jim said, "Let's go," in a stern voice.

We all walked home in silence. We would deal with the consequences in the morning.

Soon afterward, Jason started coming home late for curfew most nights and hanging out with kids we didn't trust. At first, we waited up for him. Often, he couldn't walk a straight line, staggering down the hallway to his room. He wasn't interested in participating in our family in any way. When I found out his grades had dropped from As and Bs to Ds and Fs, I called his school. They said he was hardly ever there.

His appearance changed. It looked like he had slept in his clothes. His room was littered with trash. Half-empty bags of chips, pop cans, beer bottles, and dirty clothes were strewn across his bedroom floor. A layer of half-dried vomit lay congealing in the bottom of his waste basket. He stopped speaking to us, and we only spoke to him to confront him with his behavior. Most of the time he came home after we were in bed and was gone when we woke up the next morning. It felt like living with a total stranger.

Jim thought Jason's behavior was typical teenage rebellion. My instincts told me otherwise. We argued about it to no avail. I felt utterly alone. There was no one I could talk to about my fears. I would have been too embarrassed to tell anyone what was going on in our home anyway. I was afraid to venture off the base because I didn't know the language or my way around. I stayed home most of the time, worrying about Jason and feeling trapped.

Finally, I found a book about teens, drugs, and alcohol abuse at the library. I showed it to Jim. Jason's behavior was textbook. His appearance had changed; he was hanging around with kids we didn't approve of; he had stopped participating in family activities; and his grades had fallen drastically. We went down the list, checking off every item on the page. The list went on. Finally, Jim admitted something was very wrong.

Getting Jim to recognize Jason's problem was only the beginning. Finding professional help seemed like an impossible task. About that time the Army in Europe was beginning to "draw down." Bases began closing after Congress voted to make large cuts in military forces. The Army took the hardest hit of all the branches, with mental health services the first to go.

We first approached a school counselor who was very sympathetic but whose expertise didn't include substance abuse counseling. We then made an appointment with one of the substance abuse counselors who had previously counseled Jason, but she didn't feel the problem was serious. I didn't feel she was qualified and asked her to refer Jason to the child psychologist in

Heidelberg. Instead, she referred us to her boss, Mr. Jones, who would presumably then refer us to the child psychiatrist. Mr. Jones called us the next day to tell us we couldn't see him for three more weeks.

I was furious. I was tired of being put off by one professional after another. Throughout this period, I was battling major back and gastrointestinal issues. Our marriage was failing. Both Jim and I were ready to end it at different times during the ordeal. And our fourteen-year-old son, Andrew, was being neglected, despite our best intentions not to neglect him.

Jim's feelings on getting help for Jason differed radically from mine. It seemed like he wanted to give up every time we ran into an obstacle. He was so furious with Jason, he wanted to ignore what he was doing and go on with our lives. He didn't feel we should all have to sacrifice for Jason. I was angry with Jason too, but I was driven to help him. He was only seventeen, and I felt he needed us, even though he pushed us away every time we tried to help him. I knew he needed to go into a treatment program, and that meant leaving Germany. It also meant convincing Mr. Jones to refer us to the child psychiatrist in Heidelberg, three hours away. Hopefully he would then refer us to a treatment facility in the states.

I convinced Jim to go with me to see Mr. Jones. He came out of his office as we were walking into the waiting area. I tried to explain to him why we needed to see him right away, why we couldn't wait a few weeks. He seemed confused by our presence and his manner was very condescending.

"I'm sorry, Mrs. Burton, but you'll just have to wait for your appointment!"

I cried and raged all the way home, but Mr. Jones' behavior had served a purpose for me. It strengthened my resolve to do whatever it took to convince him that Jason needed treatment. I went home, sat down, and recounted all the pertinent events of the past ten months in Germany. I then went back further, remembering things that had happened in the months prior to leaving for Germany.

The book on alcohol and drugs served as a blueprint for documenting Jason's symptoms. I took every one of the items we had checked off, symptoms that showed Jason was abusing alcohol, and possibly addicted to it, and listed his behaviors one by one. I did one more thing. The book suggested searching a child's room to look for signs of abuse or addiction. It said the behavior displayed by the adolescent represented merely the "tip of the iceberg." Parents might not see signs of actual drinking or drug use, but the behavior changes, like we had witnessed in Jason, pointed to substance abuse or addiction.

I had never invaded my child's privacy before and never would have if I hadn't believed we were facing a life-or-death situation. Jim agreed we needed to go through Jason's things. It didn't take long to find what we were looking for—pages and pages of letters to Jason's friends back in the states, ironically never mailed. They served as a journal of sorts, documenting his feelings and his drinking behaviors. In retrospect, I pondered whether Jason had left the letters out in plain sight so we would find them—a veritable cry for help.

Whenever we had confronted Jason about his drinking, he always downplayed its significance. He said he only drank "once in a while" and rarely got drunk. He accused us of overreacting and making a big deal about nothing. The letters made it plain that he had been lying to us. He had been sneaking off base and going to German nightclubs. He was drinking on an almost daily basis, usually to get drunk. In one letter, he told his friends how stupid we were for believing his lies. His only purpose in life, it seemed, was to get drunk.

Reading Jason's letters was very painful, but it was also a great relief to have my suspicions confirmed. I knew the knowledge contained in those letters would be the proof we needed to finally get help for our son and family. My main motivation now was to save our family. I didn't know if treatment would help Jason or not; I did know that Jim, Andrew, and I needed help just as badly as Jason did. He might choose to destroy his life, but we didn't have to allow our lives to be destroyed too.

The weeks passed and we were finally able to meet with Mr. Jones. I showed him several pages of information detailing Jason's behavior and outlined what we had discovered in his letters. He admitted that the problem was much more serious than he had realized. He also said he understood why I was so upset the day we had first spoken. He still didn't feel Jason's problem was serious enough for him to be hospitalized, but he finally agreed, reluctantly, to refer him to the child psychiatrist. "Hurry up and wait" is the military's favorite slogan. We were getting good at it. Our appointment to see the psychiatrist was set for one month.

When we walked into Dr. Matthews' office, I began sobbing; it finally felt safe to release the problem to someone trustworthy. He seemed to be the first truly qualified person we had spoken to in the past eleven months. We didn't have to convince him of the seriousness of Jason's problem. He didn't waste our time and only asked for the pertinent facts. He immediately began working on the paperwork needed to get us all on a Medivac flight back to Cheyenne.

Dr. Matthews told us we would leave in approximately one month, but we wouldn't know our exact departure date until a few days before leaving Germany. Each of us could bring one suitcase. Our car, furniture, and all our household goods would be left behind. Jim would come back to deal with those arrangements after Jason's initial one-month inpatient treatment, at a time to be determined by his doctor at James Everett Hospital in Cheyenne. The date would depend on how well his treatment progressed.

On a day in November, about a week before Thanksgiving, we locked the door of our apartment for the last time. An ambulance took us from Stuttgart to Frankfurt, Germany. We spent the night at Rhein Main Army Base. The following morning, we boarded the plane to begin our journey to Cheyenne. At two a.m., four days after leaving Germany, with stops at numerous stateside airbases, Jim, Jason, and I made the long walk down that hallway at James Everett Hospital.

~ ~ ~ ~ ~

I wish I could say that all went smoothly from that point on, but our recovery as a family had just begun. Jason was discharged from the hospital just before Christmas. For a while he took the antidepressants prescribed by his doctor and went to AA meetings, but after a few months he stopped doing both. Although he wasn't drinking, all of the old behaviors had returned. He had trouble getting up in the morning, wouldn't follow through with chores, and was isolating from the family again. We had all continued attending family therapy for an additional six months, but Jason refused to participate. Everyone was angry with him and there was one major incident where he punched a hole in the door in a fit of rage. Even Andrew, his staunchest ally in the past, wanted him gone. We warned Jason that he needed to make a choice. He could either change his behavior, or he would have to leave.

In May, shortly after his eighteenth birthday, Jim and I made an unbearable decision. We told Jason he could no longer live in our home. We didn't know where he would go or how he would live. We knew we had done all we could to help him, but he had refused to accept any help. Andrew was being harmed by the ensuing chaos, and so was our marriage.

Around the time Jason moved out, I started taking Andrew to Alateen meetings. One night, instead of leaving him at his meeting, I walked across the hall into the Al-Anon meeting. I decided to stay. While there I learned that alcoholism is a disease. I've also learned, as Al-Anon literature states, "I didn't cause it, I can't control it and I can't cure it."

Jim and I tried to be the best parents we knew how to be to Jason, but our efforts weren't enough to prevent our son from being affected by an insidious disease. Jason's life hasn't turned out the way we planned. I can't judge his progress, but I can say I'm proud of him today. Today Jim and I have a strong marriage and a good relationship with both our sons.

In recovery I learned I needed to let my son go to live his own life, make his own choices, and face his own consequences. I couldn't save him. Only he could do that. Asking Jason to move out may have been the hardest decision I ever made, but ultimately, it was the best one.

Rachel Hruza • Lincoln, NE

Sound Control

The rise and fall of Alfred Goesch's thin white conductor's baton carried with it the weights of the world: Mozart, Brahms, Schumann, Mendelssohn—Fanny and Felix, and the names of other composers who had changed the world with music. Each time he lifted, jerked, or swayed that lithe white instrument, notes collided and blended, molding into themselves, upon themselves, within themselves to without, until the echoes in his head were not thoughts but irreplaceable melodies.

In the evenings, after releasing his orchestra members out into the silence of the Midwestern night sky, he'd return home to his wife, Hannah, overflowing with the music of Haydn or Beethoven trapped inside his skull until he, too, thought he was deaf with sound until she'd look up from her book and say, "The wizard and his wand. Hello, dear."

"Mmmm," Alfred would answer with a florid fermata hum, passing her to his desk in his study and gently placing his baton in its protective case. Shaking off his suit coat, a slight rustling of sixteenth notes brushing down his arms, he'd drape the shoulders over the back of the leather chair, dressing it in the cheap gray polyester from the local department store.

"It was a good rehearsal then?" Hannah would call out.

Chopin for yes, Bruckner for no. Even an inaudible melody had its place, signifying if there existed any apprehension of how the rehearsal had transpired.

Weeks and months were the same as they had always been, days of the week full of instruction and lessons, with Tuesday and Thursday nights aflame with the music of men he carried in his mind. The songs he heard flowed in and out, the ebb so harmonious and logical that his brain felt full when his stomach was hungry. The music filled him, just like it had its composers. The math of it all, the way it all fit together, made him whole.

Then, on a Tuesday in mid-March, when a light mist hung in the air like Brahms' sixty-eighth opus he'd heard at Teatro Colón seven years ago last summer, the music changed—vanished even. The thin veil of water coating the grass clung to his pant legs as he trudged up the front steps and through the door. He stopped in the threshold.

"Hello, dear," Hannah said.

When he didn't move through the hallway humming the night's work, she looked up.

"Was it a good rehearsal?" she asked, surveying his damp brown coat and dangling arms.

"I—I couldn't pick it up," he said. He collapsed onto the armchair nearest the door, the one reserved for guests only and certainly not soggy-coated men. His hands were clasped loosely together between his spread thighs. "I dropped it."

Hannah sat up. "You dropped what?"

"My baton," he said.

"Is it broken then?"

"No," he said. His eyes met hers for the first time that day. "I couldn't pick it up." His head fell forward, and she half expected him to convulse into sobs. She'd never seen Alfred act this way, not even after his father died and he didn't speak for several days, lost in a dirge of being orphaned at age fifty-seven.

"I couldn't get my fingers to stop shaking," he said.

Alfred ran his now fully functioning hands over his pale face. Years of avoiding the sun made him look younger than his sixty-nine years, but now he felt much older. He thought of how he'd dropped the stick mid-song and clumsily bent down to pick it up. *Why didn't I just keep going without it?* In days past he would have laughed it off and continued with his hands, the eyes of the orchestra members gazing obediently at the nimble and graceful digits. But now, the baton was a part of him, an extension of his hands that held each musician on his or her seat, poised arms ready to pull bow along string, mouth to reed, fingers to open metal valves. His hands itched for it, couldn't move without it. Suddenly, they couldn't stop moving. The orchestra played for several more measures, nearly half a minute, before the notes slowed and evaporated altogether as their invisible timbre fell onto his back where he struggled on his hands and knees, his right-hand oscillating back and forth like the pendulum of a clock but faster, and in a rhythm of its own. The lonely bassoon reverberated longest, and the slight honk that emerged from the instrument haunted him even now.

He had found the sleek wooden tool right away, picked it up, and moved to stand, but it fell once more and then he couldn't stop his hands. Thumping them against the floor like an ape, he tried to hold them still, to cut the circuit in his brain that was causing the problem, but nothing silenced the shake. The first violinist asked quietly if he needed help. Somehow, he wrapped his vibrating hand around the baton and set it on the stand before rubbing his hands together.

"From the *scherzo*," he'd said, brushing his left hand on his pants and lifting the rescued prop in his right, clasping it tightly in his fist like a knife. The shaking had subsided, but he sensed it was still there, inside his veins and stronger than the blood pumping through them.

"Less bassoon," he'd added.

Now, he could see Hannah's eyes, much more wrinkled than his own from years of gardening out in the broad daylight without the sun hat he'd bought her that sat in dust and dirt in the garage. Her eyes were sad, and he hated seeing her crinkly skin droop into the slope near the eyelid crease. Her aging eyes confirmed his suspicions. Something was wrong with him.

~ ~ ~ ~ ~

After his appointment with the doctor, Alfred drove home despite Hannah's protestations (he even ignored her threat to walk home) with his hands clutching the wheel, trying to tell if his motor skills had indeed changed. He lifted his right hand from the wheel, still pressing against it, and looked at it. Still the same hands, thick-veined and spotted with age, but they didn't really feel that different to him.

"Look out!" Hanna shouted.

He looked up in time to see an adolescent girl running with a leashed dog a few feet from the car and slammed on the brakes. The runner didn't stop, didn't even look back, but Hannah scolded him the entire way home. He heard her but didn't comment as she muttered under her breath, "The doctor said not to let you drive."

Hannah threw open the car door and stormed into the house, her fast steps punctuating her anger. Alfred sat in the car after turning off the ignition for a few minutes. Hannah would cool off. She hated rudeness, and he'd been rude to the doctor, avoiding eye contact and questions, complaining about the pop music playing in the waiting room, and purposefully lying to try to cause a misdiagnosis.

"Do you find yourself sweating a lot, Mr. Goesch?" The doctor was young, early thirties, and had a full head of light brown hair.

"How do you mean?" Alfred said, his voice low and gruff. Beethoven's Fifth.

"Are you, um, perspiring more than you have in the past?"

"Not at all."

Hannah sighed. "He's sweatier in the bed. I don't like to put my legs against his at night."

Alfred frowned as his wife corrected every answer he gave, providing the truth. *Quasi una fantasia* Op. 27, No. 2 played through his head. He felt his chin swaying to the gentle eighth notes of the bass clef. It was a Beethoven dominated morning.

Hannah and the doctor discussed music while Alfred waited with his hand on the door.

"My daughter was devastated to hear you'd retired," the doctor said, referring to Hannah's recent end of a fifty year career as a vocal teacher at one of the local high schools.

"Yes, I miss those young voices, but it was time."

"Shelby loves music. She's only twelve, but she writes her own songs. It's cute, really."

Alfred rolled his eyes and left the room. He'd rather eat his co-pay than hear the drivel about the doctor's spoiled little girl.

Back at home, he sat in front of the piano. Somehow it felt desperate, a last plea to God or his wife or his hands or his brain itself to remember something it loved and come back to itself in its original healthy form. Symptoms the doctor had listed rushed from his memory to the forefront of his vision: losing his stamina with Hannah two nights ago, his feet cramping in sharp pains while hauling groceries up the stoop, forgetting the name of his favorite concerto last Tuesday. *Coincidence! Farce!* He wanted to shout. Didn't people get this earlier in life? Shouldn't he have known? He tried to keep his mind from saying the name of his future vanquisher, but he couldn't keep control of his own thoughts: Parkinson's. Eyes glazed over, he pushed C sharp with his right index finger, and then Hannah's voice rang out in B minor.

"There is still hope for you. Dr. Beadle was very optimistic. I don't want to hear any moping from you. You're not dead yet."

Alfred released the black key and moved to stand. The difficulty of accomplishing the simple task he wanted his body to do stunned him. Pushing his hands against the bench, he planted his feet. Nothing happened. Clutching the front of the piano, he tried to ram himself upward. Again, nothing. His muscles weren't responding. He couldn't hear the music anymore, could barely remember the sharp he'd just played. As the anger in his head grew, the more his mind grew fuzzy, less willing to listen. Mozart, Beethoven, Mendelssohn, all were gone. He kicked his foot up, and this time it listened, met with the base of the piano and he toppled over backward, scattering the music in the piano bench that now lay flopped open on his lap. As he stared at his hands, the way he had stared at his wife's eyes the night before, part of him wondered if he'd remember any music again.

~ ~ ~ ~ ~

The baton he'd always held gingerly, cradled it between his thumb and index finger, was now pressed hard, squeezed between the pads of skin to be certain it was there. The indentations on his skin might have hurt if they didn't give him the exquisite satisfaction that he still had control, their eyes still watched it, and as far as he could tell, it commanded them steadily, unwavering. He cued the cello and then brought his left hand through, welcoming the slow expressive strings. Smiling, he hadn't lost anything; he had it all, everything.

When his arm shook involuntarily at the *pianissimo*, he countered the movement by clenching his fingers tighter against the wand. The pressure was too much. The thin utensil flew through the air, narrowly missing a trombonist's tapping leg. A few eyes watched him, waiting to see if he'd stop them, but Alfred kept directing. Beads of nervous perspiration formed, immediate and harsh on his forehead. He wiped them away with his open hand and a viola came in too soon. He glanced with furrowed brow in her direction and she blushed, leaning back against her chair. After several stops and starts they finished the *Academic Festival Overture*, and Alfred ended rehearsal early. He walked through the maze of chairs and picked up his baton without a problem. *Brahms must be glad the maggots ate his ears long ago.* He thought about breaking the stick in half on his knee, but he knew the poor rehearsal was his own fault. How could an army march when their drummer couldn't keep a steady beat?

He held the score out to Hannah when he returned home that night. He frowned. "There are too many entrances. All these songs are too long. Damn show-offs," he said, cursing the men he so loved. "I don't think I can do this anymore."

"Yes, you can," Hannah said. "Beethoven didn't need his hearing to write music. You don't *need* the baton to direct."

Alfred was quiet. Beethoven was alone with his ailment. He had his piano lowered to the ground so he could feel the music. The genius didn't need to hear it, but he *wanted* to—he wanted to *feel* it because the music was most important. Alfred's body felt everything, and it couldn't handle it. The bones, muscles, and sagging skin were going to cave in on themselves and take him with it. Even now, he stared at his hand, which cast a quivering shadow.

"They'll see them shaking," he said after a few minutes.

Hannah looked at him, the yellow light from the lamp casting a shadow over her freckled nose. She took the convulsing hand in her own. "Did you ever think that maybe this is the music trying to get out?"

He pulled his hand away, but he didn't disagree.

~ ~ ~ ~ ~

The next morning, a Saturday, Hannah made Alfred sit outside with her while she started her tomatoes. She put them in separate little cups to keep inside until all the snow had passed. Sprinkling dirt from her spade into a cup, she hummed a few notes, some nonsensical song. Alfred hated her humming. It was nothing of note, no worthy composer, just whatever tone her brain selected to sing.

"I forgot the fertilizer. Would you—" She stopped when she looked at Alfred hunched over on the stoop. "Never mind." A barely audible grunt emerged from her lips as she pushed off of her knees and stood up. Alfred shifted his weight to the left so she could get into the house and then stared at a patch of dead grass a few feet in front of him. When a glint of sun glared into his eye, he looked up to see a young girl standing in the middle of his yard with a golden retriever at her side, the gold tag on its collar reflecting the light. Her long brown hair curled at the ends, and her eyes stared up, not at the sky but as if she'd caught sight of a bluebird sitting on the gutter of his house. Ghostly recognition flashed through his brain when he realized he'd almost hit this pair with his car.

"Hi," he said.

The girl didn't respond but the dog ran forward with its pink tongue out and leaned its head down for a scratch. Alfred wasn't one for pets, but he poked his fingers through the dogs' mane on its back and neck.

"You like dogs?" the girl asked.

"They're alright."

The girl walked forward and put her hands on the retriever. "Jack is my dog. We like to dance together."

Alfred looked around. This child did not look old enough to be on her own. "How old are you?"

The girl didn't respond right away but looked up at the roof again. "Twelve," she finally said.

Alfred looked at her. The thin waif was also short, and her eyes hadn't met his once. Without children of his own, he knew he wasn't the best guesser of ages, but she did not seem almost a teenager.

The door opened and Hannah appeared with a green bag of fertilizer. "Why, Shelby, right?" she said, looking down at the girl. The girl didn't respond and she didn't look at Hannah in return. Hannah dropped the bag of fertilizer by the empty cups. "The doctor's daughter," she said to Alfred. "Are you lost? Do you need a ride home?" she asked the girl.

Shelby stood, silent. They all listened, waiting.

"Do you have a piano?" she asked after nearly half a minute, setting her cheek on Jack's head. The dog let out a small whimper.

"Jack's thirsty," she added.

Inside, Alfred found himself, as per order by Hannah, showing the girl the upright in the dining room. "This is middle C," he said. He pushed it.

"I know that," Shelby said, her voice scolding.

She played a scale, slowly, but each note timed perfectly with the next. The precision with which she played the eight notes was hypnotizing; even the pressure she used was consistent, even.

"C major," she said. She smiled, this time looking at Alfred's face.

"Yes," he said.

She spent the next hour playing various scales for him, always the same rhythm and intensity of sound. Alfred didn't particularly listen, but he found the predictable scales soothing. In a way, it felt as if he was starting over.

"I know some songs," Shelby said.

He realized she'd been sitting with her hands in her lap and staring at the gold letters of *Steinway* without touching the keys for several minutes. "What are they?" he asked, not caring.

She stood up. "I'll play them tomorrow," she said.

~ ~ ~ ~ ~

Shelby arrived at the Goesch's house, Jack in tow, every day for two weeks. She played her songs, some short and sweet, the melody mostly through steady chord progressions, but others were more technical, speedy sixteenth notes cascading through the bass notes while the high notes were held long. They were so distinct and somehow so similar to every song Alfred had loved in his life that he couldn't help but sit by her on the piano bench, transfixed, waiting to hear the next note and somehow knowing exactly what it was going to be. It calmed him, steadied his twitching limbs. He added a few notes himself, here and there, tiptoed his fingers around the skinny twigs of Shelby's hands. Shelby stopped and looked at him.

"A trombone would play that part," she said. Her unprompted declaration festered inside Alfred.

"How would you like to write your songs down, Shelby?" he asked.

She stared straight ahead, her hands in her lap as they always were after playing a song.

"We could write them together; we would be composers, Shelby. You are one."

For the first time, she met his eyes, albeit briefly. "Yes. I would like that."

Alfred had arranged pieces, had written simple melodies for a single instrument, but he'd never composed an entire score before. He wrote a few of her songs from memory that night, adding his own intonations here and there, spreading the chords out amongst the instruments, the cellos carrying the melody here, the trumpets echoing it there, in harmony. The music splayed all over the living room floor; Hannah read while Alfred scribbled and scratched out, erased, and wrote anew. He stopped when his hand cramped. Crying out in surprise, he realized it hadn't suffered a tremor the entire evening. Gazing at his hand triumphantly, he looked up when he realized Hannah was speaking to him.

Her eyebrows were raised and she'd set her book aside. "Are you alright?" she asked.

"Yes," Alfred answered. "My hand just hurts from writing."

"Are you rearranging Schubert again?"

"No," he said. "Shelby."

Eyebrows raised again, Hannah smiled. "I didn't think I'd lose you to the music again."

Alfred might have heard her, but she didn't bother waiting for a reply. He shook out his hand and went back to his pages, the music flowing from his fingers, twitching with the silent bouncing rhythm in his head.

~ ~ ~ ~ ~

Shelby and her doctor father attended the orchestra practice that Tuesday. Alfred was sweaty again, not from dropping his baton, which in fact he clutched tightly in his right hand. He tapped his baton on the music stand, bringing everyone to attention. He smiled and lifted his baton. He brought in the strings, then the brass, then the percussion. The woodwinds were last, the bassoon after everything else, and he kept the baton moving throughout the entire rehearsal, his face reddening with every note.

It was abysmal. The music was awful. He had proudly presented his orchestra, his friends, his students, with the Xeroxed copies of his creation, and it was the worst thing he'd ever heard. The sounds were discordant. None of the notes matched up in harmony, and several of the instruments' music itself clearly didn't have enough measures. Cellos carried the melody sooner than he expected, the trumpet harmony sounded terrible with the horn's high peal. It was the worst music he'd ever heard his orchestra play, and their faces reflected their distaste for the amateur work.

He stopped them halfway through and opened his mouth to apologize, but the sound of the steady applause of two small hands caused him to turn. Shelby was on her feet, her face a round bastion of pride. Her father, seated next to her, was astonished.

With a deep breath in his tight chest, Alfred wiped away a few renegade drops of perspiration. This time he lowered his baton to the music stand. He lifted his hands, empty, but open.

"Again," he said to his musicians.

His hands took off like crazy, cuing the next horrible drone. His hands, tremors or not, seemed to know the music by heart; his eyes glazed over the music, unseeing. When different sections ran out of measures, he shouted at them, "Capriccio! Improvise!" And they did.

When they finished, he lowered his hands and turned his pages back to the first. Hannah had been wrong; he hadn't lost himself in this piece. After sixty some years, he'd finally found the sound of home, the sound of himself—or at least the sound he needed now.

"Again," he said.

Behind him, Shelby applauded.

~ ~ ~ ~ ~

The auditorium was sold out for the first time in years. Several faces he recognized out in the crowd, and he imagined Shelby's father had invited a few friends. Shelby sat in the front row staring straight ahead, the same straight-lip composure with her hands in her lap and her feet waving back and forth under her seat. Walking onstage, he ignored the standard applause. The eyes of his true audience, his orchestra, watched him, waited. His brain, poised and salivating, could already hear the sounds, taste them in his ear like expecting the screech of car tires when slamming the brakes or the crunch of ice beneath a heavy, determined footstep. He raised both his hands, the slight steady quiver only visible to a trained eye, and then with the downbeat, his hands, equally empty, equally in tune with his mind, broke the silence.

Janet Seegebarth • Norfolk, NE

The Writer of Dreams

My Indian grandfather was a white man. He grew up on the Great Plains, exploring and unearthing beads, arrowheads, and flint tools left by the Pawnee who had lived on that very same land so many years ago. They were the original occupants, there before the cattlemen, even before the soldiers.

Maybe my grandfather had belonged to the Pawnee tribe in a past life. Maybe that was why he attached himself to the traditions of a people he couldn't claim biologically. No one knew why he had his dreams, but my grandfather was deeply respected among both the white community and the Native Americans. He did not lie.

That is why I believed him when he told me the secret, whispered on his deathbed.

Unable to speak as my grandfather uttered his last words, I only listened. Somehow, I thought he was close enough to the other side to know how I felt and what I was thinking without the need for spoken language.

"There is a sacred place," he had said, "back on the homestead." I knew he was referring to the patch of prairieland where he had grown up, a hundred and sixty acres near the old town site of Big Tree.

"Folded within the crevices of Deer Creek Canyon lives the Writer of Dreams." As Grandfather lay on his deathbed, he saw things that I couldn't. His eyes darted back and forth, around the room. I kept turning to see what he was looking at but saw nothing.

He continued in a low voice. "Follow the canyon walls. Find the tiny man who lives there. He is the Writer of Dreams . . ." Grandfather raised a gnarled hand, pinching the air between his forefinger and thumb to illustrate the "tiny man."

My grandfather's wish was to die at home, and we honored this. His hospital bed covered most of the free space in the miniscule living room. My brother was there, his wife and little boy, a hospice nurse, but I was the only one beside Grandfather at three in the morning when he shared his last wisdom.

"A sacred place . . . Deer Creek Canyon . . . Go there . . . find the Writer of Dreams," he whispered one last time, and he was gone.

I had read stories of such places like the one my grandfather discovered: the Peruvian Puerta de Hayu Marca (Gate of the Gods), Stonehenge, Shangri-la. Could this remote piece of land, once home to the Pawnees, really hold the secret to a sacred place?

I wanted to know.

Unfortunately, I had funeral arrangements to make and a house to clear out, one that had been filled with ninety-four years of Grandfather's clutter. It was months before I could even consider getting away, and as life sometimes has a tendency to do, it got in the way.

Work was short-staffed. The garden produce was ready to be picked. Church needed help. The weather was cold. The months slipped away, and before I knew it, a year had passed.

Grandfather's death weighed on me. Anyone could argue that he was old and had lived a full life, but his death had left me orphaned at age thirty-two. No parents. No grandparents. My brother lived across the country. Sure, I had lots of friends, but shouldn't I have found that special someone by now? I fell in love once with a cheating alcoholic. Chris was selfish and unmotivated and finally ran away with someone younger, better looking, and much more fun than me, or so I was told. No one else ever came along.

I made it through the holidays alone. It was sad, but I always knew that my friends would be around again after all of their family events were over. The problem with having no family around was that *all* I had were my friends. When things turned sour at work, and people were unhappy with me, I turned to my friends, but they were often busy with family or their jobs or we lost touch.

A year after my grandfather's death, I felt more alone than ever. After a couple more weeks of going through the motions of life without really feeling anything, I spent some time thinking, just thinking, about Grandfather, trying to hear his voice and listen to his advice. The idea of the tiny man who lived in Deer Creek Canyon haunted me. What could he have meant by telling me such a strange story?

He called the tiny man the Writer of Dreams. Grandfather may have been white, but he was known as a wise old Indian. That's what everyone had called him. I smiled at the memory, the first smile in weeks. Yes, I had friends, a job, a house, and a church, but I felt no purpose. I had no reason for being. No one needed me. Not really.

During my time of introspection, I realized life could not continue like this. Nothing mattered. No one cared enough to miss me. No one loved me. I didn't want to feel this way, but I couldn't help it. I needed to stop this existence—one way or the other.

Grandfather would understand. I wondered if he would be there for me on the other side. I wasn't entirely sure he would. I hated my fear.

Grandfather had told me to go to Deer Creek Canyon, and I didn't do it. He said it was a sacred place. He wanted me to meet the Writer of Dreams. Obviously, a tiny man did not live in the wall of a canyon out in the middle of nowhere, but I wanted to figure out what he meant. Maybe Grandfather was out of his mind. No. I had been there when he died. He was completely clear. He wanted me to find a dream—an ambition, a purpose, maybe have an adventure chasing a fantasy.

Memorial Day was a three-day weekend, and I couldn't stand the thought of three days with nothing to do, so I drove the eighty miles to the old homestead. It took some time to find the place. There was nothing left of Grandfather's home site besides the skeleton of a windmill with broken blades clacking in the breeze.

I had to step out of my comfort zone to ask permission from the landowner to drive onto the property.

"My grandfather grew up out here," I said to the man on the other side of the screen door. "He passed away about a year ago, but if you don't mind, I'd like to take a few pictures of the old place." I felt like a fool standing there on his front step, the man leaning on the half-open door, a yellow lab sniffing my shoes.

"You can drive out there. I don't care. See that gate at the end of the section?" He pointed to the end of the barbed-wire fence at the last intersection. I'd been through gates like this before. A strip of wire attached to a post at one end allowed a person to undo the gate and pull the section of fence back.

"Sure," I said.

"Follow that road for a couple of miles, then head right." He pointed across the rolling hills, his other hand patting the bright green hat placed lopsided on his balding head, clearly a free gift from a seed corn company. "You should run right up against the canyon."

"I've been here before," I told him. "I was a kid. You may know my grandfather." I told him the name.

"The wise old Indian!" he exclaimed.

"That's him!" We laughed.

"Appreciate you asking permission to drive out there. Just don't forget to close the gate. I don't need my cows getting out." He smiled, and I felt some comfort at the connection we had to the land and to my grandfather.

I drove across the bumpy grassland, hoping not to get stranded out here. Then again, it wouldn't have mattered if I did. The thought gave me relief.

As the canyon came into view, I saw a few cows milling around at the bottom. I probably could have driven down into it, the slope was so gradual, but I was too cautious to try. I found the cow path gouged into the canyon from years of hooves following the same route and began my descent.

Here I was at Deer Creek Canyon looking for the tiny man who lived in its walls and was called the Writer of Dreams.

"Ha!" I shouted to the canyon.

"Ha," said the echo.

The cows stopped grazing and turned wide eyes upon me. Not one moved. They even stopped chewing, small bits of grass left dangling from the sides of their mouths.

"I have an audience," I said. "Do any of you know where I could find the tiny man? No? Some help you are." I kicked at the dirt, muddier the lower I went, and continued my exploration.

As I followed the curve of the canyon base, I spotted an area with a sheer face. It had maybe twenty feet of exposed earth, so I headed toward it. Almost there, a sound cut the silence—one I had forgotten but instantly recognized.

It was the shake of a rattle.

The snake was coiled in the shade of the canyon, maybe five feet from me.

I froze.

Would it strike me from where it was? It rattled again. The cows continued to watch the show from a safe distance.

I stared at the snake. It stared at me. I didn't move. It didn't move.

It wasn't exactly my life flashing before my eyes, but I began to think back as I stared at that rattlesnake. I had been out here many years ago with my grandfather. We had picked wild grapes and were loading our buckets into the back of the pickup when he heard a rattle. He located the snake in the grass and killed it instantly with one practiced swing of the spade he kept in his pickup for just such an event.

My brother was with me. Things had changed so much from then to now. How had it happened? I never thought life could look like this. I didn't do anything wrong. I didn't do anything right either. "I don't want my life," I said to the snake.

The blackness of its eyes and the flick of its tongue seemed to be an answer. I had thought about it many times. How would I do it? Pills? A gun? Slit wrists? Running my car into a tree? Once I heard that apple seeds were poisonous, so I thought about saving up a whole cup of them and then chowing down. No matter what scenario I contemplated, I always saw that it could fail. With my track record for failure, chances are, life would go on and be much worse after the attempt.

Now, all I had to do was step forward. It would be an accident. The farmer would find me. My brother would come and make arrangements. He would clean out my house and sell my car.

Yet something held me back. I stood there for what could have been hours. My body did not move, but my mind tumbled forward until I fell into the blackness of the snake's eyes.

The darkness engulfed me. Then I saw colors swirling through the black. Had the snake bitten me? Was I dying?

I suddenly realized I was not alone in this abyss.

"You have control," a small voice spoke. "You are still that little child who thinks anything is possible."

"No," I said, dizzy and confused by the rainbow all around me. "I'm nothing but a failure. I've been rejected. There's been nothing I've accomplished. My grandfather was not proud of me. Look at my brother. He's running his own business. He has a wife and family. I am nothing."

"You can't compare your insides to his outsides," the voice stated. "You have power and potential, but you have been complacent, comfortably living a life set by societal norms where the fear of losing what you have outweighs the hope of achieving something better."

"I don't know what to do."

"Decide to try," said the voice within the spiraling colors.

"I'll just fail."

"Good. Failure makes us grow. It's the fear of failure that has made you immobile. It's time to try. Now, tell me. What is your dream?"

"I don't know," I said in all honesty. Purple dots appeared on a pale blue background. It seemed like I once had a dream. I remembered wanting a dream, but did I ever have one? Yes! What was it?

"Stop waiting. Tomorrow doesn't exist."

"I don't remember my dream!" I yelled.

"Then I will write your dream again." There was a pause before the small voice returned. The blue now overtook the purple. "Remember the science classes you took in high school?"

"Yes."

"Did you enjoy them?"

"Yes! Yes, I did!" The colors swirled around me.

"That is your dream."

"I don't understand. What do I do?"

"Precisely," the voice stated. "You must do something. It doesn't matter what it is, as long as you act."

"So, you're saying I should do something with my love of science. I could go to school to be a teacher. Or volunteer. Or work on a project." I began to see myself going back to school and meeting new people. There was purpose.

"Once you decide, your dream will work itself out, and if it doesn't, then I will write you a new dream."

The colors dissipated, and the darkness engulfed me again. Then it lifted as suddenly as it had appeared, and I found I hadn't moved from Deer Creek Canyon. The sun was low in the sky, and the snake was no longer coiled in front of me.

My grandfather had told me the truth on his deathbed. I was ecstatic! He had once known what it was like to be alone, too, and he knew I could be trusted with the secret. Whether the tiny man I heard was an ancient Pawnee spirit, my higher self, the universe, or the still small voice of God, I learned that there was much more to life than what I had been seeing. From now on, it would be the journey to a dream that would make my life exciting and interesting, and all it took was one decision.

As I wandered out of the canyon, I pictured myself working in a lab, maybe learning about genetics. Then my mind opened to another thought. Someday, somehow, I would bring a child here to this sacred place, and maybe later in life I would share with that child the story of the tiny man who lives in Deer Creek Canyon, the man who is the Writer of Dreams.

William L. Smutko • Blair, NE

Loose Change

Sid carries his life around in the front pocket of his jeans like so much loose change. Every so often he'll stick his sun-browned, callused hand in, stir things up, and the memories will float by like driftwood on a river. One will catch his attention and he'll bring it closer and look it over to check if the memory's still intact.

> *The Gatorade he's been chugging all day has leaked out through his pores, soaked his shirt and the waistband of his jeans. It drips off his nose. A typical August day in eastern Nebraska. He digs into the sugar clay hillside to plant the last grapevine. It's a Norton, it should make a good dry red wine in a few years. It's one of the five thousand vines he planted, ten varieties, five red and five white, five hundred each. He stands up and walks down to his pickup for an ice-cold Pabst. Wine is his passion, but a cold beer slakes his thirst and signals the end of a hot sweaty day of hard labor in "Jack's Vineyard."*

One of his favorite memories, still undamaged.

The late-afternoon sun flashes off the ripples on Wyoming's North Platte River as it flows by. Trout are taking cadis flies in the slower water by the far bank as Sid sips a glass of 1985 first growth Pomerol. He and his brother Pete are guests at a private fishing lodge on the S bar S Ranch, a seventy-six-thousand-acre working cattle ranch with its own air strip capable of handling Lear Jets and Gulfstreams. He and Pete decided they should take this trip before Sid started treatment for the aggressive form of prostate cancer he's been diagnosed with. The prognosis isn't good.

Pete's still fishing but should be in shortly. Sid quit early today concerned about his left leg, red and painful to the touch. It has been bothering him since he flew to the lodge, over eight hours sitting on a plane.

The wonderful smoothness and full flavor of the wine has an anesthetic effect, and he forgets about his leg.

"Hey, big brother. How's your leg? What're you drinking?"

"It's sore." Sid holds up the bottle and asks, "Want a glass?"

"Knowing your taste in wine, definitely."

"It's nice to be able to travel again and not have to wear a mask," Sid says as he pours Pete a glass of wine. "How'd you do after I left?"

"This is *really* nice," says Pete, a periodontist learning to enjoy the good life, as he takes a sip. "I drifted a Muddler Minnow into that deep hole below a big rock a quarter mile from here and hooked a fifteen incher. Caught a couple of others, other than that, it was slow."

~ ~ ~ ~ ~

The cold water of the river flows around Sid's wader-clad legs as he casts to a slick between two big rocks. He has a Two-Bit-Hooker on the bottom of his leader and a Hare's Ear up about eighteen inches from the bottom fly. Five feet into the drift he's rewarded with a strike. Sid sets the hook and five minutes later pulls a sixteen-inch rainbow to his net. His leg still hurts. The

Aleve he took before breakfast isn't helping much, so he decides to go in at noon again.

Sitting by the river Sid picks up his cell phone and types in his symptoms. Deep vein thrombosis leads the list of possible maladies.

All that sitting at the conference and on the airplanes to get here.

Dad died from that, and suddenly.

The river rolls by, the reflected sun turning it into a river of mirrors.

A group on horseback crosses the river at the ford a hundred yards below Sid and steals his attention for a while.

But he drifts back into his memories.

A gentle Pacific Northwest rain is falling as Sid and Alison walk along the riverbank to where the Spotted Bear joins the South Fork of the Flathead in a big, deep, swirling pool. They turn to face each other, their faces barely six inches apart. Sid puts his arms around Alison, pulls her toward him, and kisses her. "I've thought about doing that since we had lunch Wednesday."

Alison says, "So have I." Then kisses him back. They slide down the tree they are leaning against and end up on the wet ground. Sid stands up, offers Alison his hand, and they walk back to the main ranch house and his bedroom.

As she accepts him, her legs intertwining with his, forming a love knot and pulling him even tighter, he realizes he doesn't want to untie the knot, ever. He wants to remain this close to her the rest of his life.

The pain in his leg pulls him from his musing. He waves a staff member over.

"Could you bring me a couple of Tylenol and a glass of water?"

This DVT could kill me. But my prostate probably will anyway, in spite of radiation and chemo. Maybe I should just let nature run its course.

The North Platte, reflecting the afternoon sun, keeps flowing by. Sid falls asleep in the peacefulness.

"Hey old man," Pete says, shaking Sid by the left shoulder. "You still alive? I landed a six-pounder, a twenty-four-inch hen fish, in the run under the rock overhang. It took me fifteen minutes to get her to the net. How's your leg?"

"Still sore. Just my old body not able to keep up anymore. Let's go to the bar and I'll buy a bottle of champagne to celebrate your catch."

~ ~ ~ ~ ~

After breakfast Sid begs off fishing because of his leg. Pete and his guide take off in a pickup headed down-river. Sid walks to his favorite chair on the bank. He unlocks his phone and downloads Ruark's *The Old Man and the Boy*. He starts to read but the glare is too much. He puts his hand in the front pocket of his jeans and nervously fiddles with the coins.

> *Alison and Sid are sitting at a table in the winery, a plate in front of each of them and beside the plate is a pencil and six note cards, one card each for the wines they'll be tasting. The plate contains several small cups. One has salt, one a slice of*

lemon, another spaghetti sauce, another beef broth, another chicken stock, and the last one a piece of chocolate.

"You'll be tasting six wines," says the winemaker. "Three white: Riesling, Sauvignon Blanc, and Chardonnay, then three reds: Zinfandel, Pinot Noir, and Cabernet Sauvignon. This is a food pairing tasting. We're going to start with the whites. So, what you'll need to do is taste a little from one of the cups in front of you, salt for instance, then take a sip of wine, then make a note about how the wine reacts with the food."

"Wow!" exclaims Sid after combining salt and Sauvignon Blanc. "The taste of the wine completely disappeared. It was like drinking water." He bends over and kisses Alison and says, "Thanks for bringing me to this. I'm having a great time."

Mid-morning one of the staff comes by and asks if there is anything he can do for Sid.

"How about a glass of chilled Albarino?"

Is it a sin to let yourself die of a disease you might be able to cure?

Sipping the wine Sid tries to read on his phone again. The glare is still too much.

The nurse hands Sid a small plastic cup with a lid and says, "We need a semen sample," and points to the restroom.

On the way over Alison playfully asks, "Can I help?"

"Of course," says Sid grinning. "We're in this together, aren't we?"

The words from the doctor three days later hit like iced buckshot. "As a couple, the two of you cannot conceive a child."

Sid takes a bite of his lunch. A bald eagle soars in, picks a fish out of the river in front of him, then lands on a branch near the top of a big cottonwood to eat it. He watches, almost forgetting his own meal.

It was like sitting in a rainbow with the sun shining through the floor-to-ceiling, stained glass windows. Father Phil announces, "One more prayer before we pass the peace. For Sid and Alison Galloway. This past week, after two years of beseeching the Lord for a child, they adopted a little boy, Jack. Please join me in saying the prayer for the adoption of a child in the Book of Common Prayer, page 440. Dear friends: It has pleased God our heavenly Father to answer the Earnest prayers of Sid and Alison, members of this Christian family, for the gift of a child. I bid you join with them in offering our heartfelt thanks for the joyful and solemn responsibility which is theirs by the joining of Jack to be a member of their family. But first, our friends wish us, here to be assembled, to witness the inauguration of this new relationship."

"Sid and Alison, do you take this child for your own?"

The joy of the moment overcomes Sid. Tears wash over his chin and soak the top of his tie and the collar of his dress shirt as he puts his arm around Alison, who's holding Jack, and pulls her closer. "We do," they say in unison.

"As God has made us his children by adoption and grace, may you receive Jack as your own son."

A kid's laughter catches Sid's attention and pulls him away from his memories. On the lawn off to Sid's left, a father watches as a guide works with the man's son on fly casting. He's trying to get the boy to wait till the line is fully extended behind him before starting the forward cast.

A mule deer buck, still in velvet, stands on the path ahead of them as Alison, Jack, and he walk around Sylvan Lake toward the dam—it must have been in ninety-one—Jack had just turned seven. Near the dam Sid positions Jack in front of him at the edge of the lake. He shows Jack how to hold the rod and line and helps him cast the leach pattern out into the lake. Halfway in on the retrieve a fish takes the fly. Sid helps him set the hook and works with him on landing the fish. Alison claps loudly and takes a picture of Jack holding the trout.

Sid looks up DVT on his phone. DVT can lead to pulmonary embolism or even a stroke. *A stroke would be quick. Would it be a sin to let it come to that??*

Sid types "Episcopal theology on non-intervention of a potentially deadly disease" into the phone.

The last sentence summarizes the article. "Each case is unique and should be looked at with its own set of surrounding circumstances." Sid's stomach churns with unresolved anxiety.

The sound of the gurgling and splashing of the river as it runs by is soothing, Sid reaches in and pulls up another memory.

The gym smells of sweat and echoes with the cheering of the parents and friends of the wrestlers. Sid and Alison are standing, shouting encouragement to Jack, who has his opponent down, the boy's back almost touching the mat. The referee, his face almost touching the mat, counts one-two-three with the fingers on his right hand and brings it down on the mat, blowing his whistle at the same time. Jack wins the eighth-grade district two-twenty weight class with a pin.

Another of his favorites.

Sid drifts off with a smile on his face in spite of the pain in his leg.

Around noon a staff member wakes Sid and asks if he would like some lunch.

Sid's stomach growls as he tells the waiter, "Bring me a medium rare cheeseburger with lettuce, tomato, mustard, and mayo, and malt vinegar for the fries, and a Sam Adams Boston Lager."

Is it suicide to allow, even hope, that a stroke will kill me quickly instead of having to endure radiation and chemo that probably won't work?

If I were healthy, not addressing the DVT would be a sin, I think. But I'm not healthy. So, it shouldn't be a sin. I think. God help me.

As good as the burger sounded Sid only eats three bites and drinks half the beer. He tries to read again but the sun is reflecting off the screen.

Sid is in his '87 Toyota Land Cruiser headed south on Highway 77 south out of Fremont.

I really don't want to go here, he thinks.

About ten miles down the road a rebuilt '66 GTO goes flying by him. Fifteen-year-old Jack is in the back seat.

This one stresses him.

The corn is high and a semi towing a grain trailer doesn't see the car and pulls out of county road V directly in the path of the GTO. The driver brakes and attempts to turn away from the truck but their momentum slams them into the side of the semi, rupturing a diesel tank. The fuel ignites causing the car's gas tank to explode.

The intense pain in his leg and the terrible memory force tears out the corners of his eyes and into his sideburns. He wipes them away with his shirt sleeve and drinks the rest of the beer as he caresses the urn pendant on a cord around his neck. He hobbles to the bar and orders a twenty-five-year-old Glenfiddich double, then limps back to his seat by the river.

Alison blocks the door as Sid tries to leave the house. "In the three months since the accident you've spent eighteen hours a day in the vineyard, crept in late, and slept in your chair. You hardly speak to me. Why are you avoiding me?"

Sid looks at the floor and answers, "How can I look at you . . . ? I can't face you. It's what I couldn't, didn't, do. I should have saved him. But I couldn't even try. I should have figured a way to get him out." Tears flow over his face like an incoming tide. "I still feel the heat of the fire and smell the horrendous odor of them burning. I'm still there."

"Sid, look at me. Look at me! Take a deep breath. Now let it out. That's it. Now take another deep breath and feel the air entering your lungs. Feel your feet in your boots. You're here, Sid, now. That is just a memory of something dreadful that happened a long time ago. Take another deep breath and let it out slowly. Sid, honey, you have no responsibility for Jack's death. The kid driving was going way too fast. The fire started before you even got stopped. There was no way you could have saved him.

"Don't go to the vineyard today. I'll take a personal day and we'll go to Bravo, have lunch on the patio, drink a bottle of wine, go to a movie, then come home and make love."

Sid puts his arms around Alison and pulls her close. "I love you so very much." Tears start flowing from them both. "Do we have to wait till after lunch?" Sid asks.

The gurgling of the river, the gentle breeze ruffling the cottonwood leaves and the double scotch puts Sid to sleep again.

Something bites Sid on his arm and wakes him. "Damn!"

A staff member hears his exclamation and comes over. "Is everything alright, sir?"

"Something bit me is all, probably a deer fly. Since you're here, bring me another double twenty-five-year-old Glenfiddich, neat." Every time Sid moves, a pain shoots through his leg.

He and Alison sit at the kitchen table, as they do every day before breakfast. She has the Book of Common Prayer in front of her, a Bible is in front of Sid.

Alison starts, "This is the day the Lord made. Let us be glad and rejoice in it." Then continues with five verses from Psalm 51. Sid reads the New Testament lesson. Alison says a list of people they are praying for. They say "The Lord's Prayer" together and Alison finishes with the Collect. "Lord God, almighty and everlasting Father . . . through Jesus Christ our Lord, Amen."

The ratcheting screech of a kingfisher flying upriver pulls him out of the memory which is still intact.

Is it ok for me to let go?

The river floating by and the scotch send him back to his memories.

"I want to close my account," Sid says to Bob Creager, their account executive at A. G. Edwards.

"Have we done something to upset you?"

"No. It's just time to sell my Berkshire Hathaway. I bought ten thousand dollars' worth in 1971 when I got back from Vietnam. Tom Beebe sold me on it. I held it for the long term, just like Warren says, forty years."

"Mr. Buffett did well for you. You should net somewhere around seven-and-a-half million after taxes."

Sid winces at a sharp pain in his leg and takes a sip from the scotch and looks at the river.

"Ladies first, Alison you get first try at a fish," says Tom, their Kiwi guide.

"Let's flip for it," says Alison. "I'm all into equality of the sexes."

"Sid, you call it," says Tom as he flips the coin.

"Heads."

"It's heads. Sid, you get the first try."

"See the flat, yellow rock about twenty feet upstream and five feet out from this bank?" Tom asks. "The fish is just to the right of the rock."

"Yes. I see it." The dark elongated shape moves easily from side to side taking nymphs as they float by.

Sid moves into position to cast; the cold water soaks his pant legs as he unhooks the fly from the keeper. The wind catches it, and his sixteen-foot leader becomes a rat's nest. "Alison, you try while I untangle this mess," he says, climbing out of the river.

Alison steps into the water, frees the fly from the keeper, shakes some line free and makes a perfect cast. The Royal Wulff drops ten feet upstream and directly in line with the trout. Like a submarine coming to the surface, the fish rises and sucks in the fly. Alison says, "God save the Queen," as Tom taught her and sets the hook. The fish runs upstream and Alison gives it line.

After a ten-minute battle, Tom nets a six-pound brown trout for her. "Good on ye! Congratulations on a nice Oriti River brown," he says.

"What're you daydreaming about? And what are you drinking?" Pete asks, disturbing Sid's reverie.

"Alison's and my trip to New Zealand in 2015 where she showed she was the better fisherman. Twenty-five-year-old Glenfiddich." Sid catches a staff-person's attention, lifts his glass, and signals two with his other hand.

"What are you thinking about for dinner?"

"The elk tenderloin, I think. With a New Zealand Pinot Noir, Rippon, if they have it. They were a little snooty in Rippon winery's tasting room but it's the best Pinot that ever ran over my tongue, and the vineyard, it sits on the shore of this gorgeous lake. We brought two cases back home with us."

The scotch arrives. "L'chaim, to life," Sid says, raising his glass. "You know, I've led a pretty good one and it became fun and worthwhile once I met Alison. Less fun without her."

~ ~ ~ ~ ~

Lying in bed, a pillow under his sore leg, he continues to fret. *Is it a sin to let this DVT go, hoping it'll kill me?*

Caressing his urn pendant, that night three years ago comes floating back to him.

> *In bed next to him, Alison punches the daily prayer app on her phone and calls up Compline. Sid and she hold hands as the soft measured words in a British accent start with, "The Lord Almighty grant us a peaceful night . . ." and finish with "Guide us waking, O Lord, and guard us sleeping; that awake we may watch with Christ, and asleep we may rest in peace."*
>
> *In the morning Alison's hand is grasping his wrist. Sid rolls over to wake her. She's not breathing; she is cold to the touch.*

A small piece of the clot in Sid's leg breaks free. The blood flow pushes it on through his lungs. The heart forces the clot up to the brain where it dislodges a bit of plaque and together, they clog an artery cutting off the blood supply to the brain. Sid stiffens in bed as a searing pain rages in his head. He sees flashes of light. His callused, sun-browned right hand sweeps across the night-stand, sending his loose change flying, then goes limp.

K. L. Riley • Lincoln, NE

Chicken in a Storm

"Look out!" Mother Margaret screamed, scattering the rest of the chickens as Admiral sped past them, not even slowing down. Next to the gray and white cat, Ginger's long collie fur blew wildly in the growing wind. As Mother Margaret fluttered to her feet she saw that Billy-Boy and Bobby-Girl were running too. Billy-Boy lived on the farm with Admiral. Bobby-Girl lived next door with Ginger. But they all worked around the farm for Uncle Ben. Uncle Ben lived in the large human coop with his hen Aunt Bea. Margaret didn't know how a human got to the level of Uncle but she knew there wasn't a higher ranking human anywhere nearby. It was Uncle Ben who had promoted her to "Mother" over the other chickens. Margaret suspected her promotion was hereditary, as her mom, Gretta, had been the past Mother. Gretta disappeared unexpectedly last November, about the same time old Friar Tom disappeared. They had a new Friar on the farm now, Friar Mort. Friar Mort was a fairly young turkey but he had broad wings and was always willing to comfort animals in trouble.

Speaking of trouble, Mother Margaret suddenly looked around and saw she was alone. Uncle Ben was closing the barn door and big drops of rain were beginning to fall. "AAAWWWKKK!" Margaret squawked. She ran for the barn but the door was closed before she got there. Swearing like a goat instead of a Mother Hen, Mother Margaret turned slowly, looking around the entire barnyard for some kind of shelter. The chicken coop door was open; it would be dry. Margaret ran for the open door, diving into the coop just as the rain began pouring.

Leaning against the rough wall, Margaret sank onto the shadowy floor. The only sound Margaret heard was raindrops against the tin roof. Finally catching her breath, the white hen blinked and peered outside. The barnyard was gray and still. The scratching spot, where her girls had been feeding when they were nearly trampled by Admiral, was drowning. On Uncle Ben, the water would only cover his ankles but for Mother Margaret and the sisters that was a lot of water. She let her yellow eyes droop, as she sighed. It was good all the other hens had made it into the barn before the rain came. She looked to the top of the barn where Chanticleer stood. The metallic rooster was spinning around faster than Margaret ever remembered.

A soft swishing sound in the back of the coop caused Margaret to freeze. Her heart stopped beating and her toes went numb. There was only one thing the old hen knew of that made such a noise—fur rubbing against wood. There was something with fur moving in the back of the chicken coop. Margaret knew better than to risk a look. With a squawk that echoed across the barnyard, she tore out into the rain.

When she'd put a considerable distance between herself and the coop, the frightened hen chanced a look behind her. From the recesses of the coop she could see the all-too-familiar visage of Chillingsworth, the fox. His caustic eyes glared into the rain. What little light there was reflected oddly off his hairless brow. Margaret did not stop to see why the fox hadn't run after her. She thanked the all knowing Chanticleer and kept running. In the back of her mind the Mother Hen knew Admiral was in the barn and Chillingsworth feared Admiral more than any other creature—even Ginger. But instead of running for the barn. Margaret turned down the garden path. Perhaps it was the memory of the last time she faced Chillingsworth, many years ago, when she had run into the garden and Admiral had mauled the fox, leaving him without fur on his forehead and a lame foot. But Chillingsworth was still lightning. Even with her head start, Margaret was only halfway down the path when she heard the fox growling behind her. There was only one way in or out of the garden, tall rose hedges fenced it in on three sides. Garden plants seemed to spin around her as Margaret looked frantically to her left and right. She'd run the wrong way, confused by the dark sky, the pouring rain, and the panic in her heart. Mother Margaret was trapped, cornered by the fox. Chillingsworth licked his lips as he ran, and Margaret knew there was no way out. She pressed her back against the thorny flowers, closed her eyes, and waited.

Pain came almost immediately. Margaret felt her wings and legs and back being scratched and torn. She felt claws grating against her beak and face. Suddenly her body jarred with impact as she hit the ground. Margaret saw stars, then there was nothing.

The darkness faded and Margaret opened her eyes slowly. She expected to see Chillingsworth glaring down at her, just waiting for her to look up and see him before he bit her head off. But there was nothing. She saw only darkness at first. As her weak eyes adjusted, she saw thorns. All around her was a tangle of thorns and roses. The plump hen struggled to stand. Red lines criss-crossed her wings, sides, and legs. Although she couldn't see them, Margaret could feel the fire of scratches on her back as well. At first Mother Margaret didn't understand what was going on. As she turned herself around and caught sight of red fur against a rainy backdrop, she realized where she was. She had stumbled backward through the brambled branches of the rose bush and was now huddled behind the protective thorns. Margaret was in shock. She stared at the brownish-red shape of Chillingsworth who stopped short of the thick bushes. He cocked his head and stared through the thorns, his eyes locked with Margaret's. The fox didn't seem to see her and the chubby chicken risked a sigh of relief. Chillingsworth began pacing the width of the path, never taking his eyes off the rose bush. His fur looked almost brown as it whipped around heavy and bedraggled. A bright blue flash illuminated the shadowed thorns. Sharp hunter's eyes caught feathered movement. With a growl Chillingsworth leaped forward, but the roses threw him back almost immediately.

There was a tool shed on the other side of the garden. Shaking the rain from his fur with a growl, Chillingsworth made his way toward it. Margaret held her breath as he disappeared into the shed through a hole in the siding. The Mother Hen still wasn't quite sure what was going on. Chillingsworth had been lurking inside the chicken coop when the rain began, but all the animals had sheltered in the barn, except Margaret. She'd been distracted and missed the closing door, something that had never happened to her before. She took shelter in the chicken coop but Chillingsworth hadn't killed her, he'd moved slowly, giving her time to escape. She should have run to the barn, but she ran into the garden. The fox had her cornered, but she'd managed to stumble into the rose bush. Understanding the unlikely series of events was beyond panicked chicken thoughts. Through the brambles she could see the top of Uncle Ben's red barn. Margaret looked up, casting her eyes to Chanticleer, but the metallic rooster, who brought comfort in times of need, just spun wildly in the wind. Watching Chanticleer spin, Mother Margaret realized that the rain was falling harder than it had before. This was her chance, Margaret decided. With the rain pouring and the wind whipping, Chillingsworth would stay inside the toolshed, she hoped. As much as Mother Margaret wanted to, she knew if she bolted across the garden, Chillingsworth would be on her in a second; he may be sheltered in the shed, but the fox would be watching the garden carefully. Margaret took a deep breath to calm her mind, looked around through the thorns as best she could, and determined her best route to freedom was through the rose bush. She picked her way through the tangled thorns and amazed herself at the ease of her progress. It wasn't long and Margaret found herself at the people coop where Uncle Ben lived. With the storm still blowing, Admiral and Ginger would surely be in the barn with the other animals. Margaret hoped, however, that Uncle Ben or maybe even Billy-Boy had returned to the people coop.

Quietly, Margaret eased out of the protective rose bush and crept toward the large people coop. She had a plan. She would peck at the back door until someone opened it. The people would either bring her into their coop or escort her back to the barn; either way, she'd be safe from the fox. It was a simple plan, to be sure, but Mother Margaret believed it would work. She approached the door, and to her amazement, the entrance was open. Margaret didn't know how or why the door would be open, and she didn't care; she could see inside the people coop. There stood Aunt Bea, in one hand she held a funny-looking basket and in her other hand hung the limp and naked body of a chicken! Margaret couldn't tell who the unfortunate fowl was, because Aunt Bea was carrying the poor hen's feathers in her unusual basket. Margaret ran back into the briars and threw up. Sitting in the mud, barely sheltered by the thick and thorny rose bushes, thoughts began swirling around in Mother Margaret's head. Things suddenly began to make sense to the sick chicken. Margaret suddenly understood why Friar Tom had disappeared and where Gretta had gone. Whenever one of her girls disappeared in the past, Margaret attributed it to Chillingsworth and changed her security plans. She made the girls learn a new scratching pattern, made them change their pecking order, all things designed to confuse a fox and give them a better chance at seeing a fox approaching. "All this time," Margaret mumbled to herself, "the fox wasn't our greatest threat." In spite of the rain and thundering storm, Margaret broke cover and ran across the barnyard. She forgot all about Chillingsworth and ignored the pelting rain. Mother Hen had to rescue the rest of her girls.

She reached the barn and scurried around to the back. There was a small gap between the boards. It was really too small for a full-grown hen, but after everything else she'd been through, squeezing through the gap was nothing for Margaret—despite the loss of feathers it caused. She forced her way into the barn and breathed a sigh of relief. All her hens were inside, along with Admiral the cat. There was no sign of Uncle Ben or Billy-Boy or Bobby-Girl. After what she saw, Mother Margaret would never trust a human again. She moved along the back wall, not wanting to draw attention to herself. She reached the area of the barn where the hens were huddled together. "Girls," she whispered when she got close.

"Mother Hen!" Angelica squawked nearly too loudly. Angelica had been Margaret's only challenger for the rank of Mother. Angelica was a large hen with dark feathers and broad wings for a hen. As young hens, she and Margaret had some epic spats, but since Margaret's promotion, Angelica had become her staunchest ally. "We were worried about you," Angelica said sincerely. "What happened?"

Margaret shook her head, "There is no time to explain," she whispered. "Our girls are in grave danger."

"Chillingsworth?" Angelica asked with venom in her voice.

"No," Margaret matched the darkness of Angelica's voice. "The fox is in the toolshed, but he is not the only threat. The humans, they have been killing our girls. I saw Aunt Bea with a corpse in her hands."

"By Chanticleer," Angelica hissed, "Wanda wasn't out there with you, was she?"

Wanda, Margaret thought to herself. *Of course that was Wanda. She was the oldest and the fattest of us all. She'd be the easiest to catch.* Aloud, she said, "No, Wanda wasn't with me. I thought she was in here with you."

"We have to get the rest of the girls out of here." Angelica nodded.

Quietly, Margaret passed the word from hen to hen. She told them only that they were leaving and to make ready. Comforted by her presence and her calm, each chicken acknowledged the Mother Hen's instructions without question. Carefully and quietly, Margaret led her girls out the back of the barn and straight into the cornfield. The cornfield was tall this time of year and grew only a short run from the back of the barn, out of view from the toolshed or the people coop. The nervous chickens made their way carefully through the field, keeping to one row between the stalks. Without warning, red fur burst forth from the row to their right. Angelica was dead before she knew what hit her. Margaret and the rest of her girls fluttered into the air and hopped away with screams of fear. Instead of carrying off Angelica's body, Chillingsworth turned his burning eyes toward the rest of the hens.

"I had given up on you," the fox growled. "I feared I'd be going home hungry as well as wet and tired. Now I will take you all with me."

Admiral wasted no energy on a challenging sound, as suddenly as the fox had struck down Angelica, the large cat pounced on Chillingsworth's back and dug in his claws. As the two rolled in the thickening mud, Admiral called out to Margaret. "Margaret, go! Take your girls and run to the trees."

Mother Margaret and her nine remaining hens ran as fast as they could through the rain and the mud to the edge of the cornfield where the farm met the forest. They disappeared into the trees, taking shelter among tangled roots and a wide trunk. The hens waited in silence until the first streaks of gray broke through the clouds and the rain began to slow. Margaret was just contemplating risking a look outside when Admiral's face filled the opening they'd squeezed through.

"Come on out, girls," the cat purred. "Chillingsworth will not be bothering you again." Admiral backed away and allowed the hens to squeeze out of their hidey-hole before he continued talking. "It will not take Uncle Ben long to figure out where you fled." To emphasize his point, Admiral turned and looked back across the cornfield. "You need to go deep into the forest. You'll have to forage for your own food and be constantly wary of predators, but," he paused again and looked over his shoulder, "you'll be safe from the people."

"Couldn't we go back to the farm?" Vera, the youngest of the hens asked.

"No," Mother Margaret snapped a little angrier than she intended. "We can avoid predators like Chillingsworth. We can't evade humans—not in their territory anyway."

"Mother is right," Admiral, the cat, agreed. "Humans have ways of taking you no matter how prepared you are. You are safer on your own."

"What will you do?" Margaret asked, giving Admiral a sincere look with her yellow eyes.

"I'll go back to the farm. Others there need my protection. I'll tell George what's happened and when Uncle Ben brings in new hens . . ."

"Send them our way," Margaret nodded. "We'll set up an escape path for them."

Not long after, with the help of Admiral, Margaret and her nine girls set up the Chicken Underground and led hundreds of doomed farm fowl to safety.

Katherine Wielechowski • Lincoln, NE

Exorcise This

Doughnutsdoughnutsdoughnutsdoughnutsdoughnutsdoughnuts

"Would you stop it, already?!" I growled. The chant had been going nearly nonstop in my head since I woke up and it was getting on my nerves.

I will stop when you get doughnuts.

"No, I'm not getting you doughnuts. I've got two weeks to fit into a bridesmaid dress so no more junk food until you figure out how to absorb the calories before my ass does." I gave the man sitting across from me a strained smile when I noticed him staring at me. His eyes widened further and he got up to move to a different seat. I really needed to stop having these conversations in public. Somebody was going to call the guys in white to chase me down with butterfly nets.

You are probably the least crazy person he's seen on the bus this week.

"True," I muttered, finally remembering to cover my mouth with my coffee cup before speaking. "Why the sudden obsession with doughnuts?"

You look ridiculous. Put the white things in your ears.

"Somebody woke up on the asshole side of the bed this morning." I could literally feel the eyerolling and had to smile as I pulled out my earbuds and stuck one in my ear. "OK, so what's with the doughnuts?"

Office Human Nadia had one yesterday. With sprinkles. It smelled sinful and I need one.

"Of course Nadia would be the cause." Nadia was the closest I could get to having a nemesis in a corporate office setting and I hated her with every fiber of my being. Which caused a heap of problems with my other coworkers, considering everybody else thought the sun shone out of her ass.

Have Humans finally evolved to do that?

"Huh? Do what?"

Emit light from their butts.

"We've talked about you eavesdropping on my thoughts."

It is hard to ignore them when you shout.

"Try harder."

This is our stop.

"Shit." I scrambled from my seat and managed to squeeze through the door before the bus pulled away from the curb.

Coffee on you.

I looked down to see I had dumped half my coffee down my front in the rush to get off the bus. "How the hell did I get it on my shoulder?" I asked as I took in the damage. I was already late for work and tried to decide which would be the lesser of two evils: stopping in the hotel boutique around the corner from my office and being even later or just smelling like a Starbucks all day.

Neither of those would be evil.

"Seriously, stay out of my thoughts." I drained the last of the coffee and chucked the to-go cup in the nearest trash can.

I am programmed to hear certain words no matter what. "Evil" is one of them.

"You're 'programmed' to hear it? When did you join the twenty-first century?"

Fourteen looooooong months ago.

"You don't have to be an ass about it."

You've met me, right?

"Unofficially." I stopped to check my reflection in the shop window and assess the damage. Of all the days to wear a yellow top and a lime green bra. "Yeah, I can't go to work like this." I texted my boss as I walked into the shop to find the cheapest shirt that wasn't covered in coffee I could find. Ten minutes and a case of sticker-shock later, I walked out in a brand new black shirt that thankfully hid the slight damp spot that my coffee-soaked bra caused.

Now doughnuts?

"No! Now work, you reprobate."

You are already late, what is a few more minutes? There is a coffee shop that sells doughnuts on the next block.

"How do you know that?"

I can smell them.

I sighed and shook my head, then deliberately turned down the alley shortcut to my office. "How about this, if you behave yourself, I will get you a doughnut on the way home."

With sprinkles?

I was a touch hurt at how suspicious the words sounded. "Yes. With sprinkles."

Fine.

"Are you going to sulk all day?"

No.

"That sounded really sulky."

I do not sulk.

"Which is what a sulker would say."

You don't have to be an ass about it.

I laughed out loud as my own words were thrown back into my face . . . well, mind. "Fine, I'll get you two doughnuts."

I accept these terms.

The words sounded happier and I couldn't help but grin.

HOST! BEHIND YOU!

My vision darkened as control was wrenched away from me and I was shoved into a corner of my own mind. I could hear a scuffle and low growling that would have made the hair on the back of my neck stand up if I had been connected to them.

what are you doing give me back control

No! The insect tried to hurt you!

what insect I swear if this was happening because of a mosquito or something, there would be no doughnuts for the rest of forever.

This insect.

I mentally blinked at the bright light as I was given back use of my eyes. A man I had never seen before was staring up at me with a combination of terror, fury, and determination on his face. He had light brown hair that was sticking up all over, framing a nondescript face. One of those guys who you couldn't pick out of a line-up even after going on a date with them. He was wearing the weird dude uniform of ripped jeans and a metal band shirt and had a black messenger bag slung across his body. He also had a trickle of blood on the corner of his mouth and the collar of his tee shirt was torn.

Then I noticed how small he was.

where the hell are we

The alley.

yeah we might be but we are not on the ground

We are on a . . . one of those noisy boxes that cools the air.

we're on an air conditioner where is the air conditioner

Approximately thirty feet off the ground.

Have you ever tried to hyperventilate without having control of your body? It is extremely uncomfortable, unsatisfying, and gives you an ice cream headache.

put us back on the ground now

The man tried to hurt us.

on the ground now and give me back control while you're at it

There was no response for a long moment and I mentally tapped my fingers as I waited.

Fine, but I'm staying close in case he tries anything else.

how can you possibly get any closer to me

You have no idea.

why do I hate how you said that

You should.

My vision dimmed and I suspected it was so I didn't freak out on the way back down to the pavement.

"Don't come any closer."

It took an embarrassingly long time to realize that the words came out of my mouth, but it definitely wasn't me saying them. It kind of sounded like somebody had taken a cheese grater to my vocal cords, then as quickly as I had been shunted aside, I was back in control. I glanced down at myself, looking for any damage and to make sure everything was where it was supposed to be, but I got distracted by my shredded nails.

"What the hell did you do? Did we climb the brick wall?!"

Yes.

"For fuuuuuOWW!" I gasped in pain as the ripped skin instantly healed itself and the peeled-up nails embedded themselves back into my fingers. Sadly, nothing could be done about the ruined polish. "What? You can't jump that high? Had to wreck my manicure?"

I . . . didn't think about jumping. I'm a crawler.

The words were more than a little abashed and I forced myself to relax with a sigh. "I can redo them easily enough. I wasn't sold on the color anyway."

The scuff of shoes on pavement reminded me I wasn't alone a second before I found myself slammed into the brick wall with an arm across my throat and the stranger's face in mine. A growl rumbled out of me that I definitely didn't have control over, but I managed to stop the other reactions, namely the one to grab the man by the throat and throw him across the alley.

"What the hell man? What do you want?"

"You are possessed by a demon!" he panted.

I stilled and searched his face for anything that would indicate he was joking or crazy but found nothing except panic masked by calm determination. "And?"

"There is a demon! Inside of you!" He raised his free arm above our heads and brandished a silver crucifix at me.

"Yeah, you said that already."

He blinked at me, clearly not expecting my reaction. "You know you are possessed?"

It would be good if you could avoid that crucifix.

"No shit, Sherlock. And yes, I know I'm possessed. He's kind of hard to miss."

No reason to be rude.

I scoffed. "Says the demon."

"What?"

"Nothing, wasn't talking to you. Anyway, how do *you* know I'm possessed by a demon?"

"I . . ." His pressure on my throat tapered off as he stared at me, completely perplexed. "I can see them."

"No way! What does mine look like?"

Host Darcy, what are you doing?

"I'm just curious. So, what does he look like?" I used his distraction to surreptitiously take hold of his forearm before he remembered to use the crucifix against us.

"The most hideous abomination you can think of, then make it uglier and scarier."

Well, now he's got to die.

"Nonononononono, you're not killing anyone. I'm sure you're a very handsome demon."

The man frowned. "I don't think it's technically killing since demons aren't actually alive."

"Oh my god, can you just get off of me already?" I shoved him just enough to make him stagger back a few paces, which didn't seem to be enough for my guest, but he was going to have to just deal. "What are you talking about?"

"You told me not to kill anybody. You can be assured you will be totally safe during the process, just demon-less by the end. I've been hunting them a long time so I can exorcise them with little risk to you."

"I wasn't telling *you* not to kill anybody, I was telling Mox-dol'th not to kill you."

"Moxdol'th?" The man frowned and pulled a ragged notebook out of his messenger bag. "Is that the demon's name? I'm not familiar with that one."

I am very glad I didn't give you my actual name.

"Yeah, me too because obviously I suck at keeping it secret." I spotted the plastic bag that contained my coffee-stained shirt a few feet down the alley and grabbed it as I walked away from the demon hunter. It was the exact opposite direction of work but I just wanted to get away from the dude before Moxdol'th did something I'd regret.

"Wait! Where are you going?" The Winchester-wannabe rushed to fall into step beside me.

"I'm going to work, and I was already late when you pulled your 'old priest, young priest' routine so now my boss is going to be pissed." My phone vibrated in my pocket and I pulled it out to see a text from my cubemate asking where I was. The excessive number of interrobangs gave me a good idea of how much trouble I was in.

"Why are you worried about work? There is a demon possessing you! We should be exorcising it right now."

"Because my job pays my bills. You just caused the death of my fresh manicure. And if I learned anything about exorcisms from Catholic school or Hollywood, they take a while to pull off and aren't always successful. Plus, my chiropractor would be pissed if my head spun around or I crab-walked head-first down the stairs with my arms on wrong."

Then, the guy did something I never would have anticipated: he took out a small white bottle and splashed something all over me.

"I hope to god that was water," I muttered as I used the hem of my new shirt to wipe off my face. I turned on my heel and headed back down the alley while the guy started muttering in Latin behind me.

Holy water, actually. Moxdol'th's tone was amused.

"Isn't that supposed to burn or something?"

If it had been properly blessed, yes. We both would be in immense amounts of pain right now. But it seems to be either unblessed or far too diluted to be of any use.

"How in the world can water be too diluted?"

Regular water, no. Holy water, yes. You bless a small amount, then put it in a large container with unblessed water and it gets diluted.

I caught myself making a disbelieving face. "I don't think that's how that works."

Oh, you're an expert on religion now?

"And you are?! You're basically the opposite of religion."

Gotta know your enemy.

I rolled my eyes at his smug tone. "I'll needlepoint that on a pillow for you."

"Wait! Come back here, I need to exorcise you!"

"Exorcize this!" I flipped him off over my shoulder as I jogged away, thankful I had resisted Moxdol'th's craving for doughnuts, and managed to badge into my secured building before the zealot caught me. I made shooing gestures at him through the glass door, then headed for my cubical, girding my loins for the tongue lashing I was sure to get.

"Where the hell have you been?! Joyce is on the warpath today."

"Good morning to you, too, Esther." My ass hadn't even hit my seat before my cubemate started interrogating me.

"Yes, where have you been?" My boss draped herself over the wall of my cubical. Her calm demeanor was a pretty good indicator of how pissed she was.

"I'm so sorry I'm late, Joyce. I texted you that I spilled coffee down my front." I pulled my stained shirt out of the bag as proof. "So I had to stop at Bozique's to get something really quick. Then this weird dude attacked me in the alley and—"

"You were attacked?!" Esther screeched.

Joyce shot to attention, concern warming her features. "What dude? Was it the alley right outside? I think we have security cameras. Did you call the police?"

DO SOMETHING!

I flinched at the voice in my head before I could stop myself. "Um, what? No, I didn't call the police. He didn't hurt me at all. He was just crazy. Kept talking about demons or something."

Anything but the truth, Host Darcy.

I could feel Moxdol'th roll his eyes in exasperation. I'm betting he was wishing he had picked a more functional human to possess right about now. "Which is insane, right? Demons aren't real." I forced myself to swallow the hysterical laughter that was bubbling out of me. "And no, it wasn't this alley, it was one closer to the bus stop."

"We can call those businesses and see if any of them have cameras. I'll call the police and see if they can find the man."

"NO!" I scared the entire office and myself with the volume. "No, that's kind but not necessary, Joyce. I'm not going to turn him in. Again, he didn't hurt me. He seemed like a mentally unstable homeless man but was otherwise unthreatening. I shouldn't have used the word 'attacked,' I was unintentionally exaggerating because of how frazzled this morning has left me."

"Oh." Joyce seemed to deflate. "Well, as long as you're sure."

"I am, thank you." The demon inside me relaxed substantially and I suddenly felt heavier.

"Very well." Joyce's face hardened. "You'll be staying late to make up the time and I expect your weekly tallies in the next thirty minutes."

"Can do. Thank you. And sorry, again."

Joyce raised her eyebrow at me but left without another word.

I hope you're proud of yourself for that performance. Ten out of ten. No notes.

I ignored the sarcastic criticism as I shoved my purse and shirt bag into my desk, then got logged in so I could add the last two stats to my tallies and get them to Joyce before something else went wrong. I could feel Moxdol'th hovering at the edge of my consciousness more than usual but ignored him as much as I could.

Office Human Esther is staring at us, he told me as soon as I hit send on the report to Joyce.

I slowly turned my chair to look at my cubemate. "What?"

"What is wrong with you?"

"So much, but what are you referring to specifically?" I grabbed my coffee mug and stood. Esther picked up her own mug and followed me out of our cubical and down the hall to the breakroom.

"What really happened this morning?"

Now would be the ideal time for you to be a good liar. Think you can pull that off?

"No," I muttered as I took my first sip of coffee, burning my tongue in the process. "It happened exactly like I told Joyce. I spilled my coffee all over myself, then the homeless dude held me up in the alley—not in a burglary sort of way—making me even later." I shifted uncomfortably while she stared at me over the rim of her mug. "What?"

Esther shook her head. "I don't know, there's just something off about you."

"Is it this shirt? I got it at Bozique's and it's very not me but everything else cost more than I make in a month."

Her eyes narrowed but she finally shrugged. "Maybe. Let's go back. You've got some serious raccoon eyes going on and I don't want anybody else to see you like this."

"Thanks?" I let my head drop forward as I shuffled back to our cubical.

Thankfully the rest of the day went without incident and, even with staying late, I made it to the gas station near my house and got the last two sprinkle-covered doughnuts left in the case. I also got a pizza because after the day we had, Moxdol'th and I both deserved a little carb therapy.

The next two weeks went by in a blur of gym visits, attempts to fly under Joyce's radar, and exorcist sightings. Moxdol'th proved himself a super accurate early warning system, and we managed to avoid the guy more often than not. The few times he did force an altercation, I would just start screaming the weirdest shit I could think of and run away. My favorites include: "I'm not interested in an extended warranty. I don't even have a car." "No, I don't want to join you and your marionettes for fondue and scrabble!" "Sir, I am not a doctor! I don't want to see your rash!"

and singing “What Does the Fox Say” at the top of my lungs, complete with an interpretive dance.

I do wish you would let me kill him and solve this problem once and for all.

We had just gotten home from our latest run-in with the nameless demon hunter and were both a bit worn out. “Oh, did you happen to grow hands when I wasn’t looking? Because there is no way you’re using mine to kill somebody, no matter how annoying they are.”

You won’t even know that it happened. You’ll just go to sleep for a while and when you wake up, it’ll be taken care of.

“First of all, Mr. Creepy McCreeperson, don’t do that. Whether I’m conscious of it or not, it’ll still be my hands committing murder and if we’re seen, it’s my ass going to prison.”

You do realize I’m inside of you? I will also be going to prison. Although, one could say I’m already in prison so not much would change.

“Hey! I didn’t invite you to possess me, you did it all on your own! Feel free to vacate this human vessel at your earliest convenience. It sure would make my life easier.” I collapsed on my bed and curled around the pile of things I had set out to take with me to the wedding but hadn’t packed yet.

We didn’t talk for a long while because how do you come back from a fight like that with the entity closest to you? We just let the soothing sounds of late 90s and early 2000s boy bands calm our tempers instead.

Backstreet Boys is better than N’Sync.

“Very controversial opinion but I agree.” I rolled over to my back and stared at the popcorn ceiling. “Do you really think I’m like being in a prison?”

If a bodyless demon could sigh, I think Moxdol'th would have.

No. You're a million times better than the last guy. He didn't even last a week.

I raised an eyebrow. "My longer shelf life is the only thing that makes me better than the last guy?"

No, you are somehow not afraid of me and are far more amusing.

"Ah, well good. Glad you think so."

Do you still want me to leave?

"I suppose not, no. You have amazing situational awareness and are really fun to annoy."

I'm leaving.

I laughed at Moxdol'th's droll tone as I rolled off my bed and went back to packing.

Where are we going again?

"My cousin's wedding in Kearney. Thankfully, it's like three hours and half a state away. The chances of running into our little demon-hunter-slash-stalker while we're there are pretty low."

Good. It will be nice to relax for a bit.

"Agreed."

We're not done talking about killing the insect.

"Uh . . . yes we are." But we both knew we weren't.

Thanks to a required after-hours meeting Joyce forced on us with only a days' notice and my inability to plan ahead, I managed to get to the bridal party's hotel in Kearney a solid forty-five minutes after the rehearsal dinner shut down. I had just enough time to get checked in and grab a beer and munchies with my cousin and the other bridesmaids before it was time to get a few hours of sleep.

With Moxdol'th's help I could stay awake for days on no sleep and very little food, but it made both of us really irritable, so we tried to stick with the human subsistence plan as much as we could. Especially when we were going to be around so many people. Don't need to go all demon-ragey when great Aunt Gerti calls you your sister's name for the fifteenth time.

Thanks to my built-in demon alarm clock, I was the first bridesmaid to show up for hair and makeup, and to cement my place as the favorite, I rocked up with the bride's favorite iced coffee.

"You are the absolute best!" Brynlee squealed and wrapped me in a hug so tight she nearly lifted me off the ground. "Ok, I have a job for you and you're pretty much the only person I trust with it."

"Suitcases in the trunk and point the car toward Mexico? I'm on it."

Brynlee laughed. "I'm not running, Darcy. I'm nervous but I'm not that nervous. No, I've got a wedding present for Asher and I need you to take it to him right now."

"Don't presents usually come after the wedding?"

"Yeah, but I want him to wear them at the wedding so it has to be now." Brynlee pressed her forehead to mine. "Pleeeeeeeease, Darcy?"

Moxdol'th made an uncomfortable sound and I had to laugh. "Yeah, I'll take it to him. Where is he and is he even awake yet? And decent? I really don't want to see a naked future cousin-in-law today. Or ever, really."

"Yeah, he's awake. We've been texting for a bit. He's in room 435, right down the hall." She handed me a small wrapped box the size of a jewelry box. "Make sure you remind him to wear them today."

"What are they?" I held the box up to my ear and shook it but didn't hear anything.

"Monogrammed cufflinks."

"Do people wear cufflinks nowadays?"

"Nobody but Asher." Brynlee sighed, then brightened. "But it did make finding a wedding present for him really easy."

"Fair. Consider it done, coz." I set my coffee cup on the dresser and headed for the groom's room. And nearly wiped out two more bridesmaids as they stepped out of the elevator.

"HEY!!!" they squealed together.

It is far too early for that particular pitch and decibel.

I snorted. "Good morning. You two ready for today? Brynlee's up and ready to get started."

"Yeah! We were made for this!" The blonde (I struggled to remember her name, maybe McKayleigh or Ashleigh or something else ending in -leigh?) nearly vibrated with excitement.

"Where are you going?" The brunette was wearing sunglasses and looked like she wanted to crawl inside of her extra-large cup of coffee.

I held up the present. "Darcy's Delivery Service on duty." When they stared at me blankly, I shrugged. "Brynlee wanted me to give Asher his wedding present so he could wear it today."

"Awwww," they drawled in unison.

"Yeah, see ya in a bit." I stepped around them and continued on to room 435.

Like nails on a chalkboard . . . did I get that Human saying correct?

I chuckled. "Yep, and I agree." I found Asher's room and knocked. It felt awkward standing outside of a groom's hotel room the morning of his wedding for some reason, especially since I had never met him before, but I was on a mission for my favorite cousin.

"You!"

As soon as the door opened, my jaw hit the carpet. "You!"

"What are you doing here?"

"Are you messing with me right now? What are *you* doing here? Stalking me in Omaha was one thing, but following me all the way out here is seriously messed up! What did you do with Asher?"

"I didn't follow you here! And I am Asher!"

Realization fell on me like a building. My annoying exorcist stalker was Brynlee's fiancé. "No. Nonononono. This can't be happening. You can't be him."

"How the hell do you know my name?"

I felt a wave of calm flood through my body and I had a strong suspicion Moxdol'th was the cause. I took a deep breath and met Asher's eye. "You're here to marry Brynlee Gartner." He stilled as the blood drained from his face. "I'm bridesmaid number two."

"You're Bryn's cousin, Darcy."

"Does Brynlee know what you do?"

Asher scoffed. "Of course not. She would think I was crazy if I told her I can see demons. Does she know you're possessed by a demon?"

My glare was answer enough.

He took my arm in a tight grip, his gaze suddenly intense. "I won't have a demon in my wedding. If we move quickly, I can exorcize it before it starts."

I started at the demonic growl that rattled through my head, but judging by Asher's unchanged expression, I was the only one who heard it. I slowly and deliberately peeled his hand off my arm. "I am Brynlee's bridesmaid, it's not your decision if I'm allowed in the wedding or not, it's hers."

"I can stop you."

I rolled my eyes. "I'd like to see you try."

"There are ways to bind the demon inside you that will render you immovable."

"You're actually threatening me right now?"

Asher's hand snaked out and he grabbed a fistful of my tee shirt. "I'll do what it takes to keep your demon out of my wedding." He yanked me into his hotel room and slammed the door behind me.

"What the hell are you doing?!" I pulled on Asher's wrist, hoping to get away before I had to resort to biting him.

Asher pressed me against the wall, his eyes cold, his breath hot on my face. "You're possessed, and if you won't let me rid you of the demon, then I'll have to be more aggressive."

Host Darcy, I can take care of this if you allow me to.

I stopped trying to pull away from Asher and smiled up at him. "Do it."

And the lights went out.

Nonfiction
and
Memoir

Catherine Baker Nicholson JD • Bellevue, NE

Thane Baker Helps Mother on Wash Day

Wash on Monday,
Iron on Tuesday,
Bake on Wednesday,
Market on Thursday,
Clean on Friday,
Mend on Saturday,
Rest on Sunday.
Wash on Monday

"Thane. Ruthene. Get up!" Mother hollered as she banged on their shared bedroom door. Seven-year-old Thane Baker sat up and looked over at the other bed where his older sister, Ruthene, slept. The coffee percolated in the kitchen. Their bedroom felt warm even though the sun had just risen. The birds chirped outside. With its hundred-degree days, the August summer of 1939 had seized Elkhart, Kansas, hard. He heard his mother turn on the swamp cooler in the living room, then walk to the kitchen.

"Ruthene, wake up! It's Monday, wash day," Towheaded Thane called to his nine-year-old sister.

"I'm not talking to you," Ruthene groused. She rolled away from him and covered her head with the goose-feather pillow Mother had stuffed for her.

"Why not?"

"My paper dolls."

Thane thought for a minute. "Sorry. I walked them acrost the table."

"What?" Ruthene asked as she removed her pillow.

"Their legs got broke," Thane said. "I said I'm sorry a hundred times."

"Mm."

"Remember, you said I *had* to play paper dolls with you, so you'd play catch with me?" Thane asked. "Sorry." Thane moved his fingers over the homemade crazy quilt folded up next to him. He liked to trace the shapes.

Ruthene, her fine hair flying around her face, sat up, pushed her sheet down, and glared at Thane. "Mother makes me sleep in the same room as you. Why can't I have a room alone? I'm nine years old."

"We only got two bedrooms in this house," Thane said.

"Go sleep in the cellar."

Thane rolled his eyes, threw back his sheets, and dashed for the only bathroom in the house before Ruthene got up. He scrubbed his face and hands in the lavatory and dressed in his short-sleeved shirt and patched overalls. Mother had darned the socks Thane pulled on by holding a lightbulb inside them. The patched parts irritated his feet. Shoes came next, leather with rubber soles glued on by Father to cover the holes. Thane combed his blond hair with water from the faucet, missed the cowlick in back, stuffed his pajamas under his pillow, and rushed to their small kitchen.

Mother already had a pot of beans with bacon, onions, carrots, and celery boiling on the stove. They ate beans every Monday because Mother did not have enough time to take care of the clothes and fuss over a meal. Thane sat for his usual breakfast, a bowl of Wheaties. Milk, delivered this morning and still warm from his neighbor's cow, covered his "Breakfast of Champions." Father, hair slicked back and dressed for work in his overalls, ate corn flakes. Mother poured coffee for Father, then a cup for herself. Ruthene soon joined them.

"Who were you talking to on the phone this morning?" Father asked Mother.

"My youngest brother," Mother said anxiously.

"He find work yet?" Father asked, his voice gentle.

"Ain't no work in this Depression," Mother answered in a deep voice. Mother sounded funny when she talked like a man.

"I'm more worried about how his wife is feeling." Mother sipped her coffee. "It must be hard living out on a farm. Expecting her first baby."

"Your brothers can always come to me for grocery money for their families. I'm able to help them because of your thrifty ways," Father said as he rubbed his hand over his face. "Working at the Ford garage doesn't pay much. But at least I have a steady job. More than most."

"Seems all we've known for the last few years is drought and dust," Mother said in a troubled voice. "I can hardly remember our last good rain."

Thane peeked from Mother to Father. Tired and careworn, their faces showed their daily struggles.

Other families had it worse. Whenever Mother had a little extra food, she often left it with a family who lived in a dugout they had clawed out of the ground. Thane joined her. Inside, newspapers covered their walls, but the hard-packed dirt floor knew the scrape of the frayed broom that stood in the corner. A thin little girl who attended school with Thane lived there. The other kids ignored her because she only had one dirty dress.

Thane's grandparents had lived in a soddy, too, until they died three years ago. When Grandmother Smith's cancer got bad, Grandfather Smith just lost his will to carry on. Mother missed them both. Father's mother, Grandmother Baker, had lots of sayings. Superstitions, people called them. No one knew if Grandfather Baker was alive. He disappeared when Father was fourteen. Father left the farm after eighth grade to work and support Grandmother Baker and his three younger siblings.

After breakfast, Father kissed Mother on the cheek and left for work. Mother stood. Her short, dark, curly hair circled her head over her rail-thin body covered with a faded cotton dress. Mother handed Thane a flour-sack dish towel. He liked to look at the pretty pictures she embroidered on them with colored thread. This towel had a kitten on it.

"Dry the dishes after Ruthene washes," Mother said. Thane dried the breakfast dishes and set them on the counter for Mother to put away in their green painted cabinets.

"Mother, I don't want to help with wash day," Ruthene said. "With school starting soon, I need to practice my reading."

"Mary Ruthene, you do enough reading," Mother said. "Everyone works 'til the work is done." When Mother used both names, she meant it.

Ruthene pouted. Mother gathered the dirty laundry while Ruthene stared at her paper dolls with their broken legs. Thane snuck over to a wall switch near their front door with its four mother-of-pearl-topped buttons. Thane pushed one button to turn on the porch light, the other button lit the living room. To turn the lights off, he pushed the button underneath each one. Push. Push. Push. Push.

"Stop playing with the lights! You'll break them," Mother called out. Thane shoved his hands into his overall pockets.

"Thane, set that cardboard wheel in the front window to tell the iceman we need ten pounds for the icebox," Mother said. "Then you and Ruthene meet me outside by the woodpile."

While Mother gathered the last load of laundry, Ruthene and Thane gathered firewood. Mother soon joined them. Mother could have carried it all herself, but she had strong opinions about "Idle hands being the devil's workshop." They all trooped down the narrow stairs to the half cellar. Mildew, malt, and earth met them, as did the welcoming lower temperature in the cement room.

Mother lit a fire in her cast-iron stove that vented to the outside. A grate in the floor above let the warm air rise to the floor above them. This helped in the winter, but not on this scorching summer day. Mother lifted a large oval tub on top of the stove and poured multiple buckets of water into it.

"Mother, why can't we use water from the water heater?" Ruthene asked.

"It never warms the water up to a temperature worth using," Mother answered. "We do things the right way." Bucket after bucket, she filled the first-rinse tub and the second-rinse tub with more water.

Thane liked to be in the cellar. Every spring, Mother bought a hundred and twenty-five baby chicks for five cents apiece. She kept them in the cellar in a big newspaper-lined box. Father did not take a newspaper, as it cost too much money, but Mother sent her children to ask their neighbors for their used ones. Thane and Ruthene liked to sit and watch the busy little fluff balls. Mother said they may not pick up a chick unless she supervised. Since Mother always did housework, that meant they rarely held them. If Thane picked one up anyway, Ruthene tattled, and Mother swatted his bottom.

Once the weather warmed up, the chicks moved out to the chicken yard surrounded by a six-foot stockade-type wooden fence. They ate kitchen scraps and chicken feed. Their manure made excellent fertilizer for the garden crops, but the wind blew feathers everywhere.

When the chickens were large enough, Mother boiled water, then caught and killed a chicken for their dinner, the big noon meal. She scalded and plucked the feathers off the chicken, then gutted it before she brought the bird into the house. Inside, Mother cut the chicken into pieces, coated them with milk and flour, and fried them in bacon grease. Thane felt hungry just remembering how good that smelled.

"Thane, stop daydreaming! Hand me the good clothes," Mother said. Thane picked up a dress of Ruthene's and gave it to Mother. She added it to the washing machine. Thane passed Ruthene and Mother's dresses and his shirts until the pile was empty.

Once the water in the tub on the stove boiled, Mother transferred the hot water from the stove-top tub using a dipper into the washing machine's round tub. It was about two feet across and two feet deep, with an agitator in the center.

"Ruthene," said Mother, "bring me my soap." Mother had left a cake of her homemade lye soap soaking in a pot of water on the cellar shelf since last week. She pulled the cake out and set it on wax paper. Then she poured some of the soapy liquid into the washing machine. She turned on the electric agitator. Thane watched the clothes go around inside the coverless machine.

The dimly lit cellar meant safety. Whenever Ruthene and Thane played outside, Mother told them to be on the lookout for a "black roller," or dust storm. If a roller hit the end of the block, they ran to the cellar, yelling to Mother. She sprinted to shut the chickens in the henhouse, then joined them. The family stayed there until the storm ended. Mother painted egg whites on white gauze masks for everyone. She lit candles when the electricity went out. Once, Thane crept up the basement stairs to peek out a window during a roller. Even though it should be daylight, Thane saw only black. Mother pulled him back down the steps and scolded him.

Mother prepared for the storms long before they hit. To protect their lungs from the dust, she had dipped two-inch-wide strips of cloth in laundry starch and covered the inside and outside of all the window frames in the house. She also shielded the door frames. Father blocked the fireplace. Despite these efforts, Thane still saw dust on the windowsills after a big roller. Some neighbors hung wet bed sheets over the windows to keep the dust out. Mother said she sealed the house well enough. Mother's precautions mattered. Those who inhaled dust coughed up black sputum. Thane heard of people going blind if the storm caught them outside. Some folks in town had died from dust pneumonia.

When Mother decided the clothes were clean, she turned off the agitator and pulled out the steaming clothes with a wooden paddle, one at a time. Now the proper work began. To keep from burning her hands, Mother barely touched the fabric as she started Thane's shirt through the wringer, which squeezed the water out of the cloth between two rollers. To make the wringer work, Mother cranked the handle round and round. The excess water slid off a lip under the rollers back into the washing machine. After she wrung the water out of that item, she put it into the first-rinse tub and fished out another. She let Thane and Ruthene take turns with the wringer handle, but she cautioned them to be careful. The wringer crushed little fingers. Because it was hard to turn the handle, they were not as fast as Mother either. They soon let her turn it alone.

"Thane, hand me the next load of clothes," Mother said after she had emptied the washing machine. He passed her the underwear, socks, and undershirts one at a time. After she filled the machine, she turned on the agitator.

Mother swung the wringer over the first-rinse tub and locked it in position. One at a time, she lifted the good clothes out of the first-rinse tub and moved them through the wringer. Ruthene helped turn the handle twice while Mother watched apprehensively, then took over. The left-over water flowed into the first-rinse tub. Mother put the wrung-out dresses and shirts into the second-rinse tub.

After Mother emptied the first-rinse tub, she stood up straight and rubbed her lower back. She sighed and turned off the washing machine. She moved the wringer back over the washing machine and forced the water out of the underwear and socks. They moved into the first-rinse tub.

Thane looked at all the food Mother had canned this summer, sitting on shelves lining the basement. She had put up peaches, string beans, strawberries, rhubarb, cabbage, carrots, asparagus, spinach, potatoes, and tomatoes. She still had more to preserve before the end of the growing season. Of course, everything tasted better fresh, but this way, the family had fruit and vegetables all winter long. Father also fermented his home brew made with potatoes, raisins, fruit, and malt in the cellar. He did not want to buy the three-two beer in town.

"Thane, are you paying attention?" Mother asked. "I need the next pile of clothes."

Thane handed Mother his dirty overalls, along with the linens and towels, to fill the machine again. She started the agitator but did not see enough suds in the water, so she poured more soapy water from the pot.

Mother and Ruthene discussed the two new dresses Mother had sewn from flour sacks for Ruthene for this school year. When it was time to make a dress, Mother and Ruthene rushed to the store whenever the grocer received a new delivery of flour to select enough bags of the same fabric. Mother reused buttons from other clothes and sewed them on, good and tight.

Thane looked over at the wall that Father had built to divide the cellar for one of Thane's uncles. A couple of years ago, when he did not have a job or anywhere to live, Father and Mother had invited him to stay with them. They had put a bed on the other side of the wall, with a small rag rug next to it covering the cement floor, and a table with a water pitcher. That uncle had since got his feet under himself and moved out. Thane thought about moving into the cellar. The air was musty, and the water froze in the pitcher in the winter, but the quilts Mother had made would keep him warm. He could have his own room.

It was time for the good clothes to come out of the second-rinse tub. Mother moved the wringer over the second-rinse tub and began moving the clothes through the wringer while the water returned below. Sometimes she took turns with her arms. Other times, she used both hands together to turn the handle. Thane tried to help with the wringer. This time, Mother kept her hands on the handle too. Mother's body felt wet against Thane. After she emptied the second-rinse tub clothes, Mother ran the clothes through the wringer a final time, then handed them to Ruthene to load into the basket.

Mother massaged her arms for a moment, then wrung the socks and underwear load into the second-rinse tub. She turned off the washing machine and squeezed Thane's overalls and the towels through the wringer. After they were all in the first-rinse tub, Mother asked Thane to hand her Father's greasy overalls, shirts, and handkerchiefs. She added extra soap and started the agitator for the last load of the day.

Ruthene grabbed the cloth bag of clothespins.

"It's my job to carry the clothespins!" Thane yelled and seized the sack. They wrestled while clothespins scattered onto the floor.

"Stop it!" Mother hissed.

The children froze.

"Thane carries the clothespins!" Mother said.

Ruthene, Thane, clutching the clothespin bag, and Mother, carrying the laundry basket with the good clothes, marched outside to the clothesline in the backyard. The sun sizzled and shimmered on the sandy soil, promising worse as the day progressed. Two end posts set in concrete stood about twenty feet apart. Crossbars near the top, but nailed on the outside of their posts, had room for four rows of clothesline spaced about six inches apart. Last week, Father had spent a couple of hours after work shoveling out the dirt that had drifted under the clothesline during a recent dust storm to keep the clean clothes out of the dirt. He piled it over to the side. Thane imagined digging into it. He could create a secret cave.

"Thane, pay attention!" Mother said. Thane snapped his head back, reached into his bag, and handed her a clothespin. He did not want to make Mother angry. A couple of years ago, Mother took Thane to the barbershop for the first time. Crying and scared, Thane fought when it was time to get up in the barber chair. Mother pulled down his overalls in front of all those laughing men and spanked him good. She let him know he should obey and not embarrass her in front of the town.

Ruthene continued to pass garments to Mother one at a time. Thane put a clothespin in Mother's hand each time she held it out. Her other hand kept the clothes on the line until the clothespins secured it. She put clothes on the two outer lines first.

"What shall we do this Sunday?" Mother asked.

"I like fishing," Thane said. "Let's go fishing!"

"I hate fishing," Ruthene retorted.

Thane enjoyed fishing with his family when they got up in the dark and drove out to a pond on his uncle's farm. Their hooks would be in the water as they watched the dawn slide over the horizon. Mother built a fire and boiled coffee and water. She added eggshells to the coffeepot to keep the grounds down, but it never worked. His parents drank their coffee through their teeth to keep from swallowing the grounds. Thane thought fresh-caught fish cooked over the open fire tasted great. Afterwards, they returned to town.

Once home, Thane dressed in his new overalls, without patches. They were too long because Mother believed in buying clothes with growing room. Mother combed his hair to make it look nice. He attended the Methodist Sunday School because they gave pins for never missing a class. His folks did not go to church themselves. But they were okay if Thane visited.

"If not fishing, what else could we do?" Mother asked.

"How about after Sunday dinner, we go hunt for arrowheads and buffalo horns?" Thane asked. "Father says we find them because all the top dirt blew away and left treasures behind on the hard ground."

"I don't want to hunt arrowheads. Why do we have to?" Ruthene asked.

"That's another good idea, Thane," Mother said. "What do you want to do, Ruthene? Sunday is our day together as a family."

"I want to stay inside by the swamp cooler, not spend the afternoon in the blistering sun."

"We'll see," Mother said. When she finished hanging the clothes on the line, cellar duties called.

Like clockwork, Mother wrung the underwear load twice and put it into the basket. Thane's overalls and towels processed into the second-rinse load after wringing. Father's work clothes moved into the first-rinse bucket. Crank. Crank. Crank. Mother's rope-like muscles stood out as she worked, huffing with each rotation of the handle. Her hair dripped from her exertion.

Thane, Ruthene, and Mother walked outside and added the underwear load to the clothesline. Mother put them on the inside lines between the outside good clothes to keep the neighbors from seeing their undergarments.

Thane looked over at the peach trees. Whenever Mother enjoyed a good peach, she would plant its pit. No matter how much she tried, she had little success. Mother said if it rained, it would help the trees. There was only so much they could water by hand.

Back inside, Mother checked the clock. “We have time to make rolls to go with our beans,” Mother said. “I’ll get the sourdough out of the icebox. Do you kids want to clean up and help me make cloverleaf rolls?” Thane and Ruthene hurried to wash their hands, jostled each other as they crowded near the bathroom lavatory, then joined Mother in the kitchen.

Mother coated the cups in the muffin pan with a little bacon grease. “Sit at the table. Remember, each muffin cup gets three balls.” Mother, Ruthene, and Thane rolled balls. Sometimes, Mother had to redo Thane’s efforts. As a reward, Mother let Thane and Ruthene each eat a ball of uncooked dough. After brushing the tops with melted butter, Mother covered them with a damp dishtowel and set them near the stove to rise. She added equal amounts of flour and water to her sourdough starter and put the bowl back in the icebox. She then turned on the oven.

“Wash up, then meet me in the cellar again,” Mother said. After another shoving match before the lavatory, Thane and Ruthene ran back down the stairs. Ruthene took control of the clothes basket as Mother double-wrung Thane’s overalls and the linens. She then moved Father’s overalls to the second-rinse tub. Back outside, Ruthene and Thane helped by handing Mother the clean clothes and clothespins.

The cellar was much cooler than the backyard now. Mother processed Father's work clothes. One last time, they hung the laundry. Mother fretted about the time. She knew Father would be home a few minutes after twelve. She wanted everything to be ready for him.

"Ruthene, go pick tomatoes for dinner," Mother said as she came back into the kitchen and handed her a bowl. "Watch out for worms. Don't forget to close the back door. We want to keep all the cool air inside." Thane wandered after his sister.

"I'm glad you're here, Ruthene," Thane mumbled as he looked at his dusty shoes. "I get lonely sometimes. Lots of my friends moved to Californee-I-A."

Ruthene lifted dusty leaves to hunt for tomatoes. She inspected those she found, checking for ripe ones. Satisfied, she picked a few and added them to her bowl.

"The Dust Bowl made them go. Their fathers needed to find work," Ruthene said. "I lost friends too."

"After we eat, you want to play with my cardboard animals and barn with me?" Thane offered Ruthene.

She nodded.

Inside again, Mother ordered Thane and Ruthene to wash their hands and set the table. She opened the oven and placed the rolls inside to bake. She glanced at the clock.

"I'll put my soap back in the soap pot with more water," Mother said as she rushed downstairs.

Upstairs, Ruthene brought the bowls and glasses down from the green wooden cabinet. Thane collected spoons and knives.

In the car repair shop where Father worked, the owner operated a steam engine to power his equipment. Father diverted pressure from it to a train whistle daily at noon to let everyone in Elkhart know it was time for dinner. When she heard the whistle, Mother began dishing out the beans. She brought her homemade loaf of butter and a jar of strawberry from the icebox and set them on the table.

Father walked in the front door and scrubbed his hands in the bathroom. Grease and dust covered his overalls. Mother sliced the tomatoes, slid them on a plate, and added a little salt, pepper, and sugar. She pulled the rolls out of the oven. She tapped them with her fingernail to make sure they sounded done, popped them out of the muffin tin with a knife, and put them in a bowl on the table. Mother pulled a chunk of ice from the icebox and dropped it in a metal bowl. She hacked at it with an ice pick to make chips for their water glasses.

Father sat down on the bench seat in the booth and drank his ice water. His cigar smoke scent blended with sweat and motor oil. He reached over and put his large hand over Mother's thin fingers.

"How were your nerves today, Mother?" Father asked. He worried about her fretting.

"Not too bad, Father," she answered. "Thane and Ruthene helped with the wash."

Mother picked up her spoon. Father told them the town news. He smiled at Ruthene and Thane and told them how proud he was of their help to Mother.

"Mother," Father asked, "how many chickens you got left from those baby chicks you bought from that catalog last spring?"

Mother thought for a moment. "I have about fifty left. I'll save the last fifteen for their eggs for until we get more next spring."

Nodding, Father added, "I'll hunt when I can at your brothers' farms. That'll make the chickens last longer. A rabbit, prairie chicken, or a few quail would contribute to our menu. We always go fishing too. That'll save us from buying meat at the store."

Mother wiped her hands on her cloth napkin. "Well, it helps to grow what we can in the garden. The children help with watering."

Thane sat up straighter. Both Mother and Father had complimented him today.

Now came Thane's favorite part of the meal. Dessert. Ruthene stood up to clear the table. Thane laid out the small plates. Mother placed the last of her two-crusted strawberry-rhubarb pie in the center of the table. She added more ice and water to everyone's glass. Everyone sat back down.

Thane bounced on his bench. "Strawberry rhubarb is my favorite."

"Sit still, Thane," Father said.

Mother cut the pie and distributed the little pieces. "It's a little late in the year to harvest rhubarb. We want it to be strong for next year. I took the strawberries from a jar I preserved a couple of months ago. You all like pie."

"You bet!" Thane enthused.

"Thane," Father warned.

"Thank you, Mother," Thane added.

After dinner, Ruthene washed, Thane dried, and Mother left the beans simmering on the stove for supper that night. Father laid down on the daybed in the living room for a brief nap.

Thane brought his wooden toy barn and cardboard animals to the rug in the living room. Ruthene soon joined him. They played together without speaking as they would get in trouble if they woke Father. Mother sat down with her embroidery. Her facial lines of worry calmed. The swamp cooler blew over them all. Ten minutes before one, Mother woke Father to tell him it was time to leave for work.

Mother stepped down into the cellar to drain the water. She filled a bucket stationed below the washing machine. She carried it up the stairs, out the door, and poured it into two buckets, one for Thane and one for Ruthene. They carried their buckets to water Mother's trees and garden until she had drained all the tubs.

Tomorrow, Mother irons.

If you want to learn more about Thane Baker, his family, and his experiences as a sprinter on the 1952 United States Olympic Team, please read *Running in Borrowed Shoes*, published in Spring 2023 by Texas Christian University Press through Longleaf Services (longleafservices.org).

Notes

1. Laura Stockett Roberts, "Wash on Monday–A Little History of Homekeeping," *Your Williamson*, January 27, 2020, https://www.yourwilliamson.com/article/690/wash-on-monday-a-little-history-of-homekeeping.
2. Walter "Thane" Baker, United States Olympian, 1952 Silver 200 meters, 1956 Gold 4 x 100 meter relay, Silver 100 meters, Bronze 200 meters, in discussion with the author, July 2019-July 2023.
3. Covault Hatchery, "Baby Chick Prices," Wichita, Kansas, 1930s, postcard.

4. Thane Baker grew up less than forty-five miles from two towns highlighted in Timothy Egan's book, *The Worst Hard Time: The Untold Story of Those Who Survived the Great American Dust Bowl* (Boston: Mariner Books, 2006).
5. "Rare Dust Storm Wednesday Night," Glimpse Back into History, *Elkhart Tri-State News*, originally published April 14, 1933, reprinted July 19, 2018.
6. Ian and Madi Wohlwend, in discussion with the author, 2019.
7. Frank Morris, "The End is Near for 3.2 Beer," Morning Edition, National Public Radio, April 5, 2019, https://www.npr.org/2019/04/05/709515770/the-end-is-near-for-3-2-beer.
8. Elkhart, Kansas, lost over 37 percent of its population from 1930 to 1940 due to "dust storms and drought." By 1939, the "cumulative departure from normal precipitation" was over sixty inches of rainfall below normal. Thad G. McLaughlin, *Geology and Ground-Water Resources of Morton County, Kansas*, Bulletin 40, State Geological Survey of Kansas (Lawrence, KS: University of Kansas Publications, 1942), http://www.kgs.ku.edu/General/Geology/Morton/04_geog.html.
9. The rains arrived in the fall of 1939, ending the Dust Bowl a few months later. "Surviving the Dust Bowl–Timeline: The Dust Bowl," American Experience, Public Broadcasting Network, accessed April 3, 2020, http://www.pbs.org/wgbh/americanexperience/features/dust-bowl-surviving-dust-bowl/.

Cathy Beck • Omaha, NE

No, I'm Not Dead

It was supposed to be a simple trip to the hardware store. Mom and I needed gardening supplies, planting soil, fertilizer, and new trowels. And we wanted to see the new hardware store.

Growing up, there was a store in our small neighborhood that had obviously been there since before dinosaurs. It had a wood floor that was aged and warped, that had seen generations of handymen, electricians, carpenters, gardeners, and dozens of neighbors working on small projects.

Every time my dad took me into the store, I could hear the floor creak and smell the sawdust of the old floorboards in this building where people came to create and build. Dad would come in to pick up a new tool or screws to fix the wagon or hang a picture or to just hang out, like I do now when I go into hardware stores. This was where he purchased his first hammer, the hammer I asked for when he died.

But then, as all things do, it came to an end. A fixture in the community, we were devastated when they closed the store for good. At the last minute, the very last second of time, it was rescued. A buyer had been found. The new owner, wanting a larger space, moved kitty-corner across the street to a vacant building that had once been the site of a grocery store, a grocery store my family shopped in when I was a child.

So, as mom and I entered the new store, the first thing we noticed was the tile floor. There would be no state dependent memory of wood and sawdust to trigger our nostalgia in this building. But at least the community kept a hardware store in the neighborhood.

We stopped by during what they called their soft-opening week. The grand opening was scheduled for the following week, so things were still a little rough around the edges.

When I was growing up, that building had been the home of a Hinky Dinky store. I'd been in there hundreds of times, as we lived a short three blocks from the store during a time when everybody walked. But the old grocery store was unrecognizable now.

Mom and I meandered around the store. "I don't see any light bulbs, do you?"

"Yeah, Mom, I saw them a couple of rows over."

"I think I see gardening stuff in the next row, shall we head over there?"

"Sure."

We walked around the corner and started perusing the long row of flower and vegetable seeds, gardening tools of all kinds, planting soil, grass seed, hoses—everything we needed to start digging our hands into the rich spring soil.

As we came to the end of that aisle, I turned the corner to go down the next aisle. And in that flash of time when everything comes together, the universe, your entire life, all your memories and loves and family, I realized I was falling to my death.

Now, obviously, I didn't die or I wouldn't be here to tell my story.

So, here's what happened. There was a deep staircase to the store basement that I didn't know existed because it must have been hidden behind walls when it was a grocery store. But there it was. An open pit, with no walls, no guard rails, no warning. And since I was looking up, my foot went off the edge.

As I fell, the first thing I saw was the cement floor about fifteen stairs down. I knew I was going to die. Really, I knew I was going to die. And I did what all people do in that moment. I thought of my kids and how this would devastate them. I thought of my mom, my family, my siblings. And I wasn't afraid. Just concerned for my loved ones.

As luck would have it, or the arms of my guardian angel, somehow I caught myself. I felt my body turn parallel to the steps and managed to stay upright. My two feet fell at the same time, solidly on the sixth step down. And in that flicker of a second, I knew to throw myself backward onto the steps behind me, landing on my butt.

I was alive.

My mother had not even seen it happen. I heard her above me ask, "Cathy, where are you?"

"Mom. Mom . . . I'm down here."

When she looked down, she was horrified. Me? I was just trying to breathe. And thank God. And find the strength to stand up.

I checked for broken bones, which I knew I didn't have. I checked to see if I was breathing, which I knew I was. And I looked down at the concrete and was grateful that I was sitting on wood.

I still shake today telling that story. Yes, we told the guy working the cash register who seemed to shrug it off, the way many of us do when we are too ashamed to feel the guilt. *No big deal. She didn't die.*

The store manager wasn't in, but I left my name and phone number, asking him to call. I received no follow-up phone call, no apology, no free-purchases-for-life coupons.

I opted not to sue. I think because at that time in my life I hadn't done the internal work to find my voice. I didn't know how to fight for myself. I'd find the courage to do that work years later.

So on that day, I had to settle with just being grateful to be alive.

William L. Smutko • Blair, NE

Where the Wild Things Are . . . Cooked and Eaten

The heavy and complex aromas of red wine and venison drifted in from the kitchen.

"Would everyone please stand and raise your glasses. . . . To the United States of America where we have the freedom to hunt, fish, and forage."

"To the United States!"

"To pan fish, bluegill, and crappie, who take a fly, fight hard, and provide this delicious ceviche."

"To pan fish!"

My annual hunter-gatherer birthday dinner always begins with a toast to the USA. Followed by a toast to each of the six courses, for which there is an appropriate wine. We pay homage to and celebrate the wild things we are about to eat.

A tablecloth of many shades of green camouflage, accented by hunters' orange napkins covered the table which was set with sparkling clear plates and glassware. There was a menu at each place announcing the dish and accompanying wine for each course.

The first course is always fish. The last time I served this celebration meal, 2019, this dish was a pan fish ceviche accompanied by a dry German Riesling.

This meal continued with "Wild Asparagus Soup Euell Gibbons." The stalks were harvested in the road ditches of northwest Iowa, blanched, then frozen to keep for this meal. A citrusy

California Sauvignon Blanc went well with the asparagus. The year before I had tried cream of nettle soup. It wasn't received well.

A pâté of morel mushrooms, gathered in the woods along the banks of the Missouri River, was served next along with a light Zinfandel which backed up the mushrooms nicely.

Whole quail, taken on a sunny day we raised five coveys, stuffed with a pearl onion and a sage leaf, draped with a half slice of bacon and roasted for ten minutes was the next dish. An Oregon Pinot Noir set off the birds.

Braised venison shanks over mashed potatoes with leeks and kale were the main course.

The first time I prepared this dish, I was butchering my deer and noticed that the shanks looked a lot like the lamb shanks I had braised a few weeks earlier. So I saved them whole instead of chunking them up for stew meat. A month or so later I cooked them and invited Tom and Renee McWilliams—they appreciate venison—to dinner. They raved about the braised shanks. So much so, the next fall Tom brought me fifteen venison shanks collected from friends of his who always threw them away as too much bother for what you got.

~ ~ ~ ~ ~

Braised Venison Shanks

Serves 8-10

Ingredients:

4 venison shanks

3 carrots, chunked

1 large onion peeled and quartered

2 celery ribs, chunked

3 quarts venison broth (beef will work)

1 Tbs dried parsley

1 tsp dried rosemary

6 juniper berries, crushed

2 Tbs tomato paste

3 bay leaves

2 beef bouillon cubes (if using venison broth)

3 tsp kosher salt

1½ tsp ground black pepper

1½ tsp garlic powder

¾ C all-purpose flour

4 Tbs extra virgin olive oil

A .75-liter bottle of a full-bodied red wine (Use the same one you're going to serve with this dish. I used an Old Vine Zinfandel from Lodi, CA.)

Directions:

Using a saw, cut all four shanks into thirds. I just washed and sterilized a hand saw to do the job. Put the shanks aside.

Combine the next ten ingredients, carrots through bouillon, in a pot large enough to hold everything (I use an eight-quart roaster), bring to a boil, reduce to a simmer, and let cook while you prepare the shanks.

Season the shanks with salt, pepper, and garlic powder and dredge in the flour.

Pour the olive oil into a large skillet or sauté pan and heat over medium high till a small piece of onion sizzles. Add the shank pieces to the skillet and brown on all sides. Brown the meat in shifts to ensure the oil stays hot. Add more oil if necessary.

Add the browned meat to the broth and vegetables.

Add 1 cup of the wine to the skillet and use it to loosen the browned bits stuck to the bottom and add to the pot with the meat, stock, and vegetables. Add the remaining wine to the pot or roaster. Bring back to a boil, then lower the heat and let simmer till the meat is ready to fall off the bone, three to five hours.

Let the meat and liquid cool, then refrigerate overnight to let the flavors mingle and the fat solidify on the surface.

Scrape any fat off, then using tongs or a slotted spoon, pull the meat and bones out of the broth and refrigerate. Remove all the vegetables from the broth and discard. Bring the broth to a boil and reduce to two quarts.

Add the meat and bring back to a boil, then simmer till the meat is hot, about one half hour to forty-five minutes.

Serve the meat and reduction over the mashed potatoes.

Mashed Potatoes with Leeks and Kale

Ingredients:

3 lbs red potatoes, skins on and chopped
6 medium leeks, white parts, chopped
8 C baby kale, chopped
2 C heavy cream
1 tsp salt
3 garlic cloves, crushed
6 Tbs unsalted butter

Directions:

Bring a large pot of water to boil, add the potatoes, and cook till they are soft, about ten minutes. A sharp knife should pierce the potato pieces easily.

In another pan combine the leeks, kale, heavy cream, salt, and garlic. Bring to a boil, then quickly reduce the heat to low—you don't want the cream to curdle—then simmer till the kale and leeks are tender, about 10 minutes.

Add the butter to the potatoes and mash. Using a slotted spoon, transfer the leeks, garlic, and kale to the potatoes. Add enough cream to loosen the potatoes to your desired consistency—some like them as loose as potato soup, others like the potatoes stiff like baked. Just remember they are to soak up the wine and venison reduction. Blend the leeks and kale into the potatoes.

~ ~ ~ ~ ~

Black walnut pie (think pecan pie with black walnuts instead) complimented by a ten-year old tawney port was served as the last course.

I base my beverage selections on *What to Drink with What You Eat* by Andrew Dornenburg and Karen Page.

~ ~ ~ ~ ~

This celebration is a combination of two events. The idea of the toasts came from an officers' dining-in I attended as a young second lieutenant at Fort Benning, Georgia, in 1968. At a Nebraska Winery and Grape Growers banquet in Kearney, Nebraska, in 2000, they served six courses, and each course had its own Nebraska wine accompanying.

One year I had thought that to pay greater homage to our quarry the dinner should be formal, men in black tie and women in formal dresses, served by liveried footmen, *à la Downton Abby*. We didn't. I didn't want to spend the money on the footmen, and I thought my friends would balk at the formal dress.

Raise a glass to all the wild things we eat.

Cathy Beck • Omaha, NE

Forks in the Road

My life is incredibly different today than how I imagined it would be when I graduated from high school. Where is my house with gardens and a white picket fence? Where is my loving, perfect Prince Charming husband and lover? Where are my two long vacations every year—to the ski slopes and then to some fascinating place like New York City or the Grand Canyon or even Europe? I wanted at least eight children and dozens of grandchildren. None of this manifested in my life.

When I graduated from high school, I couldn't wait to move out of my childhood home and be free. Independent. And away from my mom. It would be years later when I realized it wasn't my mom I was running from. First substantial fork in the road.

I ran from a free education from Creighton University, as it's hard to work full time and attend any college curriculum. I wanted to write. I wanted to be a psychiatrist. But I was told that writing will not provide me a living wage. And psychiatry is a doctoral degree. Too much for me. My second fork in the road.

I was dating a nice young man at the time, so I was still holding out for the dream. All this other stuff was just biding my time. Six weeks before our wedding day, I blew up the engagement when my fiancé discovered I was having an affair. It wasn't really an affair. It wasn't anything serious. It was just a lark. Come on. What's the big deal? Another fork taken.

I continued to work full time, taking a class here and there because I was a voracious learner, although I wouldn't call myself that at the time. I dated guys here and there, but I wasn't great at relationships. They're too quiet. They're too busy. They aren't successful enough. They're too nice. Fork.

Then, when I was thirty-two and no father/husband/breadwinner on the horizon, I decided to adopt. My first child was a six-month-old baby girl from overseas. Six years later, I brought my second child home. One more tine in the pitchfork of life's turns.

Along comes my shining knight—an ex-priest who wanted to be married and wanted children. We married after a nine-month courtship. The dream was finally coming true. And another choice/path taken.

But he didn't really want kids, and I didn't really want sex . . . from him. He was too much like my dad—in not a good way. And at the time, I had no idea what that meant.

Eight years into the marriage, at the beginning of one of my daughter's counseling sessions, I asked the therapist for five minutes at the end of the appointment. When my daughter came out, I walked into his office and sat on a brown chair. I told him that my husband had accessed porn on the internet (for all of about five minutes at a time, maybe half a dozen times), and I was hysterical about it. I didn't understand why I was so upset by it.

This perceptive therapist, who had counseled several of my siblings' families, told me gently that sexual issues were pervasive in my family. He challenged me to face this. With him. Or another counselor. But perhaps it was time.

I started seeing him the next week. My hope was that he could find a way to fix me so that I could love my husband the way he needed to be loved so that he would then love my kids. "You want me to love your kids, yet you don't want to have sex with me. Do that, and I'll try loving them." Geez!

Short story long, I was in and out of counseling with this gentle, heart-felt Jewish man for nineteen years. I came face to face with the biggest pain of my life—remembering the times my dad abused me. Counseling changed everything—who I was, how I saw myself and life, how to cope with life's curves. It was the most substantial fork taken.

Eventually, my husband asked for a divorce and another fork was thrust upon me. I lost my marriage. I spiraled thousands of dollars into debt. I fought to hold onto the house, working two, sometimes three jobs.

I discovered single parenting was difficult on so many levels. Not enough time. No other parent to back me up and give me a break. Feeling like a failure so much of the time. I had been making a very good living owning my own company. But in time, it ran its course and I was drowning financially.

But through those nineteen years, I learned to love. Me, most of all. I learned that I let people walk all over me. No! Stomp all over me. Most especially some who were closest to me. Once I learned to love and respect myself and, more importantly, see that I was loveable, I saw what people had been telling me all my life—I needed to set boundaries.

I learned that boundaries weren't a way to say No. They were a way of telling others that I had learned to love myself. And that I knew what I wanted in life and love and I was telling them I was going to create that in my life.

That was the fork in the road I found most challenging. It was a long, agonizing road. But I never once wanted to quit. Even when I couldn't see where I was going, I had enough intuition to know it was headed forward to a much better and healthier place.

I still find times where I slip backward. It is then that I go back in for a 50,000-mile therapy check-up. But I love where all the forks took me, even though I couldn't see it at the time and often fought it. Maybe fought isn't the right word. Maybe stood at the fork confused and angry is a better way to put it. But would I go back to the dream I had of picket fences, Prince Charming, and eight children? Maybe not, because who I am and who I've become is better than anything I was. And I got there by having forks in front of me. And through all those forks, I've learned it doesn't matter which way I go—left or right. Whichever fork I choose, what matters, for me anyway, is what I learn about me as I travel that path.

Johnnye Gerhardt • Omaha, NE

Garlic, My Sicilian Family, and Becoming Dead

The following is true but rearranged and related in a fictional conversation for continuity and segues into events. Using first names only, characters mentioned herein are real and my experience with them is true. All are deceased except for Anthony, who is based on a server I encountered long ago. The exchanges with him are accurate and happened at the unnamed restaurant depicted here. The restaurant shall remain unnamed because it has a large fan base, and I don't want to start a debate. The other two reminisced restaurants are no longer in existence, but their chefs are worth remembering.

"My Companion" is the only fictional character but based on several real, some still living, people. The reference to Las Vegas at the very end actually happened to one. "My Companion's" conversation and his encouragement are obviously a figment of my grandiose imagination. I know of no one as interested in my history as I have made him out to be. As for the characters who inspired this piece, I truly loved my Sicilian family and miss them terribly. "Ti recordero per sempre." I'll remember you always.

~ ~ ~ ~ ~

My first and last time going to an Italian chain restaurant, I asked the server if they had a dish without garlic. He called another server over and repeated my question. Server number two introduced himself as Anthony and stared at number one as though he'd been asked to groom lions for the Colosseum, then they focused on me. "What particular menu item are you interested in?" Anthony said with attitude.

"Something, anything without garlic." I began to think the only thing I was going to have for dinner was a cocktail since upon entering the restaurant my olfactory nerves went into garlic overload shock. I knew my ensemble that evening would have to be aired outside for days.

Anthony inhaled slowly and layered his hands on his lower abdomen like a choir boy. I prepared for what I thought would be an arrogant dismissal directed at what he saw as someone who'd never eaten or served anything more exciting than a potato casserole. He looked down at me and sneered. "I will see what we can do."

While he was sharing my apparent faux pas with the rest of the crew hovering in the kitchen, my companion asked if I was allergic to garlic. I explained I wasn't but that my first husband's mother, Sarah, was a second-generation Sicilian whose father, Nanu—I knew him only by that name, which means grandfather—made his own wine, Diego Red, during Prohibition in his basement where homemade cheese hung in the shape of wheels from the rafters. My companion showed interest with raised eyebrows and a nod, so I continued.

"Nana, the grandmother, made spaghetti sauce from homegrown tomatoes allowed to overripen outside in a screen-covered wooden box. In the middle of summer, flies covered the screen and waited their turn on the table it sat on. She'd shoo them away with a dish towel, then cover the box with it as she carried it into the house. Nana passed her recipe on to her daughters: Louise, the eldest; Sarah, my ex-husband's mother; and Lena, the youngest. Nana's three sons left the recipes up to their wives but not always the cooking.

"Nana and Nanu's house smelled wonderfully like a gourmet deli. Nanu almost got arrested for the wine but managed to slip away just before the Prohibition police arrived. Sometimes they'd chase him for half a block, then quit. The police didn't vigorously pursue him because there was an understanding.

"The Mafia, also known as the Italian mob, and Cosa Nostra, also known as the Sicilian Mafia, were generous to their communities and those with influence, also known as the police department, the mayor, and whoever else needed a change of attitude. Sarah's eldest brother, Sammy, had worked for Al Capone, so he had leverage in the Italian-Sicilian community known as Little Italy located in the southeast part of town. Police presence there was met with a wink and a nod and sometimes cash, according to family lore.

"Baptized in the Catholic church at age twenty-one so I could marry into the family, my internship in Sicilian cuisine and culture was about to begin. Most importantly I learned about family loyalties. My biological family was critically small and somewhat detached because my parents didn't marry until their forties. My baptism sponsors into the church were Sarah's younger sister, Lena, and her husband. They were my cummari and cumpari, godmother and godfather. Looking back, I found the part of the ceremony about denouncing Satan humorous since I was basically qualifying for membership into a former crime family based in Sicily. I didn't give it much thought then because I wanted to belong and learn the secrets of the best spaghetti sauce I'd ever tasted. The crime and criminals, except for Sammy, never materialized. There were a few coincidences that were suspicious though. Like a bakery opening up within two blocks of my godfather's bakery, then closing within a month."

Server number one brought water, bread, butter, and utensils. He apologized for the wait. My companion glanced up, thanked him, and gestured for me to continue. I nabbed a slice of bread, but the garlic had permeated it too, so I put it on a bread plate and ignored it.

"Returning to the garlic issue, according to Nana if you could smell the garlic, you used too much. Speaking in Sicilian, she explained it to me. Sarah translated. 'Spices should work together in harmony like a chorus in an opera. There should never be an aria.'

"The Sicilian language reminds me of music. It has a rhythm and tone all its own. I learned from the family there are significant differences between the Italian and Sicilian languages, especially in their slang, just like there are differences in their pasta sauces. Lena had married an Italian so when they argued, and they always argued loudly with lots of gesturing, the differences became apparent. Evidently Italians looked down on Sicilians and the Sicilians didn't consider themselves Italian. The Italians accused the Sicilians of being dirty, throwing garbage into the streets. It never mattered what the argument was about. The garbage issue always came up."

My companion and I laughed. It diminished as Anthony approached. "Our dishes are prepared in such a way that we cannot remove the garlic." I knew exactly what that meant. Canned or prepared the night before. Anthony layered his hands on his lower abdomen. "Our apologies." Server number one watched from the door to the kitchen which had a large circular window. He was backed by what I assumed to be kitchen staff.

In my most empathetic voice I said, "I understand." Humbly almost begging I added, "Would it be possible to get just a bowl of pasta with extra butter on the side, no sauce?" I glanced in the direction of the kitchen and made eye contact with the only man wearing a hair-covering, obviously a cook.

Having been a server myself, albeit a cocktail waitress, I empathized with his position. He was just the messenger. Anthony listened closely to my request and took notes. I ordered a chianti that turned out to be not half bad. An Irish Coffee was ordered for dessert. It felt odd ordering something Irish in an Italian restaurant, but this wasn't authentic Italian and Anthony didn't react, so I knew he'd heard it before. If all their food was pre-pre-prepared, I didn't want to take a chance on a dessert that was probably from the same vendor the local grocery store used and then thawed out that morning.

Anthony's insincere smile became sincere, and he relaxed as he took my companion's order. While Anthony discussed menu items with my companion, I drifted off into my store of favorite restaurants.

The two best restaurants at the time weren't in Little Italy. One was next to a fast-food hamburger restaurant, and the other one occupied a corner across the street from a gas station in a part of town you wouldn't want to walk in day or night. Both stood out because of their Sicilian chefs. We knew we were going to have a great meal at the first one when we'd see him standing outside the back door smoking a cigarette and drinking a glass of wine. The drunker he was, the more his hostess wife complained and the better the meal. Sometimes we'd be in the area and drive by. If he was standing outside and tipsy, we'd go in even if we hadn't planned on it.

The second restaurant's chef always came out to speak with the patrons. Opera played softly in the background and when one of his favorites came over the speakers, he'd sing along in Sicilian as he strolled among the tables. Everyone loved it because he was not only very good but sang as if it was written just for him. He eventually got engaged but his fiancée wanted to go to Las Vegas and become a showgirl, so we lost him to Nevada. A new owner took over and, even though he maintained the authentic menu, the restaurant was just a symphony orchestra without the strings. It was still better than Bach played by a kazoo, which is what I thought of the chain restaurant I was in. My reverie was broken by the sound of my companion's voice.

Anthony finished taking our orders. He sauntered toward the bar, had a rather lengthy chat with the bartender capped off with laughter, then briskly walked past us to the kitchen. I continued relating my experiences.

"The first time I met Nana, I was terrified. Christmas eve at Nana and Nanu's house was overwhelming for the uninitiated. The whole family was there except for Sammy. The adults spoke either Sicilian or Italian peppered with American English. I could guess what they were talking about just by watching their gestures and expressions. I huddled next to my then fiancé, the one I'd joined the church for, who held my hand the entire evening. At one point, Nana approached. She leaned down and with her fingertips pinched together, motioned toward her mouth, and said, 'Manciari. Manciari.' My fiancé said she wanted me to eat something. I nodded and said thank you in English even though I had practiced saying 'grazi' with the rolled 'r' and accent. After thinking it over I thought it would sound pretentious or inadvertently spark a one-sided conversation in Sicilian.

"That night I learned what real spaghetti sauce tasted like. Even after I divorced Sarah's son, later called Tricky Dicky by our children, I'd have dinner at her house. She used pork neck bones in her sauce since they were what Nana used, cheek meat being too expensive. Sarah put extra neck bones in the sauce just for me. As the sauce cooked all day, it permeated every nook and cranny of the neck bones. The little meat that clung to them was unbelievably tender and sweet. Sarah laughed at my sucking every morsel out of its hiding place until the bones were cleaner than a century old skeleton in the Sahara. Her meatballs, though, were beef and the recipe for those went to my oldest daughter who's forgotten it."

My companion inquired about Sicilian culture, the movie version, and if it was realistically depicted. I hesitated because I never experienced the movie version but once with my people, my tribe. The rest I learned by listening to the family reminisce, but before relating about that "once," I made sure no one was within hearing distance. There wasn't, so I responded to my companion's curiosity.

"There's background so you need to know before I reveal the other side. Because Tricky Dicky was abusive and I had to call the police on him when he wouldn't leave my house one evening, a judge changed his visitation privileges with our two children to take place only at Sarah's house. That meant his parents would pick up the children on Friday night from the babysitter and I'd pick them up on Sunday at Sarah's house. He rarely spent time with them. The arrangement was perfect for me. I could date without hiring a sitter and the children experienced things I couldn't afford.

"Dick had demonstrated his schizophrenic negative personality several times, even attempting to run his sister over because she had answered my call for help when he came home violently drunk one evening. The family realized the divorce had been necessary and since I didn't sue him for alimony and he wasn't responsible for any bills other than bare minimum child support, which I didn't force him to pay, I became the heroic victim."

My companion smiled with raised eyebrows, so I continued. "The Sicilian side of the family adopted me. Dick was eventually kicked out of the family Sicilian style and wasn't even allowed to see Sarah as she lay dying in the hospital. Her sisters, Louise and Lena, wouldn't let him enter her room. Louise slapped him as he tried to get by. Sarah didn't call for him anyway. She asked for my son, her grandson, instead."

Anthony interrupted my story with a carafe of chianti. My companion filled our glasses. He told me to go on.

"In Sicilian tradition, a member of the family can be declared dead to the other members. That meant no one in the family contacted, acknowledged, or even looked at the ousted member. Sammy, the Cosa Nostra-connected member, used to blow in unannounced. No one knew when or where he was going to appear, nor did they know from where, even though he and his family lived in the same city. Sammy travelled a lot.

"I met Sammy at one of Sarah's bowling tournaments where her sisters were part of the league. One night, a dangerous-looking man opened the door to the bowling alley and stood off to the side while holding the door. The cold winter air flowed past him and ahead of Sammy's entrance like a foreshadowing event in a Quentin Tarantino film.

"Sammy wore all black. His trench coat billowed behind him as he took long, quick strides toward us. Per Louise, Sammy was always escorted by two men. That night they intensely scanned the area as they stood at parade rest behind us. I half expected them to pull Tommy guns out of their coats. Too many old gangster movies, I guess. The Godfather wasn't reassuring either."

My companion laughed since that was the first image he thought of too.

"Sammy spoke in Sicilian. He looked me up and down, made another comment, and smiled. It made me extremely uncomfortable. Sarah and Lena yelled something in Sicilian at him that I knew was vile because of their gestures. Lena spat on the floor in front of him. He bowed slightly and left as dramatically as he'd arrived. I never saw him again.

"The sound of bowling balls and pins dropping paused for a minute since everyone there knew who Sammy was and what had just happened. When you lived or had a business in Little Italy, everyone knew everyone else and everyone's business. It was considered unconscionable to cheat business owners or members of the community. And that's how Sammy became 'dead' to everyone in the family. He had cheated one of his own. Lena's spitting toward him had sealed his fate.

"When my children visited Sarah, they were often taken to their other relatives' homes. One of those homes was across the street from Sammy's house. Sarah kept blankets in the car to drape over the children so Sammy couldn't see them. The dead weren't allowed to see the living, not the young ones anyway. I've met and made friends with other alleged Cosa Nostra and Mafia members throughout my life. They've always looked out for me because of my connection with and inclusion in Nana and Nanu's descendants."

My companion nervously glanced at other restaurant patrons. I assured him I was still in good standing with my Sicilian tribe and any friend of mine was a friend of theirs. Anthony brought my pasta with a side of butter at just the right time. Conversation after that turned to Nebraska football, the weather, and careers. I slathered butter all over the pasta and took a bite. At least they knew how to cook pasta. It was perfect al dente.

As I stated in the beginning, that was my first and last experience at that Italian chain restaurant. It was also the last conversation I ever had with that companion. I heard later that one of the characters he is based upon, a second husband, moved to Las Vegas because he thought his wife was showgirl perfection. It turned out she wasn't, so he became a blackjack dealer, she waitressed, and he died there from a heart condition I think. The obit didn't say. He had divorced me for that showgirl so who knows. What is it with these guys marrying showgirls and moving to Las Vegas? I wonder if the chef who migrated to Vegas ever crossed paths with my second husband. As they say, "What happens in Vegas stays in Vegas." In second husband's case, I was glad he did.

I ended up tossing my ensemble for that evening, having draped it over a fence to air it out. Even after three days, the birds wouldn't land anywhere near it. My neighbor's cat stopped coming around too.

Years later DNA tests indicated I was 14 percent Italian and shared a mitochondrial marker with Puccini. That explained a lot, even confirmed family lore, which made up for the fact that I was born in Oklahoma at a military hospital responsible for my being named after two uncles. But that's another story.

Michelle L. Howard • Holdrege, NE

A Long Story about a Quick Decision

We've all got those small number of days in our lives, a very minute amount, that are turning points. Those are the ones that dictate how the rest of our lives will play out. September 29, 1966, was one of those rare days for Harry House.

Harry was just another hick country kid. He grew up in Nebraska's breathtaking Sandhills of Loup County. Well, at the start of those hills anyway. Like most farm kids in America in the 1950s, he lived a simple life filled with work and struggles.

As the fourth child of a couple that married at the height of the Great Depression, Harry was the only one that was "planned." Born seven years after the quick succession of a son, then a daughter, then another son, Harry came into the world in March of 1946. Growing up, he often felt as if his parents were too tired by the time he came along. Jack, his father, was thirty-four years old. His mother, Agnes, was thirty-one.

The family was not well-off by any means. They had to spend two years as sharecroppers for Jack's older brother Harvey. But the family never went hungry. There was always a roof over their heads, and they had no debt. They got by, as most people they knew did.

Harry was twenty years old. He'd been living as an adult for years. Although his permanent address was still his parents' home, Harry had been coming and going as he pleased since he was sixteen. He had a complicated, sometimes cold, relationship with his mother, Agnes. He loved her, valued her opinion, and spent most of his time with her. But they would often bicker and fight. She was strict, matter of fact, and imposing. Jack, his father, was regarded far and wide as a kind, honest, and hard-working man. Although Jack was well-loved by his family, Harry never felt a strong connection with the man.

That Thursday started out with no hint that the day's events would forever alter Harry's life. He was with Roger, a friend from Comstock, Nebraska. The two of them had been down south, working in construction on a dam in Almena, Kansas. It was hard, sweaty work. Neither man was disappointed when the boss had to call it quits early in the day. They weren't about to let that disrupt their routine. They left the job site and headed straight to the local watering hole in their 1957 Ford. The car liked to backfire, and flames would shoot up out of the carburetor. It was a frequent circumstance of driving that old beast. Naturally, when it happened right as they were parking, neither man thought a thing about it.

After a couple of hours of good hard drinking, someone came running in to announce that there was a piece of Detroit machinery burning up outside. The guys stumbled out into the setting sun to see the hood was a smoldering mess. The paint was blistered off, and there was a heavy stench of burned rubber hanging in the air.

As luck would have it, just across the unpaved street was a tiny used-car lot. The paint on the building had worn away long ago. One dangling hinge was all that remained of the screen door. But the place was open and there were cars in the lot. Most importantly, the salesman was not in the least concerned with their state of advanced tipsiness. As long as they had cash, they could drive off his lot with an old clunker. The ten-year-old 1956 Mercury cost a grand total of fifty bucks. It seems ridiculous today to think about two drunks walking onto a car lot and driving away with a car they paid cash for. No questions, no paperwork, no hoops to jump through. Such a simpler time that many today cannot imagine.

At that point, the guys decided it was time to leave town and head north to go home. They were about 140 miles south of their stomping grounds. They knew they could party all weekend once they made it to Custer County. Sadly, for them, vehicle problems were not over yet. They managed to make it as far as just north of Miller, Nebraska, before their "new" car broke down about midnight. Roger, drunk enough to worry about his buddy and the cool night air, started a fire in the middle of the highway.

Once he was assured that Harry wouldn't freeze to death in the fifty-degree weather, Roger took off walking to town to call his mother for a ride. The poor dear lady was a little crazy and a lot religious, or maybe a lot crazy and a little religious. She was known to march around the town square of the county seat, Broken Bow, handing out leaflets and preaching that most of the town was going to burn in hell. Likely having her son and his friends get hammered on a very regular basis did little to help her with those issues. But, being a mother, she showed up. She gave the pair a ride on into Broken Bow, dropping them off at the Tumbleweed Café out on Highway 92.

Meanwhile, in Broken Bow, the second shift at the local Becton-Dickenson (BD) manufacturing plant had just got off work. Shannon and Janice were two local gals that worked there. They were both nineteen and neither liked to cook much. The girls decided to go to the local café. Neither of them wanted to cook.

Besides, it was always fun to go see what was going on in town, even at two a.m.

Shannon Rose, oldest child of Lester and Virginia and big sister to Colleen, was born in August of 1947 in Custer County, Nebraska. Although she'd been raised by a dominating, abusive father and a quiet, submissive mother, her character resembled neither. Shannon was a free-spirited, fun-loving, beautiful red-haired girl. Her extended family, particularly her paternal grandmother, Rosa Leona, doted on her. Shannon was her namesake.

Being born and raised in the center of the country, in the center of Nebraska, meant no excitement, ever. The most fun Shannon could hope for was going to town on Saturday night with her folks. She'd get to run off with her best friend, Nancy. A favorite pastime was going to the drugstore. It was THE place to be if you wanted to meet boys and sneak cigarettes in the back by the soda fountain.

On that cool September early morning, Shannon had long since moved out of her parents' house. She'd gone through two years of business school and loved the freedom away from her father. Working at BD was a good job. She enjoyed working the second shift, getting off work in the wee hours of the morning.

Harry and Roger walked into the café and noticed the two girls right away. After checking them out for a moment, Roger asked Harry if he'd "take the redhead" since he had a "thing for blondes." Harry had dated the blonde already. He was more than happy to talk to the pretty friend. He wasn't about to turn down getting to hit on a cute redhead, after all. That one decision was monumental to the rest of his and Shannon's life.

The guys wound up at the girls' apartment that night. Roger slept with the blonde and Harry slept on the couch. The next afternoon, the girls had to go back to work. Harry, who'd been cooking at home for years, found some chicken in the icebox. The guys thought it would be nice to cook up some fried chicken for the girls to have when they got home. Now, mind you, this was 1966. Long before a microwave. By the time the ladies arrived, the chicken was waiting for them. Nice and cold. That's how Harry learned Shannon didn't like cold chicken. She went on a rant. This one story is a foreshadowing of the decades to come. Harry would spend the next four decades doing jobs on the road but taking care of the house, projects, and their one child. Shannon always did love to work. Housekeeping, cooking, and childcare were not in her bag of tricks. Then she'd come home and not mince words if something didn't set right to her standards.

Harry spent two months on that old davenport. But there was a problem. He suffered from severe homesickness at dusk. Home was always his happy place. The homesickness was severe when he was a child. It was something he struggled with for the rest of his life. There was something about that time of day that made him yearn to be home. To be where he belonged in this world when he'd close each day down.

He'd been miserable from homesickness plenty of times before. But on November 5, 1966, that lonely, melancholy feeling was how he made the biggest decision of his life. It had only been thirty-eight days since he'd met Shannon. He'd spent most of those days with her in Broken Bow. But on that brisk, overcast day in the fall he'd gone back to Sargent for his cousin, Larry Holcomb. Harry and Larry were more like brothers than cousins. November fifth was the first Saturday of November. In Nebraska that meant the start of pheasant season. Not being much for hunting, Harry didn't care about bagging a bird. But Larry was in town and wanted to hunt. Harry left that new girl in Broken Bow to go trudging through the chilly hills of Loup County with his cousin.

When they were tired and cold enough, the guys went back to Jack and Agnes'. It felt odd to be lying there in his childhood bed again. Harry had been out of the house for quite a long while this last time. As he lay there on that Saturday night, he could think of nothing else but that crazy, beautiful, wild girl. It seemed impossible that it had been less than forty days. Harry realized it was having that old familiar feeling. For the first time in his life, he was homesick for someplace other than his parental home. He realized at that moment that his place in the world, the place he belonged, was wherever Shannon was. It didn't matter where. It only mattered that he closed down every day with her. Harry climbed out of bed, grabbed his wallet and keys, and left the house that night, right then and there. Harry became Shannon's mate for life that night.

Janet McMillan Rives • Oro Valley, AZ

Lighter

We all stood around the maple tree, the one outside our bedroom window. We were there for a summer picnic. Wow, there were lots of people—Mother, Dad, Jamie, and a bunch of men, the ones Mother had been teaching how to type and something else, shorthand. I've seen some of her books about shorthand—weird squiggly lines. Anyway, the men were soldiers. Dad called them Airmen. A few days before the picnic, Mother explained to me that our country was at war in Korea, and these men were getting ready to go fight in the war. That sounded scary.

My parents always say I'm shy, especially when they compare me to Jamie. And I was even more shy two years ago on the day of the picnic when I was only seven. I just wanted to climb the maple up to where I used to hide when I wanted to be alone. No way to do that at the picnic with all those eyes on me. Besides, I remember the men were very nice and treated me like a little sister. One of them even said I reminded him of his kid sister, same color hair and blue eyes. He was my favorite and I didn't want him going to any war.

The men kept calling my mother "Mrs. McMillan" and kept telling her what a good teacher she was and how much they learned from her. A teacher? Teachers were people like Mrs. Gray and Miss Hotchkiss—not Mother. But then I thought about it and decided she was a teacher because she taught me to write and read before I went to first grade. Mrs. Gray thought I was pretty smart! Dad was a teacher too—he taught me to hit a baseball, to throw it, to swim and even taught me how to memorize a poem. Mother said Dad taught other people too, college students. He taught them something else though, not sports or poems. Ha!

Our picnic was great—ham and tuna sandwiches, potato salad, lime Jell-O, and peanut butter cookies (my favorite). After we finished eating, one of the Airmen handed my mother a box wrapped with a pink bow. I could see how happy she was. And something else—I could see how happy Dad looked, kind of proud just the way Jamie and I felt. None of our friends' mothers had a job, so we knew our mother was special being a teacher and all that. Mother opened the box. Inside, wrapped in white tissue paper, was a silver cigarette lighter and on it LLM, Mother's initials.

All of that happened two years ago before we moved from Horsebarn Hill to this brand new house on Eastwood Road. That's when Mother quit smoking. I asked her today when I got home from school (first day of fourth grade, Miss MacArthur!) why she kept that lighter on the coffee table when she never uses it anymore. She said, "That's my résumé."

Footnote

In the summer of 1951, during the Korean War, the University of Connecticut arranged with the Air Force to prepare a group of active duty Airmen for their occupational specialties of clerk-typist or secretary-stenographer. My father, a business professor, heard about the military training program on campus (not ROTC but classes for active duty Airmen) and knew his wife would be the perfect fit as a teacher. She was a college graduate with a major in English and minor in secretarial studies. In

1951 at age thirty-six, she was a homemaker, wife, and mother. Both of her daughters were in grade school, so she had time to teach the Airmen. After I wrote this story from my own memory, I began searching through my mother's daily planners for details. I started with the summer of 1950 and then, bingo, July 1951. Thursday, July 12, 1951: *Had my class for a picnic in our yard at noon. The class gave me a very nice Ronson lighter*. Friday, July 13, 1951: *Graduation of my class at the Air Force School. Al Waugh spoke—very good talk. I told Sam I felt like a mother sending her twenty-five sons off to war.*

M. Timothy Nolting • Bushnell, NE

You Never Know . . .

You never know with first-calf heifers and early spring calving.

She must have just dropped the calf and walked away.

Dad and I found the newborn lying by the creek, all four legs in the freezing water. Dad picked the calf up, cradling her in his arms, almost like the calf was a human baby, and laid her in the bed of the pickup. Her ears were already frostbitten, I'd seen it before, the ice-caked tips, stiff and brittle, and I knew right away that she'd be a bob-eared calf.

Dad drove back to the barn, across the pasture, where the crush of frozen snow squeaked under the tires. I sat in back, legs crossed, holding the unsteady head in my lap as I rubbed her neck and shoulder. Her frost-covered lashes fluttered over her glazed eyes.

At the barn, Dad carried the calf into the stall where we were keeping the one bucket calf we already had. Dad had saved the calf but the old mother cow didn't make it. I broke open a bale of straw and scattered a thick layer into the corner of the pen, and Dad laid the calf there while I gathered up a few old gunnysacks that we'd use to dry the calf off and rub her down.

I kneeled down beside the calf with my gunnysack in hand and rubbed across her body from her shoulder, back to her flank, and down her legs. Front to back and back to front, down her legs and back up again. The calf lay flat, stretched rigid from the tip of her nose to her limp, unmoving tail. She was breathing, but barely, and the eye that I could see was a dull, cloudy orb.

Dad went on with the rest of the chores while I stayed with the calf.

It was dark when Dad came back to the barn to tell me that it was suppertime and we'd best be going in. I told him I wasn't hungry and I'd stay with the calf until she was able to stand.

There was no electricity in the old barn, but there was power in the shed nearby. Dad must have gathered up a good many extension cords to go from the shed to the barn, where he hung a heat lamp from an overhead rafter. Then he took off his heavy, old, battered, leather and sheep-wool lined bomber coat, wrapped it around me, and told me to come back to the house when I was ready.

With growing darkness and the comforting weight and warmth of that old coat, I must have fallen asleep.

It was getting light when Dad shook me awake. I was ashamed that I had fallen asleep and quickly began again the methodical rubbing of the legs and torso of the calf. She was still alive, breathing deep and strong. I thought she'd make it.

As I continued to rub her legs, I noticed that the hide was beginning to slough off of the bone. The hide was dead and there was no blood between hide and bone. The calf's legs had been too long in the freezing water of the creek. She was alive, but would likely never stand.

Dad went to the shed and came back with the old Winchester .22 rifle that stood propped in the corner beside the work bench.

"Make an X on her forehead, from ear to eye, and hit where it crosses," he said, marking the imaginary target on her forehead with his finger.

He handed the rifle to me and left. I'd be nine years old come October.

I pulled the trigger and cried.

Valerie R. Robert • Plattsmouth, NE

The Birthday Party

Every year from the time I was five, my mom planned a special birthday party for me. All the neighborhood kids were invited. Since we were baby boomers born in the sixties, there were a lot of kids on our dead-end street.

My birthday is on the last day of July. Since the weather in Vermont is usually warm and sunny then, my parties were always held outdoors on our screened-in patio. My eighth birthday stands out in my memory. Mom had decorated a special cake for me with frosting clowns set in tumbling poses on the cake. The usual crowd was in attendance—the Beaudoin twins and their sisters, Joni, Tootsie, and Patty, and Evelyn, Bonnie, Susie, Robin, and Maryanne.

Birthday parties back then were times of great excitement, whether you were the guest of honor or merely an attendee. As kids we didn't pay much attention to the gift we were bringing—our mothers usually took care of that—but eagerly anticipated the gifts and goodies we might receive. Parties always included a game of pin the tail on the donkey, dropping clothes pins in a Mason jar, and musical chairs. The winner of each game excitedly chose a wrapped prize—possibly a kaleidoscope, jump rope, pick-up sticks, or a set of ball and jacks.

Besides the prizes, we especially looked forward to the treats: cake and ice cream, Kool-Aid, peanuts, candy, and popcorn. Cake and ice cream may be old hat to today's kids, but in the sixties—in my family at least—cake was only served on birthdays, and we always drank milk with our meals. Kool-aid was a special treat, and soda was even more of a rarity. Mom kept a previously opened bottle of ginger ale under the dry sink for months at a time. I don't know how she kept it from going flat! We were lucky to get a juice glass full on special occasions.

When I look back on pictures taken that day, I recall what really made that day stand out in my memory. There were what I like to call the "before" and "after" pictures. In the before pictures, I'm sitting on a high, red, vinyl stool, wearing a flowered party dress; in the after pictures, I'm wearing an old sweater and a pair of pants and sitting on a standard dining room chair. While eating my cake and ice cream, I suddenly became dizzy. The next thing I knew I was waking up on the floor with damp underwear, shivering with cold. Hence the change of clothes. Apparently, I had fainted and fallen off the stool, landing on the cement floor below. In the process my bladder released, and I wet my pants. Fortunately, everything was intact except my pride.

As a child I suffered from petit mal epilepsy. Mom related my first couple of episodes to me. One day, as an infant in the playpen, I suddenly lost consciousness, falling backward onto the floor of the playpen. Later when I was about five, I suddenly collapsed on the grass while playing outside with my friends. When I didn't move or open my eyes, they ran to tell my mother I was dead! Fortunately, Mom realized I had had a seizure and knew what to do.

Cold food or drinks seemed to trigger seizures for me, and the day of my eighth birthday party, eating ice cream, was no exception. I remember, years later, coming home from a trip to Dairy Queen and drinking a slushy, when I started to get a headache. I put my hand on my forehead and closed my eyes. A kaleidoscope of colors began to swirl behind my eyelids. My next conscious memory was of waking up after the seizure with Dad holding me on the floor.

Despite seeing specialists who ran tests, no cause for my epilepsy was ever found. However, I was one of the fortunate children that sometimes outgrow the condition after going through puberty. I was also fortunate enough not to have had grand mal seizures. Because my seizures ended when I was eleven, I don't remember feeling different from other kids. Had it continued into my teen or adult years, it would have had a much more profound effect. I wouldn't have been able to drive, altering my life forever. The only lasting effect of my epilepsy is the memory of that day—the first time I felt what it was like to have a seizure.

Cathy Beck • Omaha, NE

When the Inconceivable Became Real

It's interesting to reflect on those first days of the Pandemic. The masks have finally come off, and yet we've learned to embrace them if needed. It is over three years since everyone at the college where I worked went home to stay safe. The entire school closed, along with every other school, business, theater, restaurant, church, airline, and doctor office. At eight o'clock at night, the streets of New York City were barren, nary a car to be seen. Empty.

March Madness cancelled in the middle of a game. The baseball season never got up and running. And unbelievably we grieved an entire year of football never played and the millions of dollars lost on beer and nacho sales.

For those with Berkshire Hathaway stock, shareholders from around the globe were left in the cold when they cancelled their yearly meeting, one of Omaha's biggest tourist events. Concerts, the swim trials, Broadway musicals, and live TV. Jimmy Kimmel, Ellen, and others began bringing out reruns or broadcasting from home. I realized how a live audience enhances live television. It was an eerie, but weirdly interesting, time. Almost as if we were living on an alternate universe, a strange weird planet.

From March 6, 2020, when they first announced the virus arrived in Omaha, to March 18, when the college closed its doors, I wiped down my desk numerous times a day. I slathered sanitizing gel over and under and through my fingers after opening any door. I washed my hands vigorously and long every time I used the restroom. If I didn't know "Happy Birthday to You" by heart then, I certainly had it down after a few days of this hell. If I sneezed, same—bring out the hand sanitizer. It was awkward having conversations standing six feet apart. So much seemed to be lost with that distance. It seemed discussions, out of necessity, became more superficial.

It was no different at the house—it, too, was cleaned thoroughly—several times a day—for a few days. In short order, I realized we were all the same three to four people living in the house, not going anywhere, and maybe I could get by with cleaning once a week.

No one could come in the house. If your sink backed up and you were lucky enough to get a brave plumber out, with mask, you might be able to do that beloved job of washing dishes again. But I made sure to stay six feet from the plumber, wifi repairman, or delivery person.

I wondered if I'd know anyone who died. Then, in late March, they announced the name of the person who suffered the most heartbreaking fate of being the first casualty in Nebraska. Although I wasn't close to him at that time, he was someone who had been a part of my life years before. His family waited until July of that year to hold the funeral.

The government stepped in with huge bi-partisan relief assistance. Everyone thrown out of work saw a glimmer of daylight, no matter how short-lived. It kept some afloat and in their homes for the better part of the Pandemic. Others? Well, they couldn't make it even with the help. Established businesses shuttered their doors. Daycares closed for good, and all schools switched to online teaching in a matter of days. It was amazing! And it was devastating!

Cloth masks became the newest and most original items on amazon.com. You could buy flowered ones, ones with the flag, and school logos. The most interesting one to me was the one with an image of a wide smile with teeth showing. Creativity run amok.

USPS, FedEx, and UPS struggled to keep up with the overflow of packages as everyone lost their brick-and-mortar stores. I could still get out and walk, although I crossed to the other side whenever I saw someone coming toward me. Everyone did. And when I noticed a UPS delivery person, I told him how much I appreciated what he did. We couldn't tell healthcare workers, first responders, and teachers enough how much they meant to us. My daughter continued to work at the hospital but stripped out of her possibly—probably—contaminated uniform in the garage when she came home. The first-hand stories she relayed to me were beyond sad.

The spring and summer of 2020 were bliss for me. A friend living with us got into high gear and took care of the yard, painted the shed, and watered the gardens. We'd sit outside in the evenings, relishing the beauty of the flowers and green carpet of lush grass. And as beautiful as my yard was, the air across our magnificent green and blue planet was equally as pleasing. Google satellite photos showed before and after views of the air. And it gave me hope for the planet that in a few short months the air could get that much better. Maybe the future of a clean planet was possible.

While working from home, I had the time to run outside for five minutes and move the sprinkler several times each day, bring in the mail, throw a load of clothes into the washer, read the newspaper at lunch, and listen to the dull drone of the news stations while working. It was 2020. The year of the Biden and Trump match-up. News could get interesting rather quickly.

I had my youngest daughter and granddaughter living with me, so I wasn't lonesome, or bored. Our lives were quiet. The house was quiet. Until the three-year-old woke up. So much for peace.

Although there was fear of this unknown and deadly plague, there was also an enigmatic blessing in life not being persistently busy, going eighty miles an hour most of the time.

I didn't miss shopping. Picking up groceries became my new thing—and I realized how much I saved by not setting foot in the store and picking up items I didn't need, want, or would ever eat. I'm not sure I'll ever go back to shopping in person on any regular basis again.

Because we were to isolate from anyone we didn't live with, I was unable to see my oldest daughter or granddaughter living in Elkhorn . . . until her fit, healthy boyfriend of seven years passed away suddenly of a heart attack in October of 2020. I needed to put my fear aside and be there for them, no matter the risk. I masked up much of the time. But a funeral is not the most conducive environment for covering your face while trying to have intimate and comforting moments with loved ones and their family and friends. In spite of all the hugs, I was fortunate not to get sick.

From the beginning, I kept daily records of statistics of how many more people tested positive in Nebraska, the United States, and the world. Numbers seemed to go up exponentially. The death rate did the same. It was unbelievable what we were witnessing. There was no way to make sense of these emotions we were all feeling. What was this? Sadness? Fear? Relief? Anger? Pity? Empathy? How do we recognize these and put them in their appropriate place? We've never been here before. Can I even trust my emotions?

We would begin to hope we were coming out of it. And then the ferocious beast would laugh at us. *How dare you not believe me? How dare you think you have more power than I?*

Death by suicide became a huge concern. Because of the isolation of learning at home? Because of the over-abundance of poison on social media? Because of the mortality surrounding everyone? Because of the confusion of this unimaginable presence surrounding us every day, when we woke up, when we talked with others, when we said our prayers at night? Whatever the reason, it was an added tragedy on top of the cataclysmic devastation around the world.

Just as we thought we were coming out of the original Covid (Corona Virus 19), there came the first variant: Delta. It raged a more deadly and vicious blow to the world than the original virus. It was followed by Omicron, which was less deadly but more contagious. A smaller percentage died, but when you have millions more getting sick, the number of those who died was barely affected.

It would be insensitive of me to list any of the good things that came out of the past two years in light of the masses we lost. The parents who loved us, the grandparents who gave us hugs till we burst, the sisters we constantly confided in, the brothers who protected us, the employer who promised security and a place to be with other people, and the friends who were always a text away. The ones who prayed for us, listened to us, held us up and were always there for us. Until they weren't. How do we even contemplate the positives from this monster in that light?

And yet there were good things. Business owners helped each other set up delivery and pickup services. For some, they actually flourished once they transitioned. Will churches ever give up streaming services online? For people who are unable to attend in person, for whatever reason, that will continue to be a blessing for years to come.

At my college, we saved thousands of trees by going paperless. We learned we could work from home and be productive. If I felt a sniffle coming on, instead of staying at work, possibly exposing others and losing my vacation days, I could work from home. I mean, I wasn't that sick.

We learned to communicate with the world through Zoom, Facetime, and all the other ways to be with our loved ones and coworkers, without exposing them to illness and even death. A group of my friends began Zooming once a week. Three years later, we still do. It has brought six more people into my life on an almost daily basis to support me, advise me, listen to me, and laugh together at all the silly things we say and do.

As a writer, I mourned not getting together with those who helped me become a better writer. Zoom kept that going also. Some people found it less of a hassle to Zoom than to have to put something nice on, take the time to drive to and from, and stay way too long chit-chatting afterward if we had other things that needed to get done. It was easier to extricate from a Zoom meeting than an in-person meeting.

Perhaps the biggest, dare I say the most anticipated, event for me was Sunday, December 13, 2020. I knew this was the day.

The whole world did. So I set my alarm. I was not going to miss it. The first trucks with the vaccines were scheduled to leave that day. It was early in the morning and I glued myself to the television waiting, waiting, waiting for the first truck to begin rolling. I must have not been the only one feeling the unbelievable anticipation, as the networks carried this live, for hours.

We watched as an assembly line of people pulled the precious vials from out of the freezers at the Pfizer plant and onto the refrigerated trucks. One by one the trucks were filled with the lifesaving vaccination. And then we waited. Are those wheels on that truck in front moving? Not yet. I was going to stay and watch as long as it took. Finally, as the large crowd of people along the road who were lucky enough to witness began yelling, we saw a truck begin to move. Then another. Then another. I watched as every truck left the plant and began their journey to Montana, Florida, Illinois, and Nebraska. Everywhere. And then I watched as the commentators turned their attention to the airports as the precious cargo was loaded onto specially outfitted airplanes.

Due to sensitive storage needed, there were 636 specially chosen distribution centers to receive the vaccines. From there they were shipped to hospitals and nursing homes first, followed by pharmacies and other distribution sites within each state. I was jubilant that my youngest daughter, who worked at the hospital, was in the first round of vaccinations. She was safe. Our household was safer. It was the biggest vaccination effort the world has ever known. It is a day I will never forget. The hope. The possible end to this nightmare. The joy.

Now it's 2023. It seems we are out of the worst of it. The question becomes have enough of us been exposed that our bodies will be able to handle future cases? Maybe we get sick. But hopefully most of us will be able to weather the few days of illness and come out on the other side.

What about those who have Long Covid? More so than the typical flu, the yearly cold, or typical human illnesses, Covid planted its foot on many for a long time. Will it eventually lift from those who continue to suffer months, even years, later?

Have we learned? Can we trust our elected officials to get it right next time? Will they keep the things they did well and fix the things that sent us backward? So much of this was impossible to predict. Is that an inevitability of any pandemic?

I hesitate to say goodbye to Covid and jinx it. But I believe . . . I'm confident the worst is behind us. I am grateful beyond belief that I'm one of the lucky ones to survive. That my family is safe, still employed, and moving forward.

I hope we remember to pray always for children and grandchildren, mothers and fathers, sisters, brothers, and friends who lost loved ones, as they have lost a future of memories, relationships, and security because of this beast. It is impossible to fathom the struggle of so much death and loss. I hope I, no we, remember to pray for them for years to come. Three years later, like many, my eldest child still grieves.

I pray that we will never experience another time like we've had since early March 2020. But if we do, I'm certain that the love and compassion of people will support and come to the aid of all. Because that's what we did. That's what we do. We rise to goodness when bad things happen. As with any tragedy, many will tell you that as catastrophic as it can be, the hearts of so many people help alleviate the pain. People are good, if given the chance. Should this happen again, I hope that, in spite of the pain, I remember and see the resilience, the generosity, and the kindness in all.

Excerpts
from a
Novel

Sandi Lyons Hoard • Alma, NE

Parallels

Part Three: Planning Her Past

Friday morning Lilly Walker entered the Vintage Coin Shop on Central Avenue in Kearney. It was her day off from the Alma library and she was intent on finding American currency from 1911 and a few years prior to that. Preparing for her adventures in the 1911 parallel, she was looking forward to spending time with Gran Sophia and Grandpa Vic. What she was experiencing must be similar to what Rod Serling describes at the beginning of each Twilight Zone episode: "a fifth dimension, beyond that which is unknown to man . . . a dimension as vast as space and as timeless as infinity." If anyone asked her how she was able to waffle between 1971 and 1911, she wouldn't be able to explain it. She didn't understand it herself. Most likely she'd be committed to a state hospital for the infirm. No matter the outcome, upon discovery it wouldn't make it any less real.

~ ~ ~ ~ ~

Nigel Walker rapidly bounced his right knee at his desk at the Aurora library. Something was amiss in this facility and he couldn't quite put a finger on it. It wasn't because of Lilly's departure, she'd left two weeks ago. The other clerks should be used to her absence by now. He sensed an unrest, discord, but why? What was going on?

Rising, he walked to Simon Hanes' office just down the hall from his. Before knocking Nigel read the name plaque on the door with irritation. "Simon Hanes: Assistant Director." What a pompous fool. No one else had a name plaque on their door, not even him, and he was the director of the whole facility.

Maybe this isn't such a good idea, to enter the office of the man he was sure was Lilly's lover. Could he be civil or would he have to fight the urge to punch Simon in the nose? Would he end up bragging that he'd been with Lilly just days ago? No, this isn't wise at all. Take time and cool down, inhale deeply, step back. He rapped two knuckles on Simon's door and ignored his subconscious' warning, his only voice of reason.

Without waiting for an invitation to enter, Nigel pushed Simon's door open. "What's going on in this library that everyone shuts up when I enter the commons area?"

Simon's brows arched and his mouth formed a small "O" as if surprised. His golden blond hair was shaggy and brushed the color of his button-down shirt. He stood and moved away from behind his desk. "I'm not sure what you're referring to, Nigel."

Nigel took two steps forward. Simon shuffled back and bumped into a filing cabinet adjacent to his desk.

"Simple question, Simon," Nigel began, his voice sounding unreasonably angry even to himself. "What's going on? Are the clerks afraid of me? Why? What have I supposedly done to receive such a response?"

Simon straightened his blue-grey tie nervously, then adjusted his glasses. "Umm," he started. "Perhaps it's your presentation—"

"Presentation?" Nigel interrupted Simon. "Presentation of what? My expectations for everyone that works at this library including you?"

"Partly," Simon said. He hesitated as if gauging Nigel's response.

Hands planted on his hips, Nigel nodded. "Go ahead. Spit it out."

"Well, Nigel, presentation . . . of your . . ." Simon wrung his hands, obviously trying to find the right words. "Your anger . . . it shows. And quite frankly, it scares us."

"Scares 'us'? Is this collective? Meaning everyone or just a few?"

"Everyone. Ever since . . . what I mean to say is—"

"Since Lilly left?" Nigel interrupted again and took another step forward.

Simon pressed his back against the filing cabinet while nodding.

"Presentation of my emotions, my anger, is causing the rift in the library?"

"Yes, so much anger. Which I don't understand. It's my understanding that you wanted her gone—"

"What do you know about it?" Nigel said raising his voice, pointing an index finger at Simon. "This is rich coming from you."

"Lilly is my friend—"

"Friend? Lover you mean."

Simon stared at him aghast. Then he laughed. Nigel lunged forward and Simon outstretched his arms to ward off Nigel's advancement. "Lilly and I are not and have never been lovers."

"Yeah, right." Nigel raised one fisted hand. "Why was it that every time I came out of my office, you two were deep in conversation? And don't lie to me, you weasel!"

"We were talking about you. You wanted a divorce with no explanation. It devastated her. She loves you more than her own life."

Nigel's raised hand dropped to his side. He pulled in a quick breath. "Go on."

"You've been very angry for months now. It's as if you didn't actually want the divorce. Which is confusing to her."

"That's none of your business."

"I agree, Nigel. But I'm merely answering your questions."

"I see. Something to ponder." Nigel opened the door. He glanced at Simon, wanting to lash out, to still punch him. Maybe he needed to ask Lilly. "I'm leaving for the day. Not sure if I'll be in tomorrow." He stepped out of the doorway, turned, and pointed at Simon. "Your hair is too long. You need to get it cut. Soon."

Walking back to his office, Nigel collected his jacket and keys and headed out the door. He was going to Alma and having it out with Lilly.

~ ~ ~ ~ ~

Lilly left the coin shop, a blue velvet bag of vintage money clasped firmly in one hand. The elderly gentleman in the Vintage Coin Shop had had a few early twentieth century dollars and coins. Enough that if she used the ten and five dollar bills to get change in 1911 that it should suffice for a long stay.

Divine intervention was driving her to decide about this drastic change in her life. After tossing and turning all night, dreaming about going back to 1911 and not returning, Lilly determined that it was meant to be. Why had God presented this opportunity if she couldn't explore it with the possibility of remaining? While she drove back to Alma, a mental list was forming for what she'd need to do. Find a place to live in 1911. Sell her car, she just couldn't leave it in the driveway of Gran's house. Giving up her job at the library was a tougher decision to make. What if she asked for time off and tried living in 1911 first? What if she kept her job and lived between the two parallels? This life choice was doable, she was certain. For as long as the brass plate held the magical quality to transport her between 1971 and 1911.

Pulling into her driveway, Lilly took her bag of vintage money and her purse and went inside. She set all of it on the kitchen counter, then headed to the attic. Quickly sorting through Gran's and Great-Gran's clothing in the trunks, she selected a few outfits with coordinating reticules that could fit inside a bag. A black carpet bag with red stitching hanging over a nondescript trunk on the west wall caught her attention. That would work perfectly. She put all the items into the carpet bag and went downstairs to her bedroom. She slipped into a long navy skirt with a timeless light-blue blouse and her black boots.

Now she felt ready for exploring 1911. The only obstacle left was how to enter the library with the carpet bag. How would she explain it? Not wasting another second Lilly hoisted her shoulder-strap purse over her shoulder, grasped the handles of the carpet bag, and opened her front door. She tensed. Nigel stood on the front porch, one hand raised to ring the doorbell.

"What are you doing here?"

Nigel lowered his hand to his side. "We need to talk."

"About what, Nigel?" She repositioned her purse. "We're divorced now."

"Were you sleeping with Simon?" Anger lined his face and his nostrils flared.

Tempted to laugh she drew in a quick breath. "Not that it's any of your business because we're divorced now."

"This isn't a joke, Lilly. Did you sleep with Simon?"

"I repeat, we're divorced now."

"Damn it, Lilly! Why can't you answer my question instead of sidestepping it?"

She set the carpet bag down and put her purse on top of it. Resigning herself to the fact that he wasn't going away without an answer, she sighed.

"Did you sleep with Simon while we were married?" His eyes were wide with visible anxiety. "Did you?"

"No," she finally answered. "I've never been with any other man, Nigel. You were my first and up to today the last man I've been with." Tears popped into her lashes, catching her by surprise. "Happy now?" She wiped the tears away with an index finger.

He stepped closer and she moved back against the closed door. If he touched her right now she'd be putty in his hands. She couldn't allow a repeat of the other night that he was here. It was too easy to give into the deep love she still felt for him.

"If that's all you needed, Nigel, I have to go."

He said nothing, just stared at her with that soft gaze of his that she knew all too well.

"Are we done now, Nigel?" She plopped one hand on her hip. "I need to go." Picking up her purse and the carpet bag, she stepped around him.

"When can we talk more, Lilly?" His voice was just above a murmur as he slid a hand in at her waist.

Lilly shifted away from him. "Call and make an appointment instead of just showing up at lunch time. Bye, Nigel."

She walked toward the library, leaving Nigel gawking at her. Had she finally grown a backbone? Entering through the east door, she scanned the large main room, willing her eyes to adjust to the shadowy interior.

Glory looked up from the log on the circulation desk and smiled. “Hi, Lilly. Enjoying your day off?”

“I am,” Lilly replied. “Just wanting to search through some of the older newspapers to find articles on my gran and other family that lived here.”

“Good luck on your search.” Glory smiled again before returning her attention back to the log.

“Thanks,” Lilly said and went to the magic table. Removing the plate with her free hand, she sucked in a deep breath as nausea crept in and the air around her started swirling. When the nausea and the chaos calmed down, Lilly glanced around to ascertain what parallel she was in. Two ladies were at the circulation desk, both attired in floor-length dresses. She’d met these two women at the library’s 1911 opening day, but she couldn’t recall their names. She slid the carpet bag under the table and went to the circulation desk.

A middle-aged gentleman in a brown plaid three piece suit was thumbing through one of the card catalog drawers. He looked up with obvious confusion and repositioned his straw hat to a jaunty side tilt. “Beth, I’m lost here.”

The tall, thin lady walked around the circulation desk. “I’ll be right with you,” she said to Lilly as she moved toward the gentleman.

“Jerry, what are you searching for again?”

The two murmured while Lilly waited patiently.

"Lilly, right?" Beth asked from behind her. "We met at the opening."

"Yes," Lilly said. "I was wondering if Sophia works today."

Beth pushed her wire-rimmed glasses up onto the bridge of her nose. "Mrs. Jensen will be in at one. Would you like to leave a message for her?" She grabbed a slip of paper and a stubby pencil and held them out to Lilly.

"No, I'll come back this afternoon," Lilly said. "Thank you."

She walked back to the magical table and picked up the carpet bag. Her first stop was the local newspaper in the hopes of finding an apartment. Opening the front door, an ad on the bulletin board in the small lobby caught her attention.

Garage apartment for rent with outside stairway. Clean and furnished. $2 a month. Stop by for a looksee at 811 First Street. Ask for Meredith.

"This is unbelievable," Lilly murmured. Just like that, an ad for an apartment was right in front of her. She took the ad down and stuffed it inside her reticule. If her memory was correct, 811 First was on the block west of her house—Gran's house, she amended.

Lilly headed to the address to a one-and-a-half-story clapboard bungalow. A two-story garage sat far back on a dirt driveway and was larger than the house. Hesitating, she asked herself if she was really going to do this, remain in 1911? If even for a little while, her answer came back affirmative. If the table and brass plate retained their magical qualities, she might possibly have the best of both worlds. Time to spend with her Gran Sophia and Grandpa Vic and her great-grandparents whom she'd never really known. And the unique opportunity to become acquainted with her mother while she was growing up. Those five people were strong magnets for leaving her life in 1971 behind. Lilly approached the front door, pulled the ad out of her reticule and knocked softly.

After a few seconds the door slowly creaked open. An older woman of about sixty with fading red hair stood on the other side, swallowed in shadows. She was short, no more than five-foot tall. “May I help you?” she asked in a voice that sounded more like a bird warbling.

Lilly held up the ad. “I’m interested in the garage apartment. Are you Meredith?”

“Yes, I am.” She extended a hand. “Meredith Sorenson. And you are?”

“Lilly Walker. I’m new to town.” She clasped Meredith’s hand and gave it a quick shake.

“Do you have any references, since you’re new to town?”

Panic floated up, Lilly pushed it back down. “I was married and lived with my husband. But now he’s gone and I’m making a fresh start.” She found it scary that she could tell a half-lie so easily.

Meredith raised her brows and pursed her lips as she studied Lilly. “Do you know anyone in town yet?” Her voice was so high and childlike that Lilly had to suppress a smile.

“I’ve met Sophia at the library and her husband Vic.”

“Well,” Meredith said as a smile spread across her face. “Sophia and Vic and her parents are dear friends of mine.” She gestured to Lilly to come in. “Let’s get the key and I’ll show you the apartment.”

Lilly followed her through her home, which was decorated with bright red and yellow curtains against pale yellow walls.

The color scheme matched Meredith's apparent sunny disposition. Taking a skeleton key off a peg by the back door, Meredith led Lilly outside and up the flight of stairs to the garage apartment.

The apartment was comprised of four rooms: a living room, with furniture that was worn but clean, a kitchen, bath, and bedroom with a four poster bed. The apartment was small, but it was perfect in both size and rent for Lilly's plan to live between the parallels.

"I'll take it. That is, if you're willing to rent it to me."

"Absolutely," Meredith said. "It's two dollars a month, to be paid the first of each month."

Lilly dug two vintage one dollar coins from her reticule and handed them to Meredith. "When can I move in?"

"Any time you're ready," Meredith said and handed the key to Lilly.

"Thank you!"

Lilly and Meredith visited for a while. When Meredith went back to her bungalow, Lilly stashed the carpet bag in the bedroom. Heading down the staircase, she walked to the library. Sophia was standing behind the circulation desk. She smiled but it didn't seem genuine, it didn't reach her eyes. Lilly entered the children's area and selected *The Secret Garden* with the hope of checking it out. *The Time Machine* sitting on an end cap in adult fiction caught her eye. She picked it up and thumbed through it. She hadn't read it since high school, which had been more than two decades ago.

Sophia approached her.

"I just rented a one bedroom garage apartment," Lilly said. "From Meredith Sorenson."

"Meredith's a close family friend. It's amazing that you found a place so quickly."

"Thank you." Lilly held out the two books. "Can I check these two books out now?"

"I'm sorry," Sophia said. "We only allow patrons to check out one book at a time."

"Oh, okay." Lilly handed *The Time Machine* to Sophia with a sense of unease.

Instead of taking it, Sophia clasped her hands and stared at Lilly, which increased her nervousness. "Who exactly are you? How can you appear then disappear without leaving this library?" She pointed to the magical table. "What time warp have you traveled from?"

Lilly swallowed past the lump that had lodged in her throat. How could she explain? Was this gift of visiting her gran going to end so soon? She moved toward the magical table but was stopped by Sophia's hand on her arm.

"Answer me, Lilly. Who are you? Where did you come from?"

Tears trickled down Lilly's cheeks. "I'm your granddaughter," she said barely above a whisper.

"What?" Sophia said incredulously. "I don't have grandchildren, my daughter's only five. What cruelty are you playing here?"

"It's true." Lilly took another step toward the table. "I'm your granddaughter. I was born August 21, 1931." She hesitated as Sophia gasped. "I worked at the Aurora library and recently started working here."

"You work at this library?" Sophia shook her head. "That can't be." Shaking her head again she pointed at Lilly. "What year did you start?"

"October 1971." Lilly wiped at her tears with a fingertip.

"1971! That would make me eighty-four years old. Preposterous! I don't believe you! Who are you?"

Lilly kept the information concerning Sophia's death in 1971 to herself. No one wanted to know when they die.

"I'm telling you the truth, Gran," Lilly said as she placed the metal plaque on the magical table. The air shifted and nausea started rumbling in her gut.

"Lilly!" Her gran called out as Lilly started paralleling back to 1971. "Lilly! Come back so we can discuss this!"

To be continued . . .

Faith Colburn • North Platte, NE

Invasion

This excerpt is from a novel in progress. The narrator is a Nebraska farm girl who took an administrative job at the US Embassy in Paris just four months before the Nazis arrived.

~ ~ ~ ~ ~

On June 10, the Parisians burned petroleum reserves on the outskirts as the last of the government left a city encircled by the Wehrmacht. When I went to the shelter that night, an oily cloud hung over everything. The sharp smell of burning oil made me cough. I tried to write home under the dim, flickering light underground.

Dear folks,

I'm sure you've already learned that the Germans have surrounded Paris. By the time you receive this, Paris will undoubtedly be occupied. Just remember, I'll be safe because the United States is neutral. American-occupied buildings are marked so they can be identified from the air. The embassy bomb shelter is even armored against poison gas.

By the time you get this, you will also know about Dunkirk. I can't say enough about British resourcefulness and willingness to step up. When Hitler's Wehrmacht had masses of British and Belgian and French troops surrounded with their backs to the sea and not enough ships to evacuate them, the Admiralty called on *citizens* with boats. The heroism of those ordinary people, with only fishing boats and lifeboats and barges and ferries, braving mines, bombs, torpedoes, and the ruthless strafing of the Luftwaffe, makes me cry. They will *never* be defeated!

Their heroism is in stark contrast with the government here. Instead of gearing up for war, French leadership is playing the blame game. The right wing (I think that's anyone who is not a socialist or a communist or a Jew) blames the "warmongers" for getting France into the war instead of accommodating Hitler. They particularly hate Leon Blum, a Jew, who is the former Prime Minister and who has tried and tried to prepare France for Nazi invasion. A military tribunal has tried communist deputies to parliament and sentenced them to five years—then changed the sentence to death for treason.

Almost a month ago, current Prime Minister Paul Reynaud ordered that Paris be defended at all cost, and military commander Maxime Weygand forbade civilian evacuation—too late. Then, the government ordered all men between eighteen and fifty to evacuate, in order to deny Hitler their forced labor for his war industries—also too late.

Just today, Churchill flew in for a conference. The French, mostly led by Pétain, are determined to apply for armistice. Churchill suggested withdrawing all remaining armies and government personnel to Brittany from which they could evacuate by sea to North Africa. He got a resounding "No!"

It appears to me that France is about to become a German colony. Imagine the resources Hitler can bleed out of France. I've only been here about four months, but the idea of Nazis walking the streets of this beautiful city breaks my heart.

Nora

On June 12, although no one told the citizens, the French government declared Paris an open city, meaning that it would receive no defense. We could hear cannon fire from somewhere to the north, but no sounds of conflict nearby. On the thirteenth, Bullitt had his last war council with Churchill while we struggled to carry out our evacuation plan and prepare last-minute documents for as many people as we could, all while packing up bales of paperwork as well as machines—typewriters, coders, everything. Sarah had already evacuated to Bordeaux with most of our staff, while I would "man the barricades" with a skeleton crew.

When I stepped outside that night at about midnight, Paris seemed deserted. I'd managed to have dinner earlier, but only one café remained open on the avenue. It was closing. From now on we might have to depend upon the embassy kitchen—assuming we could get provisions.

Nobody strolled the Champs Élysée. Lately, black-out curtains had covered all the windows, and no lights reflected off the oily cloud above the city. Smoke from the burning oil reserves made my eyes water as I stood on the threshold waiting for them to adjust to the dark. We all knew the Wehrmacht had the city surrounded and that they would overrun Paris in the morning.

I heard metal clips clanking against the flagpoles at the corners of the Place de la Concorde and an occasional snap as the tri-colors caught a breath of breeze. Refugees from farmland to the north must have lost livestock as they passed through. On the Left Bank, I heard sheep, including some high-pitched bleats from lambs calling their mamas. I even heard a cowbell or two. Nothing seemed improbable anymore.

I saw an occasional flash and heard distant artillery fire. Counsellor Robert Murphy and Commander Roskoe Hillenkotter entered the embassy's iron gates as I turned back inside to try and find a corner where I could curl up for a nap. Then the great bells of Notre Dame tolled Matins, the first hour of prayer in the holy day. Bong. Bong. Bong. Bong. Bong. Bong. Bong. Bong. Bong. Bong. Bong. Bong.

Maisie Habron-Wach • Lincoln, NE

Brave Charlie and the Awful Quiet

Sunday, September 4, 1955

The brakes hissed as the rickety bus grumbled to a stop. People hauled themselves up all around her with faint groans and commiserations about the cloudy weather, but Charlie hesitated. The street outside didn't seem to be the same one from her map.

She smoothed the wrinkled paper on her lap, nervously studying it.

"You in the right place, Ma'am?"

Charlie looked up to see a wide Chesire grin looming over her. A skinny man with short combed-over hair was leaning over the seat, peering at her map. He straightened up and nodded out the window.

"You're looking for Warston, right?"

He let his hip fall against the seat in front of Charlie, rolling up his sleeves and raising an eyebrow. His light blue cotton shirt was peppered with smudges of black grease and oil; that and the faint smell of gasoline revealed to Charlie that this friendly-looking man probably worked at a mechanic's shop.

She *hoped* that it was the same mechanic's shop that was located around the corner from where she was headed, assuming she could find it. Before she embarked on her journey, Charlie had carefully studied maps of this little town known as Warston, but somehow she was already completely lost.

Charlie smiled back at him, "Yes, I hope I'm on the right bus. I'm actually looking for Cardinal Street. Is this it?"

The man finished adjusting his sleeves and rested his dirty hands on his hips. "Yes, ma'am, *Miss America*, this is Cardinal Street. What brings you all the way here?"

Charlie cocked her head to the side, acknowledging his playful jibe at her accent. She knew that it was glaringly out of place compared to the muttering passengers that were still filing off the bus around them.

She nodded out the window. "Well, thank you, it just looks a bit different than on the map. I thought there was supposed to be a train station here and it had me a bit confused."

The man looked outside, dropping a bit of his chipper demeanor. "Well, there *was* one, until the Germans decided to wipe it off the map." He glanced down at her and patted the seat absentmindedly. "I'm sure you've seen it too."

Charlie sighed. She'd seen it too. It had been ten years since the end of the Second World War, but the scars were still visible everywhere you looked, especially here in England. Before she could answer, the man smiled broadly again and held out his hand.

"Well, where are my manners? Here we have a genuine American movie star in our humble little village, and I haven't even introduced myself. My name is Daniel Edwin, but please, I beg of you, call me '*Danno*.' I only hear 'Daniel' when I'm in trouble or, well, when I'm in trouble."

Taking his hand and laughing at his candor, Charlie responded, "It's nice to meet you, Danno. My name is Charlotte, but please call me '*Charlie*.'"

As she stood up, she looked at him over her glasses. "And by the way, I'm not a movie star."

Danno bowed dramatically. "And what a terrible shame that is, with a face like yours. Come on, I'll show you around town." He winked and heaved the bag that was directly above her in the overhead carriage. "This yours?"

When Charlie rolled her eyes and smiled, Danno clicked his tongue in fake admonishment. "What on earth do you have in here, my girl? A whole set of encyclopedias?"

He turned down the aisle and trotted down the stairs off the bus. He called out over his shoulder as Charlie followed him. "Don't tell me you're as clever as you are pretty."

Charlie rolled her eyes again at his flirtation. "Well I wouldn't say that but—"

"Oh and a modest girl too!"

"You're too kind." Charlie laughed as Danno helped her down the stairs. "Thank you very much for your help."

"And you are too welcome, my dear." Danno winked at her again. Normally, his attitude and affections would crawl along Charlie's skin like sandpaper, but she felt unusually at ease with him, as if he were an old friend meeting her after a long time away.

"Seriously though, Charlie my friend, what on *earth* have you got in here?"

"My glass set."

"Your vision must be *abysmal*."

Charlie reached for her bag, taking it gingerly as Danno put his hands in his pockets and frowned with raised eyebrows.

She held the bag against her chest, hoping that its contents hadn't been damaged on her journey. "Not *glasses*, my glass instruments. I'm a chemist, and I've been instructed to bring my own materials."

Amused disbelief tugged at the corner of Danno's mouth. "*You're* a chemist, Miss Charlie?"

Charlie cocked her head and mirrored Danno's expression by way of answer. He held up his hands in mock surrender. "Not a problem with that, just surprised, that's all. Not too many ladies at Dawnkester Industries, I'm sure, unless they're secretaries. I assume that's where you're headed then? That big, ugly industrial dung heap?"

Charlie nodded, lowering the bag to her side. "Yes, but first I need to stop by—oh what was it—Red Roof House? It's supposed to be on this street and I—"

"You're joking! Charlie my friend, don't tell me we're going to be *neighbors* as well as shockingly attractive best mates?"

A laugh bubbled in Charlie's throat. Despite his blatant extroversion, she couldn't help but find this ridiculous man to be very charming. "It would seem so, Mr. Danno. Is Mrs. Marleen Frish your landlady too?"

By way of response, Danno spun to the side and scooped his arm under Charlie's with the practiced ease of a ballet dancer. He led her down the street as he gestured widely. His arm swept side to side like a circus announcer, pointing out the noteworthy elements of his little town.

"Of course, dear old Madame Frish is simply the most excellent collector of rent you will find in all of Warston. She is very efficient and will never miss a single penny, or a single deadline."

He carried on with his tour, guiding Charlie easily through the crowded cobblestone street.

"Off to your left you will see the Black Cat, the best place in town for some food or drink, not that a proper lady like yourself would be interested in the latter. And back that direction is my own humble employer, Greasy Jim's, the best mechanic in town."

Charlie laughed. Danno continued strolling through town, slowing his stride to match Charlie's as she struggled with her heavy bag. Rainwater from earlier that morning had collected in the ruts of the cobblestone, and as Charlie was navigating a rather large puddle, she caught her toe on an uneven brick, causing her to trip. Her breath froze in her throat as Danno narrowly pulled her up in time to avoid her bag being smashed against the street.

"Easy there," he chuckled. "Too used to the smooth, smooth streets of *Cali*-fornia?"

Charlie laughed back, catching her breath. "Thank you. Can't say that I *am* used to that. Dirt roads are more like it."

"Oh? Not a city girl then? Don't tell me you're a *cowboy*!"

"Who's a cowboy? Sure, not you, Danno. You're too precious for that!"

A woman's voice called out from one of the little shops they had passed. Charlie turned around to see a lady about her height trotting toward them, gracefully skipping over the bumps in the road like sunlight over an uneven path. In the split second before she spoke again, Charlie decided that *sunlight* was indeed the correct description for her. Bottle blonde and bright eyed, the woman was more American movie star than Charlie; as a matter of fact, she wouldn't have been surprised if she claimed to be Marilyn Monroe's twin sister.

She waved a slender pale hand at the pair, urging them to stop and wait for her. Her heels clicked on the stone, and she approached them with surprising speed despite her tight skirt. Danno lolled his head back to look up at the clouds, feigning exasperation at the woman.

"Oh goodness *gracious*, Penny, couldn't you let me make *one* friend without you butting in? This is *my* very, very, very good-friend-that-I-met-five-minutes-ago, Miss Charlie from America."

The woman cupped her face in her dainty hands, gushing at Charlie, "You can absolutely *not* keep her to yourself! I heard that we had someone new coming to Dawnkester, but when they said 'Charlie' I thought—my goodness! You're even better than a *boy*!"

Her voice was breathy and sweet; Charlie admonished herself internally when the phrase *child-like* popped into her mind. However, the woman beamed with such joy that Charlie doubted it would have bothered her if she had known what her first impression had been.

"Come on now! We aren't *all* that bad!" Danno scoffed in mock indignation.

"Oh shut up, you! Sure, yes you are!" Penny waved a red-manicured hand, dismissing Danno as she beamed at Charlie. "I'm so glad to meet you, Charlie!"

The woman, Penny, spoke in such a way that you could hear her smile before it ever crossed her face, and Charlie instantly adored her. Her Irish accent had faded slightly, but the charm hadn't.

Charlie carefully set down her bag and, adjusting her glasses, held her hand out to Penny. "It's very nice to meet you, *Penny*, yeah? My name is Charlie—well, you know that. Really, it's Charlotte Ablecek. Danno was just showing me to my new apartment."

Penny took Charlie's hand in both of hers. As she glanced up at Danno, realization dawned across her face. "Oh my *goodness*! Are you at the Red Roof House too?"

"Yeah, Penny, she's staying with Frish," Danno nodded quickly at the ecstatic blonde woman, cutting her off before addressing Charlie. "Come along now, Charlie my friend, mustn't hang about with peasants."

He sniffed and turned sharply away from Penny, leading Charlie down the street. She called back toward her new acquaintance, "It was very nice to meet you!"

"And it was nice to meet you!" Penny shifted her weight, clip-clopping her heels on the cobblestone like an excited show horse, "Don't let that thick-headed idiot lead you in the wrong direction!"

Danno leaned down and whispered in Charlie's ear as she strutted away from Penny. "Pay no attention to the riff raff, let alone *bartenders*." He winked at her as Penny shook her head and disappeared into the Black Cat.

Charlie smiled to herself. *What wonderfully strange people.*

The two of them continued down the shop-lined street until Danno suddenly stopped. He gestured broadly toward a red door so skinny and so faded that Charlie almost walked right past it. As she craned her neck upward to take in the stack of grimy-looking windows that towered above the surrounding shops, Danno announced proudly, "Behold, your new home!"

He bowed dramatically, stepping away from her to pull open the creaky door. Charlie peered inside. It was dark and narrow. A collection of paintings, sconces, dead flowers, and other bizarre assorted knick-knacks coated the walls. It created a strange illusion of depth, and Charlie found herself holding back, as if she were respectfully admiring a museum exhibit.

Or as if I were leaning away from a deep canyon covered in sharp rocks.

Danno smiled to himself as he took in Charlie's fascination. "Well, jump to, *Miss America*, unless you'd prefer to sleep on the sidewalk."

He tossed his chin in toward the cramped hallway and wordlessly took her bag, allowing her to squeeze herself inside. Charlie tiptoed sideways along the hallway until she practically fell forward into a much more open room. A long, pitted, and worn wooden table took up most of the floor space. Every inch of the floor was covered in an old red Persian rug. Danno appeared behind her.

"This is the most important room in the house, Charlie my friend."

Charlie pushed her glasses up her nose. "How's that?"

Danno winked at her. "It's where we *eat*."

He said it with such stifled glee that Charlie rolled her eyes and smiled as a new voice called out from the doorway across the room.

"What'd you find outside, Daniel?"

A small woman, somewhere in her sixties, peered at Charlie from over an armful of what appeared to be absolutely gargantuan zucchini. She wore a red-and-white striped house dress with a white apron. Charlie did a double take.

It was a *black* apron, but it was coated in layers and layers of flour, streaked by countless passes of the woman's fingers. Her graying hair was pulled back from her face, revealing her suspicious expression. She nodded at Danno, urging a confession.

Danno, laughing silently, patted Charlie on the shoulder. "Madame Frish, *le poisson*, this is our American celebrity, Miss Charlie."

The woman, whom Charlie could now assume was Mrs. Frish, stared at her suspiciously, "*Miss* Charlie? Darling, *you're* the chemist?"

Charlie was getting used to this reaction, but she was wary of what came next. She had written to Mrs. Frish six months ago by the recommendation of her future employer—who also believed that Charlie Ablecek was a man—without mentioning her full name.

When she applied for the job at Dawnkester Industries, it had been on a whim. Surely this chemical factory would investigate her university, Mercy College of Detroit, wouldn't they?

Naturally they would discover that it was one of the *only* institutes of higher education in the entire country that allowed female students? Surely they would contact her professors, her current employers, her coworkers? Certainly at least *one* of them would mention that Charlie was, well, *Charlie*?

She had been wrong. Either someone at Dawnkester Industries did not mind that Charlie had been one of only four *women* in her graduating class, or they couldn't be bothered to investigate her. Whichever it was, as soon as she received the letter offering her a job, another letter fell from the envelope. It instructed her to contact Mrs. Marleen Frish, of 2400 Cardinal Street, Warston, for lodging.

And so she did. Now she stood here in her dining room, extending her hand to say hello.

Mrs. Frish still stared at her incredulously. "Charlie? Able-seck?"

"Able-*check*, yes, that's me!" Charlie tried to respond as brightly as she could. She still wasn't sure how her new landlady was going to react to being deceived, intentionally or not.

Mrs. Frish walked forward into the dining room and dumped the zucchinis onto the table. She glanced over Charlie's shoulder at Danno. Charlie didn't turn around, but she hoped that her new friend was silently vouching for her.

Mrs. Frish sniffed, briskly turning the conversation to business. "Well then, now that you're here, we have things to discuss. You *are* the Charlie Able-*check* that I've been corresponding with, yes? The one hired by Dawnkester?"

She raised an eyebrow as she started sorting out the vegetables on the dining table. Her sun-spotted hands deftly spun and rotated the green plants, quickly scanning them for spots of rot or insect damage.

"Yes," Charlie said. "*Charlotte* Ablecek. I didn't mean to deceive you, but I wasn't sure I'd be able to get a job with my full name."

"Ain't that the Lord's solemn truth." Mrs. Frish looked up at her, finished with her sorting. "They'll ask you to take a man's job during the war, but then they'll tell you you're not fit for it when they come back." She headed for the kitchen. "Come on then, we've got things to talk about."

Charlie obeyed and followed Mrs. Frish into a shockingly clean kitchen. In direct contrast to the rest of the house, this room was immaculate. Pots were hung on the wall in order of increasing height; spoons and other utensils were sorted by some system unknown to Charlie in spotless containers, carefully arranged along the massive countertops. Mrs. Frish dumped the carefully selected zucchini into the sink and called over her shoulder to Charlie.

"So, you know what your rent covers then?"

Mrs. Frish's voice was brisk and business-like but not unkind. She got to work swiftly peeling the vegetables in the sink. She glanced back over her shoulder.

"The meals and such?"

Charlie cleared her throat, trying to sound confident. "Oh yes, you mentioned that the rent covered meals, room and board, and transportation to the bus station."

"That's right. I'm glad Daniel didn't lose you on the way."

Charlie almost burst out laughing. So Danno *did* know who she was. Mrs. Frish must have sensed her stifling a chuckle because she snorted and shook her head.

"Oh, don't you mind him. He's a real practical joker. Never had a serious thought in his life. A flirt too."

She clicked her tongue disapprovingly but smiled. "There's another one of you coming tonight, so I'm sure everyone will be at dinner and you can meet all the other tenants then."

Charlie's interest was piqued. Another one? *Another new tenant?*

Mrs. Frish, who seemed to have an uncanny talent for reading Charlie's mind, answered the question as she moved on to peeling a pile of carrots.

"A policeman. He's joining us here in our sleepy little town today too. There'll be *much* talk."

Her tone was slightly self-mocking, as if she both disapproved of gossip but also indulged herself occasionally as well.

"You can put your things in the corner and I'll have Daniel take them up to your room later tonight. Your room is unlocked if you want to go in. Up the stairs, one landing up. Blue, number seven. The key is sitting on the wardrobe."

She gestured with her chin toward a doorway to her left and went back to work. Charlie tripped into a slight curtsey as she slipped by Mrs. Frish with a mumbled thank you. As she passed through the doorway, she heard a faint tut-tutting behind her.

She exhaled with a flushed face and peered up the stairway that greeted her. It was lit from above by a skylight and several old windows. She could see the sun begin to peek out from behind the clouds outside; the light beckoned her upward.

"What did she say, *one* landing up?" Charlie muttered to herself. "Or *two*?"

Charlie usually prided herself in her excellent memory, but the meeting with her new landlady had flustered her. Or more realistically, it had been the fact that she had been caught in a lie.

It wasn't really a lie, it was an omission of truth, she told herself as she climbed the sunlit stairs.

"Which is a *lie*, Charlie," she muttered aloud.

"What's a lie?" A boy's voice startled her.

Charlie spun around to see a boy spying out at her from the doorway she just passed by. His slight stature and round face suggested to Charlie that he was hovering just around the age of nine, but the cheeky grin on his face told her that he would probably try to convince her he was *actually* nine and a half.

"Oh hello." Charlie smiled. "Who are you?"

"Mike." He crept out from behind his door.

"It's nice to meet you, Mike. My name is Charlie." She paused "How old are you?"

He thought about it. "Ten . . . and a half."

Charlie chuckled to herself. "Wow, you're almost as old as me. I'm twenty-five."

"That's old. But not as old as my mom."

"I *am* old. You seem to know a lot of things, Mike. Do you happen to know where my room is?"

"Are you the policeman?" Mike was on the landing with Charlie now, and he stared up at her, seemingly content now that she was not a threat.

Charlie shook her head, "No, I'm the mad scientist."

The boy's eyes grew wide, "Really? Then you're just there," he pointed up to the first landing. "You're on the same floor as Penny."

"Oh I've met Penny. Is she a blonde lady?"

Mike just blushed and nodded.

Definitely the same Penny.

"Well, thank you so much for helping me, Mike. It was nice to meet you."

The little boy nodded again, clearly flustered at the mention of his pretty neighbor, and disappeared back into his room. As the door clicked closed, Charlie swore she heard someone step away from the door and whisper.

She shook her head and carried on up the stairs. She passed by Penny's room and stopped in front of her own door.

It was a blue door with a silver number seven in the middle. Leaning back, she studied Penny's door. It was red, with a gold number six. She leaned back further to look down at the ground floor to see Mike's door: green, number four. Charlie scanned the remaining doors and made mental note of their potential occupants. She hastily opened her own door, anxious to write down the information before she forgot. She clicked the door shut behind her, and before she even looked around, she dug around in her pocket and pulled out her little journal. Her handwriting was messy:

GROUND FLOOR
4 green (Mike) 5 black (Frish?)

FIRST FLOOR
6 red (Penny)
7 blue (me)

SECOND FLOOR
8 purple (Danno?)
9 yellow (policeman?)

Charlie shook her head at her penmanship before taking stock of her room. The light overhead illuminated the small space. It was helped by a small lamp in the corner, but the room was gloomy with the curtains drawn. A low but comfy-looking bed sat next to the window. Charlie crossed the room to look outside. She pulled aside the curtains to reveal a view of Cardinal Street. As she glanced down through the warped glass, she watched a short, well-dressed man approach the house. She stepped back, using the heavy curtains to shield herself from view.

The man wore a brown suit and round glasses. His hair was immaculately combed to the side over his square head. His nose was buried in his briefcase up until the very minute he reached the front door. When he looked up to enter the house, Charlie noted his age: approximately her own, or perhaps a few years give or take. The way he glanced around was familiar, like the schoolyard punching bag scanning his surroundings for a fist from above.

The movement seemed to be more habit than any actual perceived threat, because as he passed through the door, his nose was already back in his briefcase, digging through the papers inside.

Charlie stepped away from the window. She glanced over at the small writing desk across from the bed, accompanied by a matching wardrobe and dresser. A cynical person would call the room Spartan, but a person like Charlie would call it *neat*. Perfect, even. Everything in its place, but not sterile. She exhaled, satisfied with her lodgings.

Now time to sort out her employment. Her exhalation caught in her throat and she coughed. She wasn't looking forward to this meeting, and she had given herself too much time to sit around and worry about it. Glancing down at her watch, she cursed herself. Still another hour until she needed to leave.

She clicked her tongue three times. *What to do, what to do, what to do.* As much as she wanted to, Charlie knew she couldn't hide out in her room until it was time to walk over to Dawnkester Industries. She really ought to go downstairs and try to mingle with her new neighbors.

Charlie counted to three and crossed the room. She snatched up the key from the dresser, rushed herself through the door, and hurried down the staircase. As she reached the bottom, she was nearly bowled over by the short man with the square face that she had just been spying on a minute before.

He blinked at her owlishly from behind his enormous glasses. Charlie noted to herself that he had very sharp features, as if he had been sculpted by someone who had taken their time with his face but didn't have enough stone to make the rest of him, as he was barely Charlie's height.

"I beg your pardon," he said, scarcely sputtering out his words before another, now familiar, voice called out over him.

"Oh don't mind Braddy Wratty, he can't hurt you. As a matter of fact, you might knock him over yourself, Charlie my friend, and you're hardly heavier than your suitcase!"

Danno appeared right behind the short man, grinning ear to ear. The man rolled his eyes, but to Charlie's surprise, he barely contained a smile. If someone had called her "Braddy Wratty," she was sure she wouldn't be smiling, but just the same, the short man chuckled at the sound of Danno's voice behind him.

"And don't you mind *him*," he said, extending his hand toward Charlie. "He comes up with all kinds of horrendously asinine things to say, but you must take no notice because he hasn't the brain to do any better."

As Charlie shook his hand, he introduced himself. "My name is Bradley Wratman, even though that's near-impossible for this fool to remember."

"And you'd think I'd have the chance to learn it, wouldn't you,"—Danno winked at her—"seeing as I have to tuck him in every night."

Charlie cocked her head in surprised interest. Bradley Wratman spoke before Danno got the chance. "We are—due to my unfortunate financial circumstances—roommates."

"Well *I* just like to have someone around to pester!" Danno looked delighted at Bradley Wratman's feigned exhaustion, and Charlie smiled to herself. Their casual and good-natured bullying of each other put her at ease.

Bradley stood aside graciously for Charlie to pass them. "Please don't let us hold you up any longer. We'll see you at dinner then?"

Charlie nodded as she passed them, feeling like she was walking past a small shrubbery and a tall rickety pine, respectively, as she did so.

"Well, I'm in no hurry. I have no strong desire to go where I'm going." She flinched at her words. *No need to sound so gloomy.*

"Oh?" Danno raised an eyebrow as he looked down at her from the step above.

"Yes," she sighed, "I have to be off to let my boss know that I am, well—" she gestured down at her skirt.

"Absolutely gorgeous, my dear," interrupted Danno.

"Absolutely," agreed Bradley Wratman.

The two beamed down at her, although at his height from the stair above, Bradley barely had to incline his head.

"You're both very kind. I'll need that enthusiasm where I'm going." Charlie waved, faking more confidence than she felt.

Better be early than late, I suppose. Let's just get this over with.

"Well hold up now." Danno trotted down the stairs after her. "I'll go with you for moral support!"

"Oh there's no need—"

"Nonsense! The 'need' is that I am unbearably nosy and I *need* new gossip. Come on now, off we go!"

He practically danced down the stairs to slide his long skinny arm under hers. With a head shake and a wave, Bradley Wratman saw them off. Danno skipped deftly through the dining room, past the antique-encrusted hallway, and out the front door, dragging Charlie along with him.

Before she had the chance to catch her breath, the two of them were off again, trotting down the road in the opposite direction from the bus stop. They passed dozens of other little shops and businesses, all decorated with hand-painted wooden signs or hand-lettering on their glass storefronts. Everything about Warston seemed to be charming and she was excited to see more, but hopefully at a more reasonable pace.

"Danno," she panted, unable to keep up with his long strides, "slow down!"

"Oh come on now, I thought you were used to the fast life, Miss America!" He teased her, but slowed his pace.

They walked in silence for a few moments as Charlie slowed her breathing. As they neared the edge of town, the shops thinned and a great big building loomed on the horizon. It belched out black smoke and appeared to be covered in soot itself.

Giant bay doors were swung open wide, and canvas-covered trucks grumbled in and out, picking up and depositing deliveries. The closer they got, the more Charlie's stomach twisted.

What was she doing here? This place was a *real* chemical factory. They did *real* deals with the biggest names in the transatlantic industry. What was she, a graduate of a little women's college in the American Midwest, going to do here?

This was all a mistake, Charlie. You should hurry on home.

Danno must have sensed her slowing her pace, because for the first time since she met him, he spoke quietly. "Chin up, my friend. You don't have anything to worry about. They must have been impressed with whatever fancy college paperwork you sent them, or else they wouldn't have overlooked the fact that you're from an inferior country." He winked kindly at her. "I'll head up to the front with you."

"That's alright," Charlie said, sliding her arm away from his. "I think it'd be better if I went on my own."

She wasn't sure if she said it because she actually wanted to make a good impression by delivering herself to the front door or because she didn't want Danno to see her inevitably get fired at the front desk.

He nodded, bowing dramatically. "I'll see you at dinner then, m'lady." With that, he backed up, bounced up onto the balls of his feet and spun deftly to strut back toward midtown.

Charlie hesitated in the big gravel lot that they had been standing in. She watched the men inside the bay doors, dressed in blue denim overalls, unloading the trucks. The gravel crunched under her feet as bile rose in her throat.

Keep it together, Charlie. You can handle that much, can't you?

She tapped her thigh once, twice, three times. *And go. Go inside.*

Lucy Adkins • Lincoln, NE

Closing Down

Six weeks after Jason died, I was still pretty messed up—sleeping most of the time and letting things go—my appearance, the trailer, barely getting Michael off to school. Evenings after Michael went to bed, I drank glass after glass of wine and cried my eyes swollen. And I got pretty sick of myself.

But it was better, going back to work at the Quick Stop. One night Eddie and I were closing up, totaling up the gas sales, the snack items. I did that. Eddie turned off the overheads and we worked in the half light from the back room, that and the little glow from the coffeemakers, and it was nice working in that soft light, a little tired, the workday under my belt, and in the background, the hum of the refrigerators, the furnace clicking on and off. I was running a paper tab and there was the rustle of that and the swish of the broom as Eddie brushed the door mats.

He asked if we'd had a good day, and I said we had—over $1,700 in regular gas, $2,300 in diesel. He's the manager and keeps track of all that. Then there's the beer sales and what he calls the crunch and munch—all the potato chips and beef jerky and strawberry Twizzlers we sell. Candy bars. It can really add up.

Next I heard him checking the restrooms. One time last February we had some homeless guy hide out there and stay until morning, and I guess he had a pretty good night. Though Rosalia says he could have had a lot better one, what with all the beer we stock. But this guy, he just had a few Twinkies and used the microwave to warm up some cocoa. Then the next morning, Eddie opened up and there he was, snoozing on the floor between the snack aisles.

We never saw him again but sometimes Eddie still talked about him. Danny, his name was. He wished he'd come back, especially when the forecast said it would get down to forty overnight, maybe as low as thirty. It doesn't do that too much in this part of Texas. But when it does, Eddie said he hoped Danny would be ok, warm enough. See, Eddie's the kind of guy who'd think about that.

So I finished the day's adds and closed down the register, got my backpack, and pulled out my car keys, and it hit me. I didn't want to go home. It was still like that at times. Michael would be there, of course, sleeping, and yes, of course, I DID want to go home. I'd go into Michael's bedroom and make sure he was tucked in, watch him sleep awhile. But then I'd have to let him be and be with myself, and I guess I didn't enjoy my own company so much anymore.

"Eddie," I said. "Why don't you follow me home? Have a glass of wine with me."

He looked up. "I don't know."

"Just one glass," I said, and waited. He rolled up the door mats, walked to the back room with the broom. "Eddie," I said again.

I heard the bang of the broom as he hung it on its peg, then the storeroom door closed with a click. "I don't know if that's such a good idea." He called that out in the half-dark and I couldn't see his face, but when he came to me, he had the same look he'd worn so long after he and Sylvie split up. Kind of wanting and hurting and afraid.

And it stopped me for a moment, bothered me, but then I'd already asked.

"Come on, Eddie. It'll be fine."

So he took a breath and let it out, looked away for a moment, and I was all ready for his *I gotta get home. Let the dog out.* Or maybe he'd give me a big smile and flex his muscles. Say he had to work on his physique. That or some other joke he'd make. I was all ready for that, but then he looked up and said, "Sure. I'll follow you."

Our Quick Stop is on the west side of Houston, and as far out as we were, there wasn't a whole lot of light, and that's another thing I liked about closing up. Walking out in the dark, real dark, and on nights like this one, a billion or so stars laid out grand like it's a show put on just for you. It can get to you. So Eddie and I went out into that grand night and just as we did, a flash of star streaked across the sky and twinkled out.

"Did you see that?" I asked.

Eddie nodded and smiled and came over next to me. We didn't touch or anything, but maybe there's this little field of atoms or electrons around a person, and when you come close, that part of the other can come into contact with you, and depending on who it is, it can be kind of nice. And Eddie was a good man.

So we stood there and watched the sky, and then Eddie got in his car and I got in mine, and he followed me. He'd been to my trailer before, he and Rosalia, after Jason died, but I wasn't sure he remembered the way, and so I took it slow, making certain his headlights stayed in my rearview mirror.

Geneva Havishaw from four trailers down is my babysitter, and she sat up bleary-eyed from the couch when we came in, and then she laid her eyes on Eddie and came wide awake. Up until that point I hadn't even considered how it might look. This was Eddie, for heaven's sake. Then I remembered how he'd said his coming over might not be such a good idea. And I thought nah and handed him the corkscrew while I went to check on Michael.

He was sleeping on his side, his finger in his mouth like he still did sometimes, and I kissed his forehead, pulled his rodeo cowboy bedspread over him and shut the door.

"Everything good?" Eddie asked.

"All good."

I found some Fleetwood Mac and put it on and we sat cross-legged on the floor listening to "Tango in the Night," then "Rhiannon." And I thanked Eddie for coming over, said it was still hard, especially at night. "You're a good friend," I told him.

He looked down at his glass. I waited for one of his jokes but he didn't seem to have any that night, so we just listened to the music, tapping our toes and drinking. The first glass went down pretty easy and I poured us another.

"What happened to just one drink?" Eddie asked.

"Oh, you know."

With Jason gone, I drink alone, and two drinks can turn into three or four, then I start getting weepy, and it's pretty pathetic. But I didn't tell Eddie that. He thinks I'm screwed up enough as it is.

"So how are you doing?" he asked. "Really?"

I lifted my shoulders and let them fall.

"You know, Emmy, I know how it is," he said. "Well, not exactly. Sylvie didn't die. But I lost her." He was swirling his wine around in his glass, staring into it, and I realized that back then, when Sylvie left, I hadn't really gotten it. I didn't really know. I thought about asking how he'd done it, gotten through all that pain to get through to the other side. But maybe he hadn't. Maybe you don't ever get over it, and so I didn't say anything.

Then I decided we'd had enough Fleetwood Mac and put on George Michael. We listened to "Faith" and "Father Figure," and Eddie stood up and started be-bopping around. I joined him, and of course, I'd had too much to drink, took a few steps the wrong way, and stumbled into him, and when I did, he put his arms around me. Held me and kissed me.

I started crying, and he gently pushed me back. "What is it you want, Emmy?"

I just shook my head.

"Because you know . . ."

I put my finger to his lips so he wouldn't say it.

A slow song came on and I leaned back into him. "Let's dance, Eddie, that's what I want."

"All right." So we danced that slow dance, and when the next song was rock and roll, we danced to that one too. Two more songs we danced, and then I told him he had to go.

Margaret Lukas • Omaha, NE

A Lakota Education

Chapter 15

Even expecting Mina, the knock on Lauder's door startled her. She flung the bar up too forcefully, then jumped back as it slipped out of her hands and hit the plank flooring.

Mina stood on the small, raised step, motioned to the horse behind her, its large eyes dark as Mina's and staring. "I hid him at the end of the street."

"You rode that? There's no saddle."

"You were hoping for Dak, weren't you? That's why you threw the stick on the floor."

"Come in." Lauder picked up the bar and leaned it in the corner. "Dak's busy. He's got Neevil ordering him around, his grandmother needing watched, the farm chores."

"You don't need to explain how the man hasn't a min . . . ute"—Mina drug out the word—"to spare to come and see the woman pining over him."

"You're such a delight."

Mina stepped around Lauder to the desk and her mother's basket. She wore Uncle's army-issued coat, warmer and too big, the shoulders drooping and the sleeves hanging over her hands. She took up the basket and pressed it to her heart.

"Maybe tonight you should take it." Lauder wouldn't mention how at times the nest of thatch made her nervous and how at other times made her feel companioned.

"If it's lost, Mother will be like countless other Lakota. Forgotten with nothing to prove she ever walked on the earth. Dreamt. Wept."

"You know your mother lived. With or without the basket, you know."

Since stealing the music box, watching it night after night, Lauder's thoughts about her own mother skipped around, expanding one moment and contracting the next. Maybe there were times when the gods turned the world on its axis, when clowns rode horses backward and children were called upon to parent: giving all to those who birthed them. Maybe it was no more wrong for Mother to have failed to parent than for Lauder to have stolen the box, failing to parent Mother?

"It's my mother's breast." Mina's voice caught, scratched with emotion. "Uncle and Blackbird believe she failed her children, but I have the basket. It feeds me." She turned, her eyes full and looking through Lauder.

To what past Mina looked, Lauder didn't know. She didn't completely understand how the reeds, thatch, and bits of hair mattered so much, but she also no longer supposed she should be able to understand. That sort of arrogance shut the doors on mysticism. Had she gone to Father's library hunting for something beyond the books to speak to her, she could have opened every one of the thousand-plus tomes and still not found a wolf's whisker. Surely, that's what had slipped from between the pages, a whisper from the reservation. A wolf's call, an omen, a lost talisman.

Mina set the basket back on the desk, her hand lingering to trail an index finger around the top, then fingering a loose bit of grass, fretting it back into place. Her eyes fell on the music box, and she turned the key. She listened to several musical notes before speaking. "In our beds on the third floor, we couldn't hear the screaming in the basement. But when the piano on the first floor was being played, we knew Sister Joseph tried to block out what she was hearing."

"What are you saying?"

"They locked me in the basement. In a box too small to lie down. A dirt floor. My water sinking, but the floor never dry." She took a breath, her head nodding, "I was too young to know I didn't deserve it. I believed I did, because holy adults had done it to me." Her eyes filled and she paused to bite her bottom lip. "I never tried the door. I didn't kick at it until it came off its hinges. I was too young. I didn't know they were wrong and no child deserved being caged. I thought they saw a terrible evil in me, deserving of my treatment.

"I spent the two days pulling out my hair. One hair at a time." She struggled. "Pulling them out. A child's activity. At night, the quiet so deep I could hear a small snap tearing away with each. Feeling the sting and thinking I'm still alive because I feel pain."

"Oh Mina."

"I wrapped the strands around my fingers so I could keep them." She glanced again at the basket. "When I was let out, my fingers were so swollen and blue around the hair that a nun in the infirmary used a knife and cut into my fingers to get the hair off. She called me an animal. 'Filthy, pulling out my own hair, demonstrating the demonic behavior the school struggled to beat out of me. No human child,' she swore, 'would do such a thing.'"

"I'm sorry."

Mina nodded at Lauder's open journal. "Write it down for your stories." *What was it to be so rich?* Not having to worry about where you'd find your next meal or whether your loved ones would be murdered before the next sunrise. A life so secure you fought your boredom by fashioning stories about an exotic topic: a vanquished race. So rich you sought out more drama than was contained in your easy life.

"Mother considers my being here," Lauder said to distract Mina, "and my writing as 'irrational enthusiasms.'"

"Irrational enthusiasms? What does that mean?"

"I don't think like her."

"My mother," Mina managed, "believed she'd failed me. Yet she was the best mother any woman could be."

Lauder studied her friend. Boarding school hadn't taken just Mina's childhood, it continued to take even now. Yet, in the school records, she'd be counted as a successful graduate who'd returned to the reservation and schooled the heathen out of pagan children. On the surface, she and Mina's lives and cultures were separate as trees, but underground, threads of love and respect wove around them as sure as the clasped fingers of sisters.

"Blackbird is most unhappy with me," Mina went on. "She thinks me . . . what was your word? Irrational."

The information surprised Lauder. At the depot, the family had fallen into each other's arms.

"In the old way, as my mother's sister, she is mother to me as well."

A too-familiar pinch in Lauder's gut made her wince. "I'm sure it's just a misunderstanding." What else to say? But the hurt in Mina's voice, which matched the hurt in Lauder's gut, cut too deep for platitudes.

"My schooling has made me stupid. Aunt and Uncle see this in me."

"It's not true. You aren't stupid."

"The Indian School has cost me much." The divide between herself and her relatives didn't rest entirely on what had been forced into her but also on what she'd missed in her years away: their struggle with starvation, diseases, killings of a different sort. "I am poor in the wisdom of the elders."

"You've been given something else. You can read and write English."

"Has that made me better in the service of my people or better in the service of whites?"

"You can't wish to return to the old ways." *What of those even remained?* "You can't really believe the dancing is going to bring that all back?" Despite newspapers shouting that Indians wanted every white killed, that wasn't Mina. Nor did Uncle or Blackbird want more death. "How could dancing possibly bring back the buffalo? It's not science. And Ghost shirts? That's frankly crazy."

"As your priests believe in their vestments. Ghost shirts demonstrate our faith in being protected by the Great Spirit. When two or more are gathered . . ."

"Don't believe it."

"You suppose God recognizes only your forms of worship? That the mind of God is no larger than your own. Only fools suppose such."

Lauder crossed the small room and sat on the bed. Hadn't Darwin taught exactly that? After billions of years of evolution, the white man had arrived, the pinnacle of those eons of shifting plates and geological ages that had seen the extinction of thousands of less worthy creatures. And if evolution did continue, though God's seven days of labor appeared over, the evolution would skip over the white man. In his perfection, he remained as fixed as the stars. Now God wanted him to bring the lower races forward or destroy them. Even to those unlearned individuals who hadn't studied Darwin, wasn't it clear the white male was God's last and perfect creation? But it was all nonsense. The craniometer, the two claws of cold metal for measuring the bumps in the cranium, did science really believe that was how God spoke? "I'm no longer sure of anything," Lauder said.

Mina sighed. "There's much to be unsure of."

"You're kind. Why do you bother with me?"

"Because with you, I'm smart." She paused, gave the quip a moment. "Come to Uncle's. Tell Blackbird what you saw on the map and what you know of the army's plans."

Lauder longed to be with her friend, but going, she'd be betraying Agent Atlock, risking her job and possibly the school.

"Please," Mina said. "People are in much danger." She shifted her weight, the beads on the fur-lined moccasins Lauder admired, as did Atlock, catching lantern light. "You must help me. Blackbird must be told about the map, all the troops, and the will of the army with their guns. You must convince her."

Lauder had refused to accompany Mina to a dance, and she'd worried herself into a winter sweat every day of Mina's absence. She would not deny her this. She reached for the unattractive winter coat, wool scarf, and hat she'd purchased from the mercantile. "A Montana," the proprietor had said of the hat. The five-inch, wide brim gave protection against the sun and wet weather and featured a long leather string that fit under her chin. "A stampede string," he'd called the strap. Made for a man's larger head, the flat-topped black wool sank completely over her ears, but her long hat pin pushed carefully through the hair piled atop her head kept the hat from falling over her eyes.

Mina waved with an elaborate gesture at Lauder's attire. "So different from the silly clothing you wore on the train. If your mother saw this, what would she say?"

Lauder pulled on gloves. Mother would be far more upset by Lauder's association with Mina than any attire. She considered how she'd come to Pine Gulch in part to be free of Mother, yet Mother had been correct; living with the Lakota had changed her. Being with Mina and the children mirrored the worst of Lauder to herself. What was there to do with all she saw? "Mother would say don't come back." They'd parted that way, as if they'd not see each other again. "She'd say I'm clearly wounded and no longer welcome."

"And your father?"

"He writes to me." She wouldn't admit he demanded numbers for his work.

Mina touched the scarf of stars around her neck. "Wounded? A strange word. White families do not welcome their wounded?"

Lauder considered. The question seemed as much as if Mina asked it of her own family. But Uncle and Blackbird weren't guilty. Nor was Mina. They'd helped a filthy and broken man climb into their wagon, and Mina had sat beside the reeking creature as the wagon rolled away. No one in Lauder's family, including herself, likely not even one of the staff, would have done so. Such creatures were to be avoided. Respectable people didn't even make eye contact with such wretchedness.

"Was there no love?" Mina's dark eyes still asked broader questions.

"Maybe . . . we just didn't know how to say it, and silence carried less pain."

There'd been no hint of love in Father's last letter. *It's a great disappointment to me that you have not sent measurements per my instructions. I remind you that the purpose of your being there is my scientific and ethnological work, which will prove Euro-merican superiority is an innate characteristic, not social evolution. Papers are being published ahead of mine. Make haste.*

She turned out only one of her lanterns, thinking again of Nurse and how the woman fussed over the lamps at home. The thought of how easily one could accidentally be knocked over, the oil and flame spreading across the floor, kept the old woman edgy. Lauder had no such fear of fire, but the thought of entering the place entirely shrouded in darkness, while all around her she imagined scratching, made her shiver.

She handed the loaf she carried from the mess to Mina. "Don't say a word. I know what you're thinking: white women can take all the food they want. They aren't thieves. That truth shames me."

"*Take the music box*," Babette said.

Lauder grabbed the object, cold and too large for a pocket. She shook her pillow out of its case and wrapped up the box. The twirling and the music had pleased the children and broken the ice between them. "A gift for Blackbird," she said. "I'm expected to bring a gift, aren't I?"

They stepped back out, darkness lying deep as the cold. *A bitter dark full of omen.* Blocks of light from lanterns inside buildings splayed soft squares of pale yellow onto the frozen and snowy surface. Agent Neevil's office, where Dak worked days behind a desk, lay dark.

Lauder groaned when Mina clicked her tongue and the horse that had strayed a couple of yards came close. "I don't like horses. I wish you'd brought the wagon."

"You could walk, but maybe your white legs can't walk for three miles."

"That's very far."

"And we haven't got all night." Mina stroked the horse's long muzzle.

The reins dangled, leaving the animal untethered, able to charge or rear at any provocation. "They're fine harnessed to a wagon or carriage and a strong man has the reins and the brakes."

After Babette's death, Father ordered the horse that pulled the carriage that fateful afternoon shot. Had Nurse told Lauder, or had she heard other members of the staff talking? Voices "tsking" that the blame had fallen on the horse. Not the driver, not a faulty door latch, and not on Father, who'd been alone with Babette inside the carriage. "Horses kill," she mumbled.

Along with Uncle's coat, Mina wore a long skirt over leggings. Lauder pictured her doing some bit of fancy Indian leaping, some quick jump that landed her on top of the steed, her skirt and coat perfectly organized beneath her.

Mina's brows lifted. "Do you fear falling off?"

Lauder hadn't thought that far ahead. Now she knew that if she ever got on, she'd for certain fall off.

"You've never been on a horse?"

The trip from the depot had been Lauder's first wagon ride. "Carriages." *With a driver.*

"Oh." Mina's voice sounded full of mock pity. "You don't know animals at all?"

Lauder took a nervous step closer, a far too skinny horse, but the eye watching her held dislike enough to rear and strike. "I do know animals." She spoke to both the horse and Mina. "I have a Pekingese named Pou-sa. She's white and harmless. You have nothing over me. Have you ever had a dog?"

"Only roasted."

Lauder struggled not to grimace, not to imagine Pou-sa turning on a spit. "I'll get my chair."

"If your chair is left sitting outside," Mina lifted a sarcastic brow, "some thieving Indian is going to come along and steal it."

"Aren't we witty?"

"His name is Night, and we're wasting time."

"I shouldn't be doing this, it's dangerous."

"Riding my horse or telling Blackbird the truth?"

"Agent Neevil and Dak would forbid it."

"Tell them it's an adventure for your books." She motioned Lauder to step closer. "A man mounts from the right. A woman from the left. A man must keep his left eye closed, but a woman, her right."

Lauder took another hesitant step, her knees shaky and her right eye closed. "Now what?"

Standing at the horse's shoulder, Mina gave the reins a gentle downward tug, urging the horse to lower his head. When Night did, she tapped his belly.

Mount from the left, Lauder watched carefully, *right eye closed, tap the belly.*

The horse shuffled, moving his hind legs slightly forward under his rump, folding his front knees, and lowering to the ground. He sat sphinx like, the ridge of his backbone lower than Mina's waist. She put a leg over, sat, and gave Lauder a wry look.

"Tease all you want, but I won't forget this."

The world continued to rip open, and Mina couldn't foretell the future, but at that moment, she knew her relationship with Lauder would be short-lived. Of that she was certain. Though she was uncertain which of them would part first.

Sandi Lyons Hoard • Alma, NE

Shadow Walker

Genoa Federal Indian School
Genoa, Nebraska
Fall 1933

"Wahi . . . micinksi . . . wau . . ."* The words whispered in the night while Nathanael Walker slept. A young woman in a doeskin dress with red, yellow, and blue beads bent over him, smoothed his hair away from his face. With her black hair blowing in the wind and love radiating from her brown eyes, she planted a warm kiss on his forehead. The scent of sage and sweet-grass lingered in the air. Her waist-length hair brushed his face. Rubbing a hand under his nose, he turned toward the wall.

"Wahi . . . micinksi . . . wau . . ." The words repeated for a second time. Then a third. Nathanael jerked awake. Sitting up straight, he stared at the shadows wavering in the moonlit darkness. What did the words mean? He had no clue. Who was the woman in his dreams? There was no answer to that question either. Why did he keep having this dream? It had come visiting while he slept ever since he could remember.

He glanced around the room at all the sleeping boys. His eyes collided with Bartholomew Jordan's, who was in the rack next to his. Bart's cool brown eyes studied him with a mixture of pity and contempt.

"Wahi . . . micinski . . . wau . . ." Bart parroted back to him.

"You know the words?"

"No. But I've heard them over and over. From your mouth while you sleep," Bart said sarcastically.

"Shut up," Aaron Davies said from the rack above Nathanael's. He peeked over the edge of the mattress, the whites of his eyes hauntingly visible in the darkness. "Do you want to go to the hole? That's what will happen if you don't shut up!"

Nathanael reclined onto his pillow and pulled his thick scratchy blanket up to his chin, turning his back to Bartholomew. At eighteen, two years older than Nathanael, Bart had run away more times than anyone else. He had the scars on his back to prove the punishment that had been meted out when they'd found him. Best he stayed away from Bart, he was trouble.

"Judging me are you?" Bart hissed. "Judge not lest ye be judged."

"Leave me alone, I'm tired," Nathanael replied.

"I see the same marks on your back that are on mine," Bart said scathingly. "Or have you forgotten when you ran away? The feel of the whip against your skin? Your stomach burning from only getting bread and water for days on end after they dragged you back?"

"Leave . . . me . . . alone," Nathanael said, taking the time to enunciate each word slowly and clearly.

"So be it," Bart said gruffly. The rustling of cloth against cloth confirmed he'd turned away from Nathanael.

The seed of despair had been planted. When he'd run away more than two years ago, he'd headed north toward the Dakotas. Where his heart told him he'd find his family. But sadness warred inside of him. Even though he believed he had a family somewhere, no one ever came to visit him like the other children. He was an orphan. He'd been told that enough times by the teachers, so why couldn't he accept it? Who was the woman in his dreams?

~ ~ ~ ~ ~

Snapping awake for the second time from an unfamiliar noise, Nathanael turned over. What was Bart up to? He was always sleep walking, bumping into furniture and beds. But it wasn't Bart making the strange sounds because he was still in his bed, asleep, his mouth hanging half open.

Nathanael stared into the large room, trying to figure out where the noise was coming from. His eyes focused on a group of boys sitting in the farthest corner from the door. Aaron Davis, Rueben Redding, and Joshua Campbell were among other boys. The others' heads were downcast and he couldn't see their faces. Leaning up on one elbow, he continued watching them.

Rueben looked his way. Holding a long thin object up to his lips, he signaled for Nathanael to remain quiet. Nathanael reclined back against the mattress and closed his eyes. What were those boys doing that would most likely get them all in trouble?

~ ~ ~ ~ ~

"Thečhíȟila…"* whispered the same woman from Nathanael's other dreams early Wednesday morning. Every time he woke her vision was vague, her words still unknown to him. Who was she? She was always kind in her gestures. Was she his guardian angel? He stretched his arms above his head and yawned. The bugle sounded for first call and he jumped out of bed. Shoving his legs into his marching pants, he threw on his T-shirt and followed with the uniform jacket, then slipped on his socks and shoes. He raked a comb through his short black hair and headed outside. Just as he hit the Grinder lot, the bugle sounded again with reveille for roll call. He stepped into place amongst the other boys, standing rigid at attention.

Special Officer Joseph Henry, nineteen, a Lakota Sioux with four stripes on his sleeves, called everyone to attention. “Meyer?” he yelled crisply.

“Yes, sir!” came from the back row.

“Olsen?”

“Yes, sir!” Olsen answered from Nathanael’s left.

Joseph snapped out the rest of the boys’ names, with each responding, until roll call was complete.

“Wahi . . . micinski . . . wau . . .” Bart murmured from behind Nathanael.

“Shut up!” Nathanael hissed back.

“Attention!” Joseph yelled. “Face left; get those bellies and backsides together! I don’t want to see where one of you starts or the other one ends. Forward march!”

They did this every morning, afternoon, and evening. Just once Nathanael wished they didn’t have to march crammed together, barely able to breathe or to walk. But it was because of the boys who resisted that they had to do this exercise.

Marching forward then backward and sideways, they repeated it over and over, all the while keeping their bodies rigid, their legs perfectly straight. Nathanael’s belly rumbled from hunger. He pushed it away and focused on each step.

The bugle sounded for a third time, signaling it was time to go to the mess hall. Nathanael walked with the other students, his hair damp in the back from all the marching. He followed the boys from his dormitory to table M. They all stood stock still, shoulders squared, facing forward and staring at nothing while being silent. Administrator Charles stepped into the room and cleared his throat. As if on cue, everyone closed their eyes and clasped their hands together as Charles said the blessing.

The triangle clanged and Nathanael sat down with the others. Murmurs filtered through the once quiet room. The triangle sounded a second time and the mess hall grew deathly quiet once again. The third time the triangle was struck everyone picked up their forks and started eating.

A bugle blew four short bursts and all the children stood up regardless if they were done eating or not. This was the one day of the week that Nathanael detested more than the rest. He headed to the boys locker room and stood with the others by the showers. The stench of the lard and kerosene mixture always triggered his stomach to where he had to breathe deep to keep from vomiting. They went through this every Wednesday morning to delouse everyone. It was disgusting and humiliating and there was nothing he could do about it. Unless he ran away again.

Anthony Smith, dean of the boys' dorm, stepped up beside Nathanael. Nathanael nodded, drew in another deep breath, held it, and closed his eyes. A whoosh and a slap of a fabric pad against flesh started gagging him.

"Walker, you're dismissed," Anthony said.

Opening his eyes and blowing out his held breath, Nathanael coughed in the all-too-familiar white cloud and thick moist air from the delousing chemicals. He left the shower area quickly and headed to his footlocker to change into his clothes for the harness making class. Two more years and he could leave this place that was rampant with physical and psychological abuse. Could he last two more years? Or would he follow Bartholomew the next time he runs away during the darkest part of the night to find a new life?

To be continued . . .

*English Translation for Lakota language:
Wahi: I am here
Micinksi: My son
Wau: I am coming
Thečhíȟila: I love you

Andrea Riley • Lincoln, NE

Queen of Hearts

It started with a toothache.

John Henry Holliday was a dentist, after all. There was no such person as Doc Holliday when we first met. The gambler and shootist was a later incarnation, just as I was at the time no longer Maria Katarina Horony, the Hungarian emigre, and not yet Kate Elder, the cattle town dancing girl.

A patron at the Theatre Comique, the run-down saloon and dance hall where I worked, overheard me begging the bartender for a sip of whiskey for the pain in my jaw and suggested I should see a dentist.

"What the hell is a dentist?" I asked.

"They're doctors that specialize in teeth," he said, removing a card from his pocket along with a pencil. He wrote a name and address on the back and handed it to me. "My cousin just graduated from dental college and has an office a couple blocks from here. I'm sure he'd appreciate the business."

"And he'd be better than seeing a regular doctor?"

"Oh, most certainly." His eyes followed as I slipped the card down the low-cut neckline of my dancing dress. "You want a dentist."

What did I have to lose, I thought, other than maybe a few dollars.

The next morning I found myself making my way down Fourth Street in the middle of a rainstorm. My little black umbrella wasn't doing much to keep the raindrops off my hat and shoulders, not that getting wet mattered all that much. St. Louis in June was damp even on a sunny day, especially only a few blocks from the river. I wore the only respectable dress I owned, a dark green silk with long sleeves and a hem to my toes, so as not to draw attention to myself. I was regretting it, as the weather made the sleeves cling uncomfortably to my arms and stuck tendrils of damp hair to my forehead. It almost made me wish I'd just stayed at the Comique and waited for the old doctor that made monthly rounds to check on our health.

I finally found the building I was looking for, climbed two flights of stairs, and tapped on a door with the name "Dr. A. Jameson Fuches, DDS." painted in plain, black letters. A tall young man with dark, curly hair and wire-rimmed glasses perched on his long nose opened the door. I noted a resemblance to the tailor, so I must have been at the right place.

"Good morning," he said with a friendly smile. "How can I help you?" He was young but looked enough like a doctor to be reassuring.

"I was told you fix bad teeth," I said, still trying to catch my breath from trudging up the stairs.

"We most certainly do," he said cheerfully. "Please come in."

The room was long and narrow, papered in dark green. It didn't feel much drier than outside and smelled of antiseptic, a little bit of mold, cigarette smoke, and the scent of young men cooped up too long in the same room. I was familiar with doctors' offices, my father having been one, but the odd chair at the far end of the room and odder looking equipment laid out on the table across from the door were a bit disconcerting.

As was the young man reclining on a faded burgundy settee that was placed along the short wall beside the door. A prodigious application of pomade had failed to tame a cowlick in his reddish-blond hair so that it stuck up in places and was plastered down in others. He had the beginnings of a mustache that was struggling to come in, making him appear considerably younger than Dr. Fuches. His dark gray waistcoat and pants and pale yellow shirt were wrinkled as if he had slept in them. His eyes were closed and I thought him asleep until he lazily lifted a cigarette with long, graceful fingers and placed it between his lips.

Dr. Fuches kicked the settee as he closed the door behind me. "John Henry, I have a patient," he said under his breath.

"And I have a raging headache," the young man said, oblivious to the doctor's concern. The words came out in a drawl, not like the Missouri drawl I heard all the time but even more drawn out, from deeper in the South. "I don't know why you having a patient should matter to me."

"Maybe you shouldn't have drank so much last night," Fuches suggested, giving up on any pretense of decorum.

The other man opened his eyes to give his friend a reproachful look. He glanced over at me and a crooked smile spread across his face. "Why didn't you tell me there was a young lady present?" He arose and tried unsuccessfully to smooth out his waistcoat to make himself more presentable. "Good morning, ma'am," he said, taking my hand. "Dr. John Henry Holliday. At your service."

He lifted my hand to his, gently brushing his lips against my knuckles. I nearly burst out laughing at his gallantry, which I took for an act, until I remembered he didn't know yet what I was. I wondered if he would care. Most men in my experience did not, unless their mother or sister was present.

Fuches scowled and shook his head.

I turned to address Dr. Fuches, as Dr. Holliday continued to hold my hand. I would like to say I didn't even give him a second thought, yet I was acutely aware of his long fingers holding my own.

"My name is Kate Fisher . . ." I began.

"The actress?" Dr. Holliday interrupted excitedly. "From *Mazeppa*?" His grip tightened slightly on my hand.

I sighed inwardly. "I hate to disappoint you, but no." I often regretted taking on that particular name. The actress was a good ten years older than I was.

"Pity," he said, frowning. "I didn't think she was German anyway."

"I'm Hungarian," I corrected, finally pulling my hand away from his. I was impressed, however, that he could hear my accent, given how it had faded over the years. "Maybe someday an actress," I continued, folding my hands primly in front of me. "But for now I'm just a dance hall girl."

If I had hoped to shock them by revealing my profession, I was disappointed. Dr. Holliday's frown turned into a grin.

"A dancing girl?" he asked.

Dr. Fuches, having apparently had enough of watching us flirt or simply wanting to get on with business, squeezed in between us to turn me toward the odd chair at the other end of the room.

"Please excuse my friend, Miss Fisher," he said, trying to regain control of the conversation. "He seems to have forgotten his manners. About this tooth?"

Dr. Fuches had me sit and proceeded to examine my teeth while Dr. Holliday went back to the settee and resumed smoking his cigarette. Out of the corner of my eye I caught him watching me. The wry, crooked grin had returned. I felt flushed but attributed it to my earlier exertions climbing the stairs and the warmth of the room.

"Fuches, we really must find a place with more action this evening," he said with a slight cough as he blew out a cloud of smoke. "That place last night was a total bore. If you can't do better, I'm on the next train to Atlanta."

Dr. Fuches ignored his friend. "Miss Fisher, it appears you have a cavity that will need filling."

Holliday snorted in amusement at the unintended lewdness of the comment. He was such a boy, yet I found myself smiling as well. Dr. Fuches glowered at his friend.

"Dr. Holliday, if the lady does not mind, would you like to give a second opinion?"

"Certainly!" He set aside his cigarette as he stood up, the crooked grin still on his face.

When he leaned over to look at my teeth I caught a whiff of cologne that smelled of dried flowers, talc, and musk under the tobacco smoke. I recognized it as a scent called Jockey Club. It was something dandies typically wore.

"Are you old enough to be a dentist, Dr. Holliday?" I asked.

He stood back, his hand over his heart. "You offend me, Miss Fisher," he said in mock outrage. "I am a proud graduate of the Philadelphia College of Dentistry and nearly twenty-one years of age." He smiled and leaned in again. "But I do apologize. I am usually not this vulgar. My poor mother, God rest her soul, would be rather ashamed of me, but I suspect that you are not truly offended. I must have been carried away by your beauty. You have a lovely smile."

I raised a skeptical eyebrow, but I could feel my own smile tugging at the corners of my mouth in return.

"I suspect you say that to all the girls that come into this office."

"Just the dancing girls with foreign accents and pretty green eyes," he said quietly, as he leaned down preparing to examine my teeth.

He was charming, in a too obvious sort of way. I looked up at him again and met his eyes. They were an unusual color, a dark blue-gray, like the color of the ocean. The moment was like when I caught Janos Horvath's eye across the room on the first day of school when I was fourteen. I knew from just that look that I would like him and wanted to know him better. Janos and I ended up kissing behind his parent's barn a week later.

His examination was short and I found myself disappointed when he backed away from me. When his hand accidentally brushed my arm it raised gooseflesh, despite the warmth of the room.

"You have very fine teeth, Miss Fisher, but my friend here is correct, you will need a filling," he said.

Dr. Fuches pulled out his pocket watch and looked at the time. "I have another patient arriving in twenty minutes. Would you mind coming back tomorrow, say one o'clock? I can take care of the filling then."

I was so eager for the chance to see Dr. Holliday again that I didn't even think about what it meant to "get a filling" and quickly agreed.

“I shall see you tomorrow then,” I said, as Dr. Holliday lent me his hand to get up from the chair. I let his hand linger on mine a few more minutes than necessary, wishing that our encounter had lasted longer. Then a thought occurred to me. “If you are looking for some fun tonight, might I suggest visiting my place of employment? The Theater Comique. It’s just around the corner. You can’t miss it.”

I gave him a cheeky smile and winked. Apparently I did want a dentist.

Maisie Habron-Wach • Lincoln, NE

The Dream Delivery Service

In the early hours of November third, a heavy rain fell and coated the road that passed in front of the Premmer house. As a car passed by, its tires stirred up the rainwater on the street. Tracks of water boiled and frothed like a sea monster waiting beneath the pavement; a creature seemed to briefly consider rising above the surface before quickly thinking better of it. An old police car sloshed through the deep sea puddle in the street, disrupting whatever suburban leviathan floated beneath. The car rattled to a stop along the sidewalk. The driver's door groaned open and a heavy-set man let out a similar sound as he extracted himself from the car. Standing up, he rested his forearm on the vehicle's roof. He didn't open the umbrella clutched in his other hand. Seemingly unaware that he was getting soaked, the man squinted through the rain at the house he had pulled up alongside. He was very still and waited for a very long time.

He waited so long in fact, that the puddle beneath his front driver's tire began to stir. Something other than the raindrops began to flicker along the surface.

Just as a muddy shape in the puddle began to grow more clear, the man sniffed loudly and grunted as he shook his head, abruptly slamming the car door and shuffling toward the sidewalk.

The shape in the water lost clarity. Perhaps it had only been a shadow.

The policeman walked up to the only house on the street with its lights on as he struggled to open the old, mangled umbrella. With a violent gust from the storm, the umbrella fell to the ground, shuddered in the wind, and then scuttled off down the street. It was not carried by the wind, but by the eight legs it sprouted seconds after it touched the pavement.

The policeman blinked against the harsh rain and shook the image clear from his mind. He had seen too much absurdity, and he would take no more of it. He pulled his jacket closer and knocked on the door to 2400 Morfese Avenue.

The door flung open and a man with wide eyes stood in the doorway. His appearance bore an uncanny resemblance to that of a deer with a long, elegant face and dark, glassy eyes. He stood there in front of the policeman like he would bolt any moment, and his tall limbs looked like he could easily jump right over the visitor standing in the rain.

The man in the doorway shuffled side to side, tripping over himself to get out of the policeman's way as he let him inside. The two men entered a living room flooded with light. Despite the artificial glow, a heavy gloom had settled over the room and collected in the corners. In one of those corners sat a black cat. She blinked golden yellow eyes slowly and turned to trot up the stairs adjacent to the living room. She sat and watched from the highest step on the staircase.

As he stood in the doorway, the policeman held his hands awkwardly in front of him. Water ran down the channels of his slick coat and trailed off his elbows onto the doormat. When he took a small step forward, his soggy shoes squished on the carpet and he became suddenly aware of how much of the storm he had brought in with him. He cleared his throat as he glanced at the deer-like man and the woman who was hunched over on the sofa. With a sigh, he mentally corrected himself. The storm had already been here and gone. Like the emptiness after a tornado, the stillness in the air was absolute.

With as much steadiness as he could muster, the policeman cleared his throat. "My name is Detective Frank Abbozzo. I take it you are Melissa and Steven Premmer?"

The man who had opened the door stepped back without a word and shakily floated down to sit on the couch next to the woman, his eyes still wide and face blank. The woman nodded. She was as still as the man but with the faint restlessness of someone forcing themselves to sit in an uncomfortable chair.

Abbozzo stood rooted to the sopping wet doormat. "Your son, Peter, how long has he been missing?"

The woman spoke up hoarsely. "I went into his room when we got home at around one and he wasn't there."

She spoke so quietly that the policeman asked her to repeat herself.

"Yes, one a.m. We were—" She covered her mouth when her voice caught in her throat.

"We were on a date. We had dinner and went to a movie," croaked Steven Premmer, holding tight to her other hand. His eyelids had drooped slightly, but he somehow seemed more stunned than before.

"I understand. Mr. and Mrs. Premmer, please know that I am going to do everything I can to find Peter and—we *will* find him." As he said this, his voice caught in his throat too. He covered it with a sniffle and a cough, quickly shifting his weight and adjusting his soggy tie. It was a messy knot and much too tight.

"I am going to need to ask you some more questions. May I sit down?"

The Premmers both weakly gestured toward a recliner adjacent to the sofa. He navigated his wide frame through the tightrope-sized space between the recliner and coffee table and squeezed into the small chair. Detective Frank Abbozzo pulled a notebook from his jacket pocket and flipped to a new page. He cleared his throat before launching into his haphazard barrage of questions. Each question was answered by Mr. and Mrs. Premmer with a quiet, robotic clarity and softness, as if they were talking in their sleep.

High above the solemn conversation below her, the black cat on the stairs flicked her tail pensively. She had been listening to the people converse quietly, observing with half-closed golden eyes, and now turned her head to address the shadowy doorway at the top of the stairs.

"Bianca, my dear, how did this happen? Where is the boy?" The cat's calm, warm voice asked gently. The darkness shimmered faintly and a whisper of a draft brushed by her as she waited for her answer, as unbothered as a cat ought to be. The shimmer solidified into the shape of a child, crouched down in the doorway.

"Sweetheart, they won't be looking up here, come over please and tell me what you know."

The child crept over on all fours. She eyed the light coming from the living room nervously and answered the cat. Her voice was much different than her friend's. It was paper-thin and raspy, frantic like wind through a broken window.

"I didn't see anything. I was downstairs in the kitchen for most of the night because his parents were gone. I found out when Peter's mom started yelling, just like you did, Baggy."

The child's eyes glimmered with wisps of water and the cat's tone softened.

"It is quite alright, dear Bianca. Let's see what Bernard knows. He must have seen something."

Before the two could move, Mrs. Premmer stood up and began to pace around the living room below them.

"I think her name is Mary? Or May I think? Isn't that right, Steven? She lives north of town with her stra—eccentric parents. Peter has mentioned her a few times. I don't know much else about her . . . I don't know if she knows anything . . . or . . . I don't know . . . I don't—" Her voice was much higher than it had been a minute ago, with strange inflections and pauses.

Outside, the rain continued to lash at the windows, but inside, the air in the room had changed. The stagnant stillness of shock and disbelief had started to seep out of the cracks in the old house, leaving a vacuum of electric panic behind in its place. The dry harshness of the air was palpable. The Premmers were now breathing quickly, like they had fallen from the clouds they had been floating through and had hit the ground, hard.

The policeman stood up as well. He moved in place, subconsciously mirroring Mrs. Premmer's pacing.

"I think it would be good for me to talk to this 'May' too. Just you wait and see, Peter's probably with some little friend, off on some adventure. They'll be back any minute, soaked and wanting hot chocolate. It was just Halloween after all. Funny things always happen. Pranks."

His voice ended on a high note, like he wanted to say something else. His hands were tightly gripping his notebook, threatening to rip it in half.

Mr. Premmer rose and joined the other two standing in a circle around the coffee table. The three were all swaying slightly, like candle flames surrounding an altar. In the silence, the lethargic fog descended again and the air thickened. Damp darkness crept back from the corners of the room, suffocating the sudden lightning crack of panic and ushering in a tangible numbness.

Weighed down by returning fatigue, the Premmers both nodded meekly. Detective Abbozzo stuffed his notebook into his pocket, struggling against the sleepy spell of the room. He felt a flush of red on his forehead after his own weak assertion that the child would be so easily found. He inched away from the sofa toward the front door. The Premmers followed, unaware of their legs smacking the coffee table altar in unison.

As they walked, another voice joined the dimly lit conversation upstairs.

"Does that man know what happened to Peter?" A round, honey-thick voice drifted up from inside the doorway that the child had appeared from.

The cat's voice slid cleanly through the swamp-like thickness of the room below. "Bernard, do come out so we can have a proper conversation. This is far too serious for you to sulk behind the door," the cat named Baggy scolded the voice.

Nothing moved.

"I can talk from here just fine," the voice weakly protested from the doorway.

"Alright then, you two keep an eye on Peter's parents while I go follow this 'Detective Abbozzo.' I want to know what he knows. Keep sharp and take note of everything that happens while I'm gone."

Baggy disappeared back into the room at the top of the stairs and off to some passageway known only to nature's sneakiest of creatures.

Moving much more slowly than the cat, Detective Abbozzo and the Premmers hovered around the doorway.

"Please," the policeman straightened up and planted his feet on the ground, "Please don't worry, I'll have him back to you very, ah, very soon." He nodded and let himself out, leaving the two parents again swaying softly, like candlelight through a window.

As Detective Abbozzo stepped out into the morning, the rain began to fade into a faint mist. He shuffled quickly to his car and wrenched the complaining door open once again. Without the harsh barrage of rain, the mechanical squelching was loud enough to make him flinch. As he put the old police car into gear, his eyes were fixed ahead through his grimy windshield and he failed to notice the tentacle reaching up from a puddle toward his tire. Pulling away from the curb, he also failed to notice the glowing yellow eyes sprinting after him into the rising dawn.

~ ~ ~ ~ ~

Back inside the hollow glow of 2400 Morfese Avenue, the shadow of a child and the voice from the doorway spoke to each other in hushed tones from the top of the stairs.

"Do you think he is really *missing*? That can't be possible, he was just here last night! I saw him before I went downstairs!"

"*You* went downstairs?" exclaimed the child, still crouching in the shadow of the banister.

"Well, I can't spend *all* my time up here. It's been some time since I left the room and I thought it'd be best to do it while the parents were out," protested the doorway voice.

"Well then *get out here* and help me keep watch then!" the ghost child hissed.

"Keep watch? Keep watch?! How exactly am I meant to *keep watch* when they're never supposed to see me—"

Before they could bicker any further, one sharp knock cracked through the whole house. Louder and crisper than the policeman's knock, this sound echoed supernaturally throughout every room and seemed to shake the Premmers from their sleep. Both of Peter's parents' heads snapped up from the dazed droop they had fallen into with a start. They looked at each other for a moment before Mrs. Premmer reached past her husband and turned the doorknob.

With a creak, the door swung open and a man entered without invitation. He slickly oozed into the room, like a dense fog seeping across the floor. Despite taking only one step inside, he seemed to drift and curl around the legs of the furniture. He coated the wooden floors with an eerie coldness that cut through the suffocating air hanging around the missing boy's parents and the odd company observing them from above.

The man was dressed in a white button-up shirt, a black tie, and black wingtip shoes. The tie was simple and neat, like his black hair precisely cut around his high forehead and long neck. His nose had clearly been broken several times, and the way he purposely stepped toward the Premmers suggested that he probably set the break himself. In the crook of one arm, the man carried a completely dry jacket despite the rain outside. The other arm extended to shake Mrs. Premmer's hand. She shook it obediently as the man spoke. His voice echoed like his knock, solemn and heavy like an organ in an empty cathedral.

"Hello, Mr. and Mrs. Premmer. I am here to find your son."

Outside, the rain continued to fade. As it did, the distant thunder and eerie stillness of a quickening wind signaled a new, fast-approaching storm.

~ ~ ~ ~ ~

May clutched her backpack to her chest as she climbed out of the backseat of her parents' truck. She fell out onto the sidewalk with an unceremonious stumble and quickly looked around. No one had seemed to notice. May was grateful for that. In fact, she would be grateful if she could go the whole day without anyone noticing her at all.

"Excellent recovery, May! Now go forth and have no fear!" Her father shouted out the back door from the driver's seat. A teacher standing at the front of the school craned her neck to look in her direction, and May felt her face grow hot. She was keenly aware of how her father was dressed. Head to toe in a beekeeper's uniform that at one time had been white, he looked like an astronaut that had plummeted to earth and had been dug from the crater still covered in dirt. She was just happy her mother wasn't here, because what *she* had on this morning was definitely worse.

"Thanks, Dad. I can just walk home after school, you know. Um, you don't *have* to come back," shouted May, putting distance between herself and her father's beat-up pickup truck.

"Nonsense, honey! I'll be here right on time. See you later!"

She shuddered as the pickup groaned a curse to the automotive gods before limping away back to her new home.

May wrestled her backpack on as she trekked toward the front door. The teacher who was still watching her beamed with a sweet smile as she realized who May was. She extended both of her hands in a small wave down on either side of her hips.

"Hello, hello! Are you May, sweetie? Our *new* May?"

The bilateral flapping wave, coupled with a dramatic backward lean, betrayed the teacher's genuine excitement. It put May at ease. She had never moved schools before and was trying not to let her nervousness pin her to the ground. The lady popped her weight forward onto her toes and planted the back of her hands to her hips, looking to all the world like a very animated chicken. This image was aided by the ruffly white cotton dress, bright red flats, and her constant bobbing movement.

May gripped the straps of her backpack, willing herself to stand still and not mimic how the teacher wiggled in place. She felt a laugh bubble up from her stomach as she found herself unable to stifle a shoulder shimmy when she answered, "Uh huh, my name is May. It's nice to meet you."

The teacher smiled even more widely at May's involuntary dance. She shimmied her shoulders, too, and nodded her head solemnly. "No, it's nice to meet *you*! Well, let's go and get you started! Did your dad not want to come in?"

At the mention of her father, the image of his wardrobe this morning evaporated the laugh in her throat. *Just don't notice him. Don't notice me.*

"Um no, that's okay. I know where I need to go. I have the letter."

May pulled a carefully folded letter from her pocket. "I need to go see Miss Hadepom? She is in room thirty-four? I'm supposed to be there by 8:05."

"Yes, that's me! You can just call me Miss H if you want to. 'Hadepom' is a hard name to say, isn't it? Yours is an interesting name too, isn't it? Not 'May' of course, but your last name! What a fun name!"

Before Miss Hadepom could utter her full name, May interrupted her.

"Oh perfect, yeah, it's a fun name for sure. Do I need to check in or something?"

Her words came out sharper than she had wanted to, but the teacher just laughed.

"Nope, I'll get you all sorted out later. Let's head to class and meet everyone!" She scooped both of her arms broadly through the air to beckon May inside. The two stepped through the glass front doors of the school, and May was hit with air that somehow only exists in middle schools. It was a mixture of industrial cleaner, old carpet funk, and a cloud of body spray and body odor dense enough to leave a film on the walls.

She gulped down the dryness in her mouth that had appeared when Miss Hadepom mentioned meeting her class. A jittery wash of energy ran up her legs and settled in her stomach as she was led across the shiny linoleum cafeteria and into room thirty-four. The door was decorated with swatches of colorful butcher paper in the shape of a green hill. A smattering of laminated flowers and trees covered the scene, each with a name written in Sharpie. May quickly scanned for her name, but before she could find it,

Miss Hadepom opened the door. She led her inside where a mob of children milled around desks, chattering and jumping all over each other.

"We are still waiting on a few people so I'll wait to introduce you until class actually starts. Here is your seat, feel free to put your stuff here for now and we can go find your locker later."

May had started to attract the attention of the other children, one of whom walked up with purposeful steps. Her blonde hair was curled in very tight ringlets and the color of her shirt was carefully matched to the color of her handmade bracelets. She seemed very excited about the first day of school, and even more excited to meet May.

"Oh McKenna! Perfect! This is May! May, *McKenna* is your buddy for today. She is going to help you find your way around and help answer questions. *Of course* you should always feel free to ask me anything, but if you don't want to ask the teeeeach-er," she bobbed her body back and forth to accent each syllable, "you can ask McKenna!"

McKenna flashed braces at May that had the exact same color rubber bands as her shirt and bracelets. She spoke very clearly and purposefully, over-pronouncing each word.

"Hello, May. Welcome to our class!" She gestured across the room with her elbows tightly to her sides, as if she were giving a presentation she practiced a million times.

"My name is McKenna, like Miss H said." She inclined her body toward her teacher with a knowing nod, and her teacher nodded back with a slight smile. May found herself smiling to herself too. McKenna was clearly happy to be here, and it was rubbing off on May.

"Well, it looks like everyone is here now," Miss Hadepom noted as a few more children trickled into the room just as an off-key intercom bell blared over the speakers. "I'd like you to take your seat right up here in the front by my desk so I can introduce you. Do you want to come up to the front or stay in your seat?"

Relief pressed down on the jittery liquid percolating in her stomach.

"Um, I think I'll just stay in my seat."

Miss Hadepom nodded with her hands pressed to her hips and swayed to the front of the class. Despite the attention that she was drawing from her classmates, May felt herself relax a little. McKenna sat down near the front of the class and patted the desk next to her. Early morning sunlight glowed through the windows lining the wall adjacent to the desks and May glanced around the room, trying not to make too much eye contact with anyone else as Miss Hadepom addressed the class.

The teacher explained how happy she was to see everyone, how wonderful summer must have been, and how *exciting* it was that they had a new classmate! *May*, she said, just *May*. She could have sworn that Miss Hadepom winked at her with the obvious omission of her last name, and May decided that she really, really liked her new teacher.

~ ~ ~ ~ ~

May had never seen an adult so nervous before. The large man sitting in her living room was strangling the notebook in his hands absentmindedly while he asked her parents a series of questions. He glanced down at his notes after each question, writing and scribbling out and rewriting with each response. May shifted her weight and let her hair fall out from behind her ears to cover her face. *Why is he here?*

Her parents sat on either side of her on the sofa, like two lions guarding the entrance to an estate. Except her house, or really, the house that they had just moved into, wasn't really an estate. At one time, the big house on the farthest reaches of town had probably been very impressive, but now it was just *dingy*. May's parents had tried very hard to make it feel more homey, but to them "homey" just meant absolutely feral.

Each corner of every room housed a potted plant. Vines had been lovingly coiled around curtain rods and lamps, hanging leafy behemoths crowded the showers, and netting had been attached to the ceilings that connected every room so that tangles of vegetation could hang from it. The house smelled of the earth and morning light shone through the windows like emerald marbled sunlight on the ocean floor. May had always grown up in places like this. Places that made her feel like Nature herself would peek out from around a monstrous fern and sit down for breakfast with her. But today, instead of Mother Nature, a skittish, balding man had joined her family for pancakes and coffee.

May had seen him around the town of Mill River before, but this was the first time she had really looked at him. The man's head sat on his shoulders like a lump of dough that gravity was slowly pulling down toward his soft belly. His eyes and mouth looked like they had been sloppily indented by a child who changed their design from a bear to a person halfway through. Earlier when he entered their living room, Detective Abbozzo had sat down with the weight of a man who was wearing sodden wool clothing over lead pajamas and groaned like he was resolved to his wardrobe. Sitting across from her now, the policeman cleared his throat.

"And so, you don't remember him saying anything about running off?" he asked, gesturing broadly around the room without taking his eyes off his notes.

"Well," answered May's father, "I have to admit I've really only met the boy once, when I dropped May off at school."

The day had just begun, but he was already clothed in something bizarre. For today, he was dressed in painter's overalls and wading pants in preparation to skim some pond algae from the sad, stagnant pool in their garden. Her mother was dressed similarly but with hilariously large goggles perched on her forehead. May's parents were botanists, and they were nothing if not dedicated to their *second-greatest* passion. Their first sat on the sofa between them, desperately trying to hide behind her curtain of hair.

"I hate to say that it's the same for me," agreed her mother. "I think I've really only met him once or twice as well, but he did come here a few times. I think he found all this very interesting." She looked reverently around at all of the outdoors, inside.

"I, um, I meant May," Detective Abbozzo scratched his eyebrow with the back of his thumb and tried to meet May's eyes. She felt her stomach clench. *What?*

"Why me?" she asked the man.

"Well, you were his little friend, weren't you? His parents mentioned you by name."

He said we were friends? She peeked up at her mom and frowned. Her mom inclined her head, encouraging her to answer.

"Um, he didn't say anything like that. About running off."

"Did he say anything else? Anything that seemed strange?"

The man's demeanor had shifted slightly. A shadow of another person crossed his face. This person didn't stutter or didn't fidget with his sloppy tie. The shadow looked at May with an emotion she struggled to place. She palmed her hair back behind her ears.

"I don't know. I don't think so."

The shadow pressed on. "May, anything you can tell me might help us find Peter."

She swallowed against the dryness creeping into her mouth. "He was starting to say some weird things when we hung out. Not that he wanted to go anywhere or anything. He said that he was expecting something to arrive."

"Arrive?"

She felt the eyes of the man, his shadow, and her parents all zero in on her.

"At least, I think that's what he meant. He said something about the Dream Delivery Service. So I guess he was expecting a package."

The response from the adults surprised her. She expected some recognition, something significant in what she said that maybe meant something. But they all looked at each other with confusion.

"The Dream Delivery Service? Have you heard of that, Marshall?" Her mom looked over May's head to her dad. The tightness in her stomach coiled up further into a knot. *Was that a stupid thing to say?* Her father shook his head and Detective Abbozzo also seemed at a loss.

"It probably doesn't mean anything. I really can't think of anything else." Another thought bubbled up in her mind, but the dryness in her mouth withered up her desire to share it.

"Thank you, May. That might be something that can help. Please let me know if you think of anything else."

The shadow held its ground for one more moment before he was blinked away by the nervous man's eyes. He scratched his eyebrow again and stuffed the notebook in his back pocket. He stood quickly, patting down his pockets, and searched side to side for his coat, digging it out from underneath a pile of large elephant ear leaves cascading over the couch. Shrugging it on, he thanked them and disappeared through the vegetation like a jungle explorer. Her dad followed to let him out while her mom stayed behind on the sofa with her. She was silent for a moment.

"May, honey," she said carefully, "I'm sure your friend will be alright."

Her father returned, and her parents looked at each other through the sunbeam streaming across the living room. The sunlight illuminated her father's face from underneath with a warm, golden orange highlighting his glasses and large nose. He looked like a deep sea diver with his strange clothes, surrounded by the rich green of his plant kingdom. The leaves and flowers moved softly around him in the drafty air of an old house, like underwater plants drifting in the gentle ocean current.

"Detective Abbozzo is a smart man," he said, his hands tucked underneath the straps of his waders. "He'll find Peter." The sea life continued to sway peacefully, casting mottled shadows along the wood floors.

"Yeah," mumbled May. Her hair covered her face again. She let it stay there, obscuring the outline of her mom as she raised herself from the sofa and joined her dad in the doorway.

"Stay inside today, May. Please. Just to be safe."

"Okay." The light glowed through her hair, and she stared at her feet through the spider-web-thin strands of amber. The shapes of her parents disappeared, leaving her alone, floating in the vastness of her crowded living room. The serenity echoed with the faint rustling of leaves. A form passed in front of the window like a ship casting a shadow onto the seabed. May looked up to see a black cat sitting in her window. A halo of golden light outlined its body as a restless tail flicked silently. Its face was obscured, but May was sure it looked right at her before quietly slipping away, leaving her alone in the company of the softly sleeping world around her.

K. L. Riley • Lincoln, NE

Ben and Ada and the Order of the Raven

"I found it," Ben shouted as he crawled out from underneath the dusty workbench. In the dim light he held up the tattered old cigar box. "It was under Grandpa's workbench!"

"I looked there!" Ada hollered from the top of the stone stairs. "Twice!"

Ben tramped across the dingy farmhouse basement. Grandma called this a basement, but Ben and his sister thought it was more like a cellar. It was dark, dusty, musty, filled with oddities and tokens of long gone eras. The basement was also the best place to play when they visited Grandma and Grandpa.

Ben stomped up the stairs with his prize, carrying the battered cigar box like it was made of gold. "It was buried under a pile of old shoes and about a foot of dust," he said as Ada reached for the box.

Sneezing as she took the box, Ada turned it over in her hands. "Why is Uncle Tim so anxious for us to find this old thing?"

"Why couldn't he come find it himself?" Ben asked. "Maybe we should open it."

"Uncle Tim said not to."

"It's a forty year old cigar box, Ben! What could possibly be in here that's dangerous?"

"I didn't say not to open it," Ben smiled. "I just reminded you Uncle Tim said not to."

Ben stepped past his twin and took a step toward the door. "If anything goes wrong, I'm going to claim I warned you."

Ada rolled her dark eyes at her brother.

Ben and Ada Khangi were born twelve years earlier, ten minutes apart. Growing up, they were inseparable and often interchangeable. They both had black hair and green eyes and they were both left-handed. Ada wore her hair in a shoulder length, feminine bob, while Ben preferred a long ponytail. For ten wonderful years Ben and Ada had lived with their parents in Portland, Oregon. Then one day Mom and Dad were gone. No explanation, no funeral, no search party, they were just gone. The twins moved to Salem with their uncle, Tim Kola. Tim was an odd character who lived in his parents' old farmhouse with a cellar in the basement. Grandma and Grandpa Kola lived in town now, too old to take care of forty acres of woodland.

"Here we go!" Ada held the cigar box at arm's length, flipped up the rusty latch and lifted the lid back toward her with her eyes closed.

Ben flinched, but when nothing happened, he leaned forward and looked into the box. "A stick," he announced.

"What?" Ada pulled the box back and turned it so she could see inside.

All that was inside the box was a stick. It was a straight, smooth stick with black bark and a slightly tapered and rounded end. Ben reached into the box and lifted out the stick. He waved the stick around and shrugged before replacing the stick in the box. Ada shoved the box into Ben's hands and then lifted out the stick and waved it around herself before putting it back. The twins stared at each other across the open cigar box with the stick inside. Ben's eyes narrowed and before his lips could form the words, Ada knew he was about to cuss. She cut him off by reaching out and shutting the box.

"If Uncle Tim wants his stick in a box, we will take him his stick in a box." She shrugged as she pulled the box from Ben's hands. "Let's go."

Ben glared at his sister's back as she brushed past him and stepped outside. Uncle Tim wasn't in the house, he'd left after breakfast. The twins had watched him walk into the woods carrying his fishing pole and his .22 rifle. He left clear instructions to find the cigar box and bring it to him down by the lake. The lake was a good hour by foot but considerably less if they took the four-wheeler. There was only one four-wheeler and whoever got to it first got to drive. Ben turned, followed his sister outside, and then started running toward the barn.

"BEN!" Ada yelled as she, too, started running.

Ada was ten minutes older, but Ben was two inches taller and he could run a lot faster. He made it to the barn first and was about to open the door when the door flew open on its own, knocking Ben to the ground. Standing in the doorway, walking out of the barn, were four large men. Each of the men was dressed in a long black robe and each of them wore a tall, conical hat. Ben laughed in spite of himself. "Ya'll look like you got kicked out of Nun School," Ben said, standing up and brushing himself off. "What happened? They figured out ya'll weren't women?"

Ada skidded to a stop beside her brother and grabbed his wrist. "Hi," she said slowly. "I'm Melissa Jefferson and this is my brother Thomas." Ada paused but when the four men didn't react to her, she continued talking while slowly backing up, pulling

Ben with her. "We just stopped by to visit our friends, but they aren't here. You haven't seen them, have you?"

The men didn't move and didn't speak. If they hadn't been standing up, the twins might have believed the men were dead. For a moment, Ada thought the intruders were going to let them leave, but then the man in the middle of the group noticed the cigar box underneath Ada's arm and he seemed to come to life.

"She has it!" the man yelled. "Seize them!"

This time, Ada didn't try to stop Ben from cursing as the twins turned and ran.

Janet Seegebarth • Norfolk, NE

Shadow of the Eclipse

Hope was a thin line Garth found only in his imagination. The pain and confusion that consumed him after the accident had left him weak, like he was bleeding and bleeding, about to die. In fact, he pondered death daily, but not like his therapist thought. Dr. Johnson said he was depressed, that it was natural to feel this way after the kind of deep, sudden loss Garth had experienced.

Of course, he was depressed. The fire had destroyed his life. It took away his wife and child. It left him homeless and disfigured. No room was left in his broken heart for joy, happiness, or a loving God. He knew where he was, and he knew where he wasn't. Life was nothing but an empty prison camp.

The thing about death, depression, and disfigurement was that no one wanted to be near him, even when they said they did, he could tell they wanted to flee. Friends said what they were supposed to say, but it was obvious they'd rather be around fun people, people who were not so hard to look at. Garth didn't want to be around them either. They made him angry and even more depressed.

He tried explaining this circle of depression to Dr. Johnson during one of his sessions, but his therapist didn't actually speak much. An awkward silence was one of the techniques he used to get Garth to open up, but Garth was too smart to talk about the truth of that night. He was careful to stick to tales about being depressed and how he felt like people didn't want him around.

If he started talking about what really happened, the good doctor would be obligated to turn him over to the men in white at the funny farm.

No, Garth told Dr. Johnson what he expected to hear and kept the rest to himself. At the end of the session, he lowered his left hand from his forehead, plastered a smile on his face, and said how much better he felt after talking. The reality was he wanted to get away, to run and never look back, to get in his Jeep and drive forever.

He used to pray, but not anymore, not *after*. He couldn't quite understand why he was given his life back, and he was angry at the world and at God. Everything had changed with what Garth referred to as *after*.

"You know you did everything you could that night." Dr. Johnson urged him to talk about it, but he couldn't. He was afraid that once he started talking, he'd divulge too much.

"I know," he answered. "If I could go back, I couldn't change anything." That was what the doctor wanted to hear, so that was what he said, even if it sounded superficial.

"Except unplug the toaster," he added to fill the silence. The toaster was a wedding gift, but he didn't know who had given it to them or where it had been purchased. "I don't even have a toaster anymore. I don't eat toast."

"Are you angry at the toaster for causing the fire?"

"No, of course not," he said with an offended voice. "I can't be mad at a thing."

The accident had been eight months ago, and he couldn't bring himself to name the deep hatred he had toward what destroyed him—no, it didn't destroy him. It destroyed *her*. *Them*. It took away Carlie and Madison and left him with nothing but pain, and the culprit was God. God had taken everything from him, and if He allowed this to happen when He could have prevented it, then maybe God wasn't that great after all.

There was too much in his head after therapy that day. He drove back to his apartment, knowing the broken parts of him could never be fixed. When he was a kid, he used to stare at a neighbor who had a blotchy red birthmark across her face, wondering how she could stand to look that way.

He did the same to anyone different, a man missing a leg, a balding woman, any old person. Now, his own hideous outward appearance marked him as one of them. White scars damaged his arms and legs and his stomach looked like rotten salami. That wasn't bad though. It was his face he couldn't bear. The fire had taken his ear and placed its fingerprints on the left side of his nose and across his forehead. He'd let his hair grow to try to hide it, but that made him look even worse.

It made no sense for him to live through the fire and for them to die. Although he wouldn't have wished these burns on either of them, he ached for the company of his wife and daughter, that somehow they could be together. He knew where they were, and he felt envy. It was a longing to visit them in that place beyond this world. His home here was built of sticks, but his real home was built of jewels in a city paved with streets of gold. How he missed it.

It was lunchtime, but Garth wasn't hungry. He decided to go for a walk to clear his mind. The Loquest Trail was not far from his apartment, but it was a popular walking path. He didn't want to see anyone—or have *them* see *him*. No. He would drive out to Plum River Road and wander along a remote trail by the river.

Carlie used to love their little nature excursions there. Her adventuresome spirit was always ready to drop everything and go. She showed him how to stop taking everything so seriously and enjoy life. She taught him how to live.

"You can drive down Plum Creek Road a million times and never see as much as you do in one afternoon of walking through here," she had said. "Let's find the white mulberry trees."

"It seems early for mulberries," he'd answered.

"But the white mulberries are amazing! They're as big as plums and sweeter than any melon you've ever had." She walked backward, facing Garth and talking with her hands to emphasize her point. "Let's just see if we can find them."

"Big as plums? Really?" he teased.

"Bigger. As big as your fist!" She pushed her fist into his jaw so that he had to take a small step back.

She was spunky, but he loved her for it. The single braid of her long blonde hair whapped his chest as she spun around. She grabbed his hand and pulled him along the uneven trail in search of Mulberry Eden.

They pushed on until they found the grove, an oasis of ripe fruit. The rest of the day slipped away as Garth watched Carlie pluck the small ripe berries and pop them into her mouth by the handfuls, a special treat once a year.

He should have known they'd still be there as the sun began to color the sky. It would be close to dark before they could make it back to the Jeep, but Carlie wanted to do it all.

She wanted to float down the river on a raft and pick up bullfrogs and cast deer prints. She was forever prowling for berries and flowers, pointing out turtles in the marshy weeds, and becoming spellbound over the remarkable beauty of a spider's web. Garth would pick the flowers, make the turtles move, and marvel at the complex webs with her.

His eyes misted with the realization that this sharing was gone now. He parked the Jeep and made his way through the tall grass to the trail near the river. He would have to check his body for ticks after going home.

Home, he thought, *to the apartment*. His real home was with Carlie and Madison. He should be happy for them, but the ache of their absence was powerful. He'd never even taken Madison out here. She was only four. He had thought she was too little to go on a trail this close to the river.

Carlie. He talked to her in his head because he knew she still existed. Maybe she could hear him. *I breathe in. I breathe out. I go to work. I pay my bills. I guess that makes me alive, but this life is nothing compared to before.*

When Carlie and Madison were alive, there was a house to fix and a lawn to mow. He'd planted flowers along the fence. Irises were her favorite. He liked the lilies. Bold colors. Tall sturdy plants. What must that yard look like now? The house was gone. What wasn't burned was scraped away and deposited in the dump. He didn't want to see the empty lot. He didn't want anything to do with *after*.

After made him sick.

I still do the things I'm supposed to do, Carlie. I had lunch with JR on Friday. We talked about his kids, the food, Turner's art show at the Vernon Gallery. He asked about my music. I'm not composing. It's a struggle to even listen to music. Every song seems to be tied up in you, and if I so much as think about children's music, I see Madison's smile with her little baby teeth. It's so unfair that she never got to grow up!

Here it was again. More pain. More disappointment. He tried to block those feelings and retrieve the message lodged in the far corner of his brain, the one that told him to stop this self-pity. That message made him press on. *God granted you something big when He gave you your life back*, it said, *so stop wishing for a little life. It may feel like the wrong direction, but you're headed to that place where you need to be.*

Eight months had passed since he'd lost Carlie and Madison, and never had the tears flowed as liberally as they did today. He stumbled into the grass along the side of the trail, rolling in it and ripping handfuls from the soil. He sobbed with animal-like grunts, rubbing the grass into his face, needing to feel something, to smell something.

His eyes opened to see the broken green blades lying against the scars on his hands. In that moment, he wished he was as little and insignificant as a single blade of grass. Yet, it was each blade that made the whole green landscape around him. A handful of grass would never be missed, but if all the blades died, there would be nothing left. He picked a random blade here and there.

What difference does it make which blade I kill, for I am the god of the grass!

He wiped his hands against his jeans and lay back, ashamed of his thinking.

The sun shot flames of light through the branches of the cottonwood tree above him. After his emotions settled, Garth's senses turned to the sounds of the birds. They chirped incessantly, continuing life as normal without Carlie and Madison in the world. *How could they?* he thought.

His stomach was empty, and he was exhausted and depleted, yet he longed for neither food nor sleep. As the air cooled around him and the light dimmed, he remembered that today was the day of the eclipse. People had been talking about it for weeks, getting special eclipse glasses and making plans to travel to a good viewing area.

He hadn't given it a thought, but now that the air began to cool and the birds ceased their chirping, he realized he would be in the path of direct totality.

Carlie, are you going to watch this with me? He reached for her, his imagination clicking into the other world where she was alive and nestled against his side. He could almost feel her body there, remember the indent of her waistline and the roundness of her hip as she wrapped her leg around his. There they lay in the grass, waiting for darkness, so they could look directly at the eclipse.

It's amazing. Isn't it? I'm so glad you're here with me.

Talking to her was his comfort. Nights were spent hugging his pillow, telling Carlie about his piano students and listening to her chatter about her adventures. In his mind, he showed her around the apartment. She cleaned the corners of the cupboards and hung family photographs on the wall. Madison's perfect little fingers decorated the front of the refrigerator with wrinkled paintings of happy stick people. She would tell him little stories about cats or leaves or fuzzy slippers, and they would both laugh.

He wasn't burned in these fantasies, or if he was, it didn't matter because Carlie loved him no matter what. This invention of a continued life with his wife and little girl was the only way he could get through the long, sleepless nights. Something had to fill the gaping hole that tore apart his insides, wounding him more deeply than the flames from the fire ever could. The pain of his burns was nothing compared to the dagger that knifed through his chest, dissecting his heart into a million fragments.

The fantasies helped him process the pain. It was how he got through day by day, hour by hour, and sometimes minute by minute. He continued to breathe, knowing each breath was the passage of time, and time would heal, but never in his life had it moved so slowly. Holding onto Carlie and Madison like this kept the other thoughts away, the horrible ones where they burned to death in a fire.

As he lay in the grass along the Plum River and the eclipse darkened the sky, Carlie melted away, and he became truly alone. Like the eclipse itself, he thought of himself as a shadow. He was this thing that only followed and disappeared in the full sunlight of others. He was a second-rate musician—good, not great—always behind someone better. Other bands got traveling gigs, played in clubs. *JR and the Boys* was lucky to get a gig at the local bar, and now that their keyboard player looked like a troll, there wasn't much hope of ever doing better.

When the darkness was complete, and he saw nothing but the corona of the sun hiding behind the moon, the wildness of night swirled through cool air. A cricket chirped and the grass rustled as though an animal crept through its depths. With this perfect alignment of sun, moon, Earth, and Garth, he felt the power of the shadow.

There were people not far from him, lying in this same darkness at this very moment, and he felt somehow connected. He was one blade of grass among many that God didn't pick. The shadow of the eclipse—like life, like every life and every blade of grass—had revealed to him a vast and wondrous power.

ShennonDoah • Holdrege, NE

Lindsay Doll

An excerpt from the novel in progress: *Grey House Haunts*

"You are *not* authorized to enter my bedchambers!" A black laced-up boot offered a petulant kick to an inch-long cockroach skittering across a braided rug. "Begone or I'll feed you to Archibald."

A bulbous garden spider nested in the corner of my room where he'd chosen to spin his web, and welcomed the news. I couldn't imagine another bite passing his jaws without exploding orange and green patches all over pastel flowered wallpaper.

Shrill voices in the main vestibule grated on already tense nerves. Seriously? Couldn't Charlie have wrangled up some men? Girlish wiles worked much better on the male species. Still, I couldn't wait to shut these wenches up.

Impatient air puffed through distorted lips as I rose from my dressing table. On my way onto the upper landing, my left foot paused in mid-air, reconsidering the juicy squelch of a roach under my boot. Instead, peering over the railing, I gave the offensive bug a second kick, this time through the railing and onto a mound of tight curls.

Rising shrieks contorted my lips into a half smile. At least they'd be fun to play with. I ran to the top of the stairs and began my descent.

"Help! Help! They're after me!" My screams brought two pairs of frightened eyes up the staircase.

Opting for drama, I grabbed the banister half-way down and flipped over it, landing in a widespread stance, a tortoise shell comb falling from disheveled hair in front of me. The smaller woman clung to her companion, staring at the hair adornment like it was a second roach.

"Follow me!" I commanded, not needing to turn and check, already knowing that they would. I hustled past them into the formal dining room—the kitchen my original destination.

Swatting an insect out of my path, I turned to check out where it landed, when a shriek behind me captivated my attention. A stunned fly kicked its legs in the air next to larva- and meal worm-infested leftovers. We honestly did not use this room nearly as often as we had before papa went to war.

"This way!" I escorted them into the library to a far wall. "This leads to a secret room."

Panicked women hustled up behind me, fidgeting while I maneuvered the false bookshelf. In their haste to flee whatever evil they perceived chased them, they gladly entered the drawing room, a space with no visible exits and the precursor to a trip to father's lab. "We're safe here."

The flustered women slowed their breathing and began to relax. They turned in slow circles, taking in couches and gurneys and medical equipment. I heard the hitch in their breathing before eyes widened in disbelief to stare at me.

"You're sure this is a safe place?" The large-bosomed woman with bountiful curls touched the corner of an examination table. Tears swelled in her friend's eyes.

"Of course it is. Why else would I bring you here? Did your husbands escort you to Grey House?"

Tears splashed down the cheeks of the smaller woman when her head bobbed in an affirmative nod.

The big-busted woman vocalized the reason for their separation.

"Our husbands went to talk to Dr. Grey about charitable contributions for his cutting-edge experiments."

"Delightful." I stifled a yawn. Why was I wasting time with over powdered and perfumed ladies when there were perfectly fine and alive male specimen on the premises? "The irony, I suppose, is that Dr. Grey obeyed the draft and went to war. I assume they are meeting instead with my brother Niles?"

Uncertain eyes shifted around the room. "Dr. Niles Grey. Right?"

"My father is Joseph Grey. Niles might wish he was a doctor, but no." Mirthless laughter escaped my lips as panic anew seized the features of these women. "Have a seat, ladies. I'll be back momentarily."

With these words I pushed my way back through the secret entrance, securing the door on the library side. My last peek at the subspecies to which I belonged revealed them flitting about the room like nervous hens.

"Have a seat? Where?" Wailed one of the women.

"Don't leave us!" the other shrieked.

My mind already left these pitiful creatures behind. I went in search of their male counterparts, determined to have some fun.

Flash Fiction

Carolyn Dickinson • Morrill, NE

Open the Door

Let me begin by acknowledging that my hair is somewhere between gray and white, depending on the lighting. His hair was closer to gray. My guess is we are both from the same generation, around WWII.

My memory goes back to a time when attendants filled your gas tank, when women wore dresses, when you really did "dial" a telephone (although I'm not old enough to have cranked one), when party lines had different rings for different houses, when you could buy ten hamburgers for a dollar, when men opened the door for women, and women expected them to do so. All that goes with our hair colors.

Some time has passed.

My closet does contain a dress I have not worn in several years. Similar to most other people my age, I carry my phone in my pocket. I fill my own gas tank and pay for it with a credit card. It's been a while since I bought a hamburger, but you can get a dollar burger at McDonald's. I've been opening doors for whoever comes after me out of courtesy, male or female, young or old, or for myself.

The other day at the post office, I parked my car, walked up the sidewalk, noticed a man coming behind me, opened the door, and held it for him. As I turned to face him, he stopped. He didn't stomp his feet or put his hands on his hips, but such was his tone of voice.

"That's not the way it is!" his voice glared. "I open the door for you."

I stepped back, let the door close, and waited. He pulled it open, indicated I should go through, and I did. I smiled at him, he smiled at me. I thanked him. He responded, "You're welcome," and we both went inside to check our mail. He maintained his dignity, and I allowed him to do so.

Carolyn Dickinson • Morrill, NE

Returning Borrowed Time

I should have known better. It was a cat, a black cat, and it spoke. That should have been a clue.

But I was desperate, hanging onto a branch sticking out of the side of a cliff. And it was a looooong way down. Nobody would survive the fall from there to the rocks below.

This black cat leaned over the edge and spoke to me. “You look like you need some help.”

So what could a cat do? A tall person might have been able to reach down and grab my hand. Certainly not a cat, even a speaking cat.

“You think so?” I asked.

“Well, I can’t help the way you expect, but I can take you back in time two or three minutes to when you were standing up here, before you jumped.”

I scowled. “I didn’t jump. I fell.”

The cat shook his head. “Doesn’t matter. Either way, I can give you those minutes you need to get back up here.”

I’m not a physicist, but I knew Einstein thought time was relative. At that point, I wasn’t going to argue.

“And just to show you how helpful I am, I will grant you any wish you want after you’re back up here.”

The branch sagged a little, dirt falling on me.

“Fine. Whatever you want. Anything. Just get me back up there!”

And there I was, standing on top of the cliff.

"Wow!" I backed away and then stood quiet for several minutes, processing what had just happened.

"So what do I owe you?" I finally asked the purring cat, rubbing against my leg.

"Oh, not much. Just your soul."

That required more time to process.

"You said something about a wish?"

"Yes, is there something else you would like?"

I scratched my head, an idea forming in my mind. "Do I have to decide now?"

"No, no hurry."

"Well, I need to catch up with my friends. We've been hiking. I stopped here to rest, and they went ahead."

I motioned to the trail leading up the mountain.

"Sure." His eyes sparkled. "I can grant you a wish to catch up with them."

"No, that's fine. I'm a fast hiker." Frightened by the events, I fled up the trail. "See you later."

I did see him later, many times. Each time he asked if I was ready for my wish. I wasn't.

That was some sixty years ago. I was a young squirt then, full of life and eager to risk it. Now not so much. I married a fine man. We had a wonderful daughter. But cancer was taking me away.

So I called the cat and gave him my wish.

"I wish I had never made that deal with you."

The branch pulled out of the cliff, but I did not scream as I fell to the rocks below. I had lived a good life.

William L. Smutko • Blair, NE

The Arkansas

I need to wash away the surprise—her pregnancy test was positive.

The ***child*** *is my responsibility.*

My 1970 Scout heads south on Colorado 115 toward the Arkansas River. The red sandstone formations along the west side of the road ignited by the rising sun give contrast to the dark green junipers. At Penrose I pick up US 50 and head west through Canyon City, then follow the Arkansas River Canyon to a small collection of buildings called Texas Creek. The river flattens out between here and Cotopaxi.

Becoming a father, a new life I'll be responsible for, the joys of parenthood. A little person who loves and looks up to you. Diapers full of baby shit and three a.m. feedings. The financial drain.

The child is ***my*** *responsibility.*

There's a pull off onto the red gravel shoulder a couple of miles farther west, just beyond a roadhouse that occupies a wide spot on the river side of the road. The bitter scent of cottonwoods perfumes the air, and the river murmurs and sighs as it flows over and around the rocks.

The two pieces of my fly rod joined the front foot of the reel slides into the slot under the hand grip and I screw the nut tightening the reel to the rod. A kingfisher flies up the river screeching. The sound echoes off the ochre canyon walls. The green floating line slips through the guides. I slide my chest waders up over my jeans and field jacket, cinch a belt around my waist and put on my fishing vest.

Teaching him/her to walk and talk, to fly fish, to write stories. Big sloppy kisses and bedtime tales. Helping with homework, intervening with teachers.

The child is my ***responsibility****.*

The gin smell of the junipers rises with the heat of the sun, mixes with the bitter cottonwoods and makes me think of Dad's martinis. My rod propped against a rock, I take twenty minutes to focus on the river, blocking out everything else. The large, smooth red granite presses into my butt and the sunlight reflects off the water as I look for activity. There is none so my hands dig around in the colorful rocks and gravel in the shallows to see what's there. There are a lot of nymphs, a few caddis and mayfly, but mostly stoneflies. The April cold water has made my fingers ache. I warm them in my armpits and work at blocking out everything but the river.

I clip the last six feet from the leader, pull a slim metal fly box from my vest, choose a size 8 Royal Wulff and tie it to the end of the shortened tippet. Six feet of 4x tippet material gets tied to the hook of the gaudy dry, and a size 14 Brown Stonefly nymph tied to the other end.

The river pulls the heat from my feet and legs. Five careful steps out from the bank I cast my line toward the submerged rocks near the bank upstream to my left. It takes the flies along and drops them three feet from shore.

The child is my responsibility.

I let the nymph sink, start retrieving line, and watch the indicator drift with the current. The showy fly twitches so I lift the rod tip. The fly was just bumping on the bottom.

The rhythm of my casting, in sync with my breathing, the rod, river, and I meld. I cast again a little farther out and continue to work the water aware of nothing else.

Fishing the center of the river in six to eight feet of water, the white calf tail wings on the Wulff stop. I raise the rod tip and set the hook. A few minutes later a sixteen-inch brown trout is in my net.

I fish until I can't see the fly on the water and the river has done to my anxiety what it has done to the rocks, ground the edges off.

About the Authors

Lucy Adkins

Lucy Adkins is a writer of poetry, fiction, and nonfiction. Her poetry chapbooks include *One Life Shining* and *Two-Toned Dress*, which was the winner of a Blue Light Press Poetry Prize. She has also co-authored two books of nonfiction, *Writing in Community* and *The Fire Inside*.

Catherine Baker Nicholson JD

Catherine Baker Nicholson—Rice University BA, national champion 800 meters; University of Texas, JD with Honors; and University of Nebraska, PhD history student—homeschooled her four children. Her book *Running in Borrowed Shoes*, available Spring 2024, discusses Thane Baker in the 1952 Olympics. Nicholson prays, studies, writes, and volunteers.

Susan Baron

Susan Baron lives in Omaha, Nebraska, with her Kerry Blue Terrier, Kiss, while she hones her craft. She writes short stories and poetry and is working on a historical novel about Nebraska.

Cathy Beck

Cathy is passionate about writing. She's attended UNO Creative Nonfiction classes, as well as Iowa University Summer Writing Festival workshops. Now retired, she has more time for gardening, walking, and writing. With two daughters and three precious granddaughters calling her Nana, it doesn't get any better than that.

Lin M. Brummels

Lin Marshall Brummels earned a BS from University of Nebraska and an MS from Syracuse University. Brummels has poems in *Poet Lore*, *San Pedro River Review*, *Concho River Review*, *Oakwood*, *Plainsongs*, *Nebraska Life*, and others. Chapbooks, *Cottonwood Strong* and *Hard Times*, 2016 Nebraska Book Award. Latest book, *A Quilted Landscape*.

Marcia Calhoun Forecki

An homage to Borges set in Nebraska? With a Masters in Spanish Language and Literature, why not? Marcia Calhoun Forecki has lived on the Nebraska/Iowa border for forty years and published stories, a memoir, and three novels. A contributing editor to a Midwest literary journal, Marcia seems serious about fiction.

Deb Carpenter-Nolting

Deb Carpenter-Nolting is a writer, songwriter, and performing artist whose short stories, poems, essays, and articles have been published in various magazines, newspapers, and anthologies. She has published two books. Deb lives in Bushnell, Nebraska, with her husband, Tim, who is also a writer.

Faith A. Colburn

Faith Colburn has been a truck driver, a farmer, an environmentalist, and a mother of sons. She's a hugger of trees and lover of old folks. She has written for newspapers and magazines across Nebraska and published two family memoirs, a collection of short essays, and three historical novels.

Carolyn Dickinson

A retired teacher, Carolyn now has time to write short stories featuring her cats, her horses, and her disabled sheep (but not the chickens or the ducks). Other stories have been published in previous *Voices from the Plains* and one in the *School Magazine* in Australia.

Cambria Engstrom

Cambria Enstrom is a Wife of a Nerd, a Mother of Goblins, a Servant to her country, and a blooming author. She spends her days raising her two children to be nerds themselves. She can be found at her desk honing her writing skills with her Master's Degree in Writing.

Becky Faber

Becky Faber is the author of *One Small Photo*. She has published in *Nebraska Presence* (One Book One Nebraska 2018), *Women Write Resistance*, *Rural Voices*, the *Midwest Quarterly* (Three Generations of Nebraska Poets), *Blue Collar Review*, and *Lyrical Iowa*, with honors from the Poetry Society of Virginia and the Iowa Poetry Association.

Johnnye Gerhardt

Ms. Gerhardt has been an acquisition-and-contract editor for a small press; an editor for *Fine Lines Literary Magazine* and the Nebraska Writers Guild. Johnnye currently serves on the Nebraska Governor's Education-Outreach Speakers Bureau and has served on the Nebraska Film Association and the Nebraska Writers Guild Board of Directors.

Maisie Habron-Wach

Maisie is a physical therapist and a new mom. When she's not changing diapers and reading her favorite childhood books to her son, she enjoys writing stories of her own. As a lifelong writer, Maisie enjoys incorporating her other interests in medicine and nature into her work.

Michelle L. Howard

Michelle is a lifelong Nebraskan who loves God, family, America, words, photography, and her pets.

Rachel Hruza

Rachel Hruza lives in Lincoln with her husband and two spectacular children. She teaches English at Southeast Community College. Her first novel—for middle grade readers—entitled *Dear Isaac Newton, You're Ruining My Life*, was published by Sky Pony Press in 2018.

Waverly Jackson

Waverly Jackson lives in Lincoln, Nebraska, where she pretends to be a professional copywriter when she would rather be reading by the fire. She spends her free time going for long bike rides, occasionally with no hands! She balances parenting with cookies and lots of caffeine.

Joshua Johnson

Joshua Johnson is a poet from southeastern Nebraska. He published his first chapbook, *Silent Screams*, in February 2023. In his free time, he enjoys listening to music, studying history and current events, and writing. He is also a self-described socialist, but he assures readers that his poetry is not "preachy."

Gary F. Jones

Jones said his life seemed like a testament to bad judgment and wishful thinking. His wife of forty-five years claimed to know of nothing to justify such unfettered optimism. He worked as a veterinarian in Wisconsin for nineteen years before returning to grad school and earning a PhD in microbiology.

Margaret Lukas

BFA University of Nebraska. MFA Tacoma Washington. Professor, University of Nebraska, eleven years. Short story, "The Yellow Bird," made into a "short" premiered at Cannes Film Festival. Nebraska Arts Council, Individual Artist Fellowship Award. Novels: *Farthest House* 2015. *River People* (International Award Winner) 2019, *The Broken Statue*, 2021.

Sandi Lyons Hoard

Sandi and her husband live near Harlan County Reservoir. They have three grown children and two grandchildren. After retiring from a medical device facility, she became an NLC Certified Library Clerk. She's fully retired now and enjoys spending time with her family, reading, painting, and writing historical, suspense, and comedy fiction.

Kathleen Maloney

Kathy Maloney has been the associate editor for the Human Research Report for over twenty years. She writes poetry, reads, and creates mixed media art. Kathy also writes illustrated letters for grandsons and designs/produces greeting cards for family and friends. Kathy taught English at Central High School for twenty years.

Janet McMillan Rives

Janet McMillan Rives lives near Tucson, Arizona. She has published in *Beyond Words*, *Canary*, *Creosote*, *Raw Art Review*, *Ekphrastic Review*, and *Voices from the Plains*. She has two chapbooks: *Into This Sea of Green: Poems from the Prairie* (2020) and *Washed by a Summer Rain: Poems from the Desert* (2023).

Kim McNealy Sosin

Kim McNealy Sosin's work appears in journals and collections including *Sandcutters*, *Failed Haiku*, *Beyond Words*, *Voices from the Plains*, *Raw Art Review*, *Fine Lines*, and *Ekphrastic Review*. Her photographs are featured as the cover for several of these. She currently resides in Omaha, Nebraska, with her two cats.

Tim Moran

Tim Moran resides in rural Gosper County, Nebraska, in a refurbished farmhouse built in 1910. He is busy most days with the tasks associated with restoring nine acres of farmland to mix-grass prairie and natural habitat. In his spare time, he writes.

M. Timothy Nolting

M. Timothy Nolting is a writer from the southwestern corner of the Nebraska Panhandle, near the Village of Bushnell, along with his singer/songwriter and poet wife, Deb. Tim is celebrating the recent release of his first novel, . . . *By the Way They Treat Their Horses*, a work of western fiction. mtimothynolting.com.

Tami Olsen

She's a geek, she married a geek, and she has two geek children. She designs buildings to pay the bills but creates worlds to live forever. Animals love her, she attracts broken people, and she lost her soul to the forest long ago.

Mark M. Peyton

Mark M. Peyton lives in Gothenburg, Nebraska, with his wife of forty-nine years, Cindy. He started writing for the REA Nebraska and elsewhere in 1999. He is the author of three books with his fourth, *A Naturalist's Almanac*, to be released this winter.

Ashton Quinn

Ashton Quinn is a newly emerging writer with a passion for all things speculative and strange. He is an avid reader and spends his weekends locked in his study and dreaming up bizarre new worlds. He lives in Bellevue, Nebraska, with his lovely wife, Melinda, and their adorable Rottweiler, Dexter.

Sue Ray-Smolik

Growing up surrounded in western Pennsylvania's beauty fostered an appreciation for the outdoors. Sue has called Nebraska home since 1985. It speaks to her heart with its wide open spaces. An elementary teacher for four decades, she enjoys singing and spending time with family, including her toddler grandson in Colorado.

Andrea Riley

Andrea Riley is an archivist, wife, mom, writer, outlaw-lawman historian, and lap for a fickle black cat. She lives in Lincoln, Nebraska, with her husband, two daughters, whatever step-children still happen to call the place home, and four cats.

K. L. Riley

K. L. Riley is an author, English professor, trivia host, and Secret Service agent. He scripts every conversation a government employee has with any foreign national. Secretary of state on the phone with a prime minister to ambassador's assistant's aide's au pair on a Tinder date, he writes their script.

Valerie R. Robert

Valerie Robert is a former freelance writer who is currently writing poetry, her memoirs, and her family's history. She is a Vermont native, a former military wife, a mother, and a grandmother. She enjoys camping, cooking, traveling, reading, and attending concerts and plays.

Steve Rose

Steve Rose's writing has appeared in numerous publications, including the *Midwest Quarterly*, *So It Goes*, the *Journal of Medical Literature*, *Conestoga Zen*, *Dime Bag of Poetry*, and the Nebraska Writers Guild anthology. He has published two books of poetry: *Hard Papas* in 2014 and *Nebraska and Other States* in 2017.

Janet Seegebarth

Janet Seegebarth is a Nebraska native with a writing degree from Wayne State College. She is the author of *Norfolk*, published by Arcadia Publishing. Her work has appeared in *Splickety Magazine*, *Plainsongs*, *Nebraska Life Magazine*, *Voices Out of Nowhere*, *Christmas Prairie Tales*, *Cleanfax Magazine*, *Insecure Writers*, and more.

ShennonDoah

I am a full-time French, Spanish, and Speech teacher in a rural K-12 school. I also work part-time at a fitness facility. I enjoy reading, writing, and acting in local theatre productions. I write poetry, short stories, song lyrics, and paranormal and science fiction novels.

William L. Smutko

William Smutko is a veteran of the Vietnam War and a retired wine grape grower and loves to cook.

Nathan Sousek

Nathan Sousek lives in Lincoln, Nebraska, with his wife, Laura, and their two children. In his spare time, he enjoys the great outdoors, fishing, traveling to and exploring national parks, cheering on the Husker football and volleyball teams, reading a good book, and, of course, writing whenever he finds inspiration.

Veronica Torraca-Bragdon

Veronica Torraca-Bragdon is a poet, singer/songwriter, and special educator. Her poems have been set to music and premiered by Omaha Symphonic Chorus, along with being featured on the *REDLINE* soundtrack for lyrics and vocals. Veronica's self-published book, *Outside the Box, Inside the Wrapping*, is available on Amazon.

Katherine Wielechowski

Katherine Wielechowski is a Nebraska native and self-published author. She writes in many different genres, including romance, urban fantasy, and supernatural/paranormal. She currently has four books available, including *1-800-Henchmen* and her latest book, *Quarantine Monster Shorts*, a collection of short stories set during the 2020 pandemic.

Brittany Wren

Brittany Wren is a business writer and editor. With eight years of freelancing, in-house, and agency marketing under her belt, she is now happily self-employed. When she's not writing for others, she's bribing her kids with fruit snacks and stepping on LEGO bricks. Sometimes, she writes poetry.

About the Nebraska Writers Guild

The Nebraska Writers Guild is one of the oldest writing organizations in the country. Founded in 1925, the Guild's charter members included Bess Streeter Aldrich, Dorothy Canfield Fisher, Louise Pound, and A. E. Sheldon. In its first two years, two members of the Guild were included in the *Saturday Review of Literature*'s list of the ten writers most representative of American life. The original purpose statement from 1925, which we still maintain today, reads: "The purpose of the Guild shall be the promotion of good fellowship among Nebraska writers; to encourage the recognition of professional writing and writers in the production of fine literature; and, to foster the development of the talent of those who desire to write and who show definite possibilities of authorship."

Our Mission

Nebraska Writers Guild is a nonprofit 501(c)3 organization dedicated to empowerment and individual growth through involvement with a community of writers and related professionals; promoting authors and the craft of writing through events and publications; and advancement through professional development.

Our Vision

Nebraska Writers Guild will: advocate for literary causes; nurture creative community; expand organizational outreach;

foster personal growth through education; and increase exposure for members.

Our Core Values

Nebraska Writers Guild holds a set of values that provide the foundation for its leadership in honoring its original purpose and achieving its current mission and future vision. These include: community, through acceptance, advocacy, appreciation, compassion and cooperation; creativity; learning; motivation; and professionalism.

Our success is measured in the number of people we can help with the quality of programs and services we provide. These programs are fueled by our dedicated staff, caring volunteers, and generous donors.

For more information about the Nebraska Writers Guild, go to www.nebraskawriters.org. You do not have to be from Nebraska to join the NWG. If you're a writer and you want a community for support, check us out!

Acknowledgments

Project Coordinator: Julie Haase
Submissions Manager: Brandy Prettyman
Volunteer Coordinator: Mary Bernier
Marketing Manager: Shennon Helms
Poetry Evaluators: Amy Haddad, Ricardo Moran, Tami Wilfong,
Fiction Evaluators: Susan Baron, Margie Lukas, Katherine Wielechowski
Nonfiction Evaluators: Thomas Wenck, Michelle Huber Ulicny
Cover Design: Stephanie Cleary
Interior Formatting: Julie Haase
Proofreading: Johnnye Gerhardt

Index by Author

Index by Title

www.ingramcontent.com/pod-product-compliance
Lightning Source LLC
Chambersburg PA
CBHW070522220726
48294CB00019B/58